POWER
STABILIZED

POWER
STABILIZED

*An Urban Fantasy Filled with
Aliens, Dragonpanthers, Whales,
and One Intrepid Woman*

CATHY PARKER

Cover Design by: Bublish, based on the work of karli.foss@gmail.com
Edited by Joan Dempsey

This is a work of fiction. Names, characters, places, brands, media, and incidents are either the product of the author's imagination or are used fictitiously. Any resemblance to similarly named places or to persons living or deceased is unintentional. Except in the case of the aliens, for which none of the above applies. And I admit to a suspicious resemblance between Narcissus and a certain black cat of my own.

Paperback ISBN: 978-1-64704-258-5

eBook ISBN: 978-1-64704-259-2

for Kimmy, Pat, Deb, Wendy, Renee and Peggy
for the beautiful beluga whale Mauyak

and for Tulip
May we all learn from her sweetness and loving heart

ACKNOWLEDGEMENTS

I am deeply grateful to Shilah for her patience and support every step of the way, to my brother John for his incredible support, to Cindy and Claudia for their art and their hearts, and to everyone who has had to listen to me wail.

PART ONE

FIREWORLD

CHAPTER ONE
Incarceration

THE DRAGONPANTHER ROEBOR NEEDED SHANNON KENDRICKS' HELP, but exactly what help for what trouble, Shannon had yet to learn, and she needed to find out *now*.

She'd left Earth moments ago through a portal to RiverWorld with her cat Narcissus in her arms and the hummingbird-sized, kitten-shaped alien, Salesti, by her side. They tumbled into the cave of portals.

"Okay, Salesti, time to tell us what's happened to Roebor. Is he—"

Before Shannon could finish her question, Salesti dived into another portal: the one to Roebor's home on FireWorld. "Wait—"

But Salesti disappeared in a blazing flash of white flame. Shannon cursed under her breath and followed.

In an instant, she fell out of the portal onto FireWorld's smooth, pink-gold rock cliffs. She rolled, jumped up, and scanned in every direction for unfriendly dragonpanthers as she rubbed her rock-bruised shin.

Dragonpanthers, as large as houses, featured brightly-colored metallic fur and wings longer than oak trees. She wouldn't overlook one. Seeing nothing, she scurried to a group of boulders of the same pink-gold, crouched behind the largest, and caught her breath.

"Stay close to me, Narci. We don't know what's going on here."

Salesti, who was from RiverWorld, awaited Shannon in the bright, cold, morning sunshine, and buzzed its way to her hiding place.

"Now, please tell us why you brought us here, Salesti. Are we in friendly territory or not?"

She kept a close eye on the landscape in all directions while she waited for Salesti to speak.

not, Salesti said.

"Explain."

The tiny alien buzzed to the top of the tallest boulder and peeked at the landscape.

Behind them, a sheer cliff dropped hundreds of feet to a vast sea covered in fire. The flames burned the same silver-blue that lit her friend Roebor's blazing eyes, the same silver-blue fire he could blow from his lungs to such devastating effect.

The roar of the fire—steady, menacing, a constant warning: *do not come near, or you will burn*—carried all the way from the sea to the rock outcropping where she crouched. Shannon unzipped her lightweight sweatshirt. Cooler air could reach her already-damp T-shirt.

"Salesti? What do you mean, we're not in friendly territory?"

dangerous territory, said Salesti.

"Dangerous because of the dragonpanthers or because the dragonpanthers are under attack?"

Beyond their outcropping of boulders, the land eased upward toward the next range of pink-gold cliffs a half-mile away. Hundreds of cave entrances peppered the cliff face from top to bottom.

She crouched lower behind the boulder.

dragonpanthers unfriendly to roebor.

"Why? What do they have against Roebor?"

Salesti buzzed—its anxious buzz, not the cheerful one—and Narci glanced at the sky; her sapphire eyes grew even larger than usual. Shannon followed Narci's gaze. A group of about twenty dragonpanthers flew high over their heads. Long necks craned, and silver-blue eyes glared at them. Two peeled off from the rest and descended.

"*Odin's eye,*" Shannon said, in tribute to her beloved Norse grandmother. "Should I worry now, Salesti?"

yes, shannon worries now.

The rest of the dragonpanthers flew in a double V formation around the corner of the cliff to the left and disappeared. The two descending creatures swooped in and came to rest next to Shannon's hiding place, their great wings humming on the wind and folding inward like umbrellas next to their bodies as they settled.

"Salesti? Narci?" Shannon whispered. "You two duck under those rocks at the far end and stay there. No matter what." Narci's black fur would blend with the dark recesses between the stones, and Salesti could nestle beneath her.

3

Salesti and Narcissus disappeared into the shadows where three boulders leaned together.

Shannon pulled her silver-blonde braid over one shoulder and ran shaking fingers down to its tip. She tried and failed to stop the trembling in her legs as the two giant creatures stamped toward her—heads lowered, silver-blue eyes blazing.

Their golden fur shone in the brilliant light of the two suns rising behind them in the morning sky. The smaller of the two remained a step back as the other brought his face close to hers. Shannon stood her ground.

Please be friendly to tiny, squishable humans.

"It's one of those puny Earth things," said the nearer creature. "I recognize it from Roebor's artwork."

"Are you sure?" the other asked. "We've never had one visit here."

The larger one sniffed at her. "She carries a peculiar scent. I've never smelled anything like it. Come and smell."

The second dragonpanther stepped forward, leaned his enormous face in, and sniffed.

"I like that. Unusual. And check out her eyes—they do not carry fire like ours, and instead of our slits of blue, they are round and green. Fascinating."

Shannon *did* smell of perfume, an exotic, spice-filled, alien-made scent that never left her. The two dragonpanthers smelled as well; their scent reminded Shannon of pack rides on gentle horses in summers long past.

"Can you understand me? Are you from Earth?" The first one asked, his hot and rancid breath in Shannon's face.

Although dragonpanthers communicated without speaking, Shannon understood them; she'd become telepathic herself during the Alien Troubles six years before, catching images and emotions before they became a language.

Shannon coughed under the onslaught of their breath. "Yes, I'm from Earth. My name is Shannon Kendricks. I came here to learn what happened to my friend Roebor."

The bigger dragonpanther reared back and growled. "No friend of Roebor will find welcome here."

No, not friendly to tiny, squishable human Shannon.

One of the dragonpanther's huge front paws whipped out. He wrapped his long toes—more like fingers in length and dexterity—around Shannon's body and flapped his great, bat-like wings to lift him far enough off the ground, so she dangled beneath him. There he hovered.

Not good. Not good. Not good.

Shannon struggled in his grasp; he tightened his fist.

"What are you doing, Bale? Why don't you send her on her way and be done with her?" asked the second creature.

"No, Pak!" Bale said and growled again. "A friend of Father's murderer will satisfy me of her innocence before she may leave."

They must be talking about Tidak. That couldn't be good.

"Tell you what, my brother. We will consult with the Council," Pak said. "But what can we do with her in the meantime? The Council won't meet until after Last Meal today."

"We will imprison her, of course. Come." To Shannon, Bale said, "You have arranged for your capture right on the doorstep of our holding pen." He gestured with his free paw up the hill toward the nearest caves. "Allow me to express my gratitude."

"My pleasure," Shannon muttered.

"Wait, Bale. I don't know if we should imprison her," Pak said, his feet shifting. "She has committed no offense. Don't you think it would be easier just to send her back to Earth?"

"She claims friendship with Roebor. That is offense enough for me." Bale flapped his wings harder, lifted higher, turned, and carried Shannon toward her prison. Pak hesitated a moment before lifting off. Shannon craned her neck to watch him.

He gazed absently about while he pondered Bale's actions. As he looked around, his head jerked back, then lowered toward the shadows at the base of the outcropping.

Uh-oh. Pak had spotted Narci and Salesti. Shannon tensed. Pak cocked his head, glanced over toward Bale's retreating figure, and viewed the shadows once more. After a slight pause, he shrugged, took flight, and headed after his brother.

* * *

"This should hold you. I believe the bars fit close enough together to stop even a puny Earth thing," Bale said.

He pushed her into the cell with a flick of his thumb and forefinger.

Shannon, still off-balance from her short, none-too-gentle flight, grabbed for the six-inch-wide cell bars, missed, and fell.

She jumped to her feet and opened her mouth to argue the injustice of her imprisonment. But what did she know of the justice or injustice of this world? She held her peace and ran her braid through her fingers.

The temperature in the cell felt ten degrees cooler than outside. A faint dampness floated in the air as if the cave had trapped the moist sea breeze and held it captive, too. Shivering, she zipped up her sweatshirt.

What a mess. Sometimes her original career as a civil attorney, which she'd come to hate, didn't seem so bad after all. *Like now.*

Shannon glanced around. The cave extended far out into the shadows to either side of her, and another two hundred feet or so behind her to the rough cave wall without windows. The cell was like a rough-hewn high school gymnasium. Metal bars extended from the cave floor to the upper reaches of the cave, not quite touching the uneven roof, but coming close enough to prevent any dragonpanthers or humans from slipping over. Nothing bigger than Salesti could manage that gap.

Outside her cell, only the two dragonpanthers relieved the dreary emptiness of the stadium-sized cave.

Pak and Bale, standing midway between Shannon and the cave entrance, discussed what their next steps should be.

As much as Shannon would've wished otherwise, Salesti and Narci had likely followed her captors to the cave. Pak and Bale blocked every inch of her view of the cave entrance, so she began to pace along the cell bars like a restless tiger, treading back and forth, trying to reach a point where she could see around her bulky captors.

There! Her two companions raced into view at the lefthand edge of the cave opening. Shannon gave a quick shake of her head to warn them away.

Using her mental connection with the two, Shannon communicated without having to speak out loud. *Narci, stay there if you can find a place to hide. Salesti—it's past time you explained what's happened to Roebor.*

yes. salesti tells, said the alien. *people of roebor take roebor prisoner for death of tidak. the council sentences roebor to death. execution when sun rises.*

Execution? Shannon asked. *He should be the hero here and Tidak should be the villain. What happened?*

to the dragonpanthers, tidak not does wrong. roebor does wrong because roebor destroys head of tidak. destruction of head taboo on fireworld. terrible thing. worst crime possible.

Shannon shook her head. *But that still makes no sense because* I'm *the one who killed Tidak, not Roebor.*

The one who killed Tidak: she closed her eyes and gripped her braid. The thought of it still made her sick.

Salesti lifted its tiny shoulders in a shrug. *roebor not mentions shannon to dragonpanthers.*

Bale interrupted their silent conversation.

"Explain yourself, Earth thing. What is your connection to Roebor?"

"Our goals aligned. I wanted to stop a virus from spreading on Earth, and he wanted to take the virus away. But Tidak challenged Roebor every time they met. Help me understand why you find Roebor in the wrong."

Bale slammed his massive fist into the bars. Shannon jumped back. "Roebor left few marks on Father except the defilement of his head. No honorable fight would end in such a singular injury. . . ambush. . . treachery. . . it is impossible for it to have happened otherwise." Bale choked out the words. Whatever she thought of him, Shannon was witnessing deep and genuine grief.

"Bale, please. Let me explain. I'm—"

Shannon, no! Do not speak another word.

Roebor! The weak, distant voice of Roebor.

Can they hear us? Where are you? she asked.

No, they cannot hear us. It is our gift to exclude all but those we wish from our conversations. Otherwise, we would have no privacy. Say nothing but in direct answer to their questions. Bale would fly to Earth today and scorch it to ashes, and you with it if he had his way, but I believe calmer heads will prevail if you act prudently.

You sound weak.

I am fine. Did he hurt you? If he did, I swear by all the gods—

I'm good. He threw me in jail, that's all.

Let us speak further when Bale leaves you. Hold your words for now.

Bale interrupted again. "You said, 'I am.' You are what? Why did you stop speaking?"

Shannon stood and approached the bars. "Sorry, I'm. . . confused. Tidak didn't care if he exposed the creatures of

Earth to the virus, which would've killed us—he focused only on returning to FireWorld with enough virus cells to make the antidote, no matter what the consequences to Earth. Roebor planned to find the virus but still save my planet. Isn't that the better way?"

Bale settled back on his haunches. His eyes narrowed. "Your words might sway us *if* you spoke the truth. You do not. If you truly believe these words, then Roebor lied to you."

"Oh, I don't believe that. Roebor—"

Bale's low growl cut Shannon off. "We wished no harm to your world, puny Earth thing, but more and more of our people perished every day. Roebor was the one who proposed the method that would contaminate your world. He saw no way around it. The Council gave Roebor and my father permission to condemn your world to save our own. Then he and my father swore to the Council to work together to retrieve the virus."

"But Roebor *did* extract the virus without exposing anyone to it, so he *did* know how to do it safely."

"He played you for a fool, inventing the so-called 'process' as he went along to keep Father away, to defeat him, and to claim the glory as his own. Can you deny this?"

"Well. . . well. . . we did keep Tidak away, yes. . . ."

"And can you deny he put my father in chains, which he happened to bring along with his equipment, rather than finish the project with him?"

"Again, no, I can't deny that. But Tidak had challenged him to a fight to the death."

"Once Roebor broke the vow and endangered the mission, honor and law bound my father to challenge Roebor. A fight to the death would have bestowed honor upon them both. However, they did not engage in an honorable fight to the death, did they? Roebor slaughtered my father instead."

So much they didn't understand. And now Bale had made it clear Shannon didn't understand everything either. *Could Bale be telling the truth?* Shannon's knees weakened. She steadied herself against the bars.

"Do you know how many of my people perished while Roebor delayed on Earth with his scheme to outwit Father and take the virus for himself? Three hundred. *Three hundred.* His own mother died waiting for their return. And you helped him. I should kill you."

"His own. . . and yet he saved millions on Earth," Shannon whispered. But of course, why would that matter to FireWorld's inhabitants?

Shannon studied Bale. The glowering dragonpanther was gigantic, although not as huge as Roebor. His mouth curved over incisors the size of samurai swords. Four paws clicked to reveal lethal claws. Legs stiff, tail raised high, he radiated anger. He stepped close to the bars. Shannon stepped back. She felt like a dormouse under a tiger's intense gaze.

Behind him, his brother Pak listened and watched, but revealed none of the pure rage that radiated from his brother.

The hummingbird-kitten-like Salesti hovered quietly, buzzing behind a bulky pile of equipment next to the wide, rock-strewn cave entrance. Shannon caught a glimpse of it every few minutes as it darted out to assess the situation before zipping back out of sight. The dragonpanthers didn't seem to register the faint sound.

In the meantime, Narci had hidden well; Shannon hadn't spotted the cat again since the two arrived. She should never have brought Narci with her. True, Narci had wanted to come, and true, she'd helped Shannon out of a jam more than once since the Alien Troubles, but one misstep and these giants would destroy her sweet Narcissus in a heartbeat.

To Shannon's surprise, Narci answered. The cat had been able to connect with Shannon since the Alien Troubles but chose to stay silent most of the time. *Do not worry,* the cat said.

Can't help it, sweetheart. Get used to it.

Meanwhile, Bale continued to glare at her. "Enough of you," he said, all evidence of patience disappearing. He stood tall, opened his chest wide, and inhaled. The smell of sulphur cut the air as silver-blue sparks erupted around his nose and mouth, and for an instant that lasted an eternity, Shannon cringed, waiting for him to incinerate her. She sank onto her knees and braced for what she hoped would be a mere moment of agony before his fire reduced her to ashes.

Pak darted to Bale's side and laid a great furry paw on his chest. "Peace, brother. The Earth thing doesn't understand what has transpired here. Roebor duped her. This isn't her fight."

Shannon blushed from skin to conscience; she *had* fought with Tidak. Not only that, but she had killed him. Still, one word about Tidak's true killer would end her life in a roaring blaze. She couldn't help Roebor if Bale fried her to a crisp. She must watch her words.

"Can you tell me what happened?" she asked.

Pak took up the story, settling onto his stomach with his legs tucked under his chest. Bale paced back and forth behind him. The ground vibrated with each step.

"We all rejoiced when Roebor and Tidak pledged to work together," said Pak, "as they had been bitter rivals all their lives, each trying to outshine the other. Each carried the pride of his Clan on his back—Roebor from the ruling Blue Clan, Tidak from the once-strong Gold Clan. However, the dire straits of our people brought the two of them together—the strongest, smartest, and bravest among us—to bring back the antidote."

The two had pledged to cooperate? Whatever they might have pledged, they'd abandoned any pretense of working together from the first moment they landed on Earth. Shannon had witnessed that much.

"Their fathers came to a truce of sorts while awaiting their return. My brother and I treated Roebor's sister Jal with courtesy. It was a hopeful time."

Shannon, who'd been staring into the cave's dark recesses as she listened, turned sharply to focus on Pak; the softness with which Pak spoke Jal's name revealed his feelings for Roebor's sister.

Poor Pak. Countless Romeos and Juliets had lived that story—and it never ended well. She glanced at Bale, who had also reacted to Pak's words. The fire in his eyes flared before he narrowed his gaze at his brother.

Oblivious to Shannon's reaction before him and his brother's reaction behind, Pak continued. "They agreed with the plan to obtain the virus. You must understand that our people wished no harm to the people of Earth. But in the end, our scientists saw no way to save your world. After Roebor and Tidak departed, we heard nothing for days. The Council debated whether to send warriors after them, but we didn't know where they'd gone or what we would find."

Pak nodded over his shoulder toward his brother. "My brother, Bale, volunteered to go, despite the uncertainty, but Grandfather didn't want to lose him if our father failed to return."

The smaller brother smiled, but with sad eyes. "I'm not the warrior in our clan. If the Gold Clan is to return to power, Bale will accomplish it. Once the Council executes Roebor in the morning, Bale will challenge Roebor's invalid father to the Championship Fight; a fight Bale unquestionably will win."

"You think I could not beat Roebor in battle?" Bale roared behind Pak's back. "I would best him."

"What I believe doesn't matter, Bale. Grandfather schemes to pave your way by forcing Roebor's crippled father to face you, a battle that you cannot lose."

Bale rose onto his hind legs and smashed one great fist into the palm of the other paw. "I wish to fight Roebor! True honor lies there. True revenge for the death of our father. I can beat him."

Shannon glimpsed Pak's expression while Bale did not. Considerable doubt lingered there. Pak directed his attention back to Shannon.

"The secret Council vote on Roebor's death sentence was close. He lost by one."

"By one vote?" Shannon asked, grabbing her braid.

Do not grieve, Shannon. Death justice remains the way of my people, however hard I have fought for it to be otherwise.

"Enough!" Bale interrupted Pak's patient retelling of the story. "She is our prisoner, not a guest who's come for fireside storytelling. For aiding Roebor on Earth, I would put her to death beside him."

Pak protested, but his brother raised a paw to halt him. "I know. The Council may not countenance her death. However, if they will not, I shall ask that they force her to watch him die. And this wish they will grant."

CHAPTER TWO
Plans

SHANNON LAY CURLED AGAINST THE BARS OF HER CRUDE CELL.

Tidak's sons had departed, and despair settled over her as hours passed and the temperature dropped. But she paid no heed.

Roebor spoke at last.

Shannon. You must escape and flee to Earth.

Did Bale tell the truth about you? Shannon asked, every muscle in her body tense.

After several minutes of silence, Roebor replied. *Bale did not know one important fact: I spoke the truth when I told you that Tidak and I competed for the virus.*

But what about your vow?

He and I formed a secret pact before we took our public vow. We two took our own private oath to engage in true competition, no holds barred, and that oath took precedence over the later vow to cooperate.

So you told me the truth, Shannon said, relaxing.

Roebor hesitated. *Not entirely. Bale also spoke a truth: I told you I knew how to save Earth, although I didn't. I spoke those words so you would help me beat Tidak. It was unfor-givable. But I did struggle at every point to save your people.*

So. Shannon had left Earth to come to Roebor's aid, only to learn he'd lied to her. Was their friendship a lie, too?

Worse yet, if she'd learned the truth on Earth, would Tidak still be alive? Perhaps not. In the end, the vengeful Tidak had plucked her up with one great paw and plunged under the sea, intending to drown her. In her desperate attempt to escape death, she'd destroyed his mind. The horror of what she'd done washed over her once more. That was the desecration of which Bale spoke. The desecration attributed to Roebor, who'd hidden the truth to protect her.

To protect her.

And there lay the heart of the matter.

Roebor's lies might complicate their friendship, but his willingness to die to protect her made the friendship itself clear enough.

Right. Shannon stirred and pulled herself upright. *Time to get to work.*

* * *

I grieve that you have come here, Shannon, Roebor said, *for if you remain captive, you will endure much pain before my people release you. Did that tiny wretch, Salesti, summon you?*

"Yes." She turned to the RiverWorld creature. "Can you hear Roebor, Salesti?"

yes.

"And so, you tiny wretch, can you help me get out of this cell so that I can help Roebor avoid execution?"

yes, salesti helps shannon. narci helps as well.

"You still okay, Narci?" Shannon asked.

Am fine, the cat said.

Still not one for speechifying.

The little dragonpanther without wings has come as well? Roebor asked, indignation shading his weak voice. *Shannon, shame on you! Without wings, the small one is helpless.*

Well. Shannon wouldn't go that far. She'd seen Narci sink her small, sharp claws into creatures of significant size and to excellent effect. Not helpless, no.

Still. "Narci, if I can't get out of here and make it back to the portal, you must return to Earth without me. Understand?"

yes.

Now, how to escape this cell?

Frustrated, Shannon shook the closely-set bars. Although she could slip through tight spaces that Bale wouldn't get one leg through, some genius had spaced these bars five inches apart.

However, she conceded, dragonpanthers *did* sport incisors like saber-toothed tigers and claws that could rip a person to shreds. The jailers probably wanted to keep the sharp, pointy bits of wrong-doers inside the cell.

Bad luck.

Shannon scanned the cave for ideas. With only the limited light, she couldn't see anything that would help. Fortunately, since the Alien Troubles, she could call on her ability to cast her colors. She sent her rainbow of colors flowing to the four corners of the cave. In the glow of her casting, she could sense objects as if she were seeing them in the bright light of day.

There!

"Salesti—do you see the key hanging to the left of the cave entrance? It's on a hook. Can you carry it over here?"

too heavy for salesti, but salesti knocks key down on floor. Without further discussion, the alien flew to the key. Angry buzzing accompanied teeny, tiny grunts as Salesti worked to free it.

At last, a loud clang sounded, and Salesti's buzzing calmed as it returned and landed on Shannon's shoulder. The little creature's tinkling sound calmed and quieted Shannon. Even here, in a jail cell on a strange world, after learning her friend Roebor had betrayed her, her shoulders relaxed, the tension in her brow eased.

"Narci, can you drag the key over here?"

The small, sleek cat skittered to the key, and soon Shannon was watching Narci's slow drag, pause, drag, pause, as the cat inched the key toward the cell. Seven feet from the cell, Narci stopped and flopped down, the side of her head flat on the cave's floor. Her black whiskers twitched and stilled.

"Narci! What's the matter? Are you okay?"

Must rest, Narci replied.

Shannon studied the key, which was about as long and wide as Narci. And judging by the cat's struggle to drag the thing along by its circular end, it might weigh more than her own diminutive six pounds.

No wonder the cat had had enough. *Poor baby.* She'd given it everything she had.

"Just rest, Narci. Tell me if you start feeling worse."

Yes. The cat could muster no more.

Shannon reached through the bars, stretching toward the cat as far as she could. Still much too far.

Shannon plucked the alien from her shoulder and raised her hand even with her face. She looked Salesti right in the eye. "Okay, Salesti. Back to you. I know you possess immeasurable strength that you pretend you don't have."

Salesti spoke the word *but* and then stopped.

Shannon continued. "I never figured out why you hide it, but I bet you're strong enough to fight every dragonpanther on this planet at one time with a blindfold on and your wings glued to your sides."

Salesti sank into Shannon's palm.

"Come on, my friend. This one time, use your energy, grab that key, and haul it over here."

Salesti stilled. *shannon not knows everything about salesti.*

"No, because you don't share, Salesti. Let's see: I know that six of you live on RiverWorld with the Seladorans. You all call yourselves by the same name: salesti. I call you Salesti because the first time you came to me, you didn't share this fact. What else? I know you don't have a gender."

Shannon paused for a response. *Nothing.*

"You're all pale yellow but each of you is surrounded by a unique aura. Yours is rose-colored. And you have hidden power. That's all I know." Shannon hesitated again, giving Salesti an opening to explain why it held back its power.

Silence.

"You and your comrades split a wormhole in two. I saw that with my own eyes. That's messing with the very fabric of the universe, Salesti. If your tribe can do that, you can get a measly key across the floor. Please?"

roebor not such excellent friend, Salesti said. *lied to shannon. maybe shannon not wants to help roebor now?*

Shannon laughed. "That's not like you, Salesti. It sounds like you're looking for an excuse not to help me get the key."

Salesti emitted a tiny sigh. *yes true. salesti not wants to tell shannon that salesti cannot help shannon with key.*

"We've got to do something. Roebor saved my life. More than once. I can't turn my back on him."

Salesti, Roebor said from whatever distant place they'd imprisoned him, *Shannon should never have come here. If the truth slips out, she will die. Get her home. Please.*

The tiny alien flew from Shannon's palm and landed on the cave floor next to the still-prone Narci. It studied the listless cat.

narci not fares so well on fireworld. narci needs to go home. and salesti would help if salesti could. but for first time, salesti cannot.

cannot, it repeated.

A small hum echoed off the silent cave walls. Not Salesti's cheerful hum. Not her angry buzz. This chord struck Shannon deep in her chest. The sound of ineffable sadness.

* * *

Shannon forgot her own predicament. She pushed Roebor from her thoughts. Even her concern for her Narci moved to the back burner.

Salesti couldn't be sad. It couldn't be helpless. Everyone depended on Salesti. *Shannon* depended on Salesti.

Essi, her first alien friend, had explained the salestis to Shannon: they were wise, powerful, ancient, loving. Now that Shannon knew Salesti whole and hearty, the thought of a diminished Salesti caused her hands to tremble in her lap.

"What. . . what do you mean, you can't help?"

salesti not well.

The finality with which Salesti ended these words stopped Shannon from asking anything more. She couldn't bear to hear what Salesti might say.

"Okay. Okay, all right. Then don't worry, Salesti. You rest right there, and as soon as we can, we'll get me out and get Roebor out and get you home to your fellow salestis. They'll take care of you. I'm sure they. . . ."

Shannon wasn't sure of anything.

She inspected Narci. The cat still lay on her side, hyperventilating. Good thing her fur was short enough to help keep her cool. Poor thing. *No help there.*

The key lay about five feet beyond Shannon's farthest reach. Rising and walking the perimeter of her cell, she hunted for anything that might help her pull the key in, anything at all.

In one corner lay a huge, gray mat the size of a basketball half-court. *For errant dragonpanthers to sleep on, no doubt.* Not far from the mat lay a covered opening in the floor with a lever above it. A slight odor emanated from the space, indicating the one other bodily accommodation in the place: the toilet.

"There's nothing here I can use." Shannon aimed a frustrated kick at the mat.

To her surprise, the edge flopped up and overlapped the rest of the mat a few feet. She pulled on the upturned edge.

"I thought this would be heavy," Shannon said, "but it's lightweight. I keep forgetting that technology exists here."

At this, Roebor emitted a loud *phffft*.

Shannon pulled harder. Despite the mat's tremendous size, she could move it. She dragged the forward edge to the cell bars nearest the key.

The cell bars drove into the cave floor, so Shannon would have to prop up the mat rather than slide it under the bars. That way, she could shove part of it through the bars.

She threaded a corner through the space between the bars. The mat flopped back and forth as if alive. But after a persistent struggle—with much swearing, grunting, and mat-jerking—its corner reached Salesti and Narci. "Now, do you two think you can flip the key up onto that flat corner so I can drag it back?"

Narci and Salesti must have communicated—although Shannon didn't hear it—because, in a concerted effort, the cat took the circular end of the key between her teeth and one paw, and Salesti placed all four of her paws under the other end. As Shannon watched, fascinated, the cat stood, Salesti flapped her tiny hummingbird wings, and the key flipped over the edge onto the mat.

"Good!" *Now to draw it in.* Shannon pulled the mat back inch by inch, trying her hardest not to dislodge the key, but she had only moved the mat about two feet before the unruly mass of fabric behind her flipped, twisting the mat all the way to the edge. The key slid off and clanged onto the cave floor.

Shannon pounded the cell bars in frustration. So much work. *Wasted.*

She'd have to try again.

But first, she had to find a way to secure the key while she pulled in the mat.

After a few moments, she had the solution: She'd make a hole in the corner for the key.

She tried to poke a finger through the mat, but it was too tough. She bit it and tried to rip it apart with her teeth, but it wouldn't split.

Roebor, how can I make a hole in the mat that's in here? I'll try to get it over to Narci and Salesti so they can put the key in the hole, and I can drag it back. But my teeth can't rip the mat.

Hmmm. You can think of no simpler way to get the key?

No, I can't. I'm open to suggestions.

Do not snap, Shannon. I shall help you. Take the mat back over to the latrine. Can you see it? A large, covered, black square in the floor with a red lever above it on the cave wall.

Shannon grabbed the mat and lugged it back to the latrine. "Okay, it's here. Now what?"

Open the latrine partway by pulling that lever on the wall halfway down.

She reached toward the lever but couldn't get a firm grip on it, and a soft cry of frustration escaped. Regretting her outburst, she peeked at the cave entrance to see if the noise had attracted attention. No one came running to check on her, *thank Odin.* Shannon rolled the mat part way up, fighting its floppy length with each roll. She climbed onto it and—*yes!*—she grasped the lever. Two inches higher, she would have been out of luck. She pulled.

It didn't budge.

"I hate this place."

She tried again, swinging her feet off the mat so that she hung with her full weight on the lever.

It creaked downward.

The latrine cover opened, creating a gap of three feet.

"Okay, now what?"

If you lean over the edge into the opening, you will see two heavy black bars that support the retracting plates. Do you see that? Pull an edge of the mat to one of the bars.

Shannon laid down on her stomach and scooted to the opening. The smell from below sent her scrambling backward, and she flipped over on her back.

"So, if you've developed such good tech, why does that pit smell like a dung beetle doused in cotton candy?"

Few of my people visit that cell, Shannon, but we do not pamper those who do.

"No, you do not." Nonetheless, for Salesti and Narci's sake, as well as Roebor's, Shannon must move. She needed to get all three of her friends off this planet. Shannon inhaled deeply and held her breath. She flipped back onto her stomach, grabbed the mat, and edged forward, so her head and arms extended over the gap.

The edge of the bar will feel sharp and rough to the touch. Rub the mat against it, hard.

Shannon worked at rubbing the mat until she had no choice but to take a breath. The putrid stench caused her stomach to heave. She jerked back to struggle with her unhappy gut, pulling the mat with her. As the remains of her breakfast—which she'd consumed a long time ago now—exited her system in a great upheaval, a satisfying rip sounded from the latrine.

Again she dragged the mat to the front of the cell. She aimed the ripped corner through the space between the bars and stuffed more and more of the mat edge through, struggling to reach Narci and Salesti, who sat resting and watching her progress.

Finally, the edge with the cut reached them. Once more, they stirred themselves from their exhaustion.

Is your plan working well, Shannon?

Depends on your idea of "working well." So far, so good. Shannon hacked out one last bit of acidic bile.

She addressed Salesti, who sat on the floor, its tiny wings quiet, and Narci, who'd succeeded in lifting her head. "It's up to you two now. Can you push the key into the rip right there in the corner?—see it?—so I can pull it back." To help Narci grasp the concept, she framed a short video in her mind of what she needed. "Are you well enough to do it?"

yes, Salesti said, although its voice sounded frail.

Yes, Narci said, her voice so faint Shannon could hardly hear her.

"I'm so sorry, babies. Help me with this, and I swear I will bust out of here without asking anything else of you."

The edge lay flat enough on the corner for Narci to climb onto it. Salesti held the one end of the key steady, while Narci pushed the key all the way into the gap.

"Oh my gosh, you did it! You did it! Roebor, they slid the key into the mat!" Shannon hopped on her toes to celebrate.

Time to bring it home. She pulled the mat back at a slow, steady pace, so as not to dislodge the key. When it arrived in the cell at last, and Shannon retrieved it from the hole, she hefted its cold and considerable weight. "No wonder it tired you two out. It feels like iron."

Shannon looked up at the lock on the cell door. She'd have to bunch up the mat again to reach it. "Why don't you have a modern cell door that opens remotely with the push of a button, Roebor? This is ancient tech, even on Earth."

FireWorld retains many ancient customs, Shannon. As we intend the latrine to be unpleasant, in the same way, we intend the lock and key to be a reminder.

A roar from the cave entrance interrupted her examination of the lock and key. At the sound, the key clanged to the floor.

She looked up. Bale, followed by Pak, had returned. Bale rushed for the key.

It was too close to the bars!

Shannon snatched it up again and scurried back. She checked for Narci and Salesti. They'd vanished.

Good.

Stay hidden, little ones.

Bale cocked his head at the bunched-up portion of the mat by the cell's edge.

"How did you get that key? Give it to me."

CHAPTER THREE
Down the Chute

FOUR OTHER DRAGONPANTHERS TROOPED IN BEHIND THE BROTHERS. Stiff and scowling, they'd evidently been persuaded by Bale that Shannon was the enemy.

Bale turned to Pak. "Do you know who gave her the key? If you do, I—"

"Me? Calm down, brother. I stayed with the Golds all afternoon, right through Last Meal. She has the key?"

"Someone must have given it to her, and I want to know who."

The others behind Pak stepped back in unison, murmured denials, and shook their heads.

"Jal! Roebor's sister must have given it to the Earth thing so she could help Roebor escape. Bring Jal here."

"She does not care about the Earth thing, Bale. Jal has spent every minute lobbying the Council for Roebor's life. Don't bring her into this. Besides, what could this Earth woman do to aid Roebor if she escaped? The guards would never let her near him."

Bale paced outside the cell, clicking his thumb claw and third toe claw together again and again. "I want to find out for myself. Bring Jal here."

"You are overstepping your bounds," Pak said, placing his paw on Bale's shoulder to stop his pacing. "The Blues have many loyalists on the Council. They have allowed our retribution against Roebor to proceed, but we must treat her with care."

"Who else would have done this?" He nodded at two of the dragonpanthers. "Get her now." They dipped their chins in response and left the cave.

Pak reared onto his hind legs, a ridge of fur rising along his spine. "Leave her out of this." Bale reared to match his brother, baring his teeth.

Shannon pressed her back to the cell wall. Dragonpathers in ferocious mode was something to see. And avoid.

Pak sliced the air with one front paw. "Who else would have done it, you ask? How am I to know? But I doubt someone would give the Earth thing the key and then leave her to manage the lock alone. Perhaps she is telekinetic."

Bale rounded on Shannon at the suggestion she might have stolen the key herself.

"Telekinetic? She floated the key into the cell?" He grabbed two bars and shook them. "Did you? Are you?"

Shannon winced at Bale's questions. She'd stayed quiet during Bale's ranting, happy to remain unnoticed. *Would it serve her better to say yes or no?* If she denied it, he'd continue seeking someone to blame. If she said yes, and if they took it from her, she wouldn't get near that key again.

"Am I what?" she asked, buying time. She didn't want to cause trouble for Roebor's sister or anyone else. But she didn't want them ransacking the place in a hunt for her real accomplices either.

"Did you float the key to the cell? Do you possess the ability to move objects with your mind?"

"Okay, yes, it's true. I am telekinetic. I can definitely move objects short distances if they're not too heavy. So, yes. That's right: I stole the key from the peg over there. With my telekinetic abilities."

Just don't ask for a demonstration.

She glanced at Pak as she spoke. He came down onto all fours and contemplated her with a puzzled frown. He didn't look convinced. He knew Salesti and Narci were hiding around here somewhere. But her false confession would keep Roebor's sister Jal out of this, so he wasn't likely to give up her minuscule accomplices.

"I want the key now."

"What happens to me when I give you the key?" *Nothing good.*

Bale roared in frustration. "Do we have another key to this cell?"

Odin's eye, she prayed no spare existed. In his current bad temper, Bale would tear her to pieces like so much confetti if he found a way into the cell. Shannon shrank against the back wall.

Neither of the dragonpanthers still in the cave with the brothers had answered Bale's call for another key. One of them, smaller than Bale and Pak, with cardinal red fur, finally said, "We have so little use for the cell, if another key once existed, we may have forgotten its location. I will go ask Council Leader Faldan."

Shannon wanted all the dragonpanthers to leave so she could figure out how to escape. How could she manage that now that they knew she had the key?

Distraction.

"Did you talk to the Council about me after—what did you call it?—Last Meal?" Shannon asked.

Bale grinned like a cat about to gulp down a tasty goldfish snack. "Yes. You shall face the Council's interrogation tomorrow after the execution. You must satisfy them that you did not aid Roebor in the desecration of my father's body."

Shannon heard a distant moan. *Salesti, you must free Shannon and take her home tonight.*

Bale smacked his paws together. "I know what to do with you. You desire to see Roebor? I'll cage you with him."

"No, Bale. We do not have the Council's permission for that. Besides, Roebor strains the limits of the cage already. We cannot squeeze both of them into it."

"As if I care." Bale never took his eyes from Shannon, even as he spoke to his brother.

Would that give us a move, Roebor? Could you break out if they tried to stuff me in with you?

Perhaps.

Is he telling the truth when he says he'll put me in the cage, or is it a ruse to get the key?

Knowing Bale, I believe his desire to see me crush you to death against the bars of my cage outweighs his desire to kill you in the cell as soon as he lays his hands on the key.

Small comfort.

"All right. If you take me to Roebor, I'll give you the key."

As Shannon took a step toward the front of the cell, the two dragonpanthers who'd left to find Jal returned, walking upright, grasping a sky-blue female by each of her front legs. Her less angular head and more slender form lent her a daintier appearance than her companions. The top of her head barely reached Bale's shoulder, and Pak's huge paw could swallow hers if he took it, which Shannon sensed he yearned to do.

"Jal," Pak said. To her escorts, he said, "Leave her alone, or answer to me." He reared again, sparks of blue flame escaping from his lips, as he moved to her side and nudged the other dragonpanthers away.

"My apologies, Jal. I thought you had given the Earth thing the key to her cell, but she has confessed that she stole it herself." Bale bowed his head to her.

Jal peered past Bale into the cell. "So, the rumors prove true. This tiny Earth creature has come to Roebor's aid when not one of the cowards of FireWorld could find the courage to stand against the Golds." Her contemptuous gaze fell on each of the others. "Good for you," she said to Shannon. "What are you called?" She sniffed at Shannon. "And do all Earth things smell like you?"

"Shannon. And, no, the scent belongs to me alone among Earthlings."

"Quiet!" Bale said.

"Nice to meet you, Jal," Shannon whispered a rush of words. She'd side with any friendly face in this crowd.

Bale took a menacing step toward the cell.

Shannon flinched. *She'd keep the key until Bale calmed down. Which looked unlikely to happen. Ever.*

"Woman—Shannon—" Bale's brother Pak said in a quiet voice, "Give me the key, and I promise you will remain undisturbed in this cell until the Council requires your presence in the morning."

"No—" Bale said.

Pak interrupted. "Accept that, Bale, or I will rouse the Council from their private evening affairs to hear your proposal to stuff her in with Roebor."

Bale slammed his fist against the cell bars. "Very well." He stepped back, and Pak took his place.

Shannon trusted Pak more than his brother—which wasn't saying much, since she trusted Bale with the key about as much as she trusted Narci with an open can of tuna. But she wanted them to leave so she could find a way out.

Roebor? Is this a better option than trying to escape when they put me in the cage with you?

Yes, you can trust Pak. In any event, I have examined my wings. I do not believe I can fly. I will probably never fly again.

The great sorrow that accompanied those words twisted her heart.

She must chance it then. She gripped the key, moved forward, and handed it through the bars to Pak, then backtracked toward the cell's rear wall. *Now she'd find out if she was just another piece of burnt toast.* She gripped her braid with tight fingers.

Bale held out his palm to his brother, but Pak tucked the key into a pouch of loose fur located about where a man's shirt pocket would be. He patted his chest. "It will remain safe with me."

She loosened her death grip on her braid.

With Shannon secured again behind bars, everyone exited except one of the cardinal reds, who remained behind on watch. He settled himself on the floor at the cave's entrance, placed his head on his folded forelegs, and for a time, stared at Shannon as if he could keep it up all night.

Loki's luck. If the red stayed awake, she'd have no chance to escape. Shannon curled with her knees to her chest on the mat, her back to the dragonpanther, and remained still, giving him nothing of interest to watch.

* * *

Bright light shining from the cave entrance dimmed as the two suns set. Light fixtures on the wall to each side of the cave entrance and one above the latrine blinked on and bathed the areas within a ten-foot radius in strong amber light. The rest of the cave remained in shadows.

As the temperature dipped lower, Shannon longed for a heavier jacket. Her stomach grumbled. When she could stay still no longer, she turned, inch by inch, to view the guard.

He slept.

Thank Odin.

She reached out to Roebor to let him know that the guard on duty now snoozed in blissful ignorance of Shannon's escape plans.

Except she had no escape plans.

So, back to square one. Any ideas, Roebor? she asked.

Nothing, he said. *Salesti?*

salesti thinks of nothing.

How about you, Narci? Roebor asked.

The cat purred as if pleased that Roebor had consulted her. Slipping from the shadows, she crept along the cave's far wall and wiggled through the bars. She pattered over to the latrine and peered into the opening.

The dragonpanthers would have accounted for that route, wouldn't they? Plus, it stank down there like rotting zombies wearing bad cologne.

Narci suggests I escape through the latrine, Roebor. But that's impossible, right? Gated off to prevent such flight? A non-starter? Right?

She hoped.

Hmm. Dragonpanthers cannot fit down the latrine chute, and to my knowledge, we have never imprisoned a human. My people have had no occasion to give a single thought to escape from the cell through the sewer.

Damn, Shannon said.

I haven't seen the schematics for our sewer system, Roebor said, *but I can tell you the latrine in your cell leads to the island network. Tunnels will exist, and they will be of sufficient size for workers and, therefore, of ample size for you.*

Loki's luck. Let's try to come up with something else.

Bale's guard watches over you. Pak has taken the key. You must escape and leave FireWorld before morning. I see no other option.

Okay, I'll take a peep at it. That's all I'm promising. You realize I may die from the fumes alone.

Shannon rolled onto her knees, stopping after each slight movement to check on her captor. His eyes remained closed. She crept to the edge of the latrine, closed her mouth and pinched her nose, peering over the edge once more.

A set of dim lights dotted the circular tube that stretched down only three or four feet before opening out over a channel of sludge.

How come it's so spiffy clean up in this chute?

As I have mentioned, a limited number of prisoners means that a limited need for the latrine. The sanitation crews work diligently.

So I see.

Shannon pulled back from her vantage point and stroked Narci's tidy, shiny coat.

Your idea wins, Narci. But I'll have to swing out to try to land beyond the slop in the canal. I won't have a free hand to hold you. I could tuck you in my sweatshirt and hope not to squish you when I jump, or you could try to sneak by the guard. What do you want to do?

The cat pattered along the perimeter of the cave to the entrance near the sleeping red. Salesti flew to the other side of the sleeping figure, in case Narci needed a distraction. As if stalking a mouse, the cat crouched low, moving one foot at a time, and inched her way along the opening.

As Narci crept forward, the guard stirred, checked his prisoner, and yawned, opening his mouth much wider than Shannon believed possible, like a snake with its jaw unhinged to swallow a rat. The cat froze low to the ground, less than a foot from the elbow of the red's folded foreleg. Shannon curled on the mat, facing him, but she remained still, feigning sleep. His lips smacked, and he settled back.

Careful, kitten.

Shannon dared not move.

Go back to sleep, big fella.

She burned to find out whether he'd spotted the cat, but she figured she would hear him stirring if he went after her.

If he sees you, Narci, hightail it back to me. He can't reach you here.

After what seemed like a day and a half, Narci signaled: *Safe.*

Shannon dared to peek. The guard's head rested on his paws, snoring.

Well done, Narci. Salesti, will you stay with her? Hide at the boulders where we landed until I find a way out of here.

* * *

The latrine presented two problems: Shannon couldn't hold on to the smooth, silver tube's inner surface to climb down, and it didn't provide a rim at the bottom for Shannon to grab so she could swing out over the canal of sewage, hoping to make dry land.

She surveyed the cell again for solutions.

The mat. Shannon could make use of it once more. First, dragging it at a snail's pace to reduce the noise, she took it to the latrine. Then, standing again on a portion of the bunched mat, she wedged a piece of it behind the lever to hold the mat still.

Sliding another edge of the mat, Shannon reached the latrine opening without waking the red. She stuffed a small portion of the huge mat into the opening until the padding allowed her to inch into the chute, shoes pushing against one side, her backside and elbows against the mat on the other side. This piece of the mat filled the chute and hung down below its bottom rim.

No use delaying the inevitable.

She inched down the chute. The farther down she moved, the stronger the smell became. Twice, she came close to heaving, her temperature rising along with the bile, but both times she fought it back.

Inch by inch, she moved her feet, then her elbows, until both her back and her feet were only a few inches above the bottom edge of the chute. She planned to swing while hanging from the section of the mat's edge that hung down two feet below the rim. She pulled up that bottom edge of the mat, clutched it, and dropped until she hung under the chute. She hesitated. *Would the mat slip and spill her into the sludge?*

The mat held firm. Its immense bulk and her precaution of stuffing some of it behind the lever prevented it from budging, even with Shannon's weight attached.

Below her, the sewage flowed along in a canal with a wide pathway running along beside it. The edges of the canal sloped outward, so that the pathway was a long distance from her, at least fifteen feet.

It might as well be a mile.

She would take a plunge when she dropped, and it would be horrid. *But it had to be done.*

As she prepared to swing, she happened to glance behind her.

Wait.

To her surprise, the edge of the canal behind her rose from the muck much closer! On that side, beyond the sewage, the path itself wasn't more than five feet from where she hung. One at a time, Shannon flipped her hands around on the mat until she faced the closer canal edge. She began to swing her feet back and forth.

But before she could work up to her widest swing, she lost her grip. Momentum carried her only partway over the concrete passageway, where she landed on her side. Her hip crashed like a sack of potatoes onto the path, and her legs scraped the rock floor, but her torso, shoulder, and head still dangled over the sludge. The tip of her braid dipped into the sewage as her momentum carried her head down and into the canal wall, hammering it hard against the smooth surface.

She cried out. An echo of her moan reverberated along the tunnel. Her vision collapsed frame by frame down to black; then frame by frame, it expanded again. Everything moved in slow, slow motion. Shannon's head and upper body slid toward the canal. In a desperate attempt to pull herself the rest of the way onto the path, she clutched at the top edge of the canal wall, terrified she would plunge headlong into the sewage.

CHAPTER FOUR
Out from Under

SHANNON! WHAT'S HAPPENING? Roebor asked, his voice raw.

By throwing her left arm back over the ledge and maneuvering her legs parallel with the canal, Shannon, after a struggle, hoisted her shoulders onto the path. She laid on her back, breathing hard. She heard the words, but she couldn't process them. *What was he saying? Who was saying it?*

A sharp pain in the side of her head pierced her sluggish mind as she tried to sit up.

Shannon?

That sounded better. She grasped the meaning there: her name. The voice belonged to. . . she remembered now—Roebor.

I fell. Hit my head. Give me a minute.

Shannon sat, waiting for her thoughts to return to normal. Twenty minutes later, she shivered.

If only she'd worn her fall jacket instead of her sweatshirt.

Her chills prompted her to rise, but she stumbled as she lost her balance. When she'd steadied herself, she tested her ankles: they'd survived.

She took a tentative step. Hip protested; head protested. But she could walk. *Well, she could almost walk. Okay, she could limp.*

I can move. My head's clearer now.

The same dim lights that illuminated the vertical shaft lit the tunnel in which she stood, revealing that it led off to her left and right, a wide circle of metallic gray disappearing into darkness as the pathway curved.

The path was wider on the opposite side of the canal and narrower on her side: narrow, but still wide enough for a dragonpanther to walk. Plenty wide enough for her.

A heavy, sweet smell overlaid the terrible odor of the sewage rising from the canal. *Chemical treatment.* Shannon took shallow breaths through her mouth to stave off the worst of the stench.

When she'd first arrived on FireWorld, the sun had been rising behind the two dragonpanthers and the cliffs behind them. That put north to her right. A quick glance around the cliffs when she first looked showed her that most of the occupied caves were to the north. The waste flowed in the opposite direction. She shrugged and started hobbling south with as much speed as she could muster.

And hobbled.

Thirty minutes later, Shannon spotted an off-shoot tunnel on the other side of the canal that ended in a set of stairs.

I've passed by ladders on the wall, Roebor, but now I see a set of stairs. Do you have any idea where they might go?

Yes. I've seen sanitation workers going in and coming out of the entrances to such steps. On the outside, a worker must have a key card that allows the door to slide open. I don't know what opens the door from the inside. If you can get outside from there, it will put you somewhere on the main path along the cliff front. I suggest you try it.

The stairs it would be. But how would she get across the canal?

The dragonpanthers must cross to this side one way or another. Shannon would figure out how.

The tunnel curved out of sight about a hundred feet ahead. She trudged forward to see what lay beyond, anxious to leave the obnoxious stink behind, yet in too much pain to hurry.

Yes. Another eighty yards beyond the bend, a metal bridge spanned the canal. She struggled on, crossed the bridge, and made her way back to the staircase. There, she contemplated how to climb the giant steps.

Seeing no other option, she threw one bruised knee onto the smooth, white-tiled ledge of the first step and hauled herself on to it, then stood. She stepped to the next step and the next. At length, she arrived at the top and stopped to rub her hip, which had flared with pain at each swivel onto a new stair.

A huge, white metal door now confronted her. She searched with growing frustration but could find no key-card slot or pad, no door handle, no button, or bar.

"I don't see anything that gives me a clue how to open the door. What should I look for?"

Often such doors open when someone breaks the solid stream of a laser beam. The beam will be purple but as thin as wire, and high on the door.

Shannon studied the door.

There! I see it. Odin's eye, *it's high, all right.*

She raised her hand as high as she could, but it didn't come close to breaking the beam. She jumped, her hand held high, and winced as she landed, a sharp twinge stabbing her hip and a lightning bolt of pain shooting through her head.

Still not good enough. She backed off and took a running leap at the top of the door.

Ow.

Nothing.

She unzipped her sweatshirt and performed another running jump, waving her sweatshirt with her outstretched hand.

No. Not high enough.

Right. Time for drastic measures.

Off came her blue jeans, her blue socks, and her blue shoes. She tied the jeans to her sweatshirt and the socks to each other, and she tied one sock to a sweatshirt sleeve. Now she held one long, continuous length of clothing, which left her in her blue T-shirt and undergarments. She slipped on her shoes.

Shannon backed off one more time, took a long running start, and leaped as high as she could, swinging the jeans-sweatshirt-sock contraption in a high, overhand arc. She slammed into the door and bounced off into a heap. As she lay there, exhausted, hip and head throbbing, and praying to *Odin* that she wouldn't have to take another run at it, the door slid open.

She struggled to her feet and stepped outside, desperate to find the closest hiding spot. The door opened into an alcove designed as an entrance to the sewer system. No dragonpanthers in sight. *Thank Odin.* She sucked in great gulps of clean, fresh-smelling air.

A bit sulphuric from the sea fire, but still.

I'm out, she said to Roebor.

She dressed in the shadows at the back of the alcove, wincing as she jerked her jeans over her bruised hip, her fingers not flying fast enough to keep pace with her anxiety.

Do you have any idea what time it is? Is this path you mentioned going to be crawling with dragonpanthers between where I am and where you are? Or between here and the portal? I'll need to go down and find Narci and Salesti before I come find you.

Hah, Roebor said in a voice that held no laughter, *I cannot measure time anymore. I have inhabited this cage too long.*

Bale and his gang caught me trying to escape right after they ate Last Meal and talked to the Council. Does that help?

Indeed. If I allow time for the guard to fall sleep, time in the tunnel. . . hmm. . . I would put the time, as you measure it, at almost midnight.

So, who's out and about at midnight?

Dragonpanther biorhythms function based on natural light. You should see little activity on the path. You will see even less because you have emerged in the southern, less-populated area of the cliffs.

Sounds safe. Now, tell me how to find you.

Shannon, no. Get off the planet now. Bale will discover your absence any minute.

Tell me where you are. Then we can talk.

CHAPTER FIVE
Roebor

SHANNON CRADLED THE CAT in her sweatshirt; Salesti sat perched on her shoulder. They crouched behind a glassy, pink-gold rock wall that encircled a sunken arena so huge three football fields would fit inside. Terraced steps of the same smooth, pink-gold stone created dragonpanther-sized perches all the way around. The steps reached down to a fire pit as large as a pair of elephants.

She peered through the archway leading to the steps and stared at a contraption that hung over the fire pit. A black tower stood like a crane on one side, and a sturdy, black, metal arm jutted from it, extending over the pit. A house-sized black cage dangled from the end of the arm. Cruelly crammed into that crate and forced into a tight ball: a magnificent, Prussian-blue dragonpanther. His great wings, crushed and crumpled, bent in unnatural directions. His body mashed his tail beneath him, and his four legs jabbed into his ribcage. He couldn't move his head more than the few inches that had allowed him to flash the silver-blue fire of his eyes at them in greeting when they arrived.

Roebor.

The sight of him in that cage shook Shannon to her core.

Four dragonpanthers guarded the cage, all with fur in various shades of gold—relatives of Tidak, the dragonpanther she'd killed on Earth. The one sitting with his head high and alert on the far side of the pit might be Bale. Hard to tell at this distance in the dim moonlight. Shannon bit her lip; she'd never sneak past their alert vigil.

The walkway that encircled the arena where Shannon crouched was dark, empty, and quiet. Even so, Shannon would be exposed if a dragonpanther came along to visit with the four down below. Some distance behind her, a large building cast deep shadows. A metal retracting window ran across the side facing her.

Odin's eye. A concession stand. Shannon rebelled at the very notion that dragonpanthers might stop for beer and pretzels—or whatever the dragonpanther equivalent might be—on their way to Roebor's execution.

Nonetheless, an L-shaped corner on the structure provided a dark cranny that would offer Shannon a safer hiding spot than her current exposed position. Checking again for stray dragonpanthers, and finding the walkway deserted, she scuttled back to the relative security of the concession stand and settled into the shadowed corner.

That's how they plan to execute you? By roasting you alive?

Roebor had once explained to Shannon that FireWorld entertained a strange mixture of new and ancient ways. Roebor told her he'd urged his people to abandon public executions to no avail. But he'd spared her the details of the crane and the pit.

Are you sure they wouldn't listen to me if I were to address them in the morning and explain how it happened? I can't let you take the blame for me.

Oh, they would listen to you, but for the wrong reason. You would fascinate them. We do not visit Earth. Most of them have never seen a human.

Would they believe me?

They possess no standard by which to measure your veracity, but they would have no reason to believe that you would lie to protect a dragonpanther, nor would they believe that you would sacrifice yourself for me by lying. Most of my people do not subscribe to such virtues. No, they would simply kill you.

Maybe they won't execute me when I tell them that Tidak tried to kill me.

Shannon, the logic on FireWorld cuts in a different direction. Tidak's death and the manner in which it happened preordained the event about to unfold. Or rather, I determined the outcome when I returned Tidak's body with its destroyed head.

Why didn't you hide him?

I had no choice. It happened that a group of dragonpanthers had gathered in a vigil at the portal to await the return of Tidak and me. They all witnessed my arrival with his body. If given a choice, however, I still might not have hid his body because the absence of a body for the funeral ceremonies imposes a cruelty upon my people.

But it's not fair.

Roebor coughed a laugh filled with sadness. *This world is no fairer than the universe, Shannon. Despite my crime, they gave me the opportunity to work with the virus and develop* a cure that would save my people, and I succeeded, so I can accept the outcome. Now we must let the matter play out.

But I can't accept the outcome.

If you speak, matters will go one of two ways. Either they will not believe you, and I will die. Or they will believe you, and you will replace me here in this life-taker. And they will still execute me for not stopping you from killing Tidak.

They'd kill us both?

Remember, at the heart of their abhorrence lies the destruction of his head. This may never be allowed. No pat on the shoulder and wag of the finger for such a crime.

But I had no choice.

This does not matter.

All right. If I can't persuade the decision-makers, we must free you—divert these guards somehow and get a key to you.

You would die trying. No one can divert the guards. They have sworn to remain on Death Watch until my execution.

We might—

I have examined my chances of escape from every angle and have found no solution. Logically, the best of all disastrous outcomes will be that which stands the greatest chance of harming the fewest of us. That outcome requires that you, Narci, and Salesti leave my world before Bale discovers your escape.

No.

Please, gift to me this one comfort: Let me die knowing you three have returned to your worlds unharmed.

Shannon smacked her palm on the rock wall. *Okay, say I don't speak out. Isn't the best outcome getting you out and all of us escaping?*

Even if escape were possible, Bale and Pak and their followers would chase us to Earth and turn the planet upside down to ferret us out. Many would die. Would you wish that? Roebor paused as if waiting for a response. Shannon didn't give him one. He continued. *Of course not. No, it must end tomorrow. The people must see it end. I see no other way through.*

There must be something. . . .

Shannon hesitated.

A last-ditch tactic. . . it would work. . . but could she and Roebor live with it?

What if we bring your consciousness over to my mind? I could bring you to the Great Room I've constructed there. You've been there before, so you know what it's like. We would leave a body—your body—behind so Tidak's family could have closure. Afterward, we—let me think—we could come back and, at the moment a dragonpanther dies, we could send you into his mind?

No, Shannon. We would have zero chance of returning to find a healthy body lying around with a mind that has died moments before. The real question is whether I could bear to leave my own body and take up permanent residence in your mind.

Shannon considered Roebor's words. *Yes, I'm afraid you're right. I suppose the arrangement would have to be permanent.*

That presented a hard question for both of them.

If I had never visited your mind, Shannon, I would reject the idea out of hand. However, I have experienced it, and now you have unnerved me, for you have offered a viable alternative.

Unnerved you? Why?

To live in your mind would not constitute a good life for me or you. And it would be you and no other. No creature's mind, except yours, with your mysterious powers, could support me for more than a few hours, with the possible exception of Salesti and the others of its kind.

Roebor's voice resonated with despair. *Would it be better than no life? Would it be better than the slow, painful death I face? I cannot say. Do not speak for a time. I must deliberate.*

Shannon sank down against the wall. "Could you make it happen, Salesti? If he says yes?"

is simple. salesti flies to roebor, flies so high dragonpanthers not see, drops so quiet dragonpanthers not hear. roebor flows to salesti, salesti brings roebor to shannon, shannon takes roebor, and all return to portal and leave.

"He's a big presence, Salesti, and you're tiny and unwell. Would his presence put you in danger?"

if shannon takes roebor as soon as possible, salesti can do.

"Roebor said it himself: living with me, or anyone, wouldn't be a good life; it wouldn't be much of a life at all. What a choice: slow death by fire or life by proxy." The enormity of Roebor's predicament struck Shannon with full force. She sagged against the wall in her hidden corner.

Oh, Roebor, I'm so sorry.

For a while, Shannon and Salesti didn't speak. Shannon's eyelids grew heavy. She nodded off and jerked awake twice.

I'm sorry to bother you, Roebor. I need to move somewhere away from here, or I'll fall asleep, and someone may find me. Where can we hide?

You can walk to my lab from here.

How can we get in?

I believe the door may be unlocked. Bale and the others came there to take me prisoner while I worked at my desk. They dragged me out in haste, and I recall the door remaining open behind us.

Roebor gave Shannon directions, and she soon found the opening to a huge cavern that led into ten or fifteen smaller caves. Following Roebor's instructions, they took the first cave opening on the right and traveled down a dark passage large enough for a dragonpanther to pass through. At a point Shannon failed to notice in the dark, the passage turned into a smooth hall. The hall led to a mammoth wooden door that was slightly ajar.

Slipping inside, Shannon could see vague shapes in the faint glow of the moons that shone through holes high in the cave wall. She could make out the outlines of gleaming white counters—too high for her to reach—as well as stools, tall cabinets, equipment, and overhead lighting. Roebor's work-place appeared to contain everything a well-equipped lab should have.

We're in, Roebor. I think we're safe here. I don't dare close the door, though. I'd never get it open again.

The open door is fine. No one will come during the night. Just leave again before first light. Sleep well, Shannon.

Shannon began to say good night but stopped herself. Of course it would not be a good night for Roebor.

It was possibly the last night Roebor would ever know. Shannon shuddered.

A faint antiseptic odor seeped from every surface, and heat flowing through grates in the floor kept the room cozy compared to the chill outside.

"I can't wrap my mind around it," Shannon whispered to Salesti. "In the first place, how can a dragonpanther work in a lab? In the second place, where do they make all this stuff?"

roebor not speaks of this with shannon?

"No, the topic never came up."

digits of dragonpanthers plenty long enough to use lab equipment, no problem. dragonpanthers able to stand on hind legs, sit on stools, no problem. so why shannon not understands they work in labs?

"I. . . I don't know. In all of my time in his company, I haven't seen Roebor spend very much time on his hind legs. I always picture him on all fours."

shannon needs new picture.

"Guess I do. But what about the scientific equipment, the cabinets, the counters, all of it? I haven't seen a lot of FireWorld, but I didn't notice any factories. Do they have them?"

few factories. dragonpanthers depend on a single portal. one to distant world, advanced civilization, peaceful. fireworld trades for things they need.

"Trades what?" She paused, then snapped her fingers. "Diamonds, like the ones Roebor sent with you to Earth for me to rebuild the facility he destroyed?"

yes.

Shannon, so drowsy now she could hardly stand, slid to the floor and leaned back against what appeared to be an upholstered chair. Its soft lining reached to the floor.

Narci curled in Shannon's lap, kneaded her jeans, and purred until she fell asleep. Shannon stroked Narci as she talked with Salesti.

"Tell me more about your illness," she said, yawning. "I never imagined that you could get sick. It's nothing serious, right?"

Salesti didn't respond but flew to one of the holes high in the cavern wall; a clear window covered it. The little creature approached the covering and searched the sky.

soon sun rises, shannon. rest now. tomorrow is difficult.

CHAPTER SIX
Decision

SHANNON AWOKE WITH A JERK, Narci's sandpaper tongue licking her nostrils.

"*Odin's eye!* How many times do I have to tell you that that is the grossest thing ever, Narci? Cut it out."

Unruffled, the cat scooted back down on Shannon's chest and purred in her face.

narci tells shannon execution of roebor in short time, Salesti said.

Shannon struggled to her feet and let the cat slide to the floor, squinting at the high windows. The midnight black of the skies had lightened to deepest blue. She leaned back against the wall. Her hip ached and the headache from the knock she'd taken in the tunnel had returned with a vengeance. She fingered the lump that had formed on her head. *Ouch.*

"Has Roebor contacted you? Did he decide?"

salesti hears nothing from roebor.

"Roebor, can you hear me? We're out of time."

I can hear you, Shannon.

She waited for Roebor's decision. Death would come hard for the dragonpanther. Shannon shuddered at the notion of him roasting above the fire pit, the pain stretching out over hours and hours. But if he came away with them, he would leave his home world forever. Could he bear that separation?

For that matter, could Shannon bear to have him in her head for the rest of her life? She hadn't considered what that would mean. Roebor might be an arrogant fellow at times, but he'd also proven himself whip-smart and kind when he chose to be.

Wait. What had she been thinking? Her life might not last that long with Roebor on board. When the aliens had taken up residence with her before, they'd taken a terrible toll on her body, which eventually started to shut down. She'd nearly died. And she hadn't been able to eat enough to keep up with the energy they consumed. Her doctor might be able to find a workaround for that with Roebor to help her, but Shannon couldn't count on it.

She shook her head. It didn't matter. If Roebor decided to escape with them, she would have no choice. She wouldn't leave him behind if he wanted to live.

Roebor?

I shall tell you the logic by which I arrived at my decision.

Might we skip to the bottom line?

I prefer to explain the decision in an orderly fashion. I first evaluated the principle that I must pay for my dishonorable actions on Earth, in lying to you and betraying my promise to the people to capture the virus, no matter what the cost to Earth. At first, I thought myself honor-bound to suffer through the torture and accept my death. But it occurred to me that relegating myself to your mind, Shannon, would constitute the torture I deserve.

Wait, what?

Therefore, I moved on to the second consideration: whether I could bear to leave my homeland behind forever, and my father, my sisters, my friends. I would endure much to stay with them, but, of course, if I allow the execution to take place, I will lose them all anyway.

So, I considered the flip side: could I bear to live on Earth?

Shannon interrupted. *Earth should be different without the virus and Tidak to deal with. Or, you could live on RiverWorld if Salesti is strong enough to carry you.*

salesti not well, shannon. not able to take friend roebor.

One of the other salestis?

this not possible for salestis. sorry.

Some other Seladoran then.

Shannon, Roebor said, *the Seladorans of RiverWorld spend most of their lives in the river in their ribbon iteration. It's a most delicate form. No Seladoran could support me in that form. But you jump ahead of my logic.*

Sorry, Roebor; I only meant to say that life on Earth might not turn out to be as unpleasant as you fear.

Indeed. I have determined that I could, in fact, bear to live on Earth, despite its terrible flaws. Yet the thought of life on Earth did make the notion of death by execution sound less overwhelming.

Well, I don't know about—

That brought me to the most important consideration: could I leave your fate in Bale's hands after my death? I have made my decision based on this factor.

Bale?

Yes. If Pak were left to his own devices, he would follow the Council's wishes in the matter of your fate. But not Bale.

Right, Bale scares the beejeebies out of me.

Bale resembles his father in many crucial respects. He grieves, and his grief rules his heart; his heart in turn rules his mind.

Even after you're dead?

My death will not end his grief. However much he believes that exacting his revenge on me will ease his pain, he will remain bitter. He will remain angry, and his anger will incite him to seek you out.

All the way to Earth?

Yes, which explains why I must come with you. I need to protect you. And you are not so bad as Earth things go.

Thanks. . . I think. But I'm not too keen on this reasoning. Don't make me the factor that you use to make a decision that will turn your life inside out.

Ah, but here is the beauty of it, Shannon. Once I satisfy myself that you are safe, if I cannot tolerate life in your mind for one minute more, I have an option. I shall throw myself out into the ether and be done with it.

That's so not comforting. But what do we do about the fact that my body may not support you for very long?

I believe that if I set my mind to this problem—with the help of the doctor whose acquaintance I made previously—I might find a solution. If there is no other solution, as I said, I shall simply leave.

I'm not loving that solution. But regardless, we can't take any more time to chew this over. Are you sure this is what you want?

Yes. Now, to convince the people, I must stay with my body until I suffer acute pain, and the people see me suffer. Salesti, I will call you when the time comes for me to leave my body. Shannon, you must make your way to the portal before the entire Island walks along the pathway to watch the execution.

"Salesti? Will you be okay if I go down to the portal?"

salesti be okay, Salesti said.

Salesti will join you as soon as it can and transfer me over. Go now. Roebor's anxiety punctuated each word he spoke.

Shannon longed to sneak back to the arena one last time to see her oversized friend's magnificent form—his metallic blue fur, his proud head with those fiery, silver-blue eyes blazing at her, and those incredible wings. But she must position herself to leave the planet. Roebor was counting on her.

Shannon, Salesti, and Narci crept down the hall and back through the tunnel. Shannon peered into the adjacent cavern. Not a soul stirred.

"Wait here a second," she whispered and stepped out into the dawning day.

* * *

Shannon stepped onto the slope that would take her down to the portal.

"Stop there," a booming voice bellowed.

Farther down the path, a rust-red dragonpanther flew her way. Shannon couldn't outrun it. She froze, motioning Narci and Salesti back.

The dragonpanther flew down at her and slowed above her head. Flapping its wings, it snatched her in its front claws and sniffed her. "Nice," it mumbled as it flew off.

Five minutes later, Shannon stood behind the familiar bars of the cell she'd occupied so recently.

Again.

"We have blocked the latrine, but I will stand guard until Bale decides what he wants to do with you."

Shannon regarded this new dragonpanther. Like Jal, it was more delicate than the males who'd guarded her before, so she figured it must be a female.

Might Shannon reason with her?

"Because of the red fur, I know you don't belong to Tidak's clan. So how did you get involved in this?"

"I am Bale's mate." She raised her head and tipped out her chin. "Pip."

"Pip? I'm Shannon."

Pip nodded, turned in a circle, and curled into a ball.

"I want to go home, Pip. I'm afraid Bale will kill me. He's still so angry about his father's death."

"He is angry that the Council changed its mind and will no longer force you to watch the execution. But they still want to question you. Bale will let you live until then."

"And then he'll kill me. Bale will execute Roebor in a few minutes. Isn't that enough killing? Enough revenge? Killing me would serve no purpose. And if he kills me, what's to stop someone from coming here and seeking revenge for *my* death? Shouldn't it end with Roebor's life for Tidak's?"

Not a soul would come here seeking to avenge her, but Pip didn't need to know that.

Pip didn't respond, but the claw on the index toe—or finger—of her left paw tapped an anxious pattern on the cave floor.

shannon, salesti goes now to roebor. he feels much pain.

Then hurry, Salesti! Take care you don't get burned. Tell me as soon as Roebor's spirit boards your mind.

Roebor, Salesti, is on her way. Hold on.

Shannon returned her attention to Pip. "Nobody saw you catch me, right? If you let me out, Bale and the others would never have to know."

"Earth things are too talkative." Pip's clawed finger tapped as she continued to stare at Shannon.

"I mean, females like you and I see these things through a different lens than males. We. . . ." Shannon hesitated. She knew nothing about how female dragonpanthers saw things such as war and revenge. But before she could make up her mind whether to say more, the dragonpanther finished Shannon's sentence.

"We include the future in our thinking and do not limit our view to the moment." Pip didn't move a muscle.

Shannon opened her mouth, then closed it again.

"Yes, exactly."

Pip continued to watch her.

"We're smarter than they are," Shannon said.

"Of course. It is the same on your planet?"

"Oh yes. On Earth, the females make all the important decisions."

Hah. Shannon wished.

"And here?" Shannon asked.

Pip's brow furrowed.

shannon, salesti carries roebor now. too much for sick salesti. where shannon?

Back in jail. Be careful; I have a guard.

As Shannon pretended to study the cave, a black streak near the ground tore in, rushed around Pip's prone form, and skidded to a stop at the dragonpanther's toes.

Narci! What in Odin's name are you doing?

The cat glanced at Shannon. *Don't worry.*

Pip's head snapped up in surprise at the sight of the cat.

"Why, a tiny dragonpanther. But it has no wings."

"Yes. Why yes, we have tiny dragonpanthers on Earth. They are wingless. She and Roebor have become fast friends. She'll grieve over his death now, poor thing."

Shannon's thoughts strayed to Roebor's beautiful form. Its destruction turned her chest to sharpened glass.

Narci rubbed her side along Pip's front paws.

"So tiny. Like a baby. I would like to keep her." She leaned in and sniffed the cat. "She smells much as we do."

"I expect that Bale will kill her, too, when he kills me. Her name is Narcissus."

The brow furrowed more deeply this time.

Thank Odin. Pip was wavering.

Narci, the tiny dragonpanther replica, curled into Pip's paws and purred. The attention of Bale's mate remained glued on the purring cat.

Narci, you're as brave as a dragonpanther, I'll give you that. But be ready to run if things go south here. If you see Bale, disappear. Okay?

The cat turned her sapphire gaze on Shannon and blinked.

Yeah, not sure that was a 'yes.'

A quiet humming noise drew Shannon's attention to the roof of the cave. As Pip's attention remained focused on Narci, Salesti flew along the roof and landed on Shannon's shoulder. It brought Roebor's spirit down through its body and took him through her body to her mind, into her Great Room. Shannon had constructed the Great Room to understand and engage with the alien spirits that had joined her in her mind in the past.

As many times as alien creatures had entered her mind over the years, Shannon had never quite grown accustomed to that first moment when she could sense she was no longer alone: first, a frisson of fear slid across her consciousness; then a creeping awareness of the *other* grew in her head; a moment of panic overwhelmed her; and, finally, memory kicked in—this was Roebor, and it would be all right.

But this time, it wasn't all right in there. Roebor was in pain, and she could feel it.

roebor waits too long. burning causes roebor great suffering, Salesti said.

I will be fine. Do not worry over it, Shannon. Agony warped Roebor's voice within her head into a timbre she didn't recognize.

Listen, Shannon said, *we're back in the soup.* She explained her current situation.

This news distresses me, Shannon. You remain at Bale's mercy, and he possesses very little of it.

What do you know about Pip? Anything that will help us? Shannon asked.

She bears a soft heart for children and helpless creatures. Bale holds no patience for such things.

Right, then. "Please, Pip, I'm so worried about Narci. Let me take her home to Earth before Bale finds her. I don't suppose he would harm her in normal times, but his anger controls him now. You've felt that, haven't you?"

Remind her how he pushed Tidak's grandmother aside. When he heard I'd brought the body back, he rushed to his father. He damaged the wing of Tidak's grandmother when he forced her back. The people do not tolerate disrespect toward elders. Our Council forced Bale to bring her the best meat from the hunt for a month.

"You've seen his behavior ever since Roebor brought poor Tidak back. Look how he treated his own great-grandmother. I'm so afraid of what he'll do to Narci."

Narci climbed onto Pip's front paws and rubbed her whiskers against Pip's chest. Shannon could hear her purring from thirty feet away.

"Could she go home without you?" Pip asked.

Shannon pretended to think it over. "No. I must find the portal for her; I have a special way of making the portal visible, and then I have to carry her through. She couldn't make it home by herself."

Well. Not strictly true. Okay, a total lie.

"You can find the portal without blowing fire as we do?"

"Yes, I find it by casting my colors. I see many things I wouldn't otherwise be able to. If you want, I'll cast now and see where Bale is. Shall I? I'll tell you what I see."

Pip appeared interested, so Shannon cast her colors toward the arena and searched for Bale. "I see the arena where Roebor's body burns. He's engulfed by flames." She stopped. Her stomach churned with acid. Tears pooled in her eyes.

I am so sorry, Roebor.

Roebor paced the Great Room of Shannon's mind in silence.

Shannon wiped at her face and continued her effort to win over Pip. "I don't hear any screams, so perhaps Roebor has already died. I see a hundred dragonpanthers watching, maybe more. Bale. . . Bale. . . there, I've found him. He's perched on platform with Pak and another huge, unhappy-looking dragonpanther with a misshapen left ear—"

"Bale's grandfather, Dortan!"

"So, there's still time before anyone knows that you captured us. You could save Narci from Bale's rage, and nothing would happen to you. You can decide yourself for once."

Well played, Shannon. Females on FireWorld make few important decisions. Many of them advocate for more autonomy.

As if to seal the deal, Narci rolled over on her back and cuddled into Pip's enormous chest. She gazed into Pip's eyes, her small paws in the air. Pip grinned.

"She likes me, does she not?" She set her face into stone. "But Bale wants to punish you."

She's close to letting me go, Roebor. I can feel it. What else can I say?

Hmm. She doesn't seem close to me.

Shannon reached for Pip's thoughts. "Do you have children, Pip?"

"No. And it is not a polite topic to discuss on this world."

So, Pip yearned for children. And cuddling Narci brought her longings to the surface. Shannon could see that Pip kept her raw emotions to herself. She hated to intrude on those emotions, but she must escape, and soon. She'd compromise and tiptoe around the topic.

"Bale puts down the law in your cave, I expect. That must frustrate you sometimes. He probably wouldn't let you keep Narci, anyway, right? Because she's connected to me, and I'm connected to Roebor."

Pip's claw tapped the cave floor again.

At last, she said, "No, I will not allow Bale to hurt her."

Pip shooed the cat from her paws with a gentle push and lifted the cell key off the wall. "Let me check outside to make sure no one is nearby. Where do you have to go?"

"The portal is near an outcropping of boulders down the hill from here."

"No one is in view. Go. Hurry."

Salesti, can you fly?

no shannon, salesti tires.

Okay, into my sweatshirt pocket, sweetheart. Narci, can you run?

With one more rub of her whiskers along the cheek of Pip's lowered head, the cat took off out the cave entrance. Shannon stopped a moment to thank Pip, and chased after the streaking cat, fingers cupped over the bulge in her pocket that was Salesti.

As Shannon stretched to reach into the pull of the portal, Roebor let out a weary, ineffable sigh.

"No body. No homeland. I have never felt such pain, Shannon. Not even in the fire."

Shannon struggled to say anything meaningful in return, but as she groped for words, Salesti said, *shannon stops to help salesti. salesti very not well.*

CHAPTER SEVEN
Power

SHANNON RAN TO THE OUTCROPPING OF BOULDERS that had provided their first shelter. She stole a glance back at the cliff where it bent out of sight. The crowd at the arena hadn't dispersed in this direction yet.

The sound of the crackling fire in the pit carried to her across the quiet slope from the amphitheater and filled her with revulsion. The low rumble of a hundred voices all talking at once disgusted her, like the Roman amphitheaters where lions devoured men while the crowds engaged in casual conversation.

"What is it, Salesti? How can I help you?"

The burning fire pit's heavy smoke had settled over the island like a black fog. A swirling wind blew in from the sea, but the dark cloud persisted.

Shannon's pale braid whipped into her face, a braid so long now that she could tuck the tip under her leg. She settled below the boulders and eased Salesti from her pocket, cupped in her palm. Stray hairs snapped around her face.

nothing helps salesti. salesti dying.

The blood drained from Shannon's face. Her mind stuttered to a stop; she couldn't process Salesti's words. She rejected them with every fiber of her being.

"What? Not dying. You're not dying. You live so long it's like forever, don't you? I mean, you can't get sick, right? You're too powerful."

Shannon could fix this. There must be a way. Her mind burned, the heat became unbearable.

shannon listens to each word of salesti and shannon remembers. salesti not makes it through portal passage.

"I can carry you."

no, shannon. power of salesti too unstable for wormhole. salesti too weak.

"We must be able to do something, Salesti. I love you. I don't want to lose you."

salesti loves shannon too.

A darkness cloaked Shannon's vision, passing across the landscape of her heart: a landscape barren of light and warmth.

"I'm. . . I'm afraid of the universe without you in it. Your wisdom, your friendship, your tinkling laugh, I need that. And RiverWorld needs you. This can't be happening."

Her chest tightened with each passing second. *Surely her heart would burst.* She couldn't breathe. She couldn't move.

Roebor said, *Salesti, coming for my spirit at the fire pit took the energy you needed to return to RiverWorld. You should have left me.*

roebor friend of salesti. salesti not leaves roebor. and also salesti hopes salesti still makes it home. salesti very wrong.

shannon tells friends of salesti goodbye? apologizes for error of salesti?

Shannon's tears dripped down her face. "I promise. But I can't believe there's nothing we can do. Please, Salesti, tell us how to help."

shannon listens to each word now. salesti dies because of old wound. wound prevents salesti from accessing power of salesti. but power remains.

"All right. Can the wound be treated?"

no, shannon, no help for salesti. but fireworld in grave danger if salesti dies here without removing power of salesti. fireworld explodes. much of solar system explodes. all dragon-panthers lost.

Shannon blinked back her tears. "We'll go up like an atom bomb?"

not if salesti removes her power. gives to shannon. shannon takes power, saves fireworld. shannon only one powerful enough to share energy of salesti.

"Me?

when shannon a baby, a salesti needs to shed power. this power shared with shannon. not much. enough to make shannon strong.

Shannon couldn't grasp Salesti's words; too much, too sudden, too enormous to take in. Her tears had become rasping sobs, and Salesti bounced in her hand as she shook.

Warmth surrounded her as if Roebor had wrapped his arms around her. *Shannon,* Roebor said, *you must listen to Salesti or my planet will die.*

She steadied her trembling hand.

"I love you, little one. Always remember that. Now tell me what to do."

shannon wraps hands all the way around salesti so shannon lets no light in, no light out. critical. power comes, shannon absorbs. also critical for shannon to—

Salesti cried out and its tiny body spasmed, stilled, and spasmed again.

A small part of Shannon died with each spasm.

"Can I make you more comfortable?"

now, must do now. shannon covers salesti, no light shows. now.

Shannon wrapped both hands around the tiny creature, tucking her wings and her legs in close to her body with tender fingers. She kissed Salesti and closed the remaining gap. Peering at her hands from every angle, she checked and rechecked for cracks in the seal made by her hands.

also critical. shannon must, shannon must—

Shannon's hands warmed. Gradually at first, then more quickly, her hands grew so hot she almost dropped Salesti. But the dying creature had warned her to hold tight at any cost. The strange exotic scent of cinnamon and spices without name poured from Shannon's closed hands, stronger than she had ever known.

Hold tight, Shannon, Roebor said. *Whatever you do, do not drop Salesti. All our lives depend on it.*

Shannon tensed her arms, her wrists, her fingers.

Burning. So much pain. Hold on.

Five excruciating minutes later, the heat vanished. *Thank Odin.*

Wind carried away the exotic scent until nothing remained. She waited for several moments and opened her hands. To her surprise, they hadn't blistered or burned.

"Salesti, you said you wanted to tell us one more important thing—"

Salesti lay curled, shrunken, and twisted in her hand. As still as a photograph.

Oh no. No, no, no.

"Salesti's gone." Shannon forced the words out, as much to confirm it to herself as to Roebor.

I am sorry, Shannon.

Shannon remained still. All senses, all thoughts, her every emotion, drained from her, leaving her an empty void.

Minutes passed.

Then a murmur sounded from somewhere up the hill, pulling Shannon back to the moment. She peeked through the boulders. Dragonpanthers now straggled out in two's and three's from behind the curve in the cliff that hid the amphitheater from her sight.

"We've got to go. Now." Shannon cast her colors in search of the portal. She spotted it, ten feet to the right of them. She placed Salesti's body in her pocket, taking care to crush no part of the tiny creature, and snatched Narci to her chest. "We're going to make a run for it." With a bead on the portal, she raised into a crouch, aimed herself on a straight path toward it, and ran.

Roars emanated from behind her when dragonpanthers spotted her, and wings flapped as a dozen or more of them flew toward her position to stop her. She lifted her arm and felt herself drawn into the fire that didn't burn, blinked, then sighed with relief as she tumbled out the other end into the cave of portals. And not a dragonpanther in sight.

CHAPTER EIGHT
Essi

SHANNON'S FIRST PORTAL JUMP took her to RiverWorld. She longed to go on to Earth with a second jump, but she must deliver the news of Salesti's death, return its body to the other salestis, and ask them what do with the power Salesti had given her.

She walked from RiverWorld's portal cave through the long underground tunnel to the now-defunct temple above, and from there to the outer steps. Narci knew the way and skittered ahead.

Before Shannon could climb down the steps, she collapsed in grief.

The beautiful view from the temple's high steps of RiverWorld's emerging green valley meant nothing to her. She'd held her sorrow in check during their escape, but now it pinched her, burned her, crushed her, and filled her body with lead where there had once been light. She doubled over in pain until her face pressed into her knees and her arms hugged her bent legs. Roebor's comforting warmth wrapped her shoulders again as if he held her close. Narci leaned into her and placed a warm, whiskered cheek against her arm.

No creature like it shall ever grace the universe again, Shannon. It gave us its friendship, the greatest gift we might ever receive.

Shannon nodded. After a time, her first pangs of grief subsided. A numbness enveloped her, threatening to remain a sorrow so great she would not recover.

Several Seladoran children greeted her, looking much like colorful Earth children playing on the temple steps. She asked if they would find Essi and Toss, her first friends from RiverWorld, and tell them that she planned to visit the salestis. With her waning strength, she forced herself to move on, preparing to break the news to the salestis that they had lost one of their own.

Each time Shannon visited RiverWorld, more green vegetation covered the land, and more water returned to the great River Selador, as the planet recovered from an alien attack years ago. As she made her way along a brick path to the meadow at the crook in the River, Seladorans tending several vegetable plots stopped and nodded. She nodded back but couldn't bring herself to smile.

Does the power make you feel any different? Roebor asked.

"Strange as it seems, I feel weak and *powerless* right now. Has the power affected the Great Room?"

The soft light that used to filter down into the hall is shining so brightly I cannot open my eyes without pain. I have retreated to a dimmer place.

Shannon put aside her own grief, remembering all that Roebor had sacrificed on FireWorld.

"How are you doing? When you first arrived, you were still suffering from the pain of the fire. Any better?"

The pain vanished when you absorbed Salesti's power. For that, I thank you.

"I'm glad it was good for something. Leaving FireWorld must have devastated you.

Do not worry over it, Shannon. I shall manage.

Shannon picked at her lips as she worried about Roebor nevertheless.

She and Narci arrived at a sunny meadow nestled in the bend of the Selador River. With her first footfall, a hive of salestis rose from the deep grass and wildflowers. They flew toward her and formed a buzzing, humming, spice-smelling semi-circle around her. The soft grass gave way as Shannon sank into it. It felt cool and relaxing, and she settled in with her legs folded under her. Still, she ran her fingers down her braid, clutching the tip in her hand.

How could she tell them?

The glare of the two red suns pounded down on her. After the relative cool of FireWorld at night, the heat came as a shock. She peeled off her sweatshirt and her shoes and socks.

Narci, who had stayed with her until now, wandered off, curled into a ball, and fell asleep in the sun.

What should she do next?

She'd never spoken to the other salestis. Her Salesti had acted as an intermediary, huddling with the others and returning to discuss their conversations. She didn't know if she *could* communicate with these mysterious creatures.

The group cleared away any doubt about that.

They spoke in unison, giving Shannon the strange impression that while many were speaking the same words at the exact same time, they spoke with the voice of a single speaker.

salesti does not accompany shannon?

Shannon hesitated. What terrible news she brought. But she must speak.

"Salesti didn't make it. It died on FireWorld. I didn't know it had become so sick, or I never would've agreed to go with it to FireWorld. I'm so sorry. I've brought Salesti home." Shannon removed Salesti from her sweatshirt pocket with shaking hands and laid it in the grass.

A humming arose among the tiny creatures, a high, tense buzz. They flew to the body and surrounded it, placing their paws upon it, and patted their lifeless friend with feather-light touches. Tiny wails reached into the sky. Shannon couldn't bear it. She looked away toward the stately river and watched it flow slowly, with its ribbons of so many colors Shannon couldn't name them all.

After a time, the salestis quieted. Shannon returned her gaze to them. The salestis still hovered over the body, so close together that Shannon couldn't see her Salesti anymore. Then they moved back into a line, revealing that Salesti's body was gone. *But where?* Shannon had no idea.

The many-voices-in-one spoke again.

where did our salesti deposit the energy? not in a dragonpanther?

Roebor stirred. *I resent the implications of that statement. What would be wrong with a dragonpanther sharing Salesti's power? Dragonpanthers demonstrate great strength. If I had remained whole in body, I could have absorbed the salesti's power, I am sure of it, for I—*

The salestis interrupted. *salestis know of none who might absorb power of a salesti.*

They flew closer to Shannon. *How could salesti release its energy on a dead planet, since you brought the body home?*

"No. It didn't have the time or strength to do anything but give its energy to. . . me." Shannon swallowed and squinted through half-closed eyelids in anticipation of a salesti outburst.

The salestis scattered, landed ten feet away in a field of tall, waving grass, and buzzed in surprise. Shannon's untrained ear heard what must be distress, outrage, and mourning.

She waited.

And waited.

Her hip ached. Her head ached. She shifted positions to try to give herself some relief. Placing her legs straight out in front of her and her hands behind her, she leaned back and stretched.

The suns burned brighter as the day progressed. Still the salestis left Shannon sitting alone while they conferred. The pungent, earthy aroma of the grass intensified in the sunlight. Shannon pulled off her T-shirt and placed it on her head for shade. Sweat trickled down her face. The heat would make her ill if she didn't find relief soon.

Perhaps the mysterious creatures had finished with her. Maybe she should go home.

She'd vanished from Earth a mere two days ago, although it seemed like two hundred days. Speaking of the time that had passed—the portal had been acting up, so more or less time may have passed on Earth. She might have been gone long enough that someone discovered her absence, or she might arrive back a few moments after she left.

Should she go? No, not yet. She must find out how to either control the power or get rid of it.

Shannon laid back on the grass and draped her T-shirt over her face. She wiggled her toes in the wildflowers and struggled to forget that she'd lost her compass—her Salesti.

She struggled to forget—for the moment—that Roebor might be stuck in her head for the rest of her life. Her life might only last a week, of course, given that her body would probably shut down under the strain.

I have given thought to that problem, Shannon, the problem of the burden that I place on your body. In this regard, I have examined the flow of extra energy in your system. I find it quite extraordinary.

"Extraordinarily good or extraordinarily bad?"

Both. In fact, I can see from observing your energy that you already possessed a fair amount of power before Salesti bestowed hers upon you, with its own peculiar molecular structure. I must conclude that without that earlier power, entertaining any of those you have previously held in your mind for any length of time would have killed you without a doubt. You are alive because power already existed here.

"Strange to think that my first alien visitor, a Seladoran child, would have been the death of me if a Seladoran salesti hadn't deposited power in me as a baby. I mean, what are the odds? It's as if that long-ago salesti knew I'd need the power one day. As if it could read the future." *Could* the salestis read the future? She wouldn't be surprised, the way they always talked about time in the present tense.

It is strange, indeed, Shannon. Now that your power reserves have increased exponentially, I believe you will be able to tolerate my presence as long as necessary. Your organs will not shut down.

"There's a ray of sunshine, at least."

However, I fear that you will still require a sizable amount of food as in the past. And the more entities you take on board, and the longer any entity remains, the more caloric intake you will always need.

"What? The extra power dump didn't change that? Why not?"

Shannon sensed Roebor shrug.

Visualize your body carrying three separate sources of energy. One, your body's normal energy. This is the energy you must replenish on a daily basis with food. Two, the power given to you by the earlier salesti in infancy, not usually accessible except for unusual circumstances, like alien visitors. The third, Salesti's energy, is like a huge reserve tank from which power is slowly leaking into you, which will protect your organs. But I sense that too much energy is there. Much too much.

"Too much?"

Yes. The salestis should discuss this with us.

Just then, the salestis, back from their confab at last, rejoined Shannon and settled a few feet away in a straight line on the grass, their small yellow bodies identical, their auras a rainbow of color. Shannon slipped her T-shirt back on as she sat up.

shannon of earth. beloved salesti made no error when salesti channeled energy into shannon, for if energy bursts from salesti at death, fireworld, our solar system, and perhaps more, disappear. shannon likely the one entity able to take power of salesti.

Right.

She could have told them her Salesti wouldn't have made a mistake. Its power had to go to Shannon. But was that a good thing or a bad thing for her?

"What else can you tell me about this extra power? It will sit in my system, not causing any trouble, and leak out a drop at a time. Right?"

As one, the salestis stopped buzzing; their wings ceased to flutter, and their tiny heads stilled.

Uh oh. Brace yourself, Shannon, Roebor said.

Shannon sat straighter and clasped her elbows with her opposing hands.

A gentle breeze blew the pink and red, diamond-shaped, and peppermint-scented wildflowers at her feet toward the river's edge. Wispy clouds passed over double suns, creating momentary shadows on her toes.

The silence stretched out. In Shannon's anxiety to learn what the salestis would say, she cast her colors without conscious thought, and her mind reached out to them. . . *too much power. . . a great explosion. . . inevitable that she will obliterate a solar system—*

Unlike anyone Shannon had probed before, the salestis soon recognized that she was prying and blocked their minds, as quickly as if they'd yanked the shutters closed.

salestis decide shannon goes home to earth now.

With that, the salestis rose in unison and flew away through the waving wildflowers, across the tall, green grass, and over the slow-flowing Selador River, until, in the distance and the glare of the two suns, their tiny forms disappeared out of sight.

Shannon remained motionless, contemplating their cold, abrupt departure.

"Did you sense what I sensed when I reached into their minds?"

No. Your probe did not reveal itself to me. What did you see?

"A couple of fragments about me having too much power, exactly as you said, and then something about a great explosion and the obliteration of a solar system." Shannon ran her fingers through the tip of her long, pale braid. "I don't like the sound of that."

You saw nothing further?

"No, they shut me out. They sensed that I was probing, and they closed their thoughts to me. I have a feeling they packed up and left because they've decided to withhold something from me. Something important. Why would they do that?"

Let me ponder it at greater length, and we will talk again.

Shannon mulled over the salestis' words. They probably meant Shannon would obliterate Earth and its solar system. Nothing like *that* to darken your day.

It is time to leave. Shall we send someone else to find Essi and Toss? Roebor asked.

Shannon looked toward the village and spotted a familiar figure running toward her. "We won't need to. They've found us!" Shannon scrambled to her feet.

Essi ran toward Shannon, and Essi's friend and lover, Toss, followed not far behind.

The lavender-skinned Essi flew into Shannon's arms, and Shannon wrapped the woman in a tight bear hug. All the tension and fear and grief caused by dragonpanthers and salestis found release in that hug.

"ugh, essi cannot breathe, shannon!" Essi said, laughing, and Shannon released her.

"I've missed you!" Shannon said, holding her at arm's length. "*Odin's eye,* I still can't believe that in the five years we were apart, you aged fifteen years. And now another year is gone, and look at you, almost as tall as me. And more beautiful and mature than ever." As she always did, Shannon admired Essi's huge, emerald-green anime eyes, her tiny nose and mouth, and the scent that matched her own.

When Shannon stepped back and peered down at her T-shirt, it dripped water onto her still-bare toes. "You came here from the River, I see. But you didn't have to change your form for me. I know how much you love your ribbon form. You should have stayed in the water."

Essi laughed and tossed her wild, curly, flyaway hair. "of course essi changes! essi not sees shannon for too long! but essi sees the salestis as essi comes this way. salestis never leave meadow, and yet salestis cross river and fly away. how shannon manages that?"

"I upset them."

Essi regarded her with her head cocked. "nothing upsets salestis."

Nothing except a walking time bomb like Shannon.

Shannon glanced beyond Essi toward the lanky, dark-haired turquoise-hued Toss. "And Toss, can I give you a hug, too? It's good to see you." Essi stepped aside, and Toss, the same height as his Essi, smiled and stepped into Shannon's arms. But he remained silent. Shannon glanced at Essi, who frowned and gave her head a slight shake. An alien had captured Toss here, an experience from which Toss had not recovered. He hadn't spoken since.

Shannon held onto him. In a soft voice, she said, "I've missed you, Toss. Thank you for taking such wonderful care of Essi." He nodded and stepped back.

"Sit a minute. I have news, and it's not good."

Shannon related all that had happened on FireWorld, stopping short of the worst of it.

"roebor in mind of shannon now? essi wants to see him. can essi?"

"Sure. I'll stay out here with Toss." Essi stretched out on the grass, and Shannon placed her hand on Essi's. Shivers vibrated along Shannon's arm as the Seladoran's spirit traveled through Shannon's body to her mind.

Shannon chattered to keep Toss entertained, and soon the shivers came again, in reverse, as Essi traveled back to her own body.

"so roebor stays with shannon now? forever?" Essi's jeweled eyes, already huge on her petite face, seemed to grow larger and rounder as she spoke.

Tell her that it is unclear whether I am here forever, Shannon. I may yet figure out a better alternative.

"He's here, for now, Essi, but Roebor's a bright guy; he's working on it." She paused, clenched her fists, and then continued. "I bring grave news, Essi. I should have told you this right away, but I couldn't bear to say it. Toss, take her hand, would you?"

"shannon, what it is? shannon all right?"

"It's Salesti, our Salesti. She didn't make it home. She died on FireWorld." As Shannon related the rest of the story, Toss and Essi clung to each other and wept. The salestis formed the spiritual heart of RiverWorld; to lose one was unthinkable, unbearable.

My news has devastated my poor friends, and now they must gather the courage to tell the other Seladorans. This isn't the time to question them about the power transfer, Shannon said to Roebor so that the others would not hear.

But might they not know what the salestis kept from you?

We'll ask, but I can't bear to bother them now.

She scooted over to put her arm around Essi's shoulder as Essi leaned into Toss. They remained that way until Essi stirred and began preparations to call an assembly of the Seladorans to deliver the news.

Shannon and Narci took their leave and headed to the portal room in the cave under the temple.

Shannon gathered Narci in her arms and approached the portal, moving close enough to be drawn into its painless flames. "I have a bad feeling in the pit of my stomach about this new power, Roebor. A passenger-on-the-Titanic-watching-the-iceberg feeling."

The Titanic is a ship? Roebor asked.

"Yes. And it sinks."

PART TWO

OCEAN CITY

CHAPTER NINE
Luke

THE PORTAL DEPOSITED SHANNON AND NARCI ON THE PICNIC TABLE in her backyard, in the exact spot she'd stood—cat in her arms, Salesti on her shoulder—when she'd left Earth two days ago.

As Shannon landed, her legs folded as if made of Wonder Bread, plunking her seat without warning onto the red cedar tabletop. Her feet slipped onto the smooth-sanded bench. She released Narci, steadied, and took a moment to collect herself.

So tired.

She yawned. Her shoulders sagged as if she wore a lead jacket instead of a cotton tee and a sweatshirt. She needed a nap.

"You okay, Narci?"

The cat plopped down on the picnic table and yawned, too.

"I hear you."

The breeze blowing in from the ocean, carrying the scent of kelp and seagulls, salt and sea, caressed her skin. It cooled her after the burning suns of RiverWorld.

She studied the sky. Judging from the sun's position, morning would soon flip over into afternoon, which would make the time eleven or eleven-thirty. No matter. Shannon planned to fall into bed and sleep for a month.

A shiny, iridescent black raven flew down and landed on the table beside her.

"Hello, bird," Shannon said. She recognized this bird. He'd entertained a guest in his mind once, too: Salesti. And Salesti had left behind a touch of its essence—its residue—making him a very smart bird.

"Hello," said the bird, hopping onto her shoulder. His talons, though placed with care, pricked Shannon's sun-burnt skin. No matter; she could tolerate it for this little guy.

Time to move. She climbed off the picnic table, bird in tow.

How strange it was to be back in this familiar place after a day on FireWorld and an afternoon on RiverWorld, planets so different from her own. In her misery over losing Salesti, colors appeared muted, from the grass, the bushes, and the flower beds in her yard, to the blue paint on the back of her kitchen door.

As if in sympathy with her muted mood, the breeze died. No critters scampered across the lawn. Except Narci, who hopped off the table, dashed to the dog door, and disappeared into the house.

Shannon, I have delayed telling you something important. I apologize for waiting, but with Salesti's death, its importance diminished for a time. Now that we have returned to Earth, I must tell you that while I lingered in the Death Cage above the fire pit, I overheard two of Bale's friends laughing over a secret.

Now what? "A secret?"

When the Council rejected Bale's petition to travel to Earth in search of his father, he defied them by sending a primitive creature to wreak havoc in his stead—a species that swims in the seas below our cliffs on FireWorld. Perhaps you would call it a crocodile-tyrannosaurus rex.

"And you waited to tell me this?"

What would you have done, other than worry?

"True." A crocodile-tyrannosaurus rex. *Odin's eye.* She took her back-door key out of her jeans pocket and let herself into the kitchen.

"You coming in, bird?" The bird remained on her shoulder.

"Shannon! *Cara!* Thank god you're all right." The shout came from the front hall. Shannon had no time to consider why the person whose voice she knew so well was in her house: she found herself swept up tight in a pair of strong arms, hugged close to a broad chest, her feet lifted off the ground, toes searching for purchase.

"Cara," he said again, his head lowered to her hair.

With a squawk, the raven flapped from her shoulder and perched on a high cupboard.

Luke. She melted into the familiar beat of his heart, the fresh, clean smell of his ivory soap. She savored the feel against her cheek of the small notebook he kept in his breast pocket, the black of his police uniform against her captive eye. Color flooded back into her world.

Then it registered: he was wearing his police uniform! She'd believed he would never work in law enforcement again because of the bullet he took to his shoulder—which happened because he was protecting her. Luke was perfect for law enforcement. His manner—authoritative, calm, re-assuring—accomplished much more than the shouting and the guns, so many officers found satisfying. He loved help-ing people; he enjoyed that part of the job most of all. That he was six foot four, broad-shouldered, and muscular didn't hurt his job performance either. He thought of Ocean City as his responsibility. He would protect it, nurture it, and love it.

And Shannon loved him for it. And now he'd recovered enough to return to the force. *Thank Odin.*

But now, more than ever, she didn't dare hold him close. With Salesti's power onboard, she posed too great a danger to him.

Narci jumped onto the small kitchen storage cabinet, where her dry food bowl still contained some nuggets from her last meal and crunched a few bites. Then she stopped, her attention diverted.

At the same time, a sniffing, licking, cold-nosed creature at Shannon's ankles interrupted her thoughts. She checked her feet and discovered a puppy nosing her toes. "Oh my gosh. Who's this?"

Luke bent down, lifted the golden, brown-eyed pup, and handed him to Shannon.

"This is Gumshoe. Golden Retriever. Ten weeks old. He kept me company in your absence. He's a good boy, aren't you?" He leaned into the squirming puppy and received a shower of licks on his nose.

"Sweet!" Shannon said. "He has that special puppy smell. I love that."

She cuddled the furry ball in the nape of her neck and slipped into the nearest kitchen chair.

Luke pulled out another chair and placed it next to her, sitting close, knee to knee.

"What in the world are you doing here?" she asked.

"Dr. Moon called the police in weeks ago when he couldn't reach you on the phone or get you to answer the door."

"Did you say Dr. Moon called you in *weeks ago?*"

"Almost a month ago now."

"How weird. I left two days ago."

"It's been a month. Anyway, he was damn worried about you, thought you might have. . . he said you'd been so depressed. . . So we came in and found the note you left for Dr. Bennett."

"I'm touched that he worried about me. He's very kind."

"Yeah, I like the guy. So, your house looked like it had been empty for the better part of a week or two, and we called Dr. Bennett to see if she'd heard anything from you. She hadn't, but when she learned you'd left a note for her, she rushed over here."

"Her too? It's so nice that people bothered."

"People care about you, Shannon. I—"

Shannon laid a hand on his knee and interrupted. "Let's get back to the fact that a month or more has passed here, when for me it's only been two days."

"Maybe you're suffering from a memory gap. Have you hit your head or lost consciousness? Drugs? Or were you kidnapped?" He gripped her by her shoulders. "Are aliens involved in this?"

She leaned back in her chair, sinking down the hard slats of its back until her head met wood.

So weary.

"Yes, Aliens are involved. Salesti, Narci, and I went off-planet to FireWorld to rescue Roebor. Things did not go well. Salesti died. Roebor's body died a horrible death, and Roebor's spirit now lives in my mind."

"Roebor's body died?"

"Yes, and I also ended up with excess power—Salesti's—and there's something bad about that power that the other salestis aren't telling me. So now I'm back, but I would've sworn that I was on FireWorld for about twenty-four hours and on RiverWorld for another five or so."

"FireWorld?"

"Oh, that's where Roebor lived. Hey, Roebor? Can you explain the time discrepancy? When Essi was gone, much *less* time passed here than on RiverWorld, not *more*."

"You mean he's back in your mind? Now?" Luke asked. His voice cracked.

"Yes. Roebor. Now."

I still do not like your Luke much, although I like his intriguing little Gumshoe.

"Roebor likes Gumshoe," she said to Luke.

"Oh, I'm so relieved to hear that."

Shannon made a face at him.

But to answer your question, we can blame the time glitch on the wormhole we chose for our return. To speak in layman's terms—I suspect a rip has developed in the wormhole, and time leaks through it. When we pass the rip in the wormhole, we lose time. This, of course, is not the astrophysical explanation but a gross simplification.

"Of course."

"Of course, what?" Luke asked.

"Sorry, I was answering Roebor, who has given me the 'broken wormhole for dummies' explanation why more time has passed here than where I was."

"What did he say?"

"That the wormhole leaks time."

"But you can't keep Roebor on board. Carrying him around in your head does lethal things to your body."

"The best part of having Salesti's extra power is that my body should better tolerate his presence. I shouldn't shut down much at all this time. So that's something, right?"

Luke shifted in his seat. "I don't like it. But you said Salesti died? That's terrible."

Shannon recounted the story.

"Any idea what the salestis held back?" Luke asked as she finished.

"Yes, I think they expect the power to explode here on Earth and destroy the entire solar system."

"*What*? Is that likely?"

"No idea, really. For sure, I don't like having so much power onboard—although I feel the same as always, so far. Anyway—you didn't finish telling *your* story. Dr. Bennett came over to read the note I'd left, and then what?"

"Why her?"

"What?"

"Why not leave a note for Dr. Moon?"

"Oh, because Dr. Bennett had already heard the whole alien story. She'd met Essi and even Roebor because I bribed her with the alien meet-up to help me escape from the hospital. She and Roebor got along splendidly. Dr. Moon never learned about my extra company, so it seemed best to leave him blissfully ignorant."

Luke frowned at the comment about Roebor and Dr. Bennett getting along. "I suspect they got along because Dr. Bennett steamrolls everything and everybody in her path, including dragonpanthers." He remained silent a moment. "You could have left the note for me."

Shannon placed the puppy on the floor. He waddled after Narci, who had jumped down from the table to give him a sniff. She jumped out of reach a second before he could pounce on her tail.

Luke fiddled with a rubber band he found on the kitchen table. Shannon placed her hands on top of his. A small electric shock rippled through her. Salesti's power pulsed as if touching Luke had awakened the energy in her mind, and it sought a way to lash out.

She popped her hand off his.

"You *know* why I didn't leave the note for you. I isolated myself from you for over a year because aliens are my life now, and these alien problems will keep cropping up—like this incident on FireWorld. The whole business is too dangerous for you. That last bullet you took might have killed you. Not to mention the time I had to deliberately crash into your car during the wildfire. *I* might have killed you. I'd rather have you alive somewhere else than dead by my side. So, no note for you. Which brings me back to why you came today."

Luke listened, frowning, snapping the rubber band between his fingers, his eyes locked on her face.

"Isn't it my choice whether I want to put myself in harm's way or not?" he asked in his quiet way. "I'm a police officer, for god's sake. I put myself in harm's way every day."

"Yes, and I'm elated you made it back to the job. I was so afraid your shoulder injury would stop you. But we digress. You were in my house today why?"

"I've come every day. Dr. Bennett refused to tell us what you said in the letter you left for her, except to assure us you left of your own free will, your mission might prove dangerous, and she couldn't predict when you'd come back."

"All true."

"I suspected it had something to do with aliens, in which case things might go badly—cataclysmically badly if history is any indication. And, in fact, things did go badly. So I wanted to be here to help when you came back."

"Lucky for us, I don't need help. I'm good."

"Yes, you're good, except you came back with a male dragonpanther in your head who has nowhere else to go, and you've become a living powder keg. No problem."

"At least not your problem." Shannon shoved herself out of her chair, waved Luke out of his, and shooed him toward the front door. "I appreciate your concern, Luke, but if I'm a powder keg, that's all the more reason to keep your distance. Meanwhile, I'm exhausted and need to sleep, so goodbye."

She scooped up the puppy and handed him to Luke.

"Shannon, I—"

"You too, bird," Shannon called back toward the kitchen. The raven swept through the hallway and out the front door over Luke's head.

The door closed on Luke's retreating face as Shannon took care not to hurt him or Gumshoe. She paused, leaning with her back against the wall, savoring the comfort, the stimulation, the joy, and the heartbreak of seeing Luke again.

And good riddance, too. I fear his influence on you. Too grumpy.

"He's not grumpy about anyone but you."

Why would I make him grumpy? I am not occupying space in his tiny mind.

"Uh huh. Come on, Narci, let's go to bed and get some sleep."

Shannon crawled between soft, cool, satin sheets, and settled into her plump pillow. Narci curled into her side. But sleeping would not go well for Shannon that night or for many nights to come.

CHAPTER TEN
Marathon

SHANNON SAT IN BED, REACHED FOR HER BRUSH on the bedside table and combed out her knee-length, silver-blond hair.

So weary

She re-braided her hair, pulled a thin, soft sheet to her waist, and settled in for her nap.

But when she closed her eyes, strange patterns flashed on the insides of her eyelids—golden streaks like webs of lightning branching out across her vision, fading and flashing anew.

Her mind jittered and jumped as if she'd overdosed on too much caffeine. Pain like a cascade of mild electric shocks ran down the surface of her thighs. She couldn't bear the touch of the bedsheet against her body and peeled it away.

"*Odin's eye*, do you sense any of this? Do you know what's going on?"

Yes, Shannon, I observe. I fear your tremendous power is manifesting as it leaks into your system with increasing intensity.

"I figured I could blame the power. But I *don't* get what you mean when you say the power leaks into my system? Doesn't the power already exist in my system? Where else would it be?"

In your mind. The power resides in your mind, but too much exists here for your mind to contain it all, and it leaks out into your body.

"Okay. I guess I need to dissipate some power so I can sleep. I think I'll try taking a run. Would that work?"

It is a logical hypothesis.

Shannon scooted around the cat, who remained undisturbed on the bed. She dressed in her sweat-skimming, gray, sleeveless T-shirt, shorts, and her best pair of white running shoes. She applied sunscreen and bounced down the stairs and out the door into the warm afternoon.

Heading downhill, she enjoyed the rhythm of her shoes hitting the asphalt, her breathing steady, her arms pumping. At the marina, she turned, ran north past the city limits, and headed on to see how the countryside was recovering from a fire that devastated the area.

Shannon started down the unmarked gravel road she'd driven on the day of the Lefthand Campground Fire a year ago. Before long, blackened trees and bushes dominated the barren landscape, punctuated by occasional gullies of ash. Here and there, spots of green had grown again, but it would be years before this part of the county recovered.

No one else appeared on her lonely stretch of road, so she decided to test her legs. *Would she run faster because of the power? Farther?* She double-checked for onlookers. No one. She picked up speed.

The energy coursed through her thighs and calves. *Exhilarating.* But she wouldn't be invited to the Olympic one-hundred-meter dash trials any time soon. The power couldn't give her muscles she didn't have, and her muscles were never made for speed. Maybe she could go for duration, if not speed. She settled back into a steady rhythm. . . .

. . . . and fell into a trancelike state, pacing herself, listening to the slap of her shoes on the gravel road. Shannon relaxed into the rhythm of movement, thinking no conscious thoughts, the power propelling her forward and forward.

And forward. . . .

* * *

Thirsty. Need water.

At last, Shannon came to a stop and observed her surroundings.

Dark? How could it be dark? *That was crazy.*

But night had not only arrived, it had arrived some time ago. The moon was already sinking toward the western horizon. The cool air caused her sweating body to shiver, the scent of sage pressed at the edge of her awareness. She unhitched her water bottle from her waistband and took a long, slow drink.

How had she run from early afternoon until late night? She'd never run more than two or three miles at a time. She was no marathoner.

Not only had Shannon run for hours, now that she took a moment to study the landscape, she didn't know where she was.

She'd left the burned land behind her, though, and she smelled the sea in the near distance. That meant she'd reached the coast and headed north. The fire had started well to the south and traveled up the coast before firefighters had controlled it west of Ocean City. She'd run far enough north to escape its devastating aftermath.

Far enough north that the road had come to an end, and left her on a gravel hiking trail about three feet wide. She must have run north of Twisted Pine Bay, where the Old Coast Road ended, and onto the National Forest trail that ran along the coast to Santa Lucia. She must be twenty-five miles from home!

Wow. Power indeed.

Now that she'd snapped out of her trance, she faced two other unfortunate facts: she might possess the *power* to run twenty-five miles, but she didn't possess the trained muscles for such a run, and she wasn't wearing the right shoes.

The moonlight reflected dark patches on her feet where blood had seeped from broken blisters. Overtaxed, her legs quivered even as she became aware of their fatigue, and she collapsed onto the trail.

She pulled her feet toward her and examined them—*what a mess*—but she hesitated to take her shoes off, afraid she wouldn't be able to put them back on. Taking care to move her legs with the speed and force of an inchworm, she stretched them out and draped her feet over a rock. Before she laid back, she brushed a few small stones aside. The hard ground, covered with tiny bits of gravel and rock, prickled against her spine.

She looked up at the stars scattered across the black sky's broad expanse. The cool air flowed across her face like a gentle caress. *Better.*

But now what?

As she lay on her back, a large black bird swooped down and perched on her stomach.

"Why, hello, bird. Have you been following me?"

"Hello. Been following?"

"Listen, will you make yourself useful and go tell Luke I need his help?" Shannon didn't expect the raven to do any such thing, but it amused her to ask anyway, and *Odin knew*, she needed a bit of amusement about now.

"Tell Luke. Tell Luke," the bird said, and, to Shannon's surprise, he took off into the black night. Heading home, probably.

"You there, Roebor?"

Yes.

"What happened to me? It's like someone hypnotized me. Could you tell what was happening?"

I have access to your conscious mind alone. That part of your brain shut down as you ran. I was unable to reach you. Nor did I understand whether you knew what you were doing, so I could not tell whether I should try to break through to your subconscious. Such drastic measures might cause damage to your mind.

"Off the top of my head, I'd say next time, try to break through. If we ever experience a next time. Which I hope we do not."

Where do we find ourselves?

"Remember when I went to rescue Essi from the mouse at the SeaQuarium Maintenance Center? We're north of there, out in the boonies. We're alone. I didn't bring my phone, since I didn't need it for a quick run in town. *Hah!* Nobody knows we're here."

Ah. We have landed in the soup, you are saying.

"Yes, exactly. So when my legs stop jiggling like jello, I'll try to walk us back to Twisted Pine Bay and on to the Maintenance Center, and hope I can break in and use the phone to call 9-1-1 or somebody to come rescue us. Let's see if I can get onto my feet."

Shannon rolled to her hands and knees and then stood. The muscles in her thighs and calves exploded with bursts of pain like cracks of a whip each time she took a step. She might work with that. She couldn't, however, work with the searing pain in her heels and toes. She couldn't take another step.

Yet she must move.

Right. Hands and knees.

She knelt down, settled onto her hands and knees, and moved foot by laborious foot south toward Twisted Pine Bay. The gravel pricked her palms and knees. Shannon ignored the pain.

With any luck, she hadn't run very far north along the trail before she had come to her senses. Otherwise, a night of pain awaited.

* * *

After several hours of painstaking progress, the shape of the trailhead sign and the posts that divided the trail from the paved parking lot of the Twisted Pine picnic area rose out of the darkness.

Shannon stumbled to her feet and sat on a post at the trailhead. She picked bits of rocks, dirt, and pine needles from her stinging palms and knees and surveyed the area.

No cars remained in the parking lot. *Loki's luck.*

But did she hear shouting down by the beach?

Yes, loud voices and laughter drifted to her from the sand dunes. Someone would have a phone.

She stood and took a step forward.

Not so bad.

Her legs felt stronger, and her feet more numb. She wobbled a moment and stepped toward the sound.

CHAPTER ELEVEN
Power Rising

STEP BY EXCRUCIATING STEP, Shannon walked toward the ocean. At the west end of the parking lot, sand dunes took over the landscape, and Shannon pushed on with slipping, sliding, sinking footsteps, shivering in the cooler ocean air.

Not long after she crossed over onto the sand, Shannon spotted a car down on the beach. The state forbade driving on the sand, but kids would sometimes sneak out here. Four figures occupied various spots on the beach or in the water. They'd built a small campfire, and one figure sat there with a big bottle of wine or liquor in his hand. The two nearest to her, although separated, were shouting to one another, their voices floating to Shannon. The fourth figure was too far away to be in on the conversation.

That campfire beckoned.

"Hello," Shannon called out. "I need to borrow a phone. Can anybody help me?"

The person sitting by the fire stared at her but didn't stir from his spot. A woman on the beach near the incoming tide line began walking toward her, as did the one standing knee-deep in the waves. Another person, the farthest away, dove into the surf and swam further out. He hadn't heard her.

Unless someone put a gun to her head, Shannon didn't want to take another step, and even then, it would be a close call as to whether she'd rather take the bullet or the step. She waited for the others to come to her.

A girl of about eighteen, dressed in a black bathing suit and blue cut-off jeans approached first.

"Hi," she said. "What's up?"

"I've worked up a boatload of bad blisters, and I want to call someone to come get me, but I don't have my phone."

The girl flashed her light into Shannon's face. Shannon squinted and raised her hand to shield her eyes. Before she could protest, the flashlight traveled down to her feet.

"Oh my god, I guess you really did work up some blisters. Like, your feet are a bloody mess. Can you make it over here to the fire? I'll get my phone, and you can have a beer or something?"

"Thank you so much." Shannon very much did *not* want to move, but that fire—and the phone—beckoned. Holding her breath, she hobbled along, longing to scream at every step. The girl took her elbow in a valiant but futile attempt to help her.

"I love your perfume. Where do you get it? What's it called? Is it, like, really, really expensive?"

Shannon ignored this. No one believed her when she told them it was her natural scent.

"I'm Brittany, by the way. Here, sit over here. Don't go anywhere near Brant. He's drunk out of his mind and stopped being fun, like, two hours ago."

Shannon sat and inched close to the fire. *Ah. Warmth.*

A second girl arrived, her wavy, shoulder-length, fudge-colored hair blowing in the sea air.

Fudge-colored?—Shannon *was* hungry, now that she thought about it.

The girl wore a long, light yellow sweater over her yellow striped swimsuit.

"Are you crazy?" the girl asked Brittany. "You can't invite strangers over here like they're old pals. Who knows what kind of people are lurking out here this time of night?" She regarded Shannon with a frown.

"You're pissed because Brant is being such an a-hole, but don't take it out on her," Brittany said. "Check her out." She nodded at Shannon's feet. "She wouldn't hurt a fly."

Brittany flopped down and began searching through a backpack. "I found it." She handed her cell phone over to Shannon, who, rubbing her sore palms, took the phone and thanked her.

"Why go so soon, darlin'?" Brant mumbled.

Shannon hated to bother Dr. Bennett, but her options were limited. Dr. Bennett's number rang. Voicemail.

"You have reached the answering machine of Dr. Julia Bennett. I am out of town and will not be returning until August 15th. Please leave a message."

Okay. Then she'd try Dr. Moon.

She dialed again.

"Did ya hear me, darlin'? No need to hurry off."

"Shut up, Brant," said the as-yet-unnamed girl.

Shannon stared at the girl's huge, bright orange hoop earrings while she waited for Moon to answer. The phone rang and rang, but no answering machine message came on, and no one picked up. Desperate enough to let it ring over a dozen times, Shannon would have connected with Moon if he had any intention of answering his phone.

Nada.

He might have flown north to manage the Dickson project in Alaska. They'd started work on a new Research Center and UnderWater Complex there to rival the one that Roebor had taken down.

That was unavoidable, Shannon. I am touchy on that subject. I wish you would not speak of it.

I'll do my best. But no one blames you.

No one blames me because no one knows I did it.

I know you did it, and I don't blame you. You more than made up for it by sending the diamonds to rebuild it.

Roebor made a noise that sounded like "hmmph."

So, no Moon either. Who then?

Not Luke, not Luke, not Luke.

She must be strong for once and not rely on him. He was like an addiction she couldn't quit because he was always there for her. Every. Damn. Time. And then he'd get hurt. *Do not call him.*

Brant swayed to his feet and kept on swaying. He tried to keep his balance—with limited success, stumbled around the fire, and tried to pull Shannon to her feet by her arm. The boy reeked of whiskey. His shoulder-length hair obscured his face, so Shannon frowned at his skinny, white chest and baggy shorts. His hands, thin but long-fingered, like a piano player's, surprised her; their softness soothed her own damaged palms.

"You smell good. Let's dance."

Shannon pulled her hands out of his grasp.

"I said, leave her alone, you jerk. You came here with me," said his date.

"Yeah, but you're no fun, Jessica. This gal will be much more fun, I can tell."

"Like, check out her feet," Brittany said. "She can't dance, you stupidhead."

Roebor growled low in Shannon's throat.

It's okay, Roebor. He's a harmless drunk.

"Did you hear that growl? Sexy or what?"

Eye of Odin.

"Brant," Shannon said, "I can't even pretend to be fun tonight, and as Brittany pointed out, I can't dance, so please leave me alone."

Who might she call? She had to think.

"I said, get up and dance with me, bitch, and that's what I meant."

Uh oh. Good old Brant might be a mean drunk.

He grabbed her hands again.

"Let *go*." She pushed Brant away.

As she pushed, the colors that she would normally cast when she wanted to search for something, as she had when she was with Pip on FireWorld, came flying from her hands like a colorful tidal wave. Brant flew into the air and sailed backwards twenty feet. He landed with a thud in a deep sand dune.

"Oh my god!" Brittany said. "Is he dead?"

"Jesus, what did you do that for?" Jessica yelled at Shannon. She ran to Brant and looked him over. "He seems okay. I guess he's too drunk to get hurt."

"I'm sorry, I didn't mean to push him that hard. I had no idea I had the strength to push him that hard."

What happened there, Roebor?

Salesti's power happened. So yes, you can push him that far—and much farther.

The fourth reveler joined them at the fire. A tall, dark, good-looking boy in loose swim trunks grabbed his towel from a stack of belongings by the fire and rubbed his hair.

"What's going on? I saw Brant flying through the air like the Hulk tossed him. Who did that?" He inspected the scene as if searching for someone beefier than Brittany, Jessica, or Shannon.

"And who are you?"

"I'm Shannon Kendricks, and I'm trying to find a way home."

Brittany introduced the newcomer, Chance, who took charge.

"Okay, Brittany, take this water and make sure the fire is out. Put some sand on it too. Jess, can B-boy walk?" With Jessica's help, Brant rose to his feet, swaying side to side like a ship on stormy seas. "I'm good, bro. Watch out for that bitch there, though. She throws a mean punch."

"Shannon, you can come with us if you live in town. We can drop you off before we head back to the dorms."

"What? I'm not riding with her," Jessica said. "She's weird. Like a witch or something. You saw what she did. That's not natural."

"I'm, like, a teensy bit scared, too," Brittany said, lowering her eyes and scuffing her bare foot in the sand. "I mean, she seems really nice, but what she did was freaky."

"Pay attention, dudes. Her feet are a bloody mess, and she looks like hell. Keep your hands to yourself, Brant, and I'm sure we'll be fine. Am I right, Shannon?"

"Spot on. I'm a bloody mess, and I look like hell because I feel like hell. I won't hurt a fly on our way home. Scout's honor. And thank you, Chance." Shannon presented her three girl scout fingers.

"You all wait here. I'll get the SUV."

Chance's SUV had that new-car smell. Shannon scooted in next to Brittany on soft, beige, leather seats and laid her head back on the headrest, doing her best to keep her blood off the immaculate interior. Chance turned on the heat, and Shannon didn't move any part of her body for the twenty-minute drive into town. She never wanted to get out. After a quiet trip, during which no one spoke, they reached town, and Shannon directed Chance to her house.

When he pulled into her driveway, Luke's white Chevy sat at the curb—he'd bought a new one to replace the one she'd totaled in the fire. He sat on the front porch steps under the porch light, scratching Narci's ears. Gumshoe sat on the sidewalk, chewing on Luke's shoelaces. The raven sat on the railing that rimmed Shannon's front porch.

Shannon laughed softly. It looked as if the raven had assembled the group just for her.

CHAPTER TWELVE
Love and Hate

SHANNON KNEW HOW THIS WOULD GO, and so it did. She waved goodbye to the passengers in the SUV, took a step toward the house, and stopped cold. Every part of her body from her hips to her toes throbbed with pain as if she'd experienced the underbelly of a buffalo stampede.

Do not take his help. Do not do it. Stand tall, ignore the screaming pain, walk right past him and into the house. Feel no pain, feel no pain, feel—

Odin's eye, that hurt.

Maybe she could wait Luke out if she stood like a rock—*scratch that*—sat like a rock in the driveway until he left.

Let him help you, Roebor said. *Otherwise, we'll be out here all night.*

"No chance." Shannon stood straight and rolled her shoulders back. "He helps anytime and every time, and he almost died because I let him, so that's the end of that."

Luke rose from the porch step, stretched, and strode down to Shannon, Gumshoe on his heels. He caught sight of at her swollen, blood-encrusted feet. "My god—were you attacked by a very short wolf?"

Shannon laughed despite her hurting body. "No wolves. I ran farther than I meant to, that's all. I'm sore. I'll be all right."

"Stay right there. I'll use my key to unlock the house, and I'll be right back."

Shannon yelped in frustration. "I want that key back," she said to his retreating back. Her shoulders drooped.

She wouldn't rely on Luke to get to the house. She would not. Instead, she would—what?

No crawling—her knees had suffered enough tonight. Instead, she sat on the concrete driveway to try the butt method of locomotion: arms forward, lift, swing, butt forward, arms back by her sides; front, lift, swing; front, lift, swing. . . Her palms stung again, but otherwise it wasn't so bad.

She'd made it about three feet when Luke returned, towering above her.

"What are you doing? I mean, we're all aware you *can* do this by yourself, but the point is, you don't *have* to."

"I want to." She kept moving. *Arms forward, butt forward, arms back. Arms forward, butt forward, arms back.* Gumshoe found this to be a jolly game. He yipped and bounced along with her, trying to leap into her moving lap.

Luke peered down at her, chin jutting out as if he were giving the matter great thought.

"Beee-cause you're having so much fun?"

Shannon stopped. His silhouette hovered above her in the glow of the streetlight.

"Because in the past, when you helped me, you almost died. More than once," she said, her voice quiet. "You always want to help. I always let you help. You always stand by me. Ergo, you were standing there to take the bullet. And that—" she paused for emphasis "will *(arms)*—never *(butt)*—happen *(arms)*—again *(butt)*."

"Yes, it will."

She stopped her forward progress, such as it was. "What?"

He dropped down by her side with his ivory soap smell and his long eyelashes and draped the light jacket that she kept hanging on her coat stand by the front door over her shoulders. She pulled it on all the way. *Much better.*

"I mean, if you let me, I will stand by you when trouble comes. And trouble will come since you're a trouble magnet. I will stand by you because I love you, cara."

Shannon's eyes watered. She took his large square hand in her pink scraped ones.

"Also," he said, "you love me. But you can't control my life. Don't tell me I'd be better off without you. Been there, done that."

"But you almost died."

"And I still want to be in your life. If an alien monster swallows me whole tomorrow, so be it. We will have had today. But if you shut me out, we won't have even that."

"The alien monster consumption scenario is a distinct possibility."

"Doesn't matter. You've given me plenty of time to think about it. I tried it your way for this last year. I tried to throw my heart and soul into forgetting you."

"You just need more time to finish the forgetting."

"I didn't try to forget you because I was afraid of dying if I stayed. I tried to forget you because I thought that with your crazy life, maybe I should face the inevitable—that you would come to a tragic end sooner rather than later, so why not grieve now and be done with it?"

"Exactly. So what are you doing back here?"

He turned her hands over and studied the multitude of tiny nicks and bruises on the palm. "Did you not hear me say that I love you?"

She should say she loved him, too. *Odin knew,* she did love him. Why couldn't she just spit it out?

When Shannon didn't reply, he said, "Hey—this will give you a laugh. I was just coming in from my swing shift tonight when your bird came swooping down out of the night and landed in my driveway. Lucky thing it didn't land on my new car, or I might have had to throttle its tiny, feathered neck."

"You would never."

"Eh, close call, your bird or my car. Anyway, then—clear as a fine crystal wine glass—it said, 'Tell Luke. Hi, bird, tell Luke,' and it gave me the shivers because it sounded just like your voice. I swear to god."

"It mimicked me? Hey, bird," Shannon said, calling to the bird, which still perched on the front railing of her porch.

The raven swooped down toward them, and Luke, with one eye on the raven, said, "So I changed clothes and drove on over. He flew with me. Did you train him to do that?"

The raven landed on Shannon's shoulder. "Hey bird," she said. "No, I haven't trained him to do anything."

The raven perched there, silent, its unblinking black eyes peering over at Shannon's face.

"He has nothing to say now. I guess he's done his work for the day."

Luke hadn't turned her hands loose. "I love you."

This seems rather overdramatic to me, Shannon. I would send him away. But let him carry us into the house first.

"Stop that!" Shannon said to Roebor.

Luke dropped her hands as if they'd lit his fingers on fire. He leaned away. "What?"

Way to ruin a magic moment.

"I'm sorry. Roebor chose that moment to chip in his two cents. I meant my outburst for him. So, keep it down, will you, Roebor?" She leaned into Luke. "I worry about you risking death and dismemberment on my account, all right? Something happened out at Twisted Pine Bay tonight that I need to think about, which makes the risk very real, okay?"

"Twisted Pine? You ran all the way out there? No wonder your feet look like shredded newspaper at a crime scene. What happened? Wait. First, let's get inside. Let me help you to your feet." He lifted her to her feet and would have scooped her into his arms—again—but she stopped him by touching his chest.

"As a special favor to me, for tonight, would you get in your car and go home? Let me take care of myself. Let me think about everything you said and see if I can bear the thought of you risking your life for me."

"Compromise: I'll take you as far as your door and no further. *If* you promise to tell me tomorrow what happened tonight."

Without waiting for an answer, he grabbed her around the waist and lifted her six inches. His fingers found the ticklish spot under her ribs. She shrieked and laughed, and he rushed to the porch, spanned the stairs, twirled her around, gave her an extra tickle, and placed her back on her feet in front of her door.

"Okay, that's the only laugh out of me on this otherwise miserable day, so thank you," she said.

He leaned in and kissed her. She hesitated.

She shouldn't. She really shouldn't. . . *Well, maybe one.*

She slid her arms around his neck and kissed him back.

By the gods, too much, too soon. Slap him, Shannon.

Luke straightened, smiled, and turned away. She watched him walk to his car, the happy puppy bouncing along at his feet. She waved once more and wobbled into her front hall.

* * *

Shannon limped into the kitchen, crying out with each step since no one would hear her. She opened a can of cat food for Narci, grabbed a one-pound bag of peanut M&M's and a bag of tortilla chips, and made for her upstairs bathroom.

As she passed the front door, she checked on the raven. He still perched on her porch railing, so she fed him a handful of tortilla chips.

"You understood what I asked, didn't you, bird? But how in *Odin's eye* did you know where to find Luke?"

"How in Odin's eye?" the bird repeated.

* * *

Shannon crawled into her bathroom on all fours with the tortilla chip bag clenched between her teeth, and the M&M bag tucked in her running shorts. She revisited the decision to reject Luke's help. He could have whisked her up here pain-free.

Bad decision. Not her first, not going to be her last.

After inching her shoes off, she examined her feet. Her oozing, bloody skin stuck to her socks.

She might never walk again; the jury was still out.

In no rush to put her feet through the painful ordeal of stripping off the socks, she sat on the floor and ate the chips and candy. When she'd thrown the two empties in her trash can, she made one feeble attempt at the stripping, grimaced, and decided instead on a steaming hot bath. She eased her aching body into the water, socks and all, where she soaked for a long and luxurious time contemplating the Luke problem, the power problem, and the Roebor problem.

She peeled off her socks twenty minutes into the soak.

After she'd dried herself off and bandaged her feet, she limped into the bedroom, eased into her silkiest nightgown, and tried once again to fall asleep. To her relief, she drifted. . . drifted. . . .

* * *

Shannon jerked awake and swung her legs over to the edge of her bed.

What had awakened her? She was in her bed, in her room. Nothing looked out of place.

She listened: no noise. She grew accustomed to the dark: nothing moved. So what had disturbed. . . .

Ah. She could sense an arrival—another alien-bestowed skill—someone would come through the RiverWorld portal. . . Essi!

Shannon limped down the stairs and out the back door to the picnic table, Narci right behind her. And she waited. After a moment, she climbed on the table and lifted her arm, casting her colors. The portal flashed, though no one could see it but Shannon, and lavender light twinkled. Essi fell into Shannon, traveling through her arm and into her mind.

On Earth, Seladorans like Essi and Salesti, came through the portal in their ethereal form and wouldn't survive if they didn't find a host to inhabit right away. That wasn't true for denizens of FireWorld who came with their whole bodies. Nor was it true for her when she went to Selador or FireWorld.

Laying her head down on the smooth redwood planks, Shannon closed her eyes and went to greet Essi in the Great Room of her mind. Shannon's scent, the mysterious spicy scent that never wore off, engulfed her here. She inhaled it, savored it.

The light, once soft, now flooded the room in bright white-gold, swirling as if tossed by unfelt winds.

"Wow, we need sunglasses in here. Essi!" Shannon encircled the woman in her arms and held her there, despite Essi's random flyaway curls tickling her nose. But Essi wouldn't have come without reason. She trembled in Shannon's arms. "What's happened? Tell me."

bale comes to riverworld, forces toss to come to earth. bale comes to find shannon.

"Did you hear that, Roebor?"

The dragonpanther appeared by her side and nodded. *Good thing the Great Room stretched far out into the distance and soared high above her.* Plenty of room for his big dragon-panther body.

how long shannon back? Essi asked.

"I arrived—" she glanced at her watch "—about fifteen hours ago. Why?"

bale uses other portal, lands down at ocean same time as essi lands here.

"But I thought you would lose time in this portal and land days or weeks after you left in Earth time."

salestis make special cocoon for essi so essi protected from time leak.

Yes, Roebor said, *that makes perfect sense. When you travel through the damaged wormhole, it is as if you spend time stuck in there. But if the salestis can protect Essi from the leak—by the cocoon in this case—she can fly right through.*

"Thanks, Roebor. And Bale plans to force Toss to help him take on a human form so he can come and find me?"

yes.

"Not again! How horrible for Toss."

Bale would need to bring along a Seladoran so that he could enter a human mind because a house-sized flying dragonpanther would draw undue attention. Toss, as the caretaker of the cave of portals, had once again been the first Seladoran an invader saw.

"I was hoping Bale wouldn't bother with me now that they've executed Roebor."

on riverworld, bale rages about roebor still. shannon friend of roebor, and bale wishes everyone to do with roebor on earth to die.

It is as I predicted. I am glad I am here to help you.

"Sounds like he takes after his father, Tidak. What about his brother Pak? Has he come too?"

no. pak not with bale.

"How did he know about Toss and the need to take on a safer form here anyway, Essi?"

bale tells toss and essi that father tidak visits home one time quick during virus hunt to tell bale and pak what tidak must do.

"What? Tidak returned to FireWorld in the middle of our search for the virus? I had no clue. Did you, Roebor?"

No. Nor did my calculations suggest that he had time for such a trip. I am surprised he dared risk it. But no matter. We must assume Bale learned everything his father knew.

"Will somebody come from FireWorld to calm him down and take him back? Should we try to stay away from him until then?"

I am sorry, Shannon. No one will come to stop Bale. I don't believe he received the Council's permission to journey here, but the Council would not prevent him from seeking his revenge off-world.

"But wouldn't the Council think the time for revenge is over?"

We do not interact with other worlds except the one where we trade for modern inventions. Earth is nothing to my people, except the place where we desecrated the body of Tidak. You are nothing to my people. The Council will not interfere.

"That's just cold. What about Pak? Do you think he'll come to help his brother?"

I think not. Pak is more amenable to reason over rage. I believe he will see the unfairness and futility of seeking further revenge on Earth.

"Toss knows how to get to my house, and so did Tidak. So, Bale will come here soon if he's found a human to invade. Shall we go search for his body? He's likely to hide down on the undeveloped shoreline to the south of town or on an island, like Tidak did, since he can't traipse through town without being noticed. Would it make sense to capture him?"

Hmm. Our advantage lies in my presence here, which is unknown to him. If we entice him to enter your mind for a fight with you, I can defeat him. It would be a fight to the death, both because he would wish it, once he discovers I am still alive, and also because we cannot permit him to return to FireWorld with the news that my spirit lives.

"The chance of luring him into my mind isn't great when he'll be intent on taking me out physically. But I can defeat him alone now because of Salesti's power. I'll go into *his* mind, which I can do with a simple touch, and he need never learn you're still alive."

That plan is unwise. You would need to be prepared to fight him to the death.

"I hope I won't have to. I'll ask him to agree by an oath on his honor that if he wins, he can kill me, and if I win, he must go home. He should agree to that, right?"

I do not trust him to honor his pledge. He might well return to attack again.

"If he does, we'll devise a Plan B. But let's try Plan A. With my power, it should be a piece of cake."

She hoped.

CHAPTER THIRTEEN
Bale

ESSI INSISTED ON STAYING until they freed Toss from captivity in Bale's mind. Shannon, with Roebor and Essi now on board, returned to the kitchen and searched for breakfast fixings. She would need to consume even larger meals now that she ate for three. She pulled a zucchini lasagna out of the freezer along with several packages of frozen vegetables and a carton of chocolate ice cream with chocolate chips and fudge ripples. She ate the ice cream while the broccoli and peas cooked in the microwave, and ate the vegetables, along with a can of peaches and a package of coconut macaroons, while the lasagna finished in the oven.

Shannon turned on the radio: still no news on the crocodile-t-rex. She wondered whether Bale had lied when he boasted to his friends that he'd sent a beast to Earth.

"Roebor? Do you think the croco-saurus could possibly have stayed out of sight this long?"

I wondered this myself. I hope it was a false alarm.

After she'd eaten, she called Luke.

"This is against my good, better, and best judgment, but, your choice," she told him. "We have a mission. Proceed at

your peril and feel free to opt out of any particular activities—
or to opt out of the whole enterprise."

"I'm in," he said before she'd even finished speaking.

"Yes, well, you might change your mind when you hear
about today's schedule of events. In a nutshell, Tidak—you
remember him—big, gold, nasty beast—has a son, Bale—
big, gold, nasty beast—who seeks revenge for Tidak's death."
Shannon explained Bale's grudge and his unfortunate arrival.

"My god, Shannon, already? Aliens already? You just got
back. But okay, I'll meet you at your place and go with you
into this joker's mind."

*No, he definitely would not be accompanying her into this
joker's mind.*

"I plan to drive down to the waterfront to see if I can find
Bale's body. I bought a small runabout last year, so we can
cruise the coast. I'll meet you there."

* * *

"Are you prepared to kill this dragonpanther? Because
that's what you may have to do if things go south," Luke said
as he piloted Shannon's boat while she used her binoculars to
scan the shoreline for Bale's body. Gumshoe sat in the bottom
of the boat, chewing on the anchor chain. Shannon, clad in
a blue, long-sleeved T-shirt and jeans, barefoot to humor her
wounded feet, lowered her binoculars and studied the clouds
scudding across the sky. She turned to Luke.

"It won't come to that because I can knock him out before
he becomes a threat. Send him home."

"So, what will prevent him from coming right back?"

See? Even one as dim as he is expects Bale to return, and he doesn't know Tidak's son as I do, Roebor said.

"If he does, so be it. We'll be ready for him."

"What does that mean?"

"It means I wish Salesti were here to spy on Bale when he returns to FireWorld and to tell us when he plans to come back."

I have an idea. I can go to FireWorld to spy on Bale in Narci's body. She can pass unnoticed on my world.

"No, I can't risk Narci on FireWorld. Bale's mate already wants to adopt her. Plus, you would take too much of her energy."

"Are you kidding? I would never suggest Narci go spy on Bale," Luke said.

"Right. Roebor suggested it. He planned to go with her. But it doesn't matter because she's not going."

Luke would never suggest that Narci go because his thick wit wouldn't allow him to devise such a plan.

"It was a ridiculous suggestion," Luke said.

Shannon ignored them both.

"Will you skirt around that island there—isn't that where Tidak hid his body? He might have mapped his location for Bale and Pak when he went back."

Luke cut the engine back, slowed the boat down, and headed to the small island with its tiny cove hidden on the landward side. They curved around the island—

—And there lay Bale. He floated in the cove, intent on catching any living creature that he and Toss could board to get closer to a human. Unlike Shannon, who didn't need help to board another because of her alien gifts, he couldn't make the crossing to fish, animal, or human without Toss's help.

Bale's enormous head reared back when he spotted her, and he roared in triumph.

Shannon took two quick steps back. "Hold on, Bale. Can we talk?"

The dragonpanther lunged for the boat, flapping his great wings.

You make my revenge too easy. I did not come to talk.

He brought a massive paw, talons extended, down toward Shannon, but Luke had reversed the engine the moment Bale lunged toward them. The dragonpanther's fist smashed into the bow of the boat, missing its occupants. The entire front quarter of the boat crumpled into the sea. Luke continued to back up until what remained of the boat scraped onto the beach.

"Will you keep my body next to his?"

She trusted Luke to place her arm on the dragonpanther so she could return without mishap when it was all over.

"I'd rather come with you."

Not on your life, Luke. You will stay out here where it's safe.

"I need you here, Luke. Okay?"

Without waiting for an answer, Shannon grabbed Bale's paw, her consciousness flowing from her mind down through her arm and over to Bale.

* * *

Bale's Great Room shone in a multitude of orange tones from the palest peach to subdued sienna. Light, the color of flaming fire, beat down into the space from above. A curious scent of lime permeated the room. Like her own Great Room, it soared as high as a skyscraper.

The entire space rumbled. Shannon, looking and feeling just as she did in the outside world, found it hard to keep her footing.

She peered into the flaming light. *Where was Bale?* Her anxiety increased and the jitters of her power increased along with it. Her stomach pinched, queasy and unsettled.

One thing for sure: power did not feel good—at least not Salesti's kind.

As she searched into the upper reaches, a noise off to her right startled her.

Essi! She'd forgotten that Essi would come for Toss.

"Go back, Essi; it's too dangerous here."

toss here. essi searches for toss while shannon fights bale.

Out of the dim exterior of the Great Room, Bale loomed up behind Essi, stalking her on silent paws, intent on striking her down like an ancient saber-toothed tigers creeping up on an unsuspecting rabbit. Shannon charged forward and brushed Essi behind her.

"Leave the girl out of this, Bale." Shannon didn't dare take her eyes off Bale as she said, Go, Essi." Essi slipped away. "Bale, I want to challenge you. Will you listen to the terms?"

Perhaps Bale thought Essi meant to return to Shannon's body; he lost all interest in her, his attention riveted on Shannon.

"If I defeat you, you return to FireWorld and leave me be. If you win, you can do as you like with me."

No.

"Those are honorable terms."

I will not rest until you die.

He circled to her left.

Loki's luck. She'd have to knock him out and send him home. Then she could figure out Plan B.

Remember what Salesti taught: Cast the colors far behind him, fast and hard. Then inhale and draw the colors back, bringing the wind with them.

Shannon cast her colors, and as they returned to her, the wind increased, stronger and stronger, in a swirling mass gathering within her spread arms. She aimed it at Bale.

He crouched, swaying his rear from side to side as he prepared to leap.

Shannon's fear increased. Her power overflowed.

The dragonpanther pounced.

She set her jaw, loosened her shoulders, and threw the rainbow wind. If everything proceeded as smoothly as it had the first time she'd tried this with Roebor and Tidak, the wind would toss Bale into the wall, knocking him out for a few minutes, and she could truss him up.

But at that moment, Salesti's power unleashed itself, driving her wind like a comet and striking Bale a hundred times harder than she'd struck Roebor and Tidak.

Bale slammed into the wall of his Great Room—and flew apart from the sheer fury of her power. Came undone as if made of papier-mâché. Dissipated as if nothing could hold back the blood, bones, and brain that scattered across the wall and spattered over the floor.

He was gone.

Shannon stared, unbelieving, glassy-eyed, fingers still pointing toward what remained of him.

No, this wasn't the plan. . . make him lose consciousness. . . send him home. . . .

Giant cracks appeared in the wall where Bale had disintegrated. The cracks spread and grew until chunks of the wall fell, by ones and twos, and then in a storm of debris. Enormous slabs of the roof crashed to the floor.

Essi appeared with Toss in tow.

shannon, essi, and toss leave now. shannon remembers: salesti says shannon can die here.

Shannon moved toward Bale's remains in a daze. She knelt in the blood and other unidentifiable matter and touched her fingers to the dampness. A rancid, foul odor permeated the area where Shannon knelt. She gagged, but she didn't move.

Still warm. . . .

More and more chunks of the Great Room hailed down around her.

Essi fled, pulling Toss behind her.

The power did this. Salesti's power. No wonder Salesti always held back. But Shannon was the one who wielded it this time. . . .

Fire erupted, and falling debris scattered dust into the air, dust so thick the light from the spreading fire filtered through only dimly, giving the space around Shannon a ghostly glow. Still in shock, she stood and wandered through the strange light, paying no attention to the fire or the great blocks of debris collapsing around her.

Unable to shake the image of Bale from her mind, she sank to the floor once more.

She heard voices: Essi had returned, this time with Luke. They called her name.

She needed to answer, but her mind could not make her voice speak.

Shannon couldn't make out Luke's next words, except she caught the name "Gumshoe."

Gumshoe? The puppy?

Luke continued to call to her. The annihilation of Bane's Great Room was almost complete. Shannon must get out. . . But her legs would not move. She could think of nothing but Bane, and what was left of him.

The puppy's bark carried to her from across the Great Room. The sound moved closer. Then the puppy skidded to a stop beside her, licking her face and whimpering. Luke followed, appearing out of the smokey half-light of the fire.

"Good boy, Gumshoe." He stroked the young golden retriever. He knelt beside Shannon. "Cara, we have to go."

Shannon gazed at the floor, her hands twisting and turning. "I didn't mean to . . . ."

A cluster of small concrete-like pieces of debris rained down on her, slicing her face and shoulder. Luke stood, bringing her to her feet with him. He knew Great Rooms—he'd visited them with Shannon under stressful circumstances—but never a Great Room that was falling down around his ears. The thundering crashes of falling debris came faster now, but Luke remained as steady as ever.

"Now," he said.

As if hearing Luke for the first time, she nodded.

They navigated the collapsing room and flowed back into Shannon. Essi took Luke's spirit back to his body.

* * *

When Shannon blinked in the California sun and surveyed the scene, she was sitting next to Bale's physical shell, her shoulder and head leaning against his front leg. His torso and back legs floated in seawater; his front legs and head rested on the cove's beach. Luke nestled against her back, his arms around her, his head also against Bale's leg. Gumshoe sniffed at Bale, then backed off and scampered back to Luke's other side.

Luke stirred, and Shannon turned to watch his face.

His first expression would reveal his true feelings. *Would the terrible thing Shannon had done to Bale sicken and horrify him? Anger him? Make him sorry he'd come with her on this disastrous mission?*

Luke shook his head as if to dislodge a spider from his hair. "My god, Shannon, are you all right?" He examined her cheek and shoulder.

Her fingers found her face: something wet.

"My blood or Bale's?" she asked.

"Both, I think. Your cheek's cut, your T-shirt's ripped, and you have a bad cut on your shoulder."

Shannon nodded, her eyes wide and unblinking.

"Do you have a first aid kit onboard?" Luke asked.

"It was up front. Underwater now."

Luke pulled a handkerchief out of his back pocket. He wiped her face and her shoulder. "Keep this pressed against your shoulder."

"How did Gumshoe know you wanted him to find me? He's just a baby."

"I've been teaching him to fetch, and I told him to fetch you." Luke grinned.

"An extra hamburger patty for him next time you bring him over."

She stared over at Bale's still form. Waves lapped at his body that neither knew or cared about the ways of death. His metallic golden fur rippled as the waves pulled it first toward the shore and then back to the sea. The sun glinted off of each strand of fur on his mammoth body, mimicking life in its dazzling glow.

"Come, cara. Let's move away from here and sit on the sand for a minute."

He led her to the far side of the curved cove and settled her on the beach. A few feet away, a seagull pecked at the remains of a rock crab. Shannon turned away, but the smell of decay remained in her nose.

Luke took her pale, icy hand in his warm ones. "We need to get you warm. Is there a blanket in the boat?"

"In a storage hatch under the benches in the back, if we can get into it. But how will we hide the body. . . any ideas, Roebor?"

Since I remained here so Bale would not discover I still live, you must tell me what happened.

"Roebor wants to know what happened," Shannon said to Luke, a single tear falling from her eye. "I suppose you do, too. You had him pegged. He wanted nothing to do with oaths."

"You don't have to talk about it now if you don't want to." Luke departed to scour the boat for a blanket.

As if she hadn't heard him, she said, "He swore he wouldn't rest until he killed me. He attacked. I meant to knock him unconscious with wind summoned with my colors like I did with you, but the power appeared out of nowhere when I whipped up the wind. I cast my colors, and they annihilated him. There's no other way to say it. Annihilated him." Shannon's hand sifted through the sand over and over.

I see this turn of events has hurt you, and I am sorry for it. However, I cannot say any other outcome would be possible with Bale, once he set his heart on revenge. I wish I had met and defeated him instead of you.

Shannon's hand stilled.

An idea. . . *Would it work?*

She spoke aloud so Luke could follow along when he returned. "Roebor. This presents you with a perfect opportunity, if you want it. A body without a mind in it; a mind, yours, without a body."

You suggest I become Bale?

"Could you bear it? If you returned to FireWorld as Bale? They might accept that his experiences on this planet have changed him. You might remake the old Bale into one more like the old Roebor over time. Yes?"

Mmm, Roebor said.

"What's he saying?" Luke asked, returning with a soft thermal blanket and wrapping it around Shannon's shoulders.

"Nothing yet; he's thinking. It's a big decision. Otherwise, it'll be tough to get rid of Bale's body with the boat in its current condition."

"I think we leave the body here," Luke said, "and let it get discovered. It'll be a big mystery and big news for a while, but so what?"

"True. Although not having a body to mourn will break the hearts of everyone in his family on FireWorld. I feel sorry for Pak,"

Let us confer in your Great Room. Bring Luke with you.

* * *

Soon Essi, Toss, Luke, and Shannon sat in a circle on the soft green floor at the edge of Shannon's Great Room, where they could avoid the worst of the glare. Roebor padded in and laid down next to Shannon, facing the group.

"How are you, Toss? Okay?" Shannon asked, worried for the poor guy who'd been hijacked three times now—not only had the alien who devastated his world kidnaped him but Tidak, before Bale, had forced Toss to help him as well.

Toss didn't speak, but he shrugged, raised his hand, and tipped it back and forth, which Shannon took to mean "so-so."

"Tell us what you're thinking, Roebor."

"Two choices again: the same as on FireWorld. There, I faced these choices: 'die a prolonged and painful death or live in your mind, Shannon.' Not a simple choice. I chose life and the chance to help you escape Bale. Now it is 'live in your mind or live in Bale's body.' Another complicated choice. I wish to hear what each of you has to say on this matter. Let us start with you, Luke.

"Me? I don't have any say here."

"This is not true. You love Shannon and wish to remain in her life. If I stay in her mind, the two of you will never find complete privacy. I will always accompany you. Therefore, I wish to hear your opinion."

Luke scratched the always-present shadow of hair on his chin. "I guess I assumed you'd find another mind to share at some point. It could happen, right?"

"The possibility exists. But not a strong one. I suspect any other host, however willing, would die within days. And the odds of finding a willing host are nil in any event."

"I see. So, the next question is whether you can make yourself scarce from time to time. Can you go off somewhere isolated in Shannon's mind and keep your own company?"

"Yes. I know how to isolate myself in Shannon's mind, although not the deep isolation you might prefer."

"If you can figure out how to vanish when the three of us don't want to be 'together,' I guess I can live with it. But, if you can't solve that one, I'm all for you returning to FireWorld with a new golden skin."

"Would I still be able to visit my friends on RiverWorld as Bale? I have grown fond of you two, Essi and Toss. But I would be in the guise of your captor, Toss. This might not only fill you with revulsion but also impede your recovery."

Essi checked with Toss, who nodded.

toss not afraid of roebor in any skin, essi thinks. yes?

The Seladoran young man smiled and nodded again, this time at Roebor, who sighed and smiled.

"And now Shannon. The circumstances on FireWorld forced you to take me onboard on the spur of the moment. I find that most unsatisfactory. Now you may rethink that decision in a calmer setting. You must do so."

"Not me; it's your decision."

"The question for you is paramount, and you must answer it prior to any decision I might make: do you want me here for the rest of your days? The answer to that question is that no one would want such a thing. Am I not correct?"

"*Odin's eye*, don't put me on the hot seat. How can I answer that question?"

Shannon struggled with her thoughts for a minute. Roebor and the others waited.

"I'm still trying to process Bale's death, so bear in mind that I'm a fuzzhead right now. But I can say this. If I had no other considerations to take into account, my preference, a strong preference, would always be to keep my mind for myself. But I *do* have more to consider, don't I? First, you're my friend. A close friend. You've saved my scrawny neck on more than one occasion."

Luke stirred.

"So, the question becomes not so much what I would like, but what I could bear for the sake of a friend. If you couldn't bear to return to FireWorld as Bale, I could bear having you here, because you mean that much to me."

Roebor's face shook with emotion. "Thank you, Shannon."

"And there's another consideration," she said.

He cocked his head.

"That encounter with Bale showed me I'm in real trouble with Salesti's power. It's straining to win its freedom, escape its barriers, and explode. The salestis may not have any trouble handling all this power, but I can't keep it in check. This reaction with Bale came out of nowhere, the same as when I pushed that jerk Brant off me last night, and he sailed across the beach. Only this time, it felt much stronger."

"Somebody assaulted you on the beach?" Luke asked. "You should have told me right away!"

"He didn't hurt me—that's the point; I only meant to push him a foot or two, but instead, I threw him twenty feet. Fortunately, he was unharmed, too."

"But he didn't hurt you."

"Not at all. But here's the thing: the power that escaped today erupted with much greater force than when I pushed Brant. What about next time, and the time after that? I do need your help, Roebor. I need you to help me figure out how to deal with the power."

Roebor cocked his head. "I had not considered this factor."

"And I'm glad you call it a factor because that's all it should be. I'll deal with the power, and you can still help me deal with it if you take Bale's body. If you don't *want* to go back to FireWorld as Bale, if the very thought torments you, I'm saying you'd be more than a fifth wheel here; you'd have a role to play. That's all. It still comes down to you. All things being equal, if you would like to go back to FireWorld as Bale, you should do it. If you wouldn't like that, stay, and we'll make it work."

Roebor rose to his four paws. He paced around the circle of his friends. He let out a roar.

"I find this so difficult. So impossible. I would not hate being Bale, because, as you say, I can, over time, change his character to be what I need him to be. But I would hate *not* being Roebor. I couldn't comfort my father and my little sister; I would have to endure their hatred. My old friends would never be my friends. Nor was Bale a scientist by profession. He chose the field of food gatherer—a hunter and fisher. It would be a step too far to turn him into a thinker and a student of science. To be so close to my lab, my books, my mentors, and to have no recourse to them—*this* would break my heart."

He stalked back around to his original position and threw himself to the ground.

"I suppose these heartbreaks would ease. But it would take years. And yet FireWorld is my world. My world. My mountains to roam. My sky to fly. My fiery sea to swim. My people to aid and to love. By the gods, I find this difficult."

He quieted. The others stilled. No one said a word.

Shannon watched as he weighed his options, as he tried so hard to apply the logic he so loved to an equation that demanded his heart instead. At last, Roebor lifted his head.

CHAPTER FOURTEEN
Explosion

"I SHALL STAY," Roebor said, bowing his head. "I will help Shannon contain her power and locate a sanctuary deep in her mind where I can retreat and dream I am flying once again."

Luke's head sank to his chest.

Poor Roebor. Poor Luke. She ached for them both.

What a mess.

* * *

If they didn't wrap up things in the Great Room and get back to the outside world soon, someone would come along and see Bale's body with Shannon and Luke lying motionless nearby. Roebor's decision made, Shannon said, "I vote we call for help on my radio and say that a strange creature crashed into the boat, and that's all we know."

"Agreed." Luke still ducked his head. Shannon couldn't guess his thoughts, although she feared they'd be dark ones.

"Agreed." Roebor nodded. "I see no other practical solution, although I wish we could send him home for burial."

"Right." Shannon stood to take Luke back to his body.

wait. no one talks about shannon yet, what about power of shannon? shannon not safe, Essi said.

"Right, Essi. I don't believe Shannon is safe with Salesti's power in her. Why didn't the other salestis take it, Shannon, and share it among themselves? It would have solved the problem," Luke said.

essi knows this answer. essi asks our salesti questions one day all about salestis. essi asks who has most power of all salestis. our salesti says power of each salesti so great, no one can measure. salestis have so much power, cannot touch each other.

"No wonder they wouldn't come anywhere near me," Shannon said. "Did Salesti say what happens if they touch?"

if salestis touch, and one drop of power from one salesti reaches another salesti, solar system and far beyond destroyed. essi thinks salesti tells joke. now essi thinks salestis cannot take power from our salesti. or shannon.

"And now I have that awful power inside me. Power that leaks out at inopportune times, like when I'm tired or emotional, and I can't control it. I don't want it. How do I get rid of it?"

"Hmm," Roebor said. "I see no straightforward solution that keeps you safe."

"Let's get Shannon home, and Essi and Toss can go home from there," Luke said. "All right?"

Shannon helped Luke back to his body and restored her view of the world from her own eyes, only to be greeted by Bale's lifeless form once again. She rose, turned her back on the golden dragonpanther, and waded into her half-crushed boat to call in their mayday message.

Faking a hysterical voice, which didn't prove difficult, since Shannon kept reliving the moment Bale died, she said, "Yes, we need help right away. A strange flying creature crashed into my boat and dragged us to an island off of Preacher's Point. It destroyed the boat, but it died. . . Two of us, yes, Luke Quintana and Shannon Kendricks. . . Right. He totaled the boat. No idea what this thing is. It's got fur and huge wings and fangs the size of a pair of skis. . . No, not feathers. Fur. Not a bird. . . Yes, I'm sure. . . Okay. We'll be here."

She climbed the rocky bank to the top of the mini-island and sat where she could gaze out at the open waters. Where she couldn't see Bale's body.

* * *

A coast guard cutter, *the USCGC Willow,* arrived at the scene, and the captain invited Luke, Shannon, and Gumshoe aboard. A medic bandaged Shannon's shoulder, and they signed their written statements and asked for a ride to the Ocean City dock. While they waited in a small break room furnished with one small table and four chairs, a coffee pot, a microwave, and a refrigerator, Shannon gradually warmed up, and her head cleared. But she couldn't shake the image of Bale as he disintegrated.

In the meantime, Bale's body caused quite a stir. Excited seamen made radio calls. Another coast guard cutter and several other boats arrived. A few men in white moon-suit-looking gear debarked to examine the body.

Two hours passed, but Shannon and Luke had still not caught a ride home.

She choked down her third cup of stale, weak coffee.

"I need food, and I wouldn't turn down a pair of flip flops. I think I'll go ask the Captain—" As she rose, two men in civilian attire joined them in the cramped break room.

"My name is David Blacksilver," said a tall, gaunt, middle-aged man with a pock-marked face and sparkling white teeth, shaking their hands, "and this Jose Torra." Torra, a young, quiet, self-contained man, his face and bald head bossed to a shine, nodded and shook hands without making eye contact. "We have some questions for you."

"Walk through your testimony and don't leave anything out," said Blacksilver, taking out a recorder and placing it on the small round table at which the group of four now crowded, knee to knee.

"Please, might I get something to eat? I suffer from a metabolic disorder which requires that I take food at regular intervals."

"Yes," Blacksilver said, flipping through a thick, twelve-by-fourteen-inch notebook he'd taken from his briefcase. "I am aware of your condition. You were hospitalized in critical condition about six years ago, and again last year because of your health problem."

What *in Odin's Eye was* this?

"Right, which means I need to eat now."

"And you will, after you answer a few questions. Let's start with what happened here. Oh, and Jose, why don't you take Officer Quintana on deck and take his statement there?"

They were separating them now? Not good. Definitely not good.

* * *

Blacksilver had taken her through the story over and over. Now Shannon rubbed her temples and plodded through her story one more time with exaggerated patience. This time, however, Blacksilver interrupted her every other sentence to ply her with additional questions.

When Shannon finished telling the story, she stood up, all set to go topside and find Luke.

"Sit. We haven't finished. Now. You happened to be in Alaska at the Dickson Research Center when a creature resembling this one appeared there, didn't you?"

Ah, so that was it. They'd connected Bale's image to Roebor's and Tidak's from last year.

"I didn't *happen* to be there; I worked there until the disaster that took down the UnderWater Complex. And I will work there again once they've rebuilt it. But yes, I have heard that the Navy caught sight of an odd creature there. No one ever showed me its picture, though. So, the one at the Dickson resembled the one down here?"

"And you *won't* see any pictures from Alaska. The government has made them classified. But yes, the images, though fuzzy, resemble this creature."

Light-headed. . . Need to eat. . . Easy. Don't fly off the handle. Stay calm.

"Quintana also was in Alaska. Don't you think it's a funny coincidence that two people who were in Alaska the last time we saw one of these creatures are also the people that one of the creatures crashes into?"

"No, I don't think it's funny. My boat is a total wreck. A coincidence? Again, no. The entire crew of the Alaskan Dickson was working there when the navy spotted the other creature. And many of them came back down here to Ocean City, where they now work at the Dickson facility at the University. The coincidence encompasses forty or fifty people."

"But you *were* there when the navy sighted the creatures."

"In the same way that you were here when the coast guard found this one. Should we suspect you? I went to Alaska long before the creature arrived, and I came back home well before this one attacked us. Or do you think this one is the same one you saw in Alaska?"

"Actually, we took images of two of them in Alaska. Our experts in Washington D.C. have calculated that it's possible, although not probable, this one might be one of the two from Alaska."

He's close. The one in Alaska was Bale's daddy.

"You saw *two* of them there? And one came here? Where did he hide all this time? Or could this one be their baby? That would be cool, and it would explain why he flew into my boat, if he were still learning to fly. Maybe—"

"We do not believe this creature is a baby or that the two bat cats spotted in Alaska were a mating pair."

"Wait. Bat cats? That's what you call them?" Shannon struggled to keep a straight face.

How do you feel about that moniker, Roebor?

I much prefer dragonpanther. Bat cat sounds like something a human five-year-old would say.

Hey, if the shoe fits, Blacksilver should wear it.

"Never mind that. You are not to speak of any subject raised in this conversation with anyone. All material related to the ba—creatures is classified. Is that clear?"

"Sure. May I please have something to eat now?" Shannon was sweating; she needed food.

. . . losing it. . . .

"In a moment. Now," he said, licking his forefinger and using it to flick to a fresh page in his notebook, "you were also entangled in a murder six years ago and then last year a murder in Alaska. Another coincidence?"

"No, nothing about the two incidents are remotely the same. Here in Ocean City, one of my good friends committed suicide, a terrible thing. A serial killer was also rampaging at the time, but he had nothing to do with me."

Well, he had something to do with her. A lot to do with her. Okay, she was neck deep in it.

"In Alaska, a scientist killed my friend Kota and shot Luke because this scientist wanted to kidnap a beluga whale I worked with. The authorities must have vetted both incidents by now."

"Yes. No one found any fault on your part in either episode." Blacksilver conceded the point with a frown as if he begrudged Shannon her innocence.

Well. Her relative innocence, anyway.

"But," he said, "again, another interesting coincidence. Now, what about this research whale? I understand that all by yourself, you won the right to have it placed in the Dickson research project to free it from captivity. Is that right?"

"We're getting kind of far afield from what happened today, aren't we, Mr. Blacksilver? Why can't we continue this discussion over—" she glanced at her watch "—a late lunch or an early dinner?"

"Answer the question."

"Yes."

"Yes, what?"

"Yes, in answer to your question."

"Where was I?"

"Juneau, the beluga whale?"

"Right. And now that whale is missing, is that not true?"

"Yes."

"We'll be here a long time if you don't cooperate, Ms. Kendricks."

"I *am* cooperating, Mr. Blacksilver. I don't know what you want, what you're driving at. You asked me if she is missing. Yes, she is missing. And?"

"And isn't that suspicious?"

Shannon threw herself back in her chair. "Do you think I have her hidden in my bathtub? The UnderWater Complex exploded, a traumatic event for everyone, including Juneau. We tried to coax her down here to Ocean City to wait until we can rebuild, but on route, she disappeared."

"Convenient."

"Convenient for whom? Not for me. I lost my research partner. Our theory is that the commercial vessel traffic spooked her. I suspect she might have gone back to the far north, the belugas' natural habitat. But I haven't seen her since last year when we tried to bring her here."

Shannon had sent Juneau away to keep her from unscrupulous hands, but she'd keep that information to herself.

"I'm glad you mentioned the trip you took from Alaska down to Ocean City by boat. The U.S. navy stopped you and your companions, did they not?"

Shannon banged her head on the table. Twice. It smelled of long-forgotten cigarettes. "I can't do this anymore. Please, let me eat."

Shannon turned to a seaman who'd been standing at the door during Shannon's interrogation. "You'll be my witness. I have begged this gentleman to allow me to treat my metabolic condition—*which,* as he mentioned a minute ago, has caused my hospitalization and near death on at least two occasions—and he is responsible for whatever happens to me."

The guard shifted, glancing at Blacksilver and then at Shannon.

"No, I'm not," Blacksilver said.

"Yes, you are. You're withholding food, even though you know I need it for medical reasons, in the hopes that you can coerce information of some kind from me—but I have nothing new to tell you, so please let me eat."

"Perhaps we can arrange something once we finish discussing the incident where the navy detained your cruiser on suspicion of possession of illegal substances."

Shannon snapped. Now she not only suffered from hunger, light-headedness, and queasiness, but her fury with this petty dictator of a government bureaucrat was mounting.

"Now listen. I refuse to say another word until you let me treat my metabolic condition."

"No, you listen. The government has had its eye on you ever since your suspicious activity at the White Wolf Casino—"

Her gambling venture? *That did it.* Shannon grabbed the edge of the table until her knuckles turned white. She teetered on the edge of saying something she would really, really regret.

Be calm. Be the tree. Be the babbling brook—

"You will answer my—Ms. Kendricks, what is it? You're as white as snow. You—"

The power was building like lava forced out of a volcano's core in a violent eruption. She wouldn't be able to control it. More sweat broke out on her forehead. "This is bad. Disastrous."

Her temperature was rising.

"What are you talking about?"

"I must leave this ship. Now." Shannon stood and stumbled toward the door. The seaman blocked her way. She turned to Blacksilver.

"Please, there's no time."

Blacksilver stood there gaping at her.

She couldn't run. Where should she aim the power? People were working all over the ship.

Shannon aimed downward.

Power surged from her outstretched fingers in a rainbow of color. The floor beneath her feet exploded into a thousand splinters. Another explosion and another thundered on, as barriers in the ship below fell before the power ripping through the boat.

Klaxons sounded.

Someone shouted, "she's going down!"

Sharp pain gouged her thigh, her arm, the side of her head.

Along with twisted sheets of metal, coffee cups, shredded paper, bits of plastic, a thousand things, Shannon fell through the remains of the ship into the warm, deep water off Preacher's Point.

CHAPTER FIFTEEN
Hospital

SHANNON TOSSED AND TURNED.

She swam in shadow-black water. . . couldn't see. . . an unseen danger. . . cold, so cold. . . afraid. . . .

Shannon struggled to sit up, to get away.

". . . . Can you hear me, Shannon? You're safe now, cara. It's me, Luke."

The black water vanished.

Luke. He hovered over her, his hand on her shoulder to keep her from rising, his dark eyes, always a dead giveaway to his thoughts, half-lidded with concern.

She eased back onto what felt like a pillow.

A premonition?

She hoped not, although she did foresee impending events sometimes. Shannon laid that thought aside for now.

Where was she?

Wrapped in a white hospital gown, she lay between thin white sheets in a bed with metal bars. Soft white light lit the white room. The faint hint of antiseptic cleaner made Shannon's nose itch.

"St. James?" she croaked, her throat parched. Luke handed her a paper cup of water. She lifted her head and drank it all. "More, please."

"Yes, this is St. James." Luke poured her another cup.

In the hospital.

Again.

She ought to rent a room here.

How she hated hospitals.

"You're okay?" She asked Luke.

"I'm fine, cara."

"The puppy?"

Luke grinned. "It was all a great adventure to him. He's at home chewing on his new stuffed toy bone."

"Who's watching Narci?"

"I've been going by twice a day to feed her and make sure her water bowl is full. I usually spend an hour or so with her curled in my lap so I can give her a full report on how you're doing."

Roebor? How are you and Essi and Toss?

We, too, are fine, Shannon.

She set her jaw and asked Luke, "How serious are my injuries? Truth."

Luke pressed his lips together.

Shannon waited. Knowing him, she figured he'd rather lie than hurt her. But he'd better not.

"Cuts and bruises. No broken bones." He turned away. "A sizable chunk missing from your thigh, including muscle. You're going to get a graft, but. . . they're not sure whether you'll be able to walk unaided."

Shannon's stomach turned over.

"A long gash in your arm, a hundred and fourteen stitches. It'll leave a scar but no other serious damage. It'll be okay once it heals."

She surveyed her arms. Bandages wrapped her right arm from her wrist to her shoulder. A few minor nicks and scratches dotted the left.

"And?"

"And you hit the side of your head—hard—on something metal. It smacked you flat-on, so your head didn't get sliced, but it put you in a coma."

Two hard knocks within days of each other. *Not good.*

"How long?"

"Four days."

Four days? *Odin's eye.*

Luke turned and checked the door as if he thought someone might enter. He leaned down toward Shannon's face.

"What happened, cara? Do you remember?"

"Has Blacksilver bugged the room?" she whispered.

"I don't think so. I've been sitting in here since you came back from intensive care."

"Blacksilver wouldn't let me eat anything." Shannon's words were so low that Luke had to lean forward to hear. Tears spilled down her cheeks. "He kept badgering me, on and on, about everything that happened six years ago and everything that happened last year and today. I needed to eat. I told him."

"So, it was the power?" he whispered back.

She nodded. "I tried to stop it, but I couldn't control it. I tried to get out of there, but the security guard wouldn't let me pass. Was anybody else hurt?" She twisted her sheet in tight fists.

"The explosion hurt you the worst. Both Blacksilver and the guard you mentioned took hits, although nothing serious, and no one was working down below you, so nobody else suffered anything more than bumps and bruises."

Shannon's hands let go of the twist she'd made in the sheet. *Thank Odin.*

"Are they blaming me?"

"They suspect something, but they can't figure out how you could be responsible, since they didn't find any sign of explosives. And I heard the doctors saying they didn't find any forensic evidence on you proving that you detonated any explosive device."

"No surprise there."

"But Blacksilver says you acted crazy right before the explosion, and the part of the boat below you sustained the most damage, so I expect Blacksilver will be back for more grilling."

"We can't let them push me, or I'll lose it again. This power scares the heck out of me, Luke. When I'm angry, it tries to escape. Would you see if the doctor will prescribe me a sedative? Maybe that would help."

He nodded. "You talk like it's alive. Like it has a will of its own."

"I know it sounds crazy, but that's how it feels to me."

"I should tell someone you're awake. You okay with that?"

"Yes, if they'll let me have food. I'm famished, despite whatever's in this drip here."

Luke nodded and rose to go inform the nurse's station. "Will do."

Shannon glanced up at him. "Hey, there's something I need even more than a sedative. Can you help me find an attorney? Someone who'll put a stop to the questioning if they push too hard."

"My father will have the name of an experienced lawyer. In the meantime, you're probably still muddled, right?" He winked at her. "Maybe you don't remember what happened yet."

"Who are you again?" Shannon asked.

* * *

Several doctors came and went during the next two hours. Shannon said next to nothing to them. No food was forthcoming. Luke left for his swing shift.

"Essi, Toss, I'm sorry that you're stuck here with me. I'll find out how soon we can scram out of here so I can send you home. Everything okay in there? Roebor? Are you sure the explosion or that hit I took to the head didn't hurt any of you?"

essi and toss fine. worry about shannon, Essi said.

Interestingly, Roebor said, *the knock to your head caused substantial damage to your Great Room, but we all survived unscathed. I have examined your brain. I see swelling but no leakage of blood.*

Roebor cleared his throat. *We are glad you have regained consciousness. We were worried for a few days.*

"No wonder you were worried! If I die, you all die too. I'm sorry you had to go through that."

It is not for ourselves that we worried. We have endured nothing compared to what you have suffered. We stand ready if you want help or support of any kind.

"That means a lot to me, thanks. Is it still too bright in the Great Room? Have you come up with anything on controlling the power?"

Yes, the Great Room is even brighter now than when you visited. And no, I have mulled over the problem without success to date. He hesitated. *We knew the salestis were hiding information from you when they dispatched you to Earth and deserted you. A suspicion has taken root in my mind that they knew full well that this struggle between you and the power would emerge, that the power would fight to escape.*

"They knew and didn't have the grace to tell me?"

I fear they suspected you would not control it for long, whether they revealed it or not, and decided to sacrifice your solar system to save RiverWorld.

"That's just grand. I'm tempted to go back to RiverWorld and detonate in their faces out of spite. Well, not really. But I'm worried. I've been hurt so badly by the explosion that I'm particularly vulnerable. I'm weaker now, and I won't be able to fight off the detonation if I'm upset or angry or emotional."

No talk of detonations yet. Do not abandon hope.

* * *

A few minutes after four in the afternoon, according to the clock on the wall, Shannon's personal physician, Dr. Julia Bennett, sailed in and folded her arms over her ample chest. "So. You again. I stopped at the computer terminal outside to read your reports. You've really outdone yourself this time."

"The leg, you mean?"

"Yes, the leg. And I worry about the severe knock to your head, hard though I believe your skull to be. We'll closely monitor you for a while. No matter who," she lowered her voice, "or *what* may require your immediate attention, you are not leaving this room."

"I can't stay here too long, doc. I have problems."

"Yes, and some of your problems require you to remain in the hospital. Luke told me your memory is still fuzzy, and you're having trouble thinking clearly?"

Shannon's eyes slid toward the door. Dr. Bennett had closed it as she entered.

"I hear the feds want to interview me. I'm not ready for them yet. Luke is finding me an attorney. Until I have her or him in place, I'm befuddled, and I'm having memory problems."

Dr. Bennett's arms remained folded. "I see. Am I to take it you have committed some heinous crime against the nation, then?"

Should she tell the doc?

She paused.

Yes. Dr. Bennett had always been in Shannon's corner. Shannon could trust her.

"No, no heinous crime. Well, technically yes, maybe, since I blew up a coast guard cutter."

Dr. Bennett pulled over the visitor's chair and sank into it.

"But I couldn't control my energy level. It was an accident. I've got a serious problem, Dr. B. Maybe you can help." She paused. "Oh, Essi, Toss, and Roebor are here with me." Seeing Dr. Bennett's frozen face, she hurried on, "If you want to say a quick hello."

"I knew aliens figured into this in some way. So, they're back. I'll arrange for copious quantities of solid food for you, then, but I'll pass on the reunion. What is this uncontrollable energy, and what can I do to help?"

"Did you ever meet Salesti? The miniature creature from Essi's world? Salesti was a powerhouse. It died on Roebor's world. I happened to be there—"

Dr. Bennet shook her head.

"—and Salesti needed to offload her energy, which contained enough power to destroy Roebor's planet and solar system if we allowed it to escape into the air."

"And let me guess. You absorbed it to prevent the catastrophe."

"Don't criticize me." Shannon picked at her sheet. "Somebody had to take it."

"And this is the power that blew up the ship?"

"Exactly. We think Salesti believed I'd know what to do, but I don't. It's been leaking, and each time it does, I unleash more power. This time, they wouldn't let me eat and kept asking me questions, and I snapped and sank the boat."

"I see. So you're asking me if there is anything I can do. I'm dubious as to my ability to intercede in matters of alien energy." She tapped her blunt fingernail on Shannon's hospital tray.

"You say it's leaking. From what place is it leaking; where is it stored?"

"My mind."

"Your—my god. But nothing showed up on your MRI or EEG. I wonder why not. The molecular structure may be unknown to us, and therefore we can't detect it with our standard tests. Perhaps I'll see if I can look at the analysis of the ship's explosion. I might find a clue there. Enough power to annihilate Roebor's solar system, you say?"

Shannon's tears traced down her cheeks again as she nodded.

"And not only Roebor's solar system—this powder keg could blow everything from our sun to Uranus, and beyond."

* * *

Shannon had finished the two full dinners Dr. Bennett had ordered from Applebee's, as well as the dinner tray the hospital had sent and felt much better. A hubbub arose in the hallway on the other side of her closed door.

"I will *not* wait until I have a doctor's approval. I am this poor girl's attorney. I have every reason to believe she is being maltreated, and you will stand aside, madame, and let me pass, or I shall report you to the press at once. Give me that badge you've got around your neck. I'll need it for the reporters. . . . Oh, very good. Thank you. I shall not be long. I intend to ascertain whether anyone is holding the girl against her will in conditions that I should report to the American Hospital Association, and, once I have a quiet word, I shall be on my way again. Have I made myself clear? All right. Thank you. Please wait out here."

Her attorney had arrived.

SIXTEEN
Tourmaline Kulkarney

THE HOSPITAL DOOR OPENED AND A THIN WOMAN, six feet tall in her bare feet, entered like a prima donna taking the stage. She wore a light-weight, cream-colored silk coat that stretched to her ankles and a matching dress, three-inch black stiletto heels, and a large, black, wide-brimmed hat with a huge, black feather curling forward as if pointing the way. She looked about seventy years of age, but she'd matured well. Dark, bold eyeshadow and eyeliner adorned her face, and those long, thick eyelashes were of the artificial variety. The silver hair peeping out from under the hat was cut in a bob and contained streaks of darkest blue. She'd chosen fuchsia for her lipstick, and each long, fuchsia, polymer nail sported a navy-blue diagonal stripe. A potent perfume wafted Shannon's way as the woman approached—a musky scent, one Shannon imagined would excite the male of the species.

"Well, I never. The nerve of some people," she said, fluttering her hand toward the door. Turning her attention to Shannon, she smiled. "And you will be my client!"

Her hand plunged into a black and cream leather purse the size of Shannon's pillow, whipped out a card, and dropped it on Shannon's over-the-bed tray with a flourish.

"Tourmaline Kulkarney. Criminal law." She nodded, extending her hand for Shannon to shake before noticing her bandaging. She grasped Shannon's left hand instead. "Yes, you think it's too early for a criminal attorney, but that lovely man, Luke Quintana, explained the gist of your case to me and hinted that the story contained a few extra twists he wasn't at liberty to reveal."

She paused, a far-away look in her eyes.

"I'm quite in love with your Luke. Let me know if you ever break his heart."

Easing into the nearest chair, she continued. "No, dear, today is the precise moment when you do need me, *before* matters spin out of control, and you find yourself in chains on your way to the federal penitentiary."

Still digging around in her cavernous purse, she pulled forth a pink legal pad—*they came in pink?*—"Now. Take it from the top, leave nothing out, and recall that the rule of attorney-client confidentiality applies. Most of all, give me the 'extra twists' of which Luke spoke."

How much to tell her?

"Darling, I can tell by the look on your face that you're tempted to withhold certain salient facts. I understand you practiced law as a civil attorney before changing careers—good move, by the way, the legal profession has gone to hell—so you understand that no matter how unsavory the details, I must have them, deal with them, minimize them, bury them, and so on and so forth."

Shannon grinned. "Hi. As Luke may have told you, in the official version, we insist I'm still fuzzy from the concussion and haven't remembered the explosion yet."

"Yes, and are you?"

"Am I what?"

"Still fuzzy—ah—I see what you did there. Understood. We shall say that I introduced myself, ascertained the precarious mental state in which you find yourself, and gave strict instructions that no one may interview you outside my presence. Here. I'd better leave several of my cards for your would-be interrogators, too." She tossed the cards on Shannon's tray. "Now, I am a genius at listening, and I tend to draw out facts clients forget when talking to the cops. Tell me the story."

"If I tell you the entire story, you may think my concussion caused much more damage than the doctors suspect. Are you prepared to believe a shocker? Because if not, I'm wasting your time."

"Oh yes, I'm prepared. Believe me, child, in my line of work, I've heard it all. The stories I could tell you."

"Perhaps you haven't heard *quite* everything," Shannon murmured. She squared her shoulders and began, "It all started one evening six years ago. I volunteered at the City SeaQuarium, in the Marine Mammal Center. . . ."

Two hours later, Shannon finished her story. ". . . I concentrated the power downward, hoping to save lives that way, and caused the explosion. And that's my story."

Kulkarney had listened, one ear cocked toward Shannon, scribbling furiously on her notepad and nodding encouragement, her lips pursed. When Shannon looked up, she placed her pen and her pad back in her purse and brushed nonexistent sweat from her brow.

"Do you mind if I smoke?" she asked as Shannon sipped another paper cup of water. "Don't worry, it's marijuana, nothing harmful. You will find the secondhand smoke quite pleasant." Without waiting for a reply, she opened a mahogany-colored, bejeweled cigarette case and lit up.

"Yes. I see why telling the truth, the whole truth, and nothing but the truth, will not work in this case." She drummed her lacquered nails on the purse in her lap. "My original advice stands. You are not to speak to any strangers outside my presence. Watch what you say, even to trusted friends. The feds may have them wired."

"I'm used to keeping quiet about my alien encounters, so that won't be hard."

"Oh, but what am I thinking? You need not worry about wires: you can peer right into their minds and discover their motives."

"No." Shannon swiped the hand of her unharmed arm back and forth as if to erase the very suggestion. "I stay out of people's minds except in the most extreme cases. I'll watch my words."

"Even the luscious Luke?"

"He'll signal me if they force him into anything."

"Very well."

As if it were a casual afterthought, Tourmaline withdrew a set of documents from her purse. "Our legal contract. Worthless, of course, since you could claim diminished capacity if you ever wanted out of it. The important clause is my fee—a $20,000 retainer and $750 an hour. Worth every penny. Google me."

Shannon had come into a substantial sum of money courtesy of the White Wolf Casino with Essi's help back during the Alien Troubles and then courtesy of Roebor and his diamond gift. The fees didn't bother her.

"Hand me a pen, will you?"

The door opened behind Kulkarney, and in stormed Dr. Bennett, her face red and hot. Tourmaline slid the marijuana cigarette behind her back.

Shannon recognized Doctor Bennett's glare. She quickly scribbled her signature and handed the contract back to Tourmaline.

"Oh, Dr. B.," she said, attempting to get ahead of the incoming missile. "Let me introduce my new attorney, Tourmaline Kulkarney. Ms. Kulkarney, my all-time favorite doctor, Julia Bennett."

"Get out," Dr. Bennett said. "I gave strict orders that Shannon have no visitors at this time."

"I'm not a visitor," Kulkarney said. "I'm her lawyer. And call me Tourmaline." She addressed these last words to Shannon while keeping a wary eye on the doctor.

As Dr. Bennett approached, she sniffed the air and zeroed in on the cigarette. "Put that out this instant. This state has a law banning indoor smoking, and you're in a hospital, for god's sake." She sniffed the air. "The law applies to cannabis, as I'm sure you are aware."

Kulkarney stubbed out the reefer in Shannon's paper cup, which Dr. Bennett swept off Shannon's tray with a moue of distaste and carried to the trash bin in the adjoining bathroom.

"Well, perhaps I shall take my leave now," Kulkarney said as if the doctor had not ordered her out. "It will be a treat representing you, Ms. Kendricks. Good day."

She gathered her bag and offered her hand to Dr. Bennett as she departed. Dr. Bennett crossed her arms over her chest in slow motion and tipped Kulkarney a sharp nod. In one smooth gesture, Kulkarney's offered fingers rose to her hat, and she adjusted the feather, nodded, and strode out the door.

Dr. Bennett watched Kulkarney's exit. "Now. Regarding your excess power, I'm afraid my preliminary research has proven useless. This phenomenon is far beyond my abilities. I have found no way to measure it or view it, let alone direct it."

"I wonder if visiting my Great Room to see the stuff would be any help. Roebor?"

Hmm. I have located the construct where the power re-sides in your mind. There is a small chance that Dr. B. may gain some useful insight if she were to view it. I am doubtful, however.

"He says, sure, come on over."

Dr. Bennett shrugged. "It couldn't give me any *less* infor-mation than I have now." Knowing the drill, she pulled her chair next to the bed and laid her head next to Shannon's ban-daged arm. Shannon flowed down from her mind to retrieve the doctor's spirit and brought her over to Shannon's Great Room.

Come this way, Roebor said. He had shrunk to the size of a horse—much less frightening to humans. So much light poured into the Great Room now that they made their way forward only by placing their hands on the wall and sliding along, eyes squeezed closed.

From the Great Room, he led them through several corridors. At length, they came to a black, metal barricade the size of a garage door. Shannon couldn't find any way to open it, but around all four sides, bright white-gold light—too bright for the eye to contemplate for long—leaked from the gaps between the barricade and the corridor walls. She sensed the vastness of the cavern beyond the door, filled with Salesti's power, and her hands began to shake.

"My god, I can feel the power behind this door. It's immense." Dr. Bennett moved to place her fingers in the flow of power, slipping along the vertical left edge of the barricade. Roebor swatted her hand away with one quick flick of a furry paw.

Pardon, Dr. Bennett. I, too, tried touching the stream. Your hand will burn. I found the pain excruciating. He lifted his other paw. Two toes—or as Shannon now thought of them, fingers—had blistered red and raw.

"Why didn't you say something? I can conjure ointment here for you. Have you seen enough, Dr. Bennett?"

"Enough to scare the daylights out of me. I'm afraid the scientific tools at my disposal can't solve this mystery. I'm sorry."

"No worries, I didn't hold out much hope. Let me take care of Roebor's hand, and we'll head back."

* * *

Shannon whiled away the night dozing on and off while she watched an all-news channel: no alien creatures had been reported. A quiet young nurse, a Miss Amy Scarlett, checked on her six times. She peered at the size of Shannon's pupils and asked her questions: what year it was, who the president was, and so on and so on and so on.

In the morning, Dr. Bennett shipped in a large breakfast from Shannon's favorite pancake house, which she devoured along with the hospital's less generous fare.

"The swelling has diminished, which is what I wanted to see—" Dr. Bennett was saying later in the morning when two men familiar to Shannon interrupted her, bursting into the room and leaving the protesting Nurse Scarlett in their wake.

Blacksilver sported a gauze dressing above his right eye, and Torra wore a wrist cast. Shannon winced.

Yeah, wounding the feds would do nothing to help her case.

"Gentlemen," Dr. Bennett said. "I am not allowing my patient to receive visitors yet, although she is improving, and I might allow you to speak with her later this afternoon."

"The Department of Homeland Security trumps your credentials, doctor, and when we say we need to talk to Ms. Kendricks, we will. We won't be long."

Dr. Bennett was gathering steam to roll right over these two unsuspecting feds when Shannon intervened.

"Even if Dr. Bennett said you could speak to me, gentlemen, in my current condition, I refuse to talk to you without my attorney present. Her card is there on my tray. Please take it. Why don't you contact her, and perhaps you can set a time for us to meet?"

As if she hadn't spoken, Blacksilver moved to her bedside. "How are you feeling today, Ms. Kendricks? We have a couple of questions. Routine matters. You won't need legal counsel for this. Let's go through what happened when the *Willow* exploded. Now—"

"When my legal counsel is present, Mr. Blacksilver. A chunk of my leg is missing here, and I don't feel well. Would you like to see?" She flipped her sheets back to reveal her thigh, with its thick bandaging and an unnerving dip on top where she'd lost part of her leg. As she gazed at it, her stomach pitched. She picked at the tape holding the bandage as if to show them the wound. As she fussed with it, her stomach's unpleasant acrobatics increased.

Torra had ventured forth to stand by Blacksilver, and he blanched at her injury. Blacksilver found his shoes suddenly of great interest. He halted her with a well-manicured hand.

"All right, Ms. Kendricks. No need to show us any more."

Yet, he took one more crack at her.

"Did you, in fact, know in advance someone had planted a bomb on the ship? Simple yes or no."

Dr. Bennett handed Kulkarney's card to Blacksilver and shooed them toward the door. "No attorney, no conversation. That agrees with my medical judgment. Out you go. So good to meet you."

"I can have you taken into custody." Blacksilver tried to make his voice carry as he backed out the door.

"She still has a right to a lawyer, so don't bother," Dr. Bennett said as she closed the door in their faces.

"Damn Homeland Security thinks it can throw its weight around. Not in my hospital. If they come back, I'll be ready for them." She moved back to Shannon's bed. "As I was saying, I want to keep you overnight again tonight, but we're hopeful you'll be able to go home in three or four days to await your first leg surgery."

"Leg surgery?"

"Yes. They've scheduled it for ten days from now. A consultant will come in later today to talk to you about it, and then you'll receive information in the mail. You do understand that you'll need to return for several more surgeries and other treatments, yes? When will you be ready for lunch?"

"What time is it?" Shannon asked, glancing at the clock. "Ten thirty? I can hold out until ten forty-five, ten fifty max."

"I'll see to it."

* * *

I like your new lawyer, Roebor said, as they chewed over the ramifications of Shannon's various visitors. *She strikes me as more than sufficient to hold her own against Blacksilver.*

"Me too." Shannon shifted her bandaged arm in a futile attempt to stop it from hurting. *Her super-drugs must be wearing off.* Her arm and leg throbbed, and pain sliced through her thigh with the slightest movement. She'd developed a headache that could drown out a tsunami siren, and her good wrist now throbbed too, for reasons unknown.

She shifted her hips, trying to maneuver her leg into a more comfortable position.

"She'll do a great job. I liked the reconstructionist, Dr. Singh, too, although he depressed the heck out of me."

Jagmeet Singh had visited her an hour ago, explaining the severity of the damage to her leg. He set forth a treatment regimen that would include surgery, physical therapy, and muscular tissue engineering. This plan, he said, should produce a reasonable facsimile of the leg muscle she'd lost.

"It will be a long path to travel," he had cautioned, "one for which you will need great patience and perseverance. But from everything Dr. Bennett has told me about you, I believe you can achieve great success."

Shannon dismissed Dr. Singh from her mind for the moment. "Blacksilver and Torra will be back, but I haven't yet concocted a convincing lie that explains how I knew I needed off the ship before it exploded."

Perhaps the best course is to say you were simply referring to your need to eat. Plead ignorance of the ship altogether.

essi thinks shannon say she sees blacksilver throw bomb.

"Oh, there's a thought, sort of blame the victim but in a deserved way. Splendid idea, Essi."

Essi giggled.

"Torra has remained quiet through all this. Let's pin it on him. Still waters run deep and all that," Shannon said.

What has that to do with Torra?

"It means that just as you can't see the turbulence below the calm surface of deep waters, we might not see what turbulence lies in quiet Mr. Torra. A joke. We can't pin the explosion on him."

I see. Deep waters. Very good.

"Anyway, the problem is that if I say nothing, they'll never figure out what happened. But they'll also keep me in their sights when I want them to forget all about me."

Mmm. But I do not see another choice.

Luke pushed open the hospital room door. "Knock knock. Okay to come in?"

Tell him no; he is interrupting. We are in still waters running deep, and his waters run very shallow.

Shannon waved him in.

"How are you? How's the head? Did anyone say anything about the damage to your leg yet?"

Shannon brought him up to speed. "What did you and Torra talk about while Blacksilver turned the thumbscrews on me?"

"He succeeded in depressing me inside ten minutes. I doubt the man has ever smiled. We talked about the decline of the salmon fishery and the rare appearance of an abundance of tuna offshore here in recent weeks. When the explosions sounded, I was telling him about one time when I had a marlin the size of Miami on my line down in Mexico."

"What happened up on your deck when the ship exploded?"

"The detonation didn't damage the upper deck. But I raced for the stairwell to get to you, with Torra right behind me, and we ran out of boat—the stairs ended at the waterline because half the boat had already sunk. Debris floated everywhere; the cove was thick with it. I waded down in there, and I came across the coast guard guy first, then Blacksilver. It took us over half an hour to find you."

He squeezed the hand of her uninjured arm.

"One of the longest half hours of my life."

Shannon squeezed back, smiling, though fatigue was settling in again.

"Have you talked to Blacksilver?"

"After they checked us all out and treated us for minor injuries here at St. James, I waited for you to get out of surgery, and Blacksilver nailed me and spirited me off to an empty office."

"What for?"

"He wanted to know what I knew about the explosion. I was telling the truth when I said I didn't know anything, although I had a solid suspicion, of course, which I didn't mention."

"Has he talked to you since?"

"No, but I've overheard plenty, sitting right out in the open in the waiting room. They can't figure out any way we could have known that particular boat would come to answer our S.O.S., and they seem sure you didn't have the bomb on you. Blacksilver claims he was staring right at you when it happened, and he didn't see you holding anything."

"So, do they have a theory?"

"The experts believe that the blast came from within the boat, not underneath it. But they haven't identified the source yet. They can't pin anything on you."

He grinned. But his smile faded. "That's not to say they won't keep close tabs on you. They think you're suspicious as hell."

"I gathered." Shannon shifted on her bed again.

"What is it?"

"I can't get comfortable."

"Too much pain?"

"That and the energy is jazzing my nerve-endings again. We've got to solve my power problem and soon, or something will happen that will make the explosion on the *Willow* seem like a firecracker."

CHAPTER SIXTEEN
Power Defined

TOURMALINE KULKARNEY STOOD WITH HER FEET WIDE AND HER HANDS ON HER HIPS. Her wide-brimmed, cardinal-red hat sported a veritable garden of long, stiff, matching feathers, which in turn matched the eye-popping red of her floor-sweeping designer skirt and blouse. The perfume of the day reminded Shannon of a midnight garden.

"No sir. You may *not* interrogate my client. I don't care how innocent you say the questions would be. She possesses no information that would be of any value to you. Ergo, we will waste neither her time nor yours as she monotonously repeats the phrase, 'I don't know.'"

"Why can't she tell me that herself?" Blacksilver took a step toward Kulkarney. Torra hovered at the edge of the action near the door.

"Ms. Kendricks has informed me of the despicable manner in which you treated her on the ship, denying her food for her known metabolic condition despite her pleas. After that? No sir, you will approach her person over my dead body."

The two of them turned and stared at Shannon as she lay sprawled on her living room couch, the injured leg propped up on pillows covered with pale pink pillowcases, Narci in her lap with her head stretched out over Shannon's good leg. They'd caught her with a peanut butter snickerdoodle halfway to her mouth. She froze, cookie wavering in the air.

"There! You see? Her metabolism requires food, dammit. You don't mind if I smoke in here, do you, darling girl?" She pulled out one of her marijuana cigarettes and lit it.

"Marijuana is a controlled substance under federal law. I could have you arrested."

Kulkarney blew an O-ring of smoke in his face.

Shannon wanted this conversation to end. Her thigh screamed as if someone were just now sawing off the missing chunk. She'd banged her bandaged arm on the doorframe when Luke had brought her home from the hospital an hour ago to find Tourmaline and Blacksilver shouting over one another on her front porch. Her head felt as if someone had taken her brains out, run over them with a lawnmower, and shoveled them back inside.

Her T-shirt and jeans took a hit during the explosion, so she'd relied on Luke to bring her a set of going-home clothes. He'd been afraid to bring anything with a close fit, so here she sat in her silky nightgown and matching bathrobe. It *did* feel cool and comfortable. But still. She had guests.

Besides, she needed to get out in the backyard to send Essi and Toss home. They'd agreed Essi would try sounding out the salestis on her own first for more information about the power—she would be less threatening than Shannon, with her exploding head.

So she wanted the federal idiots out of her house.

Shannon concentrated on Narci's soft black coat. *Okay, now. She mustn't lose her temper; she must stay calm. Let Tourmaline take care of it.*

"You are standing in my personal space, fed boy. Back off," Kulkarney said.

Blacksilver turned to Shannon again and shook his fist.

Really?

"If you think we're going away, think again. I'll come here every day until you talk to me. Every single day."

"Not unless you've arranged it with me first, you won't," Kulkarney said.

In her red stilettos, she towered four inches over him. She used that to full advantage. He took a step back.

Shannon stared at him as he blustered again, refusing to back down and leave.

Blacksilver must go.

The power beckoned. She should not use it. . . *Well, just a bit of power. . .* she bent her little finger. She'd give him a tiny nudge.

"Tourmaline, might I have a word over here?"

Kulkarney stepped toward her with the grace of a ballroom dancer, clearing the path between Shannon and Blacksilver.

Shannon brushed her finger in his direction.

The power lifted him like a sheet of tissue and blew him toward the living room window.

Odin's eye. Too much!

With her index finger, she pointed at her favorite over-stuffed reading chair and, pushing her finger, slid it across the floor. She lifted it with her energy, caught the agent in it as if she were a shortstop on a line fly ball, and dropped both chair and occupant onto the carpet.

To cover what she'd done, she flicked her thumb and blew out the sliding glass door in her adjacent dining room almost simultaneously.

"What in the hell did you do?" Kulkarney asked Blacksilver.

"Me? What happened?"

"No, it had to be the wind," Torra said. He pulled Blacksilver out of the chair. "Come on, boss."

"That was the weirdest thing," the flustered fed said. "But I'm not sure—"

"Come on, boss," Torra said. "Let's get out of here."

Shannon watched as they made their way to the door. Torra turned at the last minute and stared straight at Shannon, fear on his face. He didn't say a word.

Still waters run deep, Shannon. I think he suspects. What possessed you to do that?

He suspects. Blacksilver will suspect, too, when he calms down. You ask what possessed me? I'm hurting. I'm tired, but I can't sleep, the power pushed, and I wanted them gone.

Tourmaline said, "As your counsel, I would have strongly recommended against that."

Shannon pressed her head back into the couch.

"Never mind. I could file a restraining order alleging he broke your sliding glass door in a fit of temper. A 'he said, he said, she said, she said' kind of thing?"

"No. Don't worry about it. What I did, I did. And I'll deny it. Who's going to believe them? We have a bigger problem.

And as to that problem, let's start by sending Essi and Toss home pronto."

"I'm counting on you, Essi, to find out from the salestis if they believe I will blow, and if they do, how we can stop it."

Outside now, balanced on her crutches and standing on the picnic table, Shannon lifted her good arm toward the portal.

"Where are you pointing? I can't see a thing." Tourmaline squinted into the sky.

"It's a portal. And they're gone. Help me down, will you?"

"Now what?" Tourmaline asked as Shannon folded onto the picnic bench.

"Now we wait for Essi to return."

They hadn't yet settled on the picnic bench when Shannon glanced up, the sharp blush of surprise on her face. "They're back." Shannon frowned. "Someone's back, anyway. Not Essi."

She struggled back onto the table and used one of her crutches to steady herself on her good leg. Why the portal remained so high off the ground here was something Salesti had never explained to her. It had just shrugged when Shannon asked and said, *portals end where portals end, high, low, in between.* On days like today, she yearned for a nice waist-high wormhole entrance.

I am ready if someone unwanted appears, Roebor said.

"Well, don't keep me in suspense." Tourmaline wrung her hands as she stood beside the picnic table, her back stiff and her chin up.

A salesti, the one with the pale magenta aura, buzzed into Shannon's hand and flew on to her Great Room.

"It's one of the salestis," Shannon explained to Tourmaline. "You want to come with me? Might as well."

"With you? With you where? What's a salesti again?"

"I'm going inside of my mind. Here, come lay your head on the table by me."

"Well. I don't know. I might get splinters."

"Come with me." Shannon rested her bandaged arm on Tourmaline's ring-bejeweled hand and flowed to her mind, snagging her spirit. Then they flowed back through Shannon to Shannon's mind.

Tourmaline studied her surroundings. "Oh, my lord. This is even better than the night Roddy smuggled me aboard the back seat of his F-4 fighter jet. So. Everything you said is true. Rather too bright, but otherwise manageable."

Roebor stalked into the Great Room at full size and squinted down at the tiny form of the hummingbird-kitten-like creature resting with still wings on Shannon's shoulder.

"And now I'm ready to go home," Tourmaline said. The attorney backed to the wall and tried to fade into invisibility.

The others moved into a dimmer corridor.

salesti not stays long. comes with apology first. salestis should tell shannon whole truths on RiverWorld but salestis sad for dead salesti. sad for shannon, not knows best words to say, so say nothing. now ready to say. shannon asks questions?

"Am I going to lose control of this power and unleash it all?"

yes.

"Will it destroy Earth?"

yes.

"The solar system?"

yes.

"Can I do anything to control it?"

salestis think no.

"Can I pass it on to anyone who *can* control it?"

salestis think no.

Roebor let out a roar and slammed his fist to the ground. "The salestis don't think anything useful at all. Will they give us any help?"

Shannon gripped a handful of fur on Roebor's long leg and gave it a slight tug.

"Does a place exist in space where the explosion wouldn't cause any damage—or at least damage nothing but dead stars?"

yes.

"How would I get to such a place?"

the cave of portals.

"Toss's book! Of course. Have you seen it, Roebor? Over the centuries, the Seladorans have mapped the wormholes in the cave of portals. They've learned which ones lead to inhospitable places, which is exactly what I need."

salesti goes now. The salesti rose into the air.

"Wait, can you tell us anything at all that might help us?"

salesti not knows.

"I see. So, I might as well tie up my affairs, return to RiverWorld, and take a portal to a dead planet or a broken wormhole that ends out in space."

Roebor swiped the tiny creature out of the air and into his large paw. He opened his fist and glared down at it. "I supposed the salestis to be wise and powerful, attuned to the universe. And you have nothing? Nothing for us? You're telling Shannon she will explode into oblivion and take a chunk of the galaxy with her, and you have nothing?"

He dropped the salesti and swept Shannon into his oven-sized paw.

"Salesti thought you could deal with its power in some way, Shannon. It tried to tell you, but it died too soon. I refuse to believe it would have given you the power if it thought it was giving you a death sentence. We must figure out what Salesti's plan was. Do not surrender yet."

"I'm already too dangerous for Earth. You saw what happened on the *Willow*. We have very little time. I'll have no choice but to take a portal to a dead world soon."

"Then we must control your environment so you can remain calm. You must avoid Blacksilver and Torra at all costs. A few days, at least. Give me a few days to find a solution." He put her down, taking care with her injured leg.

Shannon sat by the dragonpanther, who shrank until he reached horse-size and plunked down beside her.

"I'm sorry I dragged you into my self-destruct problems. It isn't right," Shannon said, laying her head against his shoulder.

"Me? Much of what I am died along with my body back on FireWorld. I am rather a ghost here in your mind. No, the injustice of this power threat is that Salesti asked *you* to bear this burden—you, who have struggled so hard for so many.

At least you will consider calling Juneau one last time, will you not? You should not miss your chance to see the whale."

"I'm not sure I can find her, but I would love to. We'll try it your way for a day or two. You're right; Salesti had figured something out she thought would work. Something the other salestis haven't. What does that tell us? The other salestis are homebodies, am I right, salesti?"

"homebodies" means what?

"It means that, unlike our Salesti, who traveled to Earth, FireWorld, and who knows where else, they stay on RiverWorld. So maybe somewhere she went gave her an idea that wouldn't occur to the salestis who don't travel. Could this be right?"

The salesti buzzed and flew over Roebor's head. Back and forth it flew, in greater and greater arcs, as it struggled with Shannon's question.

yes. this salesti thinks shannon understands departed salesti, the traveler.

"Then we have a chance," Roebor said.

CHAPTER SEVENTEEN
Endangered Species

SHANNON RUMMAGED AROUND IN HER UPSTAIRS OFFICE FOR A MEDITATION TAPE she used to listen to when she attended the university. To help her stay calm at all costs. Barefoot, she wore a lavender tank top and loose black shorts to avoid aggravating her various wounds.

Tourmaline Kulkarney had emerged dumb-struck from her encounter with Roebor and the salesti in Shannon's mind. Shannon dispatched her to throw her considerable intellectual powers at keeping the two agents from Homeland Security at bay.

Sensing her doorbell would ring in a moment, Shannon arose from her dusty, neglected video discs and headed downstairs on her crutches, one painful step at a time. Her visitor hadn't yet parked at the curb by the time she reached the door. She leaned against the wall, queasy from the pain, and waited. The doorbell rang.

"Dr. Moon. Great to see you. Come in. Things have been hectic around here, or I would have called you to tell you I'm fine." The Director of the Dickson Research Center and

Shannon's sometimes boss looked her up and down and cocked a quizzical eyebrow.

She frowned at her arm and leg, bandaged mummy-style. "Relatively speaking."

"My sympathy for your injuries."

"Thanks. I'll live."

"I heard about the explosion at the site of the discovery of a strange creature. Did you see it?"

Shannon loved that Moon focused right in on the mysterious "bat cat."

"Yes, I saw it. Come on in, and I'll tell you all about it. Do you want tea?"

She fixed them each a cup of Moon's favorite tea. He brought it out from the kitchen and set it on her blue-tiled coffee table, and then sat on her reading chair. She sank into her couch, propping her leg on its pillows. Narci lay across the top of the couch back, one paw batting at Shannon's hair.

Moon received her fabricated version of the explosion and her accurate description of Bale.

He could not hear enough about the creature.

"Mammal, though, not reptilian?"

"Yes, mammal, for sure. Fur, not scales, warm-blooded."

"Not avian?"

"Not a bird, no."

"But not a marine mammal?"

"Not like a dolphin or a seal. Although I think it could dive into the ocean with no trouble."

She sipped her tea. These were odd questions.

Of course we can dive, Roebor said. *Without question. Why do you hesitate? Dragonpanthers are excellent divers. We hunt in the ocean. Swim underwater, too, as you have seen.*

Roger that, but I can't let on how much I know.

Oh. Sometimes I forget the games we play and with whom we play them.

I'm with you on that, Shannon said.

"Not related to my alien," Moon said under his breath.

Shannon cocked her head. But before she had the chance to ask him what he meant, Moon slapped his knees. "Enough about the bat cat. I cannot stay. However, before I leave, I must seek your help. I came today on an unrelated, but urgent matter."

What now?

"Are you familiar with the North Pacific Right Whale?"

"Not very. They live in the Alaska area, and a related species lives over in the North Atlantic, right?"

"Quite so. The most eastern group of the North Pacific Rights lives in and around the Gulf of Alaska, where we are building the new Dickson Research Center. Two days ago, one of our research boats motored out to explore the shoreline north of us. The crew came across a deceased North Pacific Right Whale on a rocky beach."

"Oh, how sad. They're endangered, right? And I mean, among the most endangered animals in the world?"

"Exactly. We suspect less than fifty of them still exist in the eastern population, perhaps as few as thirty."

"What caused its death?"

"That is why I have sought you out. Certain experts think someone killed it."

"Someone *killed* it? Why?"

"Someone took the poor animal's brain. They removed it without disturbing any other part of the whale but leaving no part of the brain behind. They removed it with surgical precision. We can only speculate as to their purpose."

Shannon dropped her teacup on her light blue-and-gray berber carpet, spilling her tea and splashing Narci, who'd come down off the couch back to sit on Shannon's feet. The cat stood and walked with great dignity to the other end of the couch for a wash.

* * *

As Moon helped her clean up her spill, she asked, "Removed the brain but nothing else?"

"Yes. I am sure you agree that with so few of the population left, we must apprehend the perpetrators of this outrageous travesty before any more right whales die."

"Who do you mean by 'we'?"

"Government funds to mount an investigation are scarce. NOAA and the Navy have together arranged for a patrol ship to scan the area, but the Gulf of Alaska covers something in the neighborhood of 600,000 square miles. I hold out no hope that a single vessel will find the culprit."

"I agree. Sounds hopeless. But why have you come to see me?"

"Because we need Juneau, and you are my one hope to contact her."

What? Moon knew about their telepathic connection?

"What do you mean, 'contact her'?"

"I wasn't born under a banana tree, Ms. Kendricks. Long ago, I concluded your connection with Juneau had as much to do with telepathy as a special working relationship with the beluga. But it suited my purposes to allow you to maintain your pretense."

If Shannon hadn't already dropped her teacup, she'd have dropped it now.

"You knew?"

Dr. Moon smiled a brief thin-lipped smile, and gave a curt nod.

"I can't believe it."

"Let us move past this revelation and concentrate on the current question: can you contact Juneau? And if you can, will she communicate with other belugas to search for whoever has done this?"

Shannon, we should help Dr. Moon. The whale's killer might be the alien that Bale sent to Earth. If so, we must catch it before it does more damage.

PART THREE

GULF OF ALASKA

CHAPTER EIGHTEEN
Becky

SHANNON STARED AT DR. MOON. He wanted to know if Juneau would help in the search for the right whale's killer. Would she?

"I can contact Juneau. At least I could, as of about four months ago. Right now she has the freedom to be a beluga in the far north, and after what happened with that fruitcake trying to steal her. . . ." Shannon's voice faltered. "I wanted everyone to think she'd gone for good."

Dr. Moon stared down at his steaming teacup. "Yes. This, I understand."

Shannon's teacup shook. She shivered so much her fresh cup of tea spilled everywhere. That fruitcake was also a murderer. She steadied herself.

"But I don't know what Juneau can or will convey to other belugas or whales."

Dr. Moon stood. "Will you come to Alaska with me and find out?"

Moon is holding something back; I can sense it. If an alien killed the right whale, Moon may think he has to hide that information, Shannon said to Roebor.

The facts fit. A crocodile-tyrannosaurus features an appendage as sharp as any human tool, sharp enough to cut the brain cleanly. As for taking only the brain—the crocodile-tyrannosaurus has evolved in such a way that each population has specific food preferences. I have no way of knowing from which population Bale's creature came.

Shannon hesitated before answering Moon's question. To cover her pause, she dabbed at her spilled tea with her napkin. The danger of her doomsday explosion made the trip risky. Her surgeries could wait a short while, but she'd feel pain, plenty of pain. And yet—to communicate with Juneau again—for one last time if she didn't survive the power Salesti had given her—perhaps to see her! Then too, Bale's creature was Shannon's responsibility: she'd killed Tidak, triggering Bale's rage.

Roebor said, *I suggest we go. I shall like to say goodbye to the beluga, too. And to be fair, the responsibility for the creature does not fall to you, but to me. It comes from my world, sent by my enemy.*

"All right," she said to Moon. "I'll come. Let me throw a few clothes together and make a few calls."

"Very good. I will arrange matters and pick you up here tomorrow morning at 7 a.m."

* * *

Shannon called Luke to explain her trip to Alaska, and to see if he would watch Narci.

"I feel like a broken record here, but I'll say it anyway. Are you crazy? You've just sustained serious injuries. You ought to be at home on your couch for the next month. I know you're all about 'I can do it,' but this is over the top. And you're a loose cannon in the most literal sense. It's too dangerous for you to fly on an airplane, ride on another boat, or run around in Alaska chasing after god knows what."

"You're not saying I should ignore the problem?"

"Yes, of course you should ignore the problem. You should spend every moment working on getting well. We should spend every moment while you're sitting on your couch figuring out how to fix your power leak. I mean, yes, right whales are endangered, bless them, but right now, you're endangering the entire planet. You won't help the whales much if the planet blows."

"My leg can hold for a few days, which is all this should take. If I'm about to lose control, I have a plan. I'll get off Earth through the portal that sticks with me and find a safe place to go ka-pow. So, we're good." One of the two portals in Ocean City had been designed by the Salestis to follow Shannon. When she traveled to Alaska, she would find it close by.

"Good? You call that a good plan? Where you run off to a dead planet and blow yourself to bits? I don't call that a good plan. I call that a horrible plan. Can you hear me in there, Roebor? Why don't you make yourself useful and talk her out of this ridiculous side trip? And find a way for her to beat this power threat?"

Tell him I hear him. Tell him he must know by now no one can tell you what to do. He wastes valuable time by trying.

"Roebor agrees with you one hundred percent. But this is a *harmless* 'side trip,' and Roebor's work on a solution can continue as well in Alaska as here."

Luke emitted a long, weary sigh.

"I'll take care of the cat. You'll call me? I'd come, but I didn't return to duty until a few months ago, I already took time off when you were in the coma, and, as you know, I have my detractors on the force."

Yes, and the blame for Luke's detractors rested at Shannon's feet. Luke should stay here. That he would also be safe from alien monsters was purely coincidental.

She smiled.

"Thanks so much, Luke. Narci sits here as we speak, preening like a cat in a salmon factory at the prospect of your attention. I promise I'll call."

She clicked off and pulled the cat into her arms. "I'm sorry to abandon you, baby, but I have one more thing to do before I go north."

* * *

An hour later, Shannon's uber driver dropped her in a parking lot at the Central California Institute for the Criminally Insane. Shannon wore loose-fitting khakis and a loose tunic to hide the worst of her injuries. She stared at the CCICI's austere brick facade and, determined to succeed where she'd failed so many times before, she pressed forward on her crutches. She would try for the hundredth time to get in to see her former best friend, Becky Anderson. Becky had lost control of her thoughts and actions when two sick and evil alien actors left behind a residue—powder, Shannon called it—in Becky's mind.

Each time Shannon visited, Becky had refused to see her. But it was crucial that she get in to see Becky because Shannon had learned a new alien-acquired skill that might cure her friend.

Today would be the day she succeeded. She *would* convince Becky to see her. Because this might be Shannon's last chance before she and her power must leave Earth forever.

The receptionist at the front desk, Penny Pink, was playing a game of checkers with herself. She hovered over the board, a frown on her face, her hand poised as if to make a move, but she wasn't quite sure the move was wise. She'd braided her thick, wild hair into six plaits that faded from black at the roots to pale aqua at the tips.

"Hi, Penny. The hair looks nice today. Who's winning?"

"Me. So you're here to have your heart trampled on yet again." She shook her head. "I'm surprised you have any heart left. It's pretty pancaked by now, I would guess?"

"Flat as a ping-pong paddle. And yet here I stand." Shannon smiled, finished signing in, and went to sit in one of the dusty, beige upholstered armchairs in the waiting area.

Each time she came to the CCICI, the same routine played out: Penny called Becky's ward. Mr. Tabatabai took the call and checked his paperwork to see if Becky had earned the privilege of visitors. If she had, he forwarded Shannon's request to Becky, and Becky refused to see her. Mr. Tabatabai called her refusal down to Shannon, and Shannon dragged herself home. She'd tried sending notes, ever since she'd learned the skill that would help Beck, but each had come back unopened.

"No note today?" Penny called over to her.

"Not today."

She settled back into her chair and concentrated on the image of her friend—her long-legged, short-waisted, broad-hipped, wide-shouldered frame, her wild, curly, black hair that she wore in a ponytail on top of her head, her light brown eyes flecked with green.

Shannon reached for a sliver of her new white-gold power and cast her colors with it. As she watched, the colors flew through the institute, up the stairway to the second level, the third level, down the hallway, and through three sets of locked double doors. The colors came to a large sunny room. People sat around a television set. Others had taken to the couches to read or to chairs in front of jigsaw puzzles, chess boards, pinochle games, or decks of cards. Her colors searched on, over to the far window, where a lone woman stared out at the leafy green trees in the courtyard.

Becky.

Becky. It's Shannon.

Her friend jumped and clapped her hands over her ears.

It's okay, Beck. A lot has happened to me since we last talked. I can boost my thoughts with a high-energy power I've acquired.

"I don't want to talk to you. When will you accept that?" Becky said to the window.

Look, I'm bothering you because I want to try something I've learned, something that can clear those two creeps' residue from your mind. Let me try it, and then I'll leave.

"No."

Do you like it here so much you never want to get out?

A cruel thing to say, but Shannon needed to jolt Becky into a reaction.

"What the hell, Shannon? Why can't you leave me alone?"

Because I'm your friend. When you're free, I'll leave you alone if you like. Let me help you. That's all I want to do.

"Free? Won't happen. I've got the residue. I'll never get right in the head."

Not if I get rid of the residue, which I can do now. I did it for Luke. You remember Luke? The police officer who helped me get to the pool to save Juneau.

"Good looking, tall dude crushing on you? Yeah, I remember him. What about him?"

He tangled with a different unpleasant alien. I removed his residue, and he's fine now. What can it hurt? I can do it. You'll see.

"You took his alien residue away? Where did you put it?"

Scattered it to the wind. Now he's fine.

Becky continued to stare out the window. For five long minutes, she didn't move or speak.

What if she said no? Shannon might never get another chance to help her. Her stomach pinched, and her hands tightened on the well-worn arms of her chair.

Mr. Tabatabai appeared in the room, accompanied by several husky men in tan uniforms. He approached Becky and spoke to her, giving her Shannon's request. He turned away, looking as if he'd been through the drill too many times to waste a moment more on the fruitless plea. But this time, she nodded and said to his tan-suited back, "Yes." The manager turned back, his mouth open and eyebrows raised, and spoke again. "Yes," Becky repeated.

Yes! Shannon remained still in her chair as if she hadn't just witnessed her small victory, picking at her fingernails and waiting for Mr. Tabatabai to call Penny.

Penny's phone rang. "Hello, Mr. Tabatabai. What?" Penny's elbow brushed several checkers off her board. "Are you certain?" A pause. "Okay."

"Shannon! Today's your lucky day. Don't forget to buy a lottery ticket later. Becky said yes!"

Shannon wobbled to her feet and pumped a belated fist in the air. She grabbed her crutches and headed for the door beside Penny's desk. Penny buzzed her through.

* * *

Becky had retreated to her room. Mr. Tabatabai led Shannon to the door.

"Leave the door open, please. I will wait here a moment to see that Becky remains comfortable."

Becky's cold, brooding eyes stared at a point somewhere over Shannon's right shoulder. Shadows haunted those eyes, her forehead, and her mouth. She'd lost a lot of weight—too much. Her shoulders slumped as if all the fight had seeped out of her. Around her neck, she wore her mother's emerald. The one Shannon had lost and found again.

Her small, clean room held few traces of the fun-loving, kind, artistic woman Shannon had known. A faded print of picnickers and boats, painted by an impressionist who seemed to find his way onto the walls of every mental health facility, hung above her bed. Light tan walls bore too many scuff marks. The thin brown carpet had suffered from too many footsteps.

Shannon shivered with the cold—a kind of cold that couldn't be measured in degrees.

Becky perched on her neatly made bed covered by a lavender bedspread and gestured Shannon toward the white oak straight-back chair at a small matching desk by the door, the only furniture in the room other than the bed and a matching white oak bureau.

She sat and slid her crutches to the floor.

We have to make small talk until he goes away. Shannon tilted her head toward the door.

"How. . . how is Juneau?"

"She's free! And doing well. She lives in the north of Alaska with a pod of belugas. The best thing I could have hoped for."

"What about your grand plan for a place she would come in for husbandry and then go free?" Cruel bitterness tinged her voice.

Remember, the two aliens controlled Becky sometimes.

"Long story," Shannon said, her voice unperturbed and airy. "The quick version is that somebody tried to steal her, so I sent her away where she would stay safe. She may come back, though."

"What happened to you?" Becky asked, gesturing at Shannon's crutches.

"Another long story. The quick version of this one is that I was standing on a boat that exploded. Ended up with a long cut along my arm, and it took a chunk out of my leg. I'll be having reconstructive surgery soon."

If I live long enough for it.

"I expect it. . . expect it hurts."

Shannon curled her fingers into a fist and pulled them to her face. That was the kindest thing Becky had said to her in six years.

Shannon smiled. "Like the dickens."

Becky leaned to her left and surveyed the hallway.

"He's gone."

"Good." On one leg, Shannon hopped the short distance to Becky on the bed.

Becky flinched.

"I have to flow into your mind to locate the residue. Remember?"

Becky frowned. "Oh, I remember all right. But go ahead."

Shannon took Becky's hand, and the two women laid back on the bed, side-by-side. She flowed down through her arm, across into Becky's mind.

Shades of gray swathed Becky's darkened Great Room. Hard, jagged walls met a rough, uneven floor. It smelled like a damp cellar. Sparse light filtered into the room. Shannon's heart clutched at the size of it: small, like a cramped studio apartment. Shannon would have cried at the bleakness of it, but she had no time for that.

Becky's form joined her. "Now what?"

"We go to the room where your brain has stored the residue. Have you ever visited it?"

"I don't think I can. But if I could, I'd never go there. Ever."

"Okay, I'll find it. Do you want to come with me or wait here?"

Becky hesitated, stared down at her toes, and then looked straight at Shannon. "I'm coming."

Shannon and Becky exited the Great Room and located corridors—complex, winding, intersecting corridors without doors or windows. At one point, they found themselves back at the Great Room without ever having turned around.

"Let's try this way," Becky said, pointing to another exit from the Great Room. They walked by more doorless corridors, each the same as the last, until finally, down an offshoot of an off-shoot, they found a dead-end with a door to the left and a door to the right.

Shannon crossed her fingers and opened the door on the right. This room stored Becky's sky-blue essence, along with the essence of anyone who'd visited Becky's mind, including Shannon's cobalt blue.

But it stored none of her two evil visitors' dark residues.

Shannon returned to the hall to try the door on the left. She turned the nob and pushed, but it resisted; the wood had warped. She pressed hard with her shoulder until it finally popped open.

A dark and musty interior greeted her. But, yes, in the taupe light filtering through from the gray corridor, lumps of dark residue glistened with slime. The residue that plagued Becky's nightmares, that still sent her into uncontrollable rages and burdened her with impulses to do unspeakable things. The charcoal gray residue of the twisted alien who had murdered with pleasure, and the green-mixed-with-brown residue of the one whose primitive instincts dictated only *hunt, kill, eat, mate.* Shannon heard the faint, low strains of a cello, unrelenting as it repeated the same four sour notes. Becky shrank back from the door. Shannon could no longer see her.

Softly, ever so softly, Shannon cast her colors and shaped them into a light breeze that tinkled and swirled around the heaps of residue, swirled and stirred the residue into a small whirlwind that rose as she willed it into a tight ball. She made sure her whirlwind caught every single mote of the repulsive powder within its circling flow.

So much residue!

Ten particles of ash lifted from the whirlwind, floating away free into the room.

No! Shannon gritted her teeth and borrowed once again from her leaking white-gold power. She aimed her power at the stray bits, gathering them in, encircling them all, until not a single mote floated free.

A sudden rush of heat bathed Shannon in sweat. *The power! Trying to escape.*

Let us out, out, out, let us. The power pushed at her.

Shannon concentrated on holding onto the gathered residue, but she must rid herself of all anxiety.

Be calm. Happy and calm.

She would be titanium. A wall of titanium, past which no power could escape that she did not control.

Seconds ticked away. Shannon struggled against the power. Becky might have spoken to her; she did not hear it. She must regain control.

Let us out, out, out.

No, Shannon said.

Think of Becky. She owed her this. She *would* control the power. She would.

Fifteen minutes of skirmishing ticked by, second by slow second. Shannon weakened. Another minute and she feared she would have to yield to the power, ending the world. She gritted her teeth.

No, she said again.

Finally, the power relented and yielded to her control. She shivered. The sweat cooled on her brow before her hand steadied.

After subduing the power, she again reclaimed each ash that had wandered while the power diverted her attention, and wrapped the whirlwind of residue with her colors. She surveyed the room, hunting for any last trace of the monstrous powder.

A light violin concerto whirled through the room.

After she assured herself that not a trace of powder remained loose in the dark, swamp-smelling room, she moved past Becky, who stood transfixed in the corridor. With calm, deliberate movements, Shannon directed the whirlwind out of the corridor, through the Great Room, down through Becky's shoulder and arm. At the moment she would usually cross the barrier into her own hand, she blew the whirlwind out between their linked fingers into the air. For good measure, she used a spark of her power to speed the residue in a wide arc throughout Becky's CCICI room.

She watched her colors in the whirlwind scattering the dark residue, mote by single mote. It flew through the ventilation system and out into the California sun. From there, it would fly to the far corners of the planet where the single particles of two primeval beings possessed no power to influence even the smallest creature.

As the last of the residue drifted away from her whirlwind, Shannon hiccupped. A dozen motes of that evil residue escaped Shannon's grasp and floated into Shannon's hand.

"Oh, no you don't." Goosebumps prickled her arms at the thought of even one tiny ash of the old, corrupt beings seeping into her brain. She hurried after them, but where had they gone? Dashing around her body, she found nothing until she reached her own mind and inspected her own residue room where the powder of so many of her visiting favorites resided—Salesti, Essi, Toss, Becky, Luke, Narci. And there she found the sinister motes. They had nestled on the top of Becky's residue pile.

Creepy.

The unwholesome nature of the powder and its putrid smell suffused her residue room. These former enemies had held so much evil that even this small amount of residue would affect her, would give her the same sort of nasty, debauched thoughts Becky suffered if she didn't rout them out.

She'd have to remove a small amount of Becky's residue to collect them. She frowned. She didn't want to lose any of her friend's residue. But she also wanted nothing to do with the powder of those slimy creatures.

Never mind. The real Becky would return; she could afford to lose a bit of residue.

Again summoning her whirlwind of power, she whisked the evil residue away, regretting the sizable portion of Becky's residue that she must sweep away with it. In a matter of minutes, she had spread it to the four corners of the room and out the ventilation system. She checked her mind one more time for any stray motes of the terrible residue.

When she confirmed not a single mote floated in her system, she awakened, sat up, and hopped back to her chair. Still flat on her back, Becky stared at the ceiling and shook her head in disbelief.

"I feel a hundred pounds lighter. I feel like sunshine has reached my soul for the first time in years. Oh my god, Shannon, I feel peace. I'll sleep tonight without nightmares for the very first time since Andy's death."

She scooted back onto her pillow, a new lightness shining forth as if someone had turned on a light bulb inside her.

Shannon watched her friend for any sign she'd missed lingering residue. Becky looked good. Even her face had improved; in the span of a few minutes, heavy lines had disappeared from her face, transforming her to the woman of six years ago.

At last, Becky looked over to her former friend, her smile widening. "Do you know what this means? I *will* get out of here. It'll take a while, but I'll win my freedom. My freedom!"

She flew from the bed, pulled Shannon to her feet, and hugged her as if she meant to break her in two. Pain shot through Shannon's leg. And Becky had caught her injured arm inside the fierce hug, but Shannon didn't utter a sound.

She'd worked for this day for six long years. *Her friend restored!* She savored the moment.

Well done. Your power did not interfere. I feared the whirlwind would go awry because of the leaking energy.

I was determined to make it work since it might be my only shot. But, Roebor, I was within seconds of weakening so much the power could have overwhelmed me. I only got away with the solar system intact because the power didn't realize how weak I'd become. If I hadn't wanted this so badly, I don't think I could have pulled it off.

At length, Becky let her go and slipped back, suddenly shy. She swung her arms behind her back as if she hadn't hugged anyone in a long time.

"David's still here, too, right? I can do the same for him if I can get into see him."

Becky fixed her gaze on the wall behind Shannon. "He committed suicide three years ago. I'm sorry nobody told you."

"What?" Shannon shuffled back until she banged into the oak desk and sank onto it. "Oh, poor David." Shannon tugged on her braid. "If only I had known what to do sooner."

"No, that wasn't your fault. Put the blame where it belongs. That bastard alien. And David. . . I went to see him once, not too long after they incarcerated us here. He'd gone pretty far down the rabbit hole, Shannon."

Shannon's eyes and nose burned.

"All the time that alien spent controlling him broke him into tiny pieces. I'm not sure removing the residue would have solved his madness."

The two remained quiet, thinking of the young man the aliens had invaded and destroyed.

"Well. You have a lot to mull over. I'll leave you to it. Will you let me come again?"

"Yes, any time. But it won't be long before I can come see *you*."

Perhaps.

Shannon gathered her crutches. "Juneau may help me with a problem Dr. Moon has to deal with—the death of a North Pacific Right Whale. He wants to find out who killed it. I'm leaving in the morning to go to Alaska to see if I can call her to shore. I'll let you know what happens."

That is, if Shannon didn't blink out.

Tears formed.

"Oh my gosh. I have to plan a future now." Becky sat back down on the bed.

Shannon wiped her face so Becky wouldn't notice.

"Yes, you do. I'll say something to Moon. The new Dickson Research Center in Alaska might be one possibility you'd be interested in. Keep it in mind, anyway."

Shannon arranged herself on her crutches to leave. She and Becky gazed at each other, and then each glanced away.

An awkward silence arose between the two former friends.

After everything that had happened to them, this distance between them came as no surprise. She could live with it because Becky would get well.

* * *

Shannon Ubered home, asking the driver to stop at the fast-food restaurant near her house for three double veggie burgers, three large orders of fries, three salads, three fruit bowls, two chocolate shakes, and four cherry turnovers.

"You need me to pick up your other friends, or are they meeting you at home?" the Uber driver asked.

"Oh, everyone who's coming will be there."

That would be Shannon, Shannon, and Shannon. And Narci would get a couple bites.

As she came in the door, she sensed the phone would ring. She pulled her cell phone out of her purse and waited.

Come on, she didn't have all day.

Her leg throbbed, so she tossed the phone back into her purse, and used the crutches to make it to the couch and collapse.

The phone rang.

"I'm coming," Luke said without preamble.

"You're coming over?" Shannon said, digging into her bags of take-out. "Great. Your timing's good; I just came in the door a second ago. And guess what? I went out to see

Becky for the eleventy-eleventh time, and she finally let me in, and I rid her of every ounce of her bad juju."

"You dispelled the evil residue that had driven her mad? That's great! Really great. But I mean that I'm coming to Alaska."

"What about Narci? And Gumshoe?"

"I've arranged for a vet and one of her assistants to check in on them four times a day, and the assistant will stay over-night at your house with both of them if that's okay. I know the assistant; you can trust her. You've met the vet. She—"

Oh her. Shannon didn't love that Luke's ex would look after her cat. "I don't know. . . What do you think, Narci?"

The cat licked her paw and elected not to say.

"I suppose it'll be okay since it won't be for more than a few days. But how are you able to come? You've got work."

"Oh, I came down with something. My doctor gave me a note. I may be ill for what? A week? How long do you plan to stay?"

Shannon laughed. "I don't want to bring any more trouble down on your innocent head. Not after all the other trouble you've suffered because of me."

"No worries, cara. I told the absolute truth. I get sick thinking about the trouble you're bound to get into in Alaska."

CHAPTER NINETEEN
Magenta

SHANNON, LUKE, AND MOON ARRIVED AT THE OLD DICKSON RESEARCH CENTER late the next morning.

Because Roebor had once tumbled into the old Dickson Research Center's premier attraction, the UnderWater Complex, laying waste to the entire structure, Moon had undertaken the venture of building a new facility, the New Dickson, a few miles away.

The Old Dickson infirmary, the cafeteria, and the rooms—both the overnight hotel-like accommodations and the staff residential apartments—remained operational for support staff and for the construction workers who toiled at the new site.

"Your apartment remains as you left it, Shannon. We have not needed it for workers, but someone may require it when the most active construction phase begins. I would recommend that before you leave, you place your belongings in our storage area for future safe-keeping. If we stay on schedule, I estimate that the new residential units will be functional, along with the new dining hall, in about twenty-eight months. One unit will have your name on it."

"That soon?"

"Construction workers will continue to live on this site, but I wish to attract research staff at the New Dickson as soon as work exists for them to do, and they have a place to lay their heads at night. Why don't you settle into your apartment, and I will show Luke a room in the hotel quad? Unless he is going to—"

"That'll be great. You say the cafeteria is open? Can I get something to eat this time of day?"

"The cooks are preparing for dinner, but I have left special instructions pertaining to you." He removed a card from his wallet. "Show this card to Mrs. Inlender. She will see to it you eat well."

"Let me help you get settled in," Luke said.

Moon handed him a key to her old quarters, and Luke unlocked the door, carrying in her duffel bag. Shannon eased through the door on her crutches and examined her old digs. Someone had dusted the place, and the air smelled fresh: evidence of Moon's thoughtfulness. Still, being back here after everything that had happened at the end of her last stay, all of it bad, made her stomach turn queasy. She stared at the carpet without seeing it.

She blinked. She couldn't think about that now, not with a whale killer out there.

Luke and Moon departed. She pulled her belongings from her duffel, and tucked them into bedroom drawers and tossed them onto bathroom counters. In fifteen minutes, she was making her way to the dock; she always had her best luck contacting Juneau from there. She could hardly wait.

Juneau, she imaged, *where are you? Can you hear me?*

The beluga whale immediately imaged back, showing Shannon her pod, three females, a male, and three young ones.

All the darkness in Shannon's mind lifted at the image of Juneau and her pod. For those moments, her leg didn't need surgery, no one had killed a right whale, and she didn't threaten the solar system. She existed, and Juneau existed, and that sufficed to fill her with lightness.

Juneau imaged a coastline, as Juneau might see it from the water, but that didn't give Shannon much of a clue to her whereabouts. She gave herself a mental slap in the head.

What a ridiculous question: 'Where are you?' She might as well have asked Juneau if she was swimming in the ocean at the moment.

Juneau, I'm at the Dickson, where you used to swim in your sea pen—where the UnderWater Complex exploded. Do you remember? Would you come here to help me again?

This time Juneau's response came in the form of emotions: reluctance and curiosity.

Why? Juneau asked.

Someone or something murdered a whale. I want to find him and stop him.

A rush of surprise; whatever Juneau had expected, she hadn't expected murder. The belugas communicated among themselves. Shannon waited. *We are coming,* Juneau imaged. *This light and dark, next light and dark, in the next light we arrive.*

They'd travel today and tomorrow and arrive the day after. She'd see her Juneau one more time before the power forced her to journey to a dead planet.

* * *

"*Can* belugas communicate with other whales?" Luke asked through his headset as he and Shannon sat on opposite sides of the Dickson's helicopter. They were scanning the waters west of the old Dickson site, searching for evidence of whatever had taken the right whale's life. "I mean, do you think Juneau can enlist help in covering all this ocean out here?"

Even with headphones, Shannon had trouble hearing Luke over the *chop chop* of the helicopter.

"I've read about a dolphin helping a couple stranded pygmy sperm whales get back into the sea down in New Zealand. Different dolphin species team up to hunt fish. So, yes, the possibility exists. I don't think Juneau wanted to come to us, but when she found out the mission, she agreed. So, there's that."

"Shouldn't this be a matter for NOAA and whoever watches out for the marine life in Canada? Why you and Juneau? You sure Moon hasn't concocted this story as a ruse to lure Juneau back?"

"Moon wouldn't do that. Besides, the timing's off. If Moon wanted to use this mission to scam me and recapture Juneau, it would've made more sense to do it either right after she left, a year ago, or when the new Dickson is functional. And if Moon does anything, he does it sensibly."

"True, he's not a wild and crazy guy."

"Why did Moon want Juneau and me on the job? Maybe because the North Pacific Right is one of the most endangered species on the planet, which Moon cares deeply about, and NOAA doesn't have the resources that the Dickson does to throw at such a critical problem." She shrugged. "We may find out more at dinner."

Luke nodded and turned back to scan the green-black waters of the Gulf of Alaska.

* * *

When the chopper landed back at the Old Dickson, Luke and Shannon wandered toward the cafeteria once more, intent on finding a snack for Shannon. They'd made it from the helipad as far as the marina parking lot when Shannon grabbed Luke's arm.

"Somebody's using the portal. Come on; it's down on the pier again."

They hurried to the pier and stood waiting. And waiting.

"Well?" Luke asked.

"In a minute. I've gotten so good at picking up someone's arrival, I've been arriving earlier and earlier."

At length, Shannon cast her colors so she would see the portal as it opened, took a step closer, and raised her arm just in time to catch the salesti with the magenta aura. The Seladorans, including the salestis, could only visit Earth through the portal by coming in their ethereal form. As a result, they must find a host as soon as they arrived, or they would perish, but Salesti didn't have the same trouble on Roebor's world.

Why was that, Roebor? Do you know?

There is a rare element found on Earth that is fatal to the Seladorans in their physical form. The element does not exist on my world.

"It's the new salesti," she said to Luke. Turning inward to her Great Room, she said, "I can't call you Salesti, because that was our salesti's name. Can I call you—oh, how about Magenta?"

strange, the naming obsession of humans. naming of salestis matters not at all. It shrugged its tiny shoulders. *yes, magenta may be name shannon gives salesti.*

"I'm calling it Magenta," she said to Luke. "I want to find out why it's here, so I'll be quiet for a minute." She sat on the edge of the pier and leaned into Luke's shoulder.

In the corner of her Great Room, she found Roebor studying the tiny creature with his magnificent head cocked.

"I cannot tell the difference between them, Shannon, except for the color of its aura. This one seems identical to the one we lost." He poked a toe at the tiny form as it buzzed at the height of Roebor's head. "Except this one doesn't act very friendly."

Magenta buzzed in a tiny, angry circle. *salestis not meant to be friendly. salestis meant to be respected.*

The hummingbird-kitten flew right up to Roebor's eyes and glared at him—at Roebor, whose thick eyelashes could crush magenta if he blinked.

"Hmm," Roebor said.

"And we *do* respect you, Magenta, because you, at least, have tried to explain my fate to me. For this, I thank you. What brings you here today? Is Essi all right?"

essi not all right. essi comes here and falls into fish mind. fish eaten by shark.

Essi, like Magenta, could visit Earth only by finding the nearest host as soon as she arrived.

But why hadn't Shannon's extra skills warned her Essi was coming? Something had interfered. Was it the power? Perhaps she'd been incommunicado up in the helicopter.

"Essi's on Earth," Shannon said to Luke, "and she hooked a ride with a shark since I wasn't there to catch her."

Luke took a quick step away and put his hands on top of his head, elbows akimbo. When he turned back, his dark eyebrows had lowered in thunderous fashion. "That sounds like Essi."

"Why did Essi come? Are you going to stay here to help bring her back, Magenta?"

essi comes to see if essi can help shannon with power issue. but magenta different from salesti of shannon. magenta not likes travel to earth, spend time in head of shannon. magenta likes riverworld meadow in own body. magenta goes now.

"Wait, can you tell me where to find this shark, what kind it is, what size, anything?"

shannon casts colors. shannon finds. bye.

With Luke's assistance, Shannon rose from her perch on the edge of the pier and lifted her arm. Magenta disappeared as quickly as she'd come.

"*Odin's eye*. We could have done without a search for a shark carrying Essi on board interrupting a search for a brain-snatching alien interrupting a search for a cure to an overdose of power." Shannon lowered her arm and frowned at the sea.

CHAPTER TWENTY
Whitechair

MOON PEERED AT SHANNON THROUGH HIS THICK, BLACK-FRAMED GLASSES with a perplexed frown on his face. He took off his glasses and polished them with his white cloth dinner napkin, but this left a thin sheen of peanut oil from his shrimp dinner on the lenses. He put the blurry glasses back on, blinked, took them off, folded them with precision, and placed them beside his plate.

The director had joined Shannon and Luke for a late dinner at the cafeteria. Shannon wore a long-sleeved, black shirt with a loose pair of silky black pants. She informed Moon that Juneau would arrive the day after tomorrow, which delighted him. She also announced she wanted to take a boat out in the morning—with a shark tank if he happened to have one handy, which led to Moon's mishap with his glasses.

To avoid questions about the shark tank, she raced onward. "And, I have the strongest feeling, Dr. Moon, that you have more to say about this whale killing tale than you've spilled so far. Will you tell us the rest?"

"Yes," he said at length, "I do have more to tell you. But why in the world would you need a shark tank?"

Now it was Shannon's turn to squirm. She took a moment to align the edge of her cafeteria tray parallel to the edge of the table. She positioned her glass of soda pop adjacent to her plate at a forty-five-degree angle. Next, she planned to put her napkin on the table, aligning it with the short edge of her dinner tray. . . .

Luke placed his calm hand over her jittery one with enough, but only enough, pressure to still her nervous movements.

He smiled at Moon and said, "We figured that unless you have something specific planned for us, we're useless until Juneau arrives. People have spotted a shark in the vicinity they say is worth viewing, so I thought we might see if we could find it tomorrow."

Moon nodded, but said, "First, you must attend a meeting that shall convene at 9 a.m. tomorrow in my office in a trailer at the new facility. We can ride over together in the morning. At this meeting, Dr. Chet Whitechair will give a brief talk on the North Pacific Right Whale and show you some slides that identify the known members of the eastern group. I will also have more information for you then. If there is time, your afternoon will be free."

"Whitechair. I've heard of him. He's a whale expert with the University of British Columbia, right?" Shannon said.

"Indeed. He has joined us for the summer. You are certain Juneau will help us?"

"I'm certain. How much she can help, I don't know yet. I hope we can get a wide communication web going." Shannon's eye strayed to the dessert counter, where a lone remaining piece of chocolate mousse cake called out to her.

Moon's near-sighted vision brightened. "Think what it would mean if we could document that." He thumped the table. "We shall have hydrophones out on boats over as wide an area as we can manage. I must see to this." He placed his napkin on the table and rose.

"But you promised to tell us more about the right whale killing."

Moon hesitated. It appeared he wouldn't give them any more information, but then he shrugged, his shoulders relaxed, and he took his seat.

"There are things I must tell you. I did not wish to raise this at dinner, but at least now we have finished."

So much for the chocolate mousse cake. With a sigh, Shannon returned her full attention to the small, tidy man sitting across from her.

"First, someone or something did indeed make a precision cut into the brain of the whale with a sharp instrument. No teeth could have managed the incision through the head."

Luke hadn't removed his hand. She liked how it felt on hers. She liked its large square size and the warmth it offered.

In fact, she liked the wrist attached to it, the arm, the—

"But I am afraid I must report that no one removed the brain; something ate it. Ate it with precision. When we moved the whale to the old Dickson for further investigation, we identified sharp tooth marks on the interior only. Even so, remarkably, the creature consumed no tissue apart from the brain itself."

Shannon's attention to Luke's anatomy dropped like a stone, and she turned an astonished face to Moon.

"Eaten by what?" Luke asked.

"Unidentified. The experts agree the consumption took place in the water and not on the beach where our team found the whale. The tissue left behind had absorbed a great deal of saltwater."

"Could it have been Native Americans? Or members of a First Nation?" Shannon asked.

"All those who might have been in the area have denied it, and we believe them. The local people would have put the whole carcass to use if they had killed one; they would have taken the wax, the fat, the meat, all the rest. Whatever perpetrated this vile act left these precious parts on the animal to rot. In addition, the tribes do not place a premium on the brain. They also realize the precarious state of the right whales in these waters. They would have honored the treaties that prohibit harming the rights."

Shannon frowned. This sounded more and more like the crocodile-tyrannosaurus.

"Human, or nonhuman?"

Moon hesitated. "We cannot be sure."

"But best guess, human or nonhuman?"

"Nonhuman." This time Moon did rise, sweeping his coat off his chair and plucking up his greasy glasses. He took his leave with a short bow. "I will see you at 8:30 in the parking lot. After our meeting, I will show you the New Dickson site. In the meantime, I will see what I can do about arranging a boat, two drysuits, and. . . perhaps a shark tank."

Neither of them spoke for a beat after Moon departed.

Shannon glanced at Luke and caught him staring at her.

"Suddenly I'm glad I came with you. I don't like the sound of this."

* * *

"A whacked-out human *must* have done it," Luke said as they sat at opposite ends of the well-worn couch in her apartment. Shannon had dimmed the lights, then propped her mangled leg on the couch where Luke massaged her foot. Soft jazz played on her stereo.

She had compensated for missing out on the chocolate mousse cake by serving herself a bowl of chocolate ice cream with peanut butter balls that she and Luke had purchased during the afternoon at the commissary—along with a few days' supply of more nutritional groceries.

"We'd never run into another person as obsessed with whale brains as our last demented tormentor. He was one of a kind," Shannon said.

Why do you not tell him of our suspicions that the creature responsible for the right whale's death was sent by Bale? Roebor asked.

I wanted to spare him another alien ordeal. But I guess I might as well ease him into the truth.

"Yes," Luke said, "he was one of a kind. But this whale killer is just another crazy variety. The first guy wanted to study Juneau's brain. This time, our mystery man wants a rare meal."

"But a man would take the brain out and cook it, I would hope. Whoever took this one ate it raw and didn't bother to go ashore for the meal."

"How do we even know someone or something ate the brain?"

"The internal teeth marks, remember?" She spooned another scoop of ice cream into her mouth. "What if it turns out to be an alien? The ice cream tastes really yummy, by the way. You sure you don't want some?"

"Very sure. In the same way that it would be a big coincidence if we had another madman on our hands, wouldn't it be as big a coincidence if we had another alien on our hands?"

"I have aliens on the brain these days, but maybe it's not coincidental. Maybe it's connected to Bale."

A deep, rumbling laugh arose in her mind. *Good pun, Shannon. Do I have that right? You have made a joke about having aliens on the brain both because you are thinking so much about aliens, given all that has passed in these last few days, and because I am literally on your brain as well? Funny. Did Luke get the joke?*

Very good. You beat me to that one. A subconscious pun, you might say.

Tell Luke I beat him to the grasping of this pun.

No, I think I won't.

"Roebor says hello, Luke."

Luke waved.

"Roebor, do you have any ideas about what caused this whale's death? An alien?"

Dr. Moon withholds yet more information, but the facts still make Bale's creature the likely suspect.

"What did he say?" Luke asked.

"Roebor said 'no.'"

"He took a long time to say no."

You misrepresent me, Shannon.

"That's Roebor's way."

"Shannon."

Shannon.

Her jaw tightened. "Okay. You want to know what Roebor said? He heard that the dragonpanther we encountered the other day, Bale, also sent a creature from FireWorld to terrorize Earth, and that creature may have killed the right whale. I had hopes of sparing you that jolly news. Now you know."

"What? *Another* alien ate the whale's brain?"

"We're not sure yet. It's our working hypothesis."

"Why didn't you tell me? An alien from FireWorld? A dragonpanther?"

"No, a predator that hunts in the FireWorld sea. Roebor calls it a crocodile-tyrannosaurus rex because of its similar body parts." Shannon watched as Luke's face lost color. "I didn't tell you sooner because I hoped you would never have to find out. One less alien in your personal repertoire. But I was fooling myself. You need to know."

"Of course I need to know! A crocodile-tyrannosaurus?" he said, letting go of her foot.

"You can opt out. Alien business doesn't have to be in your wheelhouse."

Yes, tell Luke to opt out. I would prefer it.

"Were *you* planning to opt out?" Luke asked.

"No, I can't. Since I angered Bale by destroying Tidak, I have to step up and take responsibility for the creature he sent from FireWorld. And these poor right whales are dying off. I won't let a crummy alien come in here and finish the job."

"Has Roebor pressed you to go after this FireWorld monster?"

"No, Roebor can't press me to do anything I don't want to do."

He annoys me, Shannon. Let us opt him out. Get him out of our wheelhouse.

"I need time to absorb this news, so let's talk about something more pleasant, like a shark hunt," Luke said.

"We'll have time to talk about it on the boat tomorrow. I'm too tired tonight if that's okay."

Luke placed her foot back on the couch without disturbing her injuries, rose, and came down to her end of the couch. "Scoot forward and let me slip behind you, cara. You can put your head on this pillow in my lap and fall asleep."

"You do understand why I can't let you sleep here, right? If I get all hot and bothered—which always happens when you sleep over—it would send us all ka-blooey. A glorious way to go, but still."

"I understand. Now, go to sleep."

Shannon awoke an hour later as Luke carried her from the couch to her bed. He deposited her, pulled her quilt to her shoulders, and left without a sound.

* * *

"Right whales are baleen feeders, meaning they sift the water for small zooplankton such as copepods and krill larvae. Unlike some baleen whales, the right whales skim the surface of the water to ingest their food. So, you might think you have an excellent chance of seeing them on the surface when you go out searching for them tomorrow. Am I right?"

Shannon, Luke, and Moon sat in a row watching Dr. Chet Whitechair's PowerPoint presentation, their hands folded neatly on the long wooden table in front of them. Dr. Whitechair was a man of average height, average weight, and bald as a croquet ball, with a small beard that came to a point just below his sharp chin. His head looked like a puffy pyramid with the pointy end down. Shannon couldn't take her gaze off it. *So very triangular.*

He stood, flicking his pencil at her now. She hadn't been paying attention because of the head thing. "Right," she said.

"Wrong," he shouted.

Shannon jumped in her straight-backed wooden chair. She hated being here. Essi's shark could be traveling farther and farther away, and Essi would not be enjoying the ride. *Poor Essi.* But if she wanted Moon's boat, she needed his blessing. And he wanted her here, so here she would stay. *For a while. Within reason. Not much longer.*

"These eastern North Pacific Rights are so rare you'd be lucky to sight them once in your career. I have certainly never seen one, you will never see one, and what you hope to do out here, I don't know, although I do know you will make fools of yourselves. However—"

He paused and glared at Shannon, who glared at him. "My associate, Dr. Moon, has asked me to tell you about the species, and here I am." He returned his attention to his PowerPoint. "People call them black whales. They have a long pectoral fin, although not as long as a humpback's, and an expansive fluke with quite an inverted "v" between the two sides. . . ."

As exhausted as Shannon had felt the night before, she'd only slept about an hour before the sweating, the tossing and turning, the tingling in her legs, and the brain fever started again, driving her from bed. She'd plugged in her laptop and studied the rights for several hours. She didn't need this lecture. Her mind wandered, reaching out to Juneau.

I am so looking forward to seeing you, Juneau. It's been so long.

Her psychic reception in Moon's trailer wasn't the best, but soon the faint rejoinder sounded: *Me too.*

". . . think they sing like the humpbacks? Well, do you, Ms. Kendricks?"

Oh, for Odin's sake. What now? She turned and searched Luke's face, her eyebrows raised in the unspoken question. He gave a slight shake of the head, no.

"I'm guessing no."

"Wrong!" he shouted. "Although it *is* true that the rights don't create songs as the humpbacks do, they *do* create a variety of sounds such as groans, pops, and belches. And who can say those sounds are not songs to them?"

Okay, now he was being petty.

"So, what you're saying is that if we don't see a right, we might still hear their—" Shannon made a pair of air parentheses. "—'songs?'"

He pinched his face, as if unwilling to spit out the next word: "Correct. Now the steam of the right is quite interesting because it makes a distinctive V shape and. . . ."

Shannon's leg throbbed. She shifted in her chair. At this rate, they wouldn't set out in search of Essi until mid-afternoon. Whitechair had started out well enough, showing photos of the known right whales, but the presentation had devolved into a boring, pedantic, and unimpressive lecture too long ago.

". . . . the head accounts for a quarter or more of the whale's body length. . . ."

She stole glance at Moon. He was sketching a nice facsimile of a right whale on his notepad. . . now he was adding some sea gulls. . . .

". . . . rights are the only whales known to have callosities on their heads. And what causes them, Ms. Kendricks?"

"Whale lice, technically cyamids."

"Ah." Whitechair frowned when he could not yell "Wrong!" into her face once more.

Why was he picking on her, anyway? Jealous of her bond with Juneau? Or maybe he thought she hadn't earned the research privileges she enjoyed working with Moon, having no marine biology degree. Whatever the reason, Shannon couldn't bear much more of him.

"Cyamids. Correct. But that is a minor point. Can you tell me—"

That clinched it. But she couldn't lose her temper.

She lurched to her feet. "I'm sorry to interrupt (*not*), Dr. Whitechair, but I'm about to throw up (*not*). It's the pain from my leg. I need the nearest restroom, now!"

Dr. Moon, appearing quite relieved, showed her to the restroom down the hall. She fiddled about in the immaculate powder room that smelled of lavender and antiseptic— smoothed her hair, picked her teeth, checked her bandages. When she thought she'd killed enough time, she exited and found Moon and Luke chatting down the hall. Whitechair had mercifully vanished.

"We have thanked Dr. Whitechair on your behalf, and ours, and released him to his other duties. I should have known you would research the rights on your own, Shannon. My apologies."

"Not a problem. I liked seeing the slides of the known whales."

"Shall we take a quick tour of this site and return to the Dickson cafeteria for an early lunch? Then you may have the afternoon to yourselves."

"We're willing to go up in the helicopter again if you need us. It seems hopeless, though." *Please, Dr. Moon, say you don't need help.*

"I agree that another day of helicopter scanning would be unproductive for you two. Various staff members have gone up with the helicopter pilot with no luck. I had hoped you, with a fresh perspective, might notice something. Dr. Whitechair and his teaching assistant will fly today. But I fear we must pin our hopes on Juneau."

"You all right?" Luke asked Shannon. "When did you have a chance to study the whales?"

"I'm fine. Fabulous now."

Luke winked at her. "Thought as much."

"I woke about an hour after you left last night. Thanks for putting me to bed, by the way. I couldn't sleep, so I hopped on my laptop and researched the whales to pass the time. If Dr. Whitechair didn't finish, I can get you up to speed."

An alarming thought occurred to Shannon. "Dr. Moon, when we go out on the research boat to search for the whale killer, will Dr. Whitechair join us?"

"Of course."

Shannon looked at Luke and crossed her eyes.

* * *

After grabbing a quick lunch, Shannon and Luke hustled down to the eighteen-foot research boat Dr. Moon had allocated to them, wearing drysuits they'd scooped up with Moon's permission from the racks that remained at the old Dickson. Shannon's arm and leg protested the tight fit of her suit, even though she'd chosen one too large for her slender frame in order to accommodate her bandages. The pain left her queasy, despite her heavy protective bandaging.

Luke was right: she *should* be home in Ocean City cuddled under a throw blanket on her couch, but she would never admit it: the stakes were too high.

Moon hadn't found a shark tank—or he claimed he hadn't—but a young, agreeable skipper, D'eriqwa Stove, came with the boat.

When Luke boarded first, D'eriqwa failed to notice that Shannon followed. Luke affected women that way. With his towering frame, thick, unruly black hair, irresistible five o'clock shadow, his soft brown eyes, long, thick eyelashes— he couldn't help it; he left women pining wherever he went.

It irritated Shannon.

I don't see it, personally, Roebor said.

You wouldn't.

Shannon watched as Luke helped D'eriqwa cast off in record time, although she seemed quite capable of managing the boat on her own, and he continued to help her move out into the bay that protected the old Dickson from the worst of the Alaskan winter storms. When D'eriqwa took the helm, Luke made his way to the back where Shannon perched on a heavy barrel stowed behind the wheelhouse.

"How will this work? What if the shark has gone too far for us to reach him?"

"I cast my colors back on shore, and the shark hadn't gone far. I'll cast again when we clear the shallow water. With the power boost I have now, I'll find Essi even if the shark has traveled all the way down to Canada."

"What if something goes wrong with your power again? Are we going to just suffer our losses out here where no one's available to rescue us?"

"Nothing should go wrong. That jerk Blacksilver wouldn't let me go on deck where I would have channeled the power into the open water. Out here, I should have plenty of room to release any excess power threatening us."

Fifteen minutes later, Shannon cast her colors in a sweeping motion around the boat until color stretched away in every direction. She hoped Essi's ride hadn't taken her too far. Shannon wanted her friend out of the shark as soon as possible.

She spread her circular pattern farther and farther outward, and concentrated until all other sounds—the rumble of the boat's motor, the crash of waves against the hull of the boat, even Luke's words—faded away. Soon, she could no longer smell the exhaust fumes from the motor or the tang of the sea. As if she floated above the boat and viewed the circular pattern all at once, she watched it stretch out, seeking shallow and deep, from surface to floor of the ocean.

"Where did you go, Essi, you and your shark?" she murmured.

Ten minutes later, she called out. "*There*. I have her." She turned to Luke, sure her face and voice reflected her surprise. "Essi's not far from here, maybe two miles off to the southeast. The shark's feeding in a school of char, or maybe salmon. It's huge. Might be a Great White. Do they range this far north?"

"I'll ask D'eriqwa. What heading should I give her?"

Shannon blurted out a laugh. "Heck if I know. Let me show you." With Luke's steadying hand gripping her arm, she slid off the barrel and hopped over to the boat rail. She pointed off to the left of their current heading.

"Okay." Luke had to shout above the engine clatter. He passed on the directions to D'eriqwa. The boat changed course.

Turn, turn, yes, just about right.

She nodded at Luke and gave him the OK sign. She would give more precise directions as they approached the shark.

Now, how would she get close to the beast to touch it so Essi could board her mind?

CHAPTER TWENTY-ONE
Shark

THE SHARK STARTED MOVING AGAIN, and it took longer than Shannon had expected for the boat to draw close. Her arm and leg throbbed against the drysuit's rubbery skin by the time she spotted it. Her blistered and banged-up feet chafed in her dry suit booties.

They'd closed the final distance and now approached the shark.

"Essi, can you hear me?"

essi hears shannon. essi ready to leave fish. essi not likes fish. reminds essi of old salty.

"I bet it does." Old Salty, a crocodile, had tangled with them back during the Alien Troubles. None of them had come away with fond feelings for Old Salty. "Similar primitive brains. Are you okay?"

essi okay.

"Have you tried to communicate with the shark? Can you make it understand that all it needs to do is glance off my hand to transfer you, and then it can go on about its business?"

essi tries. fish mind wild. essi afraid of fish. always moving. always hunting.

"Essi's afraid of the shark," Shannon said to Luke.

"You mean it won't come over and poke its head up for a nice rub the way Juneau does?"

"I wouldn't count on it, no."

"Can you communicate with it?"

"I'm as afraid of its primitive brain as Essi is. It's just too different. But I'd better try. I'll send simple images, see if I can get through."

Shannon cast her colors out to where the shark swam on a track parallel to the boat, about thirty yards off their bow.

Found you.

She sent an image of the boat and sensed the shark's vague awareness turn their way. *A good start.* She sent an image of herself: no response; tried an image of herself in the water in her dry suit: still no response.

Try the important one: she sent an image of herself in the water touching the shark's side as the shark brushed past her and swam away. She sent the image again. And again.

The shark turned their way.

"Ask D'eriqwa to stop here."

As the boat came to rest, pitching in the rough sea, Shannon climbed down the back ladder, adjusted her goggles, and slipped into the choppy water. She floated in a harness Luke had rigged up. He let out rope he would use to haul her back if the shark threatened her.

"I'll need to concentrate now, so stay quiet, Roebor."

I shall. But may I say I cannot support this course of action.

"Lack of support noted."

Are you sure I cannot convince you—

"Quiet, now."

The water ran cold against Shannon's drysuit, and fear made her colder. She'd entered the water with a Great White! Her adrenaline was pumping overtime.

"I don't like this. It's crazy," Luke said, leaning over the boat railing. "I'm pulling you out at the first sign of trouble, and you're not going back in, if I have to hogtie you to the bow, Essi or, no Essi."

She continued to send the images over and over: *the shark comes and brushes by her; she touches the shark; the shark moves on past.*

D'eriqwa had come around the stern to stand by Luke. She pointed out to sea. "It's surfaced. It's heading this way."

Essi? You ready to move in a big hurry?

essi ready.

Shannon did her best to send a sense of friendliness to the shark.

She was not the enemy, not the enemy, not the enemy.

"Look at the size of that thing! I'll get fish bait in case we need to distract it," D'eriqwa said, making her way back to the pilothouse.

The Great White's fin moved in a steady straight line above the water, mesmerizing Shannon. It headed toward them as if the waves it cut through provided no resistance at all.

Closer. . . closer. . . .

Then it vanished.

Shannon cast her colors; that way she could sense its location, even when she couldn't see it.

"Where is it?" Luke's voice faltered. "Is it coming?"

Shannon concentrated on the shark.

"No, it veered off. My images confused it. It assumes the images are its own, but they make it uneasy."

Shannon kept sending them anyway. *Shark brushes by, Shannon touches, shark moves on past.*

"I don't think we want an uneasy shark over here, do we?" Luke asked, his hair whipping in a steady easterly wind.

"Just be ready to pull me out." She paused. "Right, here it comes again."

She would need to reach underwater, but when she ducked below the surface, her drysuit—which was too roomy for her slender frame—prevented her from staying down, kept afloat by accidental air pockets. However, the lowest two rungs of the boat's ladder reached below the waves, so she dipped below the surface and stayed down by clinging fast to the lowest rung with her good arm. She peered into the murky water.

The shark raced toward her.

She reached out.

Coming.

Odin's eye. Could she do this?

Before Shannon could react, the shark rushed her.

And veered off at the last second.

So close.

Shannon surfaced.

"Did you grab Essi?"

"No, the shark slipped by me too fast. I'll try again."

She sent the images once more.

Come on. Brush by, that's all you need to do. Brush by.

The fin appeared again, this time off to starboard. It raced toward her.

Was it swimming faster?

She promised herself she would touch it this time, so she let go of the ladder and stuck both her arms out straight and stiff, palms facing away. She concentrated on the images she sent out and the images her colors brought her.

The shark closed in.

As it approached, Shannon knew, *knew from the shark*, it would veer again. It was too uneasy, too agitated.

Shannon had to do something to get to Essi. At the last minute, she pushed off from the ladder and lunged forward, arms reaching, striking the shark.

Essi flowed into her outstretched hands.

She surfaced. She'd drifted about ten feet from the boat. "Got her!"

In the next instant, a chilling truth registered: to the shark, her contact felt like a blow. Shannon *knew* this. And the shark interpreted the blow as an attack. As *danger*.

The Great White surfaced about thirty feet away, swimming in a wide, swift arc, and headed back for her.

"Pull me in," she said, her voice loud and strained. "Now."

She scrambled for the ladder. She wouldn't make it.

The shark approached. She couldn't watch.

As Luke and D'eriqwa hoisted her by her harness, she curled herself into a protective ball, flippers out.

Just as the shark lunged for her, her two companions jerked Shannon toward the deck. The Great White, jaws open, surged three feet out of the water and ripped the rubber flipper from her foot, reopening her shredded blisters and lacerating the back of her ankle.

She screamed.

"It's still right there," D'eriqwa said, pointing, as Shannon tumbled into the back of the boat. Adrenaline, fear, and pain flooded Shannon's system. The power surged and drove Shannon to the boat railing. The shark lifted out of the water to strike again. She lost control and shot a bolt of energy at it. The power struck just as its great jaws opened.

The shark had no chance.

No, no, no. The shark had done nothing wrong, poor thing; none of this was its fault.

The water frothed and turned red with blood. A new wake formed behind the boat from the churning energy, twenty feet deep, with walls of water rising high above the vacuum on both sides. Their boat lifted from the water, pushed by the power, and sailed above the waves like a hydroplane. When it landed, it hit the surface of the sea with enough force to toss its three passengers into the air. They fell back to the deck in a heap.

Unpleasant hunks of shark and fish rained into the boat.

CHAPTER TWENTY-TWO
Baby Beluga

"THAT SHOULD KEEP YOU FROM BLEEDING all over my boat, but you'll need stitches," D'eriqwa said as she finished wrapping Shannon's foot in gauze. "I'm sorry I don't have enough bandaging to re-wrap your arm and leg."

After their short above-boat flight, Shannon had landed on her injured leg. The pain had exploded, and Shannon had passed out. Luke had carried her into the cabin. Her leg still throbbed.

"This is great, thanks," Shannon said. The other dressings could wait.

D'eriqwa hadn't escaped their short airborne flight uninjured. Luke had bound her wrist in an ace bandage and treated a cut below her left eye.

"You sit still," D'eriqwa said to Shannon. "I'll take the helm. Luke will come down in a jiffy. . . Oh, and you've got a gob of something unpleasant in your hair, above your right ear. There's a mirror in the head if you want to take a look."

A strong, fishy odor *had* pestered Shannon since the shark's untimely demise. She hobbled on her crutches to the head and studied her hair.

Ew. She definitely saw a shower in her future.

She used a paper towel to remove as much of the gunk as she could. It wasn't enough.

essi causes shannon so much trouble. but essi worries about shannon and power. essi wants to help.

"I know, Es. And I'm glad you've come. Things have not gone well with Salesti's power, and I wanted to see you one more time before. . . before things get worse."

Shannon made her way back to the table and sat down in one of the four chairs at the small table in the cabin, propping her foot on a pillow on another chair. She closed her eyes and traveled to her Great Room. The light blinded her; she couldn't see Essi or Roebor until the two appeared inches from her face. Roebor had again reduced himself to horse-sized dimensions.

essi sad for roebor. nothing shannon can do to return roebor to fireworld?

"Not now, anyway."

what essi can do to help shannon?

"I can't hold Salesti's power. I need to find a way to release it on Earth, or, if I don't, I'll have to ask Toss to consult the Book of Portals and tell me which one I should take to reach a dead world. The weaker I get with these injuries—and now I have this new one—the less control I have. If I'm injured again or run into a situation that makes me angry or upset, the power will break free, and we'll lose everyone. Do you have any ideas?"

Essi thought about this. *essi knows this much: salesti not gives shannon its power unless it believes shannon can do right thing.*

"But the other salestis don't agree with our Salesti. They think I'll obliterate my solar system."

The Seladoran woman frowned. *other salestis not knows shannon as salesti who dies knows shannon.*

"Then let's think about what our Salesti knew that the other salestis do not," Roebor said, settling down on his belly.

"Aren't you going blind in here?" Shannon asked him.

"Not at all. I have found a quiet room nearby where I can rest in a pleasant light. Recall that my world depends upon two suns, both bright. At the height of summer, the light intensifies. Not as glaring as the light in your Great Room, but at least good preparation for such powerful brightness."

Luke interrupted them as he stepped down into the small square cabin and eyed Shannon's bandaged foot. She turned her consciousness outward. Blood had already seeped through the bandage from the deep slash where the flipper had cut her heel.

Luke hadn't escaped injury either. His jaw had swelled and purpled, and he limped as he walked over to her. "I checked out your heel when we yanked you aboard. Your flipper strap tore your Achilles tendon if I'm not mistaken."

"Unfortunately, I think you're right. The good news is that I'm already on crutches for that foot. However, for the record, it hurts worse than my thigh, and my thigh, what's left of it, hurts like somebody just now tried to saw it off. How's your jaw? Painful, I bet. And you're limping?"

He waved his injuries away. "I'm okay. A couple bruises. Be fine by morning. But I should never have let you go into the water with a shark." He smacked his palm onto the table next to Shannon's chair. "I've hung around you too long. These wacky, life-threatening stunts feel like just another day at the beach with Shannon."

Shannon shrugged. "We had to pick up Essi, no choice. I'm sick about the shark, though. Poor thing. I didn't want to hurt it. This power has a will of its own."

"You and Essi need to have a talk about timing her arrivals better. You hear me in there, Essi?"

essi hears luke. essi crying, essi so sorry.

Do not listen to him, Roebor said, giving Essi a gentle pat with his oversized paw. *I do not like him much. You need not like him either.*

"Luke, I'm a menace now. That shark should never have died. That means my time's up." She updated him on the internal conversation. "Any ideas?"

He pulled out the chair opposite her and sank into it, leaning his elbows on the table and shaking his head. "I've been wracking my brain. There must be a way you can manage this power without detonating yourself. But I don't see what more you can do."

"Let's all keep working on it. We'll brainstorm tonight. Right now, I need to lie down on that cot over there."

* * *

The group didn't brainstorm that evening, as it turned out. Shannon spent the night in the infirmary, as well as the next two nights, under Dr. Kelly Killian's care. Dr. Killian confirmed that Shannon had torn her Achilles tendon and that it would take months to heal. The doctor studied her other injuries. She sat on a stool by a small computer screen, her arms crossed against her chest, her fingers drumming.

"Shannon, I've never encountered a person with the number of serious injuries you have sustained in the two brief periods of time I've known you. I worry about you. One of these days, you won't come back from these death-defying feats. Have you talked to anyone—a professional—about your continual injuries?"

Shannon stopped chewing on the apple Dr. Killian had brought her and stared at the doctor. "You think I have a death wish? Or some sick need to injure myself for attention?"

"Yes, these suspicions have crossed my mind."

Shannon shook her head. "I have my problems, Doctor Kelly Killian—many, many problems—but none of them involve a desire to injure or kill myself. Although I can see why you might think so. Believe me, I wish with all my heart to stay alive and in one piece, although sometimes circumstances conspire against me."

"Well, I hope you're right. But think about seeing someone. In the meantime, the pain killer I've administered will make you drowsy. I recommend you go with the flow and sleep as much as you can tonight."

* * *

Two days later, Shannon awoke in her hospital bed after another fitful night to find that her pain killers had worn off. Her heel radiated pain much worse than the day before. Her thigh also throbbed the worst since she'd regained consciousness after the explosion.

She spent two minutes feeling sorry for herself and then moved on to more important business.

Juneau, have you made it to the old Dickson yet?

Here. Juneau sent the image of her pod of seven, swimming among the remnants of the UnderWater Complex infrastructure that still littered the ocean floor.

Wait for me. I'll make it down to the dock later this morning. Thank you for coming. I can't wait to see you.

Dr. Killian came in to check on her, and three hospital breakfasts followed—Dr. Killian knew all about Shannon's extraordinary metabolism and the caloric intake it required.

Shannon had just finished two candy bars the generous doctor had supplied to supplement her breakfasts and was crumpling the wrappers when Luke and Dr. Moon came to visit.

Moon shook his head. "I shouldn't have let you go shark hunting. Now I have lost you for our whale killer search. We waited for you while the installation of the harpoons in our longboat and the rough weather delayed our departure, but we must go today."

"You haven't lost me, Dr. Moon. You've known me long enough that it should come as no surprise I already asked Dr. Killian to discharge me this morning. Although she isn't happy about it, I can depart with you right away. True, I can't single-handedly chase down any suspects who take off across the tundra, but I'll do my part, promise."

Moon remained doubtful.

As if to prove her point, Shannon added, "Juneau and her pod have arrived, so if you gents will excuse me, I'll throw on my clothes, and we can get underway."

Luke had brought her duffel bag, and soon Shannon was dressed and made her way to the dock on her crutches, where her lovely, white, round-headed beluga waited by the wooden pier. Luke helped Shannon lay flat on her stomach, so her arms hung down from the dock planks. Now she could rub her sweet friend despite her injuries.

Juneau's head rose under Shannon's dangling hands, and Shannon touched the whale for the first time in over a year. Shannon grinned like a fool from the sheer joy of contact with Juneau, her fingers feeling as alive as if a doctor had reattached her hands after she'd spent a year without them.

The whale, too, squeezed shut her small, dark, intelligent eyes as Shannon's gentle fingers traced around them and down to her mouth, where the whale opened up to reveal her widely spaced teeth and thick, pink tongue. As Shannon rubbed Juneau's tongue for her, she whispered, "I've missed you so much."

Another small form popped its head up beside Juneau.

"*Odin's eye*, is this who I think it is?"

The pint-sized figure replicated his mother in miniature, the smooth, rubbery skin, blowhole, and bright eyes. But, where Juneau glistened in her pristine white, with a few yellow cracks where her skin needed to slough, the baby, still young, retained the gray color of a newborn. Over time, he would turn as white as his mother.

Shannon felt Juneau's warmth and love for her calf through her fingertips. The immensity of Juneau's love turned Shannon's heart to melted butter.

"Can I touch him, do you think, Juneau?"

Communication passed between the two whales, but Shannon didn't understand it. She moved her hand with slow deliberation to the water beside Juneau and held it there. The baby floated closer, dipped below the surface, and rose right under Shannon's outstretched palm. Although it seemed impossible, his small, round, rubbery head felt even smoother and softer than his mother's.

Shannon sent her emotions to the baby—her wonder at this new miracle and fondness for Juneau and her new offspring. And—

The young one messaged an emotion back that reverberated with trust, nervousness, and curiosity.

Shannon sent an image of her hand rubbing along the edges of the baby's pectoral fin where it met his body. The baby turned on its side and offered its flipper. Shannon rubbed in all the places she knew Juneau liked best.

Juneau! He's perfect.

She looked back up at Luke and smiled so wide her lips should have split. He winked at her.

Long ago, Juneau had learned to do a bow, where she arched out of the water, much like dolphins do, although it took a powerful start deep beneath the surface to work up the energy for the blubber-coated belugas to achieve it.

"Shall we show your baby how it's done, Juneau?" She imaged the bow to her friend, and she gave the trainer's sign for the bow for the sake of the onlookers who had no idea she communicated with the whale telepathically.

Yes, the whale imaged back and ducked beneath the waves. The calf followed her.

"Watch out there about fifty feet straight in front of me," Shannon called to Luke and Dr. Moon.

She waited.

Juneau broke the surface in a beautiful arc, and, to Shannon's surprise—and *oohs* and *ahhs* from those on the dock—the *calf* arced out of the water right by her side.

The crowd clapped and whistled as Juneau and the baby reappeared below Shannon dockside.

Juneau! That was fantastic. Thank you so much.

Shannon reached out and gave Juneau another good tongue rub, and did the same for the baby.

And thank you, little one. Your timing was perfect.

Behind her, Dr. Moon inched closer. He bent down and reached out, unable to contain himself as he watched this wild baby beluga interacting with Shannon.

The baby splashed at his approach and ducked into the black-green waters, followed by Juneau, who sank from Shannon's hand, leaving coldness and emptiness behind.

* * *

"My sincerest apologies, Shannon," Moon said as Shannon cast the colors to see where Juneau and her pod had gone. "I quite lost control of myself, but you, of all people, recognize how extraordinary it was to see Juneau's wild baby come to you as if you'd trained it all of its life. Which of you prepared the young one for the interaction?"

"That was all Juneau." Shannon grinned. "Was he cute, or what? Did anybody get a picture?"

Now it was Moon's turn to grin. "Better than that—we have video. I will show it to you onboard the *New Moon*."

* * *

Moon and Shannon sat on the dock where the belugas had disappeared. Luke stood behind them, arms folded across his chest, listening as Moon said, "But now, allow me to present my search plan so that you can convey it to Juneau." He handed her a two-page document.

"In stage one, Juneau will alert her pod and as many belugas as possible to the danger to the North Pacific Right Whales—and to all cetaceans, in fact, because we don't know if the creature limits his attacks to the rights. In stage two, she will alert the rights and other whales and dolphins in the Gulf of Alaska to our need for them to find the attacker."

Shannon leveled a hard stare at Moon. He would not face her.

"Dr. Moon, if you know anything else that would help me explain this to Juneau, or would help the cetaceans search, tell me now. We're friends. Please don't hold back on me."

Moon checked whether anyone could overhear him. The research staff and crew who had been standing around had gone ahead to the ship and other boats when the belugas departed. Only Dr. Whitechair stood nearby, watching, it appeared, for the belugas to resurface.

A shadow crossed Moon's face.

"Luke," he said in a near-whisper, "Will you ask Dr. Whitechair to show you aboard the *New Moon* so you can stow your and Shannon's belongings? We shall come in a moment."

Luke nodded and said in a quiet voice, "I'll keep him out of your hair."

Turning to Shannon, Moon said, "It will be impossible for me to prevent many on the research team and crew from guessing the truth about you and Juneau after this voyage—Whitechair in particular. He has nagged me about your connection with Juneau ever since you appeared here, followed in rapid order by your beluga."

"I'm not overly fond of Dr. Whitechair. Can we drop him overboard when we get out into the middle of the gulf?"

Moon allowed himself a subdued laugh. "I did not hear you say that. But back to the problem. I'll never admit the truth of your bond, but rumors will spread. I fear she'll need to return to her northern habitat, or she will attract unwanted attention. It may—" Moon studied his hands "—also be impossible for you to work with cetaceans at the New Dixon for the same reason. That remains an unknown. But you will always be welcome here in any event."

Shannon's eye filled with tears. She'd thought the same thing herself, but it became more real, a harder truth, when Moon spoke the words out loud. Yet, he'd just presented her with her one chance to back out. If she and Luke flew down to Ocean City now, the rumors floating around about the connection between Shannon and Juneau would die down.

But she'd be turning her back on the endangered right whales and the croco-saurus.

She blinked back the tears, nodding at Moon. "Let me get your plan off to Juneau."

"Wait. First, I must confess one more thing Juneau should know." Moon surveyed the expanse of ocean washing in along the shore

A lone gull cried out from above.

"We believe an alien is behind the first attack." He held up his hands as if to stop her from protesting the absurdity of alien involvement.

"The story is classified, and you did not hear it from me. Fishermen first spotted the alien creature off the coast of Canada, three hundred miles south of us. No one believed their story in the beginning, but a U.S. submarine caught sight of the creature not long after. Three days after the creature's arrival, we discovered the whale's carcass on the beach here, and the next day, I sought you out in Ocean City."

"You think it swam all the way up here? What does it look like?"

"It appears to be amphibian with an appendage that is either a natural part of its anatomy or is a device it carries. I believe that the appendage cut through the right whale's skull, allowing it to feast on the brain. I have obtained an artist's rendering of the creature." He pulled a fifteen by eighteen-inch drawing from his briefcase.

Shannon studied the drawing. The creature's color ranged from light blue to black in a camouflage-like pattern. The artist portrayed the coat as slimy, with neither scales nor fur.

Six appendages: two short legs extending from the shoulders, and two longer, thicker legs extending from the hips; yes, much like a tyrannosaurus rex. Midway between those four legs, though, two more legs emerged from its flanks. On one side, a long, thin leg ended in a sharp-edged mass shaped roughly like a curved saw. The final leg, positioned across from the weaponized one, and of a similar length, ended in a hand with seven long fingers, five joints in each finger.

Its small head did resemble a crocodile's, but with a longer, thinner snout and a mouthful of longer, sharper teeth. It had a fluke like a whale's, but paddle-shaped and much larger than any whale's.

"Please tell me they estimated the overall length at a foot and a half?"

Moon shook his head. "Forty to fifty feet."

Odin's eye. It came from FireWorld, right, Roebor?

I'm afraid so.

"Why hasn't the navy sent out half the fleet to search for it?" she asked Moon.

Moon took off his glasses and held them in the light as if searching for spots. The glasses looked clean to Shannon. "That is a more delicate question. Naval and other government vessels do search the waters well south of us off the coast of Canada. They did not expect the creature to travel this far north in three days."

"A hundred miles a day—I don't blame them. But you think it swam here to the Gulf of Alaska? And that massive fluke is what propelled it here so fast?"

He nodded.

"Team members on one of our research boats believe they spotted it the same day the whale washed ashore. Government experts discount their sighting. I do not."

"It surfaced?"

He nodded.

"What are you going to do if you find it?"

"Harpoon it. With whale harpoons."

Thirty minutes later, she'd finished imaging all Moon's information to Juneau and had shown her the drawing.

"We know it has a taste for rights," said Shannon, "So they must keep their distance at all costs, Juneau. But we don't know if it feeds on belugas, so you and your pod shouldn't go anywhere near it either. Long-distance reconnaissance only. Remember, it can cover a lot of ground in a big hurry."

Juneau disappeared, and Moon helped Shannon to her feet to board *the New Moon*.

* * *

Shannon and Luke watched from the observation deck as the Dickson's fleet of fifteen vessels, including *the Moonbeam*, spread out before them, assigned to disperse and monitor the whale callings. She wore her drysuit now, along with two pairs of wool socks on her feet.

"Moon gave me rotten news and more rotten news. Which would you like to hear first?" she asked Luke.

* * *

Shannon recorded each time Juneau sent out whistles, clicks, clacks, and other sounds. The Dickson ships would attempt to record the calls and sounds made by the other whales to coordinate later with Shannon's data. They hoped the whales who heard Juneau's message would also pass along the warning about the alien to yet more whales.

About mid-afternoon, Moon approached her, beaming as if he'd won the lottery, and, knowing him, the news he brought probably gave him greater joy than any money prize could.

"It's working! Our boats have recorded the whales messaging immediately after Juneau's original messages over a broad area. We will have much to study in the days to come."

"But no word on the croco-saurus?"

Moon stopped grinning. "'Croco-saurus.' Very good. I like the nickname. But, nothing yet, although one of our boats did report finding a submerged carcass in our area. A fin whale. Our divers inspected the body. The alien had removed the brain."

"So, the creature isn't picky about what kind of whale he eats."

"It would appear not."

Not good.

Juneau. How far are you from my boat?

Far. Searching.

It's not safe. Bring in your baby.

End search?

You and the baby should come. To protect him. The rest can continue if they want.

Coming.

Shannon settled in to wait for her.

Several hours passed. *The New Moon* pushed farther and farther west.

Are you close now?

Close.

For an hour, the beluga sent no new messages. Then:

Shannon, Juneau imaged, *Whales tell us, the creature swims on your land-side up the coast.*

She conveyed the message to Moon, who conveyed it to the Captain. He changed their heading and swung northeast to intercept.

Continuing to cast her colors, Shannon searched for the alien and tried to pick up Juneau's location. *Nothing yet.* She cast for any other whales or dolphins in the area as well, for they'd all be in danger.

There—a whale way out off the bow. Judging by the shape. . . Yes. That might be a right.

Still no sign of the croco-saurus. More and more anxious, she kept a close eye out for Juneau and monitored their boat's progress toward the right whale.

Yes! Juneau and her calf came into view of her colors at last.

After another half an hour, Shannon spotted the distinctive V-shaped plume of the right whale when it surfaced.

"Right whale," she called to the upper deck. Moon rushed to the railing with Dr. Whitechair at his side. Shannon pointed where she hoped the whale would next surface, a tricky calculation.

And then it sank in: she had glimpsed the rarest whale on earth, an eastern North Pacific Right! Goosebumps prickled up and down her arms.

"Whatever you saw, it's not a right whale, Ms. Kendricks. I've been out on these waters innumerable times. The few rights that exist do not frequent this area," Whitechair said. Moon scanned the horizon with his binoculars.

You cockroach. "Possibly, but the whale killer may have influenced their movements," Shannon said.

"I see the plume!" one of Moon's researchers shouted to Moon, "At two o'clock." Moon spoke to one of the crew members with new instructions for the captain, and the boat turned in a wide arc that would bring the whale into view.

"Another one!" someone called out, pointing to the same area. "Definitely a right."

Shannon watched for the croco-saurus and monitored the progress of Juneau and the baby. They approached the boat now. *Thank Odin.*

Shannon, the whales see the creature coming straight for us, Juneau imaged.

She cast her colors beyond the rights and spotted the croco-saurus far off in the distance.

Loki's luck, it's coming in fast.

"Dr. Moon! The creature is heading this way."

Moon leaned over the upper deck railing to look down on Shannon. She pointed. He ducked away and shouted orders. Crew members readied a long, wide boat to lower over the side of her deck. Two huge harpoons would fire from a device attached to its bow.

"Shannon, go with them," Moon shouted down to her.

Luke grabbed her arm. "Hell no."

Juneau appeared at that moment beneath Shannon's spot on the rail.

Shannon pointed. "Look. Juneau and her calf. I pulled her in to the boat, thinking she'd be safer with us, so I can't let anything happen to her. Or the calf. Or the right whales." She made for the longboat as the crew lowered it over the side.

"Then I'm coming too," Luke said.

A Tlingit tribe member, weathered and silent, climbed down a rope ladder to the longboat and took his position behind the harpoons. Luke followed, and Shannon came down after him, one rung at a time, using her good leg on the ladder while letting her injured leg hang free. Another crew member followed her and made her way to the outboard motor at the rear.

"Let's try to get beyond the rights," Shannon said, "and move between them and the creature."

"I don't see it. Where is it?" The pilot asked.

"Not close enough yet. But it'll be visible soon. I'll tell you when I see it." The pilot cocked her head. Shannon figured she was thinking, *then how do you know it's there?*

They motored at high speed until Shannon called out for the pilot to cut the engine.

One of the right whales surfaced next to the longboat before the motor had died. He was twice the length of the boat. His broad, dark back rolled forward above the waves, splashing them as he released his blowholes with a "poosh," and the air above the two adjoining blow holes created V-shaped mist. Shannon's heart lifted; to be so close to that much gentle beauty and majestic size and power!

"Oh my god," the pilot said. "He came so close I could have touched him. A right! I can't believe it."

The harpooner continued to scan for the creature.

The right whale had distracted Shannon, but now she cast her colors for the alien once again. It had made a slight adjustment to its course. It would pass behind the rights as they traveled south. Would it turn and attack one of them from the rear, or did it intend to go for Juneau and the baby?

Shannon reached out for its mind, giving her thoughts a power boost.

. . . Chaos enveloped her thoughts—the creature shrieked and uttered guttural noises, alien to Shannon in a way Roebor's and Essi's thoughts would never be. Roaring, twisting, attacking urges swept over her, a hundred images at once. But within that hurricane of thought, she caught one brief glimpse of a small gray whale swimming several feet from a bigger white one.

The alien wanted the calf.

Shannon, leave its mind. It will drive you mad; its mind differs too much from yours for comprehension. Roebor's voice rose above the din in her head created by the croco-saurus.

"Shannon! Whatever you're doing, stop it. Your face has turned as white as Juneau's." Luke shook her by her arms.

"It's going for the baby! Turn the boat, turn the boat! Back toward the *New Moon*. We'll catch it coming under us. Beeline for the white beluga by the ship."

As the pilot turned them in an arc back toward the *New Moon,* the creature sped toward their position. Shannon directed the pilot to line up the boat between the alien and the belugas.

Wait. . . wait. . .

"Now, fire now!"

Shannon didn't have much faith the harpooner would aim far enough ahead of the alien for his harpoon to reach the water at the same point as the flashing creature, but he surprised her. He loosed both the harpoons, aiming well in front of the racing croco-saurus and both of the shafts hit the creature.

Yet the alien didn't slow down.

The boat jerked hard, pulled forward by the croco-saurus, throwing both pilot and harpooner overboard. They fled from the alien's path, their drysuits protecting them from the freezing water. Luke and Shannon held fast to the boat edges and managed to stay aboard.

The creature pulled their boat as if the harpoons had never hit it, as easily as a draft horse pulling a plow.

Luke and Shannon gripped the sides of the longboat with white, clenched hands. She couldn't aim her power at the alien; it was too close to Juneau and the calf—and the *New Moon*—to risk it.

Shannon had no choice: she gathered herself and leaped. In normal times, she would have landed mere feet from the boat, but she sprang across the water a hundred feet or more, with a terrible surge of power—straight toward the surfacing creature.

CHAPTER TWENTY-THREE
Alien

SHANNON LANDED ON THE ALIEN'S BACK. Her injured leg bathed her in agony. She slipped down its slimy, mucous-laden back.

Where was something she could grab? *Nothing.*

She scrambled, trying to grasp the skin.

Can't get a grip. . . slipping. . . .

Bristling with white-gold power, she plunged her hands through the creature's skin, ripping a hole in its back. It halted and howled, and the sound pained Shannon. But she needed the handhold, and she needed to divert the alien's attention.

Her revulsion at tearing into the croco-saurus pulled her stomach into knots.

Still, no way would she let it hurt Juneau or her calf. *No way.*

Her actions created the desired effect: the croco-saurus reared above the surface, clawing at its back with its two long legs—arms, more like—and the one with the saw appendage tried to slice her, but it swiped at an angle that missed Shannon by inches. Its other hand, closer to her position, felt around its back, trying to find a body part to grab.

Its arms bent *that* way?

Seven slim fingers found the ankle of her unharmed leg and clasped it like an iron shackle. As it tried to wrench her off, she clung with both hands to the rupture she'd made in the creature's back. A slippery, reddish-brown liquid oozed from the opening. The discharge smelled like the sulphur of the FireWorld seas. Shannon gripped the wound with all her strength as the croco-saurus yanked hard on her leg, but its slimy skin and oozing excretions loosened her hold. Inch by inch, her hands slipped out of the wound. Grimacing, she plunged her hands farther into the creature until she found bone.

The creature roared out its pain, and the slicer came for Shannon again. It had forgotten about Juneau and the baby.

Good.

Now what?

She didn't want to kill the thing, although she might have accomplished that with the wound she'd created. It wasn't the creature's fault that Bale had forced it onto this planet or that it didn't know or care about Earth's endangered species. Still. She couldn't let it kill another whale.

The croco-saurus turned toward the open sea and dove deep, taking Shannon with it. Shannon had no choice but to relinquish her hold and surface, splashing and gasping for air. As if she had not mangled its back, as if it didn't have two harpoons buried deep in its side with a boat attached, it continued to dive until the excess chain from the harpoon ran out, and the bow of the longboat dipped beneath the waves. The boat tipped twice, taking on water, then sank for good. Luke jumped out as the boat disappeared, his orange life jacket bobbing momentarily below the waves before resurfacing.

Shannon cast her colors.

As the croco-saurus came into focus, Shannon gaped when she saw that it was bee-lining for one of the fleeing right whales.

Why wouldn't it quit?

Perhaps it possessed a greater capacity to heal if it consumed food. Why else would it want to eat at a time like this?

Shannon was not unsympathetic. She, too, could use a five-cheese lasagna pan about now.

The rights could move along at about six miles per hour, faster with a brain-eating croco-saurus in pursuit, but they couldn't match its speed—even though it towed a boat along behind it. It would seize one any minute.

Suddenly it ducked away from its relentless hunt.

With her colors, she saw now that he was a male. He churned the water with his two thick back legs to keep him in place while his tiny arm-like legs held taut the chain that attached the harpoons to the boat. His fingered hand clutched the harpoons as the sharp appendage sawed away. He had not forgotten Shannon; he kept glancing her way, although, in the murky waters, he wouldn't be able to see her.

She cast her colors to gauge his emotions. She had pegged him in her thoughts as the villain, and so it surprised her to find nothing but fear, pain, and confusion in his mind. This made sense; the harpoons and Shannon's attack had left him bleeding and broken. On FireWorld he was an apex predator of sea creatures. He had probably never experienced what it was like to have other creatures hunting and hurting him.

Poor thing.

And what would happen to him if Shannon succeeded this time in merely stunning him? An alien in the hands of the military, the object of poking, prodding, drugs, experiments. Dissection. People would see him as an object, as property, as a research subject. He didn't deserve that ending. And she'd injured him, possibly mortally. Shannon had no way to rescue him and send him back to FireWorld. Like a wolf trapped by a bitter rancher, like a mink trapped by a seller of coats, he didn't stand a chance.

In an instant, she decided: she would end his unhappy voyage to Earth in the most decent way she could. With a sorrowful heart, she aimed her power at the croco-saurus and readied herself.

Goodbye, big boy. I'm so sorry for your pain.

She angled her power to the ocean floor and hoped she would send only enough power to end the creature with no extra fuss. But "no extra fuss" wasn't in the cards. Seeing Juneau and the baby in danger, jumping onto the creature's back, suffering its slimy fingers on her ankle, the adrenaline in her system had built to dangerous levels. Her power answered to that over-stimulated hormone, not to her heartfelt intentions. Her time in the water had exhausted her, despite her drysuit. The power took advantage: it surged and sped toward the croco-saurus.

A split-second before a giant cyclone of water rose from the spot where her power met the ocean floor and rebounded, Shannon yelled to the three who'd jumped from the longboat. "Duck!"

A second after the warning left her lips, a whirling tower of water full of fish, longboat pieces, harpoons, broken sections of chain, croco-saurus parts, rocks, kelp, and other bits of flotsam and jetsam soared over two hundred feet in the air before falling, not only onto those in the water but also on the research ship. Shouts from the ship floated over to her despite the sound of the waterfall of debris crashing into the sea all around her.

It was the croco-saurus's massive fluke that drubbed her.

Pedaling in the water, she looked skyward, muttered *Loki's curse,* and had started to swim out of the way, when the heavy, slimy, fleshy fluke knocked her unconscious and pushed her beneath the waves.

She regained consciousness with a jerk. The fluke still held her down. She went with her first instinct—the wrong one—to take a breath of air. She sucked in water, then tried to choke it back out.

She needed oxygen. . . her brain wasn't working right. . . couldn't think. . . needed air. . . .

A powerful arm wrapped around her and pulled her to the surface.

Luke.

But the arm across her waist. . . . .

Blood gushed from a jagged wound even in the cold Arctic water. *it must hurt like hades.* But he didn't let her go.

She surfaced, choking and gasping. She couldn't catch her breath. More water poured into her mouth every time she tried to choke out the water in her throat.

"Look at the sky, cara." Luke pulled her head into his chest, trying to protect her from the slapping of the waves as he swam for the *New Moon*.

Her limbs leaden and frozen, she couldn't swim six inches. He must feel as cold and tired as she did. Yet still he swam. Still he held her above water. *But the blood. He was losing so much blood.*

Steady hands reached for her. A crew member pulled Luke's arm free of her chest and slid a harness around her shoulders. They lifted her up the side of the *New Moon*.

Her face, so wet.

She wiped off saltwater. Her fingers came away red.

Oh. The croco-saurus fluke.

She arrived on the deck, and more hands reached for her, strapping her to a stretcher. "Luke, he's hurt. Someone, please."

"Do not worry, Shannon," said Dr. Moon. "I shall see to Luke personally."

Crew members carried Shannon to the medical bay, where a doctor stitched up the gashes that ran from her cheek to her forehead. "You'll want plastic surgery on that soon. I'm sorry, I'm not a plastic surgeon by a long shot, but this'll hold you until you can see someone." Shannon's vision had doubled; she couldn't read his name tag. "In the meantime, I'll have to change your other dressings and bandaging, so bear with me. It will hurt a bit."

"Where's Luke? Why isn't he here?" Shannon said, panicked now.

"Is Luke the other casualty they pulled from the water? He needed immediate triage on deck. He's still there. He'll be here in a minute."

"What does that mean, immediate triage?"

"Just lie back and let me take care of this leg. Let's get these wet bandages off and see what we've got here. . . Whoa, what are you even doing out on a boat with an injury like this one, Ms. . . . ?"

"Shannon. What kind of immediate triage?"

"And a ruptured Achilles tendon. And. . . ." The doctor glanced at her over his face mask. "I came down to the med bay with you, so I know no more than you do."

"He lost so much blood in the water. I need to make sure he's okay. You can finish me up when I come back, okay?"

"Ms. Kendricks, there's nothing you can do up there but watch. In the meantime, this leg needs attention now, unless you want a major infection that'll put you on your back at a minimum and, at worst, put you underground."

That got Shannon's attention. "An infection could kill me?"

"It could, yes."

Shannon's head was clearing, bit by bit. Dying in a hospital bed without getting rid of the power would not be good: if she died, the power would explode. Her Salesti had made that much clear.

She settled back. "Please finish as quickly as you can. And thank you for helping me. Does anybody have my crutches?"

The unnamed doctor called to an assistant and asked him to look for her crutches. "The other patient? Is he your husband?"

"No, he's my. . . he's my Luke."

* * *

Dr. Throckmorton, according to his tag, had finished attending to Shannon. Her head, her face, arm, leg, and foot all throbbed.

Mother of throbbing Odin. And that made three concussions now. *Not good.*

At last, two crew members carried Luke in on a stretcher and transferred him to the other med bay bed. Luke had lost consciousness. A man in scrubs rushed in alongside the stretcher and gave orders at a rapid pace. Her ears perked up.

"In shock. . . having trouble recovering from hypothermia because of the blood loss. . . needs a transfusion. The ship isn't equipped. . . ."

Dr. Moon entered and received a quick, hushed update from the doctor, his back turned to Shannon.

"At least we might solve one problem," Moon said in a voice loud enough for Shannon to hear.

Bless him.

"We've received a message that my helicopter is inbound, only minutes away now, with two HSD agents on board along with an attorney for Ms. Kendricks." Moon nodded toward Shannon.

Blacksilver and Torra. *Oh, swell.*

"The minute it lands, we will ship Mr. Quintana back to the Dickson Infirmary, where—correct me if I am wrong—we have enough blood to stabilize him, and then, if necessary, we can send him on to the hospital in Juneau."

Dr. Whitechair chose this moment to barge in and confront Shannon.

"You've chased away two of the rarest whales on earth, in the stupidest stunt ever perpetrated by womankind."

Shannon wanted this annoying man to jump overboard.

Be calm. Whitechair can't help being a jerk; that's just who he is.

"I believe that will be all, Dr. Whitechair," Moon said.

"But who knows what we—"

Moon's cold expression chopped Whitechair off mid-sentence.

Shannon's respite was brief, however.

When Whitechair disappeared, Moon approached Shannon's bed.

"What happened out there? What caused the explosion?"

"No idea. I didn't have any explosives. Have you talked to the others? Maybe someone left chemicals on the longboat?"

"Yes and no. Yes, I talked to them—they don't know what happened either—and no, nobody left chemicals on the boat. I oversaw the placement of the harpoons myself. The crew cleared the boat of everything extraneous to improve its speed."

Moon seemed to take Shannon at her word regarding her involvement, *thank Odin.*

"Pity. I should have liked to examine the creature before the federal government reasserted control." He sighed.

Sorry, Dr. Moon.

A helicopter sounded off to the southeast.

"That would be Luke's ticket out of here, Shannon. I shall go to meet them."

"Dr. Moon, wait. I want to go with Luke."

Moon nodded. "You need the attention as well. I will arrange it."

Shannon flopped her head down on her pillow.

CHAPTER TWENTY-FOUR
Blacksilver

"SO, A FEW MORE THINGS HAVE EXPLODED since last we spoke," Shannon said to Tourmaline Kulkarney, explaining why her face looked as if Dr. Frankenstein had visited and why her arm and leg sported fresh bandages. They sat in the bed in the small stateroom Dr. Moon had lent them for Shannon's interview with Blacksilver and Torra, their backs against the bed's headboard, their feet stretched out before them. Shannon had dressed in her baggy sweats from her duffel after the medical officer had finished caring for her. "I happened to be in the water during the last one."

"What things?" Today Tourmaline had dressed for the occasion in nautical-themed blue and white attire—white heels, sleek white sailor pants, and blouse with navy trim. The coat that fell to her ankles today, however, flashed bright orange, as did her magnificent hat sporting five large white plumes. She wore a breezy scent.

"A shark and an alien."

"The shark I know about. That is why the boys felt it necessary to come out here to bully you again. But an alien? Not one of yours, I hope?"

"No, not mine. It had killed endangered whales in the region, so we went after it. We found it, and I blew it to smithereens."

"*You* caused that spectacular water spout we saw on our way out here? Fantastic! Fabulous! I've never seen anything like it." She stopped pacing and threw her curled hand to her chest. "But not at all good for our case, you realize."

"Why do they care about the shark?"

"I believe they care about the explosion, dear girl. And now they have yet another one. I wonder if you shouldn't come clean and take responsibility for the accidents, but assure them there's nothing sinister about it. No foreign government plot, that sort of thing."

"But wouldn't that draw more interest by the government? The last thing I want is the attention of HSD or anyone else."

"Oh, my poor child, I'm quite afraid the ship has sailed on that desire."

A rap on the door interrupted them.

Tourmaline opened the door and admitted Blacksilver and Torra. Shannon rested on the bed, and Tourmaline remained standing. Blacksilver sat in the room's only chair, and Torra stood leaning on the door.

"First things first. Moon informed me that you had plans to evacuate on the helicopter we came in on. We already disabused Moon of that notion. You are going to sit here and talk to me as long as I need you to."

"But—" Shannon began.

"I protest—" Tourmaline began.

"You can save your breath. I told the helicopter pilot that I would arrest him if he flew you anywhere."

Shannon sank back against the bed pillows. *Luke.*

"What happened to your face?" Blacksilver said.

"Cut it when about fifty pounds of alien tale fluke hit me. I got knocked in the head yet again, too, Mr. Blacksilver, so please forgive me if I'm not at my wittiest."

The sound of Moon's helicopter taking off reverberated in the close quarters.

"Wait, that's not *our* helicopter, is it? What's it leaving for?"

"It is my understanding, gentlemen, that the helicopter left to transport an emergency medical patient to the Dickson," Tourmaline said. "It will return in due time."

Blacksilver looked miffed. "We came out here to talk to you about the shark destruction. Another explosion? A few days after a boat explodes with you on it, a shark explodes with you nearby. Don't you think that's rather a strange coincidence?"

And he's back to the strange coincidences.

"Of course, it's strange. And nobody wants it to stop happening more than me. If you could do something about it, that would be great."

"And today, for yet a third time, you find yourself at the epicenter of an explosion, this one destroying government property, mind you. Don't you find *that* rather a strange coincidence?"

"Again, yes. What government property?"

"The alien. From the moment it landed on Earth, it belonged to us. So how did you destroy it?"

Property. From the moment he came to Earth. Poor thing.

"Since you don't believe the truth, maybe you'll believe me when I tell you I have a superpower. I'm like Wonder Woman, except I don't have the lasso and the suit, which tends to the skimpy side for me. The tiara is cool, though. Mr. Torra, do you—"

"Oh, come on, superpowers?"

"I protest. You're badgering my client. Do not mock or belittle her, or there will be consequences."

"Don't you threaten me, you old—" Blacksilver stopped himself.

"Go ahead; say it. Give me a reason to sue Uncle Sam, which would be so pleased to know how its employees break the laws of this county against age discrimination. So, go ahead. Say 'you old biddy' or 'you old battle axe.' That's what you meant, didn't you?"

Shannon sat back and relaxed.

A master at diversion, her Tourmaline.

"I was about to say, 'you old bat,' but you'd never prove it. Who would believe you over Jose and me?"

"Oh, that's right. Silly me, forgetting the matter of evidence. After all, I've only been in litigation for as many years as you've lived. I suppose what I've recorded on this cute little device would have to do." Tourmaline unpinned a brooch she wore on her left coat lapel and studied it on her flat palm. "Marvelous what they can fit a recording device into these days, isn't it?"

Torra went over to take a closer look at the miniature recorder.

"Nifty. SR-75 series?"

"SR-90."

Torra whistled.

"That evidence is for later. Now, where were we?" Tourmaline said, pinning her brooch back on and beaming at Blacksilver.

"I believe Ms. Kendricks here had claimed to be Wonder Woman," Blacksilver said, still smarting over the recording.

"No, I made a comparison, me to her, and was asking Mr. Torra what he thought of Wonder Woman's tiara."

"That's the best you can give us? We come all the way out here to ask you serious questions about the explosions you keep finding yourself in the middle of, and you're telling us it's superpowers?"

Shannon nodded. "'Superpower' is only a word, Mr. Blacksilver. But it's as good as any. I possess a superpower, but it comes whenever it wants. I've no control over it. True statement."

"While you were having your face stitched up—looks creepy, by the way—we talked to the crew. They say you were nowhere near the water geyser when it blew and carried nothing. Do you deny this?"

"No, they are correct on that point."

"So, did you have anything to do with it or not?"

"If you can't accept the superpower, then I deny any involvement."

Blacksilver stood. "We're wasting our time here. We'll go with the crew now to search for evidence. But don't think we're fooled by your nutcase act, Kendricks. We're on to you. You have some way of planting explosives we haven't uncovered yet. But I promise you, we will."

"And I promise you, you won't. There's nothing there. See my leg here? You think I did this to myself on purpose?"

Blacksilver glanced around, everywhere but at her leg. Torra kept his eye on Blacksilver.

"As to the cutter, we think you hid the explosives on you, and it exploded by accident, unlike yesterday and today when you damn well intended to destroy the shark and the alien. We'll keep after it; you can count on it."

Tourmaline Kulkarney stood and stretched to her full six feet and stepped forward, chest-to-chest with Blacksilver. "Shannon has given you a full statement, and you will stop blaming the defenseless victim of a shark attack and an alien attack of imaginary crimes. And she's suffered brain trauma. Out with you. Shoo." She waved them out, stepping on their heels with her stilettos to emphasize the point, and slammed the door behind them.

"They haven't found enough evidence to justify serious action against you, Shannon, but you really must stop blowing things up, or the circumstantial evidence will suffice."

"I don't have control of the power. That's the problem."

"As long as they're content with mere questioning, I'm not too worried. They've been using the tried and true method of bullying to see if they can scare you into a voluntary statement. But if they arrest you or take you in for questioning,

I'll have to bring out the big guns. I've been researching the HSD powers and procedures, and I find them, frankly, frighteningly un-American for the average innocent citizen. Not that you are one, but they don't know that. I have some connections I'm putting to good use, and I have prepared several legal documents to be ready if they move on you. Now," she said. "Let's talk about something more uplifting. Are those rare right whales still in the area?"

* * *

Shannon stayed in Moon's stateroom and tried to nap, but her concern for Luke kept her wide awake.

He had to be okay. It wasn't fair for him to die because of the mess Shannon had managed to create for herself. He'd saved the world by saving her, and no one would ever know.

After staring at the ceiling for an hour, Shannon fetched her crutches and made her way to the deck. The ship now headed due east toward their port at the Old Dickson. She cast her colors for something to do, something to take her mind off Luke. Interesting. . . the rights still traveled in front of the ship on a course that would allow it to cross paths with them once more if they headed northeast. Shannon couldn't work up any enthusiasm.

But then Moon received word that Luke had stabilized at the Old Dickson infirmary. He told Shannon that while she'd been talking to the two HSD agents, he'd arranged a blood drive for Luke. Between the donations of the nurses, doctors, support staff, and construction workers, they didn't have to send him on to the hospital in Juneau. He was resting and recouping.

Thank Odin. Shannon cried pent up tears from a rough day—tears of relief that once more, Luke had saved her sorry kiester without paying the ultimate price for it.

Now she could concentrate on those right whales. One more chance to interact would be an excellent idea. She talked Moon into traveling a few more hours out of the way to search for the right whales that had fled the alien. She directed the boat straight to them and pretended that Juneau led the way.

Tourmaline Kulkarney delighted in the sight of the dark, beleaguered whales. Whitechair insisted they'd seen a record four rights on the same day, although Shannon explained to him with great patience that they had instead seen the same two whales twice.

"Tourmaline," Shannon said as the sun lowered in the western sky above the waves. "Juneau tells me the two rights would be comfortable with me going out on an inflatable to see them. Will you come? Moon too—that goes without saying. And I suppose we must take Whitechair."

"After everything that happened today, you want to go back on the water?"

"To be with the whales? Yes, right back on the water! Once in a lifetime thing."

If only she didn't feel like a coffee bean after a visit to a power grinder.

"Will I have to wear one of those awful looking drysuits?"

"Just a life vest."

"That would simply crush my blouse. I shall be content to watch from here. Your Dr. Moon will lend me his binoculars, will he not?

And so it was that Juneau arranged for Shannon and her party to take the *New Moon's* inflatable out onto a calm sea to visit with the rights, who popped their heads up within four feet of the vessel and allowed Shannon, and then the others, to rub their great heads and smooth sides.

Shannon just wished Luke could have shared the moment with her.

* * *

Later that night, as the ship headed back to shore, a sore and tired Shannon lay on her bunk in the otherwise empty four-bunk cabin assigned to her.

"So with Essi on board and the right whales rescued, we're back to the elephant in the room."

Elephant? Roebor asked.

The big, obvious topic nobody wants to discuss.

I see. In a room, the elephant would be quite large. Good. I am enjoying these strange idioms.

"I'm coming into the Great Room."

The room's oppressive light had grown brighter. Roebor met her at the entrance.

Come. Essi awaits us in our hideaway.

The three settled in a pleasant and cozy room—pale green light filtering in and classical music turned down low—to discuss yet one more time what to do to get rid of Shannon's power without causing a major calamity.

Shannon started. "Salesti knew two things that the other salestis don't know: she knew Earth and she knew me. The answer could lie in one of those two places."

"I agree," said Roebor. "As a matter of note: I have attempted to measure the energy expelled from your power system during the three explosions, and your energy did not decrease much at all."

"Not much?" Shannon said. "*Loki's luck.*"

"I have also continued to explore your mind to see if other potential repositories for the power exist—to spread it out, so to speak, within your brain. I found this endeavor difficult because, in the end, you alone can know your own mind, Shannon. And I will request that you spend time when we have finished talking, after first taking care of yourself, of course, to take a look at your mind's hidden recesses. Still, I doubt we can ease the building power that way."

"Essi? Anything?"

essi studies earth to see if shannon can feed power into water, soil, or air. too dangerous, all. in water, causes worldwide tsunamis. in soil, causes instability all way to center of earth. earthquakes, volcanoes, earth's magnetism lost. in air, burns hole in atmosphere, sun's radiation arrives, hole enlarges, radiation kills life. plus, unknown damage when power continues through space.

"In sum, we can't dissipate the power on Earth and, subject to a last examination by me, we can't spread it out in my brain. What else would Salesti have thought I could do?"

No one spoke.

"We must face the possibility that Salesti erred in her assessment. Another elephant in the room. We must confront it."

no, salesti never wrong. salesti knows. comes from way salestis see. salestis see all time at once. other seladorans see a minor part of time. shannon now sees small bit of time—sees phone about to ring, visitor about to come. sees essi about to come through portal. shannon understands?

"I think so: I can see the 'future' by seeing time, but only an insignificant amount of it, a short way into the future. Salesti saw the future too, and much better, because it saw time all at once, or at least a long way out."

yes.

"So, you deduce that because Salesti saw the future, it must have seen Shannon succeeding in managing the power," Roebor said.

yes.

"Then logically, at some point, we must figure out what Salesti saw."

"But we haven't figured it out yet, and we're running out of time. Today made that even clearer to me than before. If I'm hurt again or lose control of my emotions, the power will win. We're that close to disaster. What if," Shannon said, trying to work out her thoughts, "what if Essi and I start with our ability to see a small amount of time all at once, and try to see more time, try to see me in the future doing whatever I do to contain the power?"

Roebor sighed. "I have never placed myself in the role of naysayer in my entire life, but it is possible what Salesti saw is that you would be wise enough and brave enough to take the power to a dead star in a dead solar system and burn it—and you—away. I do not find it palatable for you to go searching for your future because you might see this terrible outcome."

"Thank you, Roebor, but I'm envisioning that outcome anyway. I understand it's the likely outcome. Let's do this: Essi, work on trying to see more of time than you can now—try to see time for a week, say, as it applies to me. Can you do that?

She paused, and Essi nodded.

"And we have to get you home so Toss can research the Book of Portals to see which of the dead-end planets would work best for me if all else fails."

"And me?" Roebor said.

"Can you double-check Essi's work, trying to think of every possible alternative way to ease this energy into Earth's environment in a way that does no harm but relieves the excess I'm carrying?"

"Normally, you would have an assignment for Luke. Why didn't he come?"

"He cut his arm and lost too much blood, so they air evacuated him to the infirmary. Dr. Moon says he's all right, but I want to see for myself." Thinking of Luke, Shannon struggled to go on, but managed to say, "And I'll do as Roebor suggested; I'll spend some time exploring my mind and where I might spread the power, to see if the answer lies there."

As she stood to hug Essi and Roebor, she said, "One thing I do know for sure—we can't have any more incidents of any type. No sharks, no aliens, no Blacksilver and Torra. Nothing but perfect calm."

Of course, she'd said that before and look how *that* had turned out.

* * *

The *NEW MOON* docked at midnight, and a weary but satisfied group of researchers and crew members made their way to their beds. Shannon arranged a room in the hotel quad for Tourmaline and said good night to Dr. Moon.

"Okay, Essi, let's get you back to RiverWorld to help Toss with his research and to try to see a week out in the life of Shannon. We'll find the portal out on the pier."

Shannon hopped along on her crutches to the end of the pier and cast her colors. The portal, with its white flames, lit the sky. She sent Essi and Toss home, turned, and began making her painful way along the pier on her crutches.

She'd be glad to fall into bed. Every part of her body hurt.

But first—a call to Dr. Kelly Killian to find out when she could see Luke and how he was faring—

What—?

—A great furry paw snatched her from behind.

The fur shone metallic in the moonlight, a deep sable.

The Clan of Bale and Pak.

Others crowded in with her captor, but her view of them disappeared as a giant toe moved into place over her eyes.

Her crutches clattered to the wooden planks of the pier.

CHAPTER TWENTY-FIVE
Kidnapped

DO YOU HAVE ANY IDEA WHAT'S GOING ON, ROEBOR?
No. But the sable fur that blocks our vision belongs to Dortan, Tidak's father, and the grandfather of Bale and Pak. But why. . . Roebor stopped speaking. *Oh, by the gods, how could I have been so distracted—of course they have come. Bale came to your world and disappeared in the same way Tidak had done before him. They have abducted us for an accounting.*

The very thought made Shannon queasy. She feared the gargantuan dragonpanthers and especially the tempestuous Gold Clan. This Dortan who held her now could squish her like a grape if he wanted to, or even if he moved his fingerlike toes too carelessly. And now, fatigue overwhelmed her. Any disruption and the power could seize the chance to break free.

Shannon would have only a few seconds more to stop Dortan and his accomplices with her power before they dragged her through the portal. Her fear, her adrenaline skyrocketed. Her power was building within her; if she wished, she could reduce them to dust, but she must act now.

No—too dangerous. Her fear and her fatigue would ruin them all.

Although she didn't see matters going well for her on FireWorld, she held herself in check and fought the strong urge to stop them, to blast them with her power.

In any event, Dortan had lost his son, Tidak, and his grandson, Bale, and he was playing fair by the rules of his world. She wouldn't be a party to his slaughter—if she could contain the power. She'd find another way to escape.

With Bale, the ship, the shark, even the croco-saurus, she hadn't maintained control over the power; it had controlled her. This time, she would find the strength to stay in charge.

She stopped struggling against Dortan's grip and focused inward, seeking the barricade that restrained the power.

So much power leaked from it now. *So much!*

Back, she said, commanding the power. *Today, I say when you will be released, not you. I say how much power. I say when. Not you.*

The power swirled around her as she stood before the barricade.

Let us out. You want it. Free us, use us, destroy your enemies. Free us, and we will explode for you; we will expand and destroy for you. Let us out.

As if hypnotized, Shannon swayed before the barricade, before the power.

So easy, so simple to let the power explode, to defeat her enemies, to free herself from danger. So simple: free the power and send a bolt of power that would annihilate Dortan and his dragonpanthers. . . so easy. . . .

Her face grew heavy. She couldn't feel her arms, her legs. But she did feel the power. It was as if she were in the grip of a mesmerizing narcotic.

Shannon lifted her hand, a monumental task, brought it to her mouth, and bit down, hard, on the flesh below her thumb, and again. A third time. She drew blood. Pain lanced through her. And the grasp in which the power held her loosened.

Not today. Today I will not let you out.

The power searched for her fear, her adrenaline, her anger. It sought to seize them, use them, channel itself through them. It desired the same destruction it had wrought with Bale, the boat, the shark, the croco-saurus.

But no. Shannon cut off the power. She tamped down her fear. Her adrenaline subsided.

Not today.

The power curled away from her, back under the barricade door, around its edges, into the deep cavern beyond.

Perhaps you can control us today, but you cannot keep us at bay. We will be free.

Shannon sagged in Dortan's grip.

You did it, Shannon! You controlled it. Well done.

We're not out of the woods, though. I don't want to annihilate your world, so help me stay calm here.

While she'd fought the power, Shannon and her captors had passed through the portal and traveled some distance. Dortan thrust Shannon down on the now-familiar smooth, pink-gold tile, and right onto her injured leg and foot. She cried out and rolled in agony. No time for that, though, so she pulled herself to a sitting position and, wary of the power, monitored her condition: disoriented, hot, sweaty, but calm. As calm as a person could be surrounded by mammoth hostile creatures. Stripping off her heavy winter jacket, which had suited her fine out on the waters of the Gulf of Alaska, she felt the cooling breeze of FireWorld upon her skin. *Better.*

"Someone has injured you. Bale? Dortan?"

She peered up into the face of an ancient dragonpanther covered with white fur dotted with a few patches of emerald green.

Faldan, the leader of the Council of Elders. He will be fair and just, but because you come from off-world, he will be no fan of yours. Don't expect pity from him.

How shall I address him?

First of the Elders.

"No, First of the Elders. Neither Bale nor Dortan injured me."

Faldan's fiery eyes sparked. "You know my title?"

"Roebor taught it to me."

Faldan glanced up—a look of shame on his face. She followed his glance and saw the cage that held Roebor's remains. She winced.

They'd brought her to the floor of the arena.

"You may address me as Faldan. How did you come by these injuries?"

"An explosion injured me; the same explosion that—" she cleared her throat and raised her voice "that took Bale's life." *So many lies.* A murmur from higher ground arose behind Shannon. Dortan groaned.

Shannon twisted as she sat on the stone-tiled arena floor and glanced beyond Faldan.

Full house. They had expected her.

She stole a longer look at the metal crate dangling above the fire pit behind her: *something black and charred still in it.* Shannon's stomach flipped.

Odin's eye. I can't do this.

Erase the crate from your mind, Shannon. It matters not at all—not anymore. Try to concentrate. You can do it. And thank you for fighting the power. By fighting the urge to kill Dortan, you honor my people.

It was as if a gentle arm wrapped around her waist, holding her steady, helping her focus.

She owed a show of heart to Roebor; if he could gut his way through his death by fire, she could gut her way through this ordeal. Her face turned back toward Faldan.

"I regret I must bring this news to Bale's grandfather and his brother. Are they here?"

Choose your words with care, Shannon.

"I stand behind you. I am Dortan of the Gold Clan."

At the sound of his voice, Shannon twisted to peer at him from her position on the floor. The heaviness around his eyes spoke his grief.

"Why did he die?" Dortan said.

"I am questioner here, Dortan," Faldan said, his voice commanding and compassionate. "But let the question stand. Earth thing?"

Because of his temper and my power. "Bale came after me, and I hoped to talk to him. But as he landed, a big boat drew close to us. They'd seen Bale and followed him to me. We don't have any creatures like you on Earth, so he caused quite a stir."

"As you do here," Faldan said. Titters emerged from the crowd.

Shannon ignored the comment and the laughter. "But, unrelated to him, a problem on the big boat led to an explosion, injuring me and killing him. Forgive me for saying it, but you'll want to know—the explosion was so powerful it left no remains that I might bring to you. If I could have brought him to you I would have. I'm so sorry it wasn't possible." *That much was true at least.* Gasps rained down from the terraces of the arena.

Dortan roared behind her, and she shivered. "How are we to know she speaks the truth?"

Ask Faldan for permission to speak.

Shannon stared at Faldan and waited. He nodded.

"You can see the results of the explosion." She unwrapped her arm and showed him the thin, straight, angry-red wound that ran from her wrist to her shoulder. "Not thick enough for Bale's claw, would you agree? A smooth-edged tile from the boat, much like these—she pointed at the tile floor beneath her—injured my arm."

"That proves nothing." Dortan shook his head at Faldan as he spoke.

"Do you think that Bale, catching me unaware, as you did, would ever fall by my feeble efforts? Even if I had seen him, do you think I would best him? No." *Yes.*

Dortan sank into silence, contemplating Shannon's words. Faldan also remained quiet as he gazed down on Shannon.

You have done well to refer to Bale's skill and size. Now Dortan cannot continue to accuse you without tainting his son's honor by insisting a puny Earth thing would best him.

Faldan spoke at last. "Dortan, we cannot know for certain what happened to Bale on Earth. But recall that he journeyed there without permission, accepting the risks. And I believe the Earth thing. She has suffered much in the days since she escaped from our containment cell."

Wasn't that the truth.

"The matter of Bale's passing shall be closed. We grieve for you, friend, to have lost son and grandson both, and we rejoice that you have one grandson remaining still."

Shannon heard Dortan let out a great sigh that hitched at the end as if he struggled to hold back his grief. She'd been regarding Faldan as he spoke but turned back to Dortan as Pak stepped to his side and placed a comforting paw upon his back.

"But what of Tidak?" Dortan asked. "The Council ordered her to account for her part in Tidak's terrible death."

I am safe now. No need now to protect me. Disavow any knowledge, or they will not let you leave unpunished, Roebor said.

"Speak, child."

"Bale explained to me how Roebor and Tidak had vowed to cooperate in bringing the virus home, even if it meant the end of my people on Earth. Whatever Roebor's reasoning may have been, he befriended me and saved my life at least twice.

He also extracted the virus without injury to the Seladoran child who carried it, and without infecting a single one of my people."

Shannon, enough.

"And so, this is why I told Bale that Roebor was my friend, and why I came to your world to help him. Whatever happened to Tidak happened in the ocean after Roebor had secured the virus and was waiting for the portal to open and take him home. I could not view it from land." *Or, alternatively, it happened right before my eyes, and I know exactly what happened.*

How easy the half-truths and lies came to her. *Not good.* But her life depended on them today.

"If all you knew of an Earth thing was that he had saved your people and saved you, would you not also come to his aid if he encountered grave trouble? Is that not the honorable thing to do?"

The crowd murmured at these words. But Faldan's stare remained upon her, and this time, his eyes squinted to slits.

"You hide something. It may matter, or it may not, but you have not told us the entire story. What do you withhold?"

The battle between Tidak and me within your mind and your interference with it. Hurry.

"You are a keen observer, Faldan. Something occurred that will be hard for you and your people to understand. My part in that event, I now know—but didn't know then—did not honor the ways of your people." She lowered her head in acknowledgment of that mistake.

"I am telepathic in a way most Earth things are not. I can ferry the consciousness of others into my mind. For various reasons, Roebor and Tidak found themselves in my mind and determined between them to fight to the death. It was a fierce battle."

Shannon risked a glance at the terraces. *She had their attention now.*

"They flew high in aerial combat for much of it, but also grappled on the ground, and I saw how they ripped into each other. Roebor told me their actual bodies, outside in the physical world, would not show the effects of this battle, but if the consciousness of one of them died within my mind, he would truly die.

"I didn't wish death for either of them. So, when I saw how they had injured each other and how close to death they'd come, I interfered with the fight and prevented either of them from winning or dying. They left my mind and reentered their own bodies. Now I understand that both of them would have preferred death to my stopping the fight. For this, I apologize."

"Who would have won?" Dortan asked, eagerness and anger both rippling in his voice.

Roebor, of course. "This, I do not know," Shannon said. "Blood covered them both, and I couldn't tell grave wounds from superficial ones. And, as I mentioned, when they left my mind, no wounds showed on their physical bodies. Each went his own way."

"You ask us to believe Tidak and Roebor fought inside your mind? Nonsense," said a voice from among the assembled listeners.

Invite Faldan in. I shall hide.

"I can prove that much. Do you wish to bear witness, Faldan, by coming into my mind? You will feel no pain. We needn't stay long."

Faldan's head jerked back in surprise. "Me?" He thought about it. "Very well."

Shannon struggled to her feet to come to Faldan.

"Wait!" another among the listeners said. "We can't risk Faldan. Send another."

"Let me go," said Dortan with a growl.

Shannon, no! Do not trust him.

"I'll agree if he takes a vow before Faldan that no harm will come to me."

Hide, Roebor.

"I swear by all my forefathers, by my son Tidak and by my grandson Bale, I will not harm the Earth woman if she takes me to her mind."

"Let it be so," Faldan said.

Shannon stepped to Dortan, sat by his paw, and asked him to lie down beside her. She touched his paw, and her spirit flowed through her, entered him, and met his consciousness. She led him back to her Great Room.

"It is so bright here; I cannot see," he said.

"My power causes this light. I do not wish to use this power on FireWorld. But come, we will go somewhere less blinding. Shrink down to a more reasonable size, and we can leave."

He lifted an eyebrow. "I can shrink?"

"Yes, in here. It doesn't affect your actual body outside."

He scrunched his brow in concentration—replaced by surprise when he shrank to a height that allowed him to meet Shannon eye to eye.

She led him away from her Great Room and into a forest green corridor. "Better? I can show you where I keep my power locked away, if you like."

His mouth remained open as he gazed around, and he nodded without hearing Shannon's words. Shannon led him to the barrier from which her power continued to leak. Four times as much energy escaped it now.

Dortan took one look and said, "I have seen enough. Take me out." He turned from the blazing light.

Shannon turned her back to return to the Great Room to depart.

"Die, killer of Bale, friend of my enemy! If I must die here as a result, let me die," Dortan said.

A terrible pain ripped down her back: the pain of a dragonpanther's razor-sharp claw tearing her flesh.

Before Dortan could finish the job, a deafening roar behind her drew Dortan's attention away. She collapsed to the floor.

Roebor.

He matched Dortan's size.

"Treacherous bastard. Your son wanted to fight me; your grandson wanted to fight me; what about you? Do you wish to fight? For harming her, I shall kill you."

Dortan answered with a roar of his own.

"You live? Here in the Earth thing's mind? Who commits the greater treachery, you or I?"

"I came here to live; you came to kill. You know the answer. Observe—in life, I stood five feet taller than you at the shoulder—I have become equal to you in size to make ours a fair fight."

He pushed himself between Shannon and Dortan.

"Shannon, this time, there shall be no interference. One of us shall die."

"And it shall be you because I fight with the spirits of Tidak and Bale behind me."

Dortan sprang at Roebor, but he had already moved, maneuvering to make his first strike.

And so it started again. They would inflict wounds on each other like the vicious ones Tidak and Roebor had endured. She couldn't bear to watch such bloodshed again.

Her head became woozy, and her legs buckled. She slid down the wall and pressed her back against it to stem the flow of blood from the gash in her back. Dortan and Roebor rolled into the Great Room, still flooded with blinding light.

The pain in her back had stirred the power awake once again.

Let us out, Shannon. Let us out. We will come, we will, we will. End your pain; let us explode in all our glory. Let us out.

Shannon called upon every ounce of her will power and strength. She imagined pulling strength from every cell in her body, from the tips of her toes to her fingertips. She pulled strength from the very wound Dortan had given her and from the screaming wound on her thigh. She dug as deep as she could and gathered all of her strength at the barricade. She pushed back against the door. She pushed back and held. As her strength waned, she called upon her every ounce of will power.

She could do this. She had to.

She could do it for Roebor and all the dragonpanthers who would die if she could not hold.

She held.

The power pushed back.

But she pushed harder. She pushed longer.

At last, the power subsided.

Her head rocked back against the wall. Every fiber of her being ached with weary pain. There would be no more battles like this one. The next time, the power would win.

She struggled to her feet and searched for the fighting dragonpanthers. She couldn't see because of the power's blinding light.

She couldn't do much, but she might do something about the glare.

She staggered to the Great Room and designed a dark, filmy covering, like a dark-tinted plastic wrap, and used her colors to spread it over the upper reaches. The glare faded. The Great Room now reflected the light of a normal day at noon.

Better. At least for now.

But what could she do about the fight?

She studied Dortan as the two flew at each other, not far away. Dortan looked huskier than Roebor, but her friend appeared stronger and superior in the air, both faster and more agile. Although a grandfather, Dortan didn't look or act any older than Roebor. This must have something to do with their long lifespans.

But it hardly mattered who won.

If Roebor won, she'd have to go back to face a world of dragonpanthers with a dead Dortan, and they'd dispatch her in short order. Then, the end of the world.

If Dortan won, against the odds, he'd divulge Roebor's ruse and his own victory. Shannon would still be in the soup for harboring Roebor. She could try to prevent Dortan from leaving her mind, but then the Dortan body would not respond, and she'd have no hope of explaining *that* away.

A lose-lose situation.

The two dragonpanthers crashed to the ground, tight in each other's grasp, rolling, bucking, snapping, clawing, each trying to gain the advantage over the other. She looked over in time to see Roebor sitting atop his foe, ready to use his great jaws on Dortan's neck. But Dortan's front claws found Roebor's eye, and as Roebor roared and pulled away, Dortan rolled him off to the left and took flight.

This would end poorly, nightmarishly poorly. Solar system obliteratingly poorly.

* * *

Their battle raged. Each time the two dragonpanthers came near enough for Shannon to observe them, their wounds and the blood that bathed their bodies increased, while their energy and ferocity decreased.

Someone touched her physical hand in the outside world and shook it.

Uh oh. Dortan had been in her mind too long. His friends grew uneasy.

She returned her attention to the outer world. When her vision returned, she found Pak shaking her still form. Shannon pulled into a sitting position.

Poor Pak. To first lose Tidak, then Bale, and now, probably Dortan. How terrible. She hoped they would permit Jal to comfort him.

"Sorry, everyone, Dortan finds the inner workings of my mind fascinating. He'll return in a minute. But I must go back to facilitate that." She grasped Pak's leg. "I'm sorry about everything, Pak."

She rejoined the raging battle. The two giants now stood toe-to-toe, like two prizefighters in the tenth round, neither able to take the other to the mat. Their paws grasped each other's shoulders, each holding the other's snapping jaws from his neck. Blood and gore covered their bodies, as when Tidak had fought Roebor. She couldn't make out all their injuries, but, as in the last fight, Roebor's opponent appeared to have taken the worst of it by far.

Sick: the sight made her sick—sick to her stomach, sick in her thoughts, and sick in her soul.

To know she could stop it by rendering them both unconscious! But the result would be the same; she would die, and the world would fly apart.

Nothing she could do, nothing at all. So damned helpless.

Shannon pulled her knees to her chest, buried her face in her folded arms, and cried.

A few minutes later, a paw touched her shoulder.

"It is over."

Roebor had assumed the horse size he preferred when he visited with Shannon. She stared past him at Dortan's broken body.

"He's dead?" she asked, her voice quivering.

"Yes."

She stood with weary deliberation. "Let's go get you bandaged. We can't have you bleeding to death in here." Shannon had created a storage locker of first aid supplies the first time injuries had occurred in her mind. She went there now. He limped after her.

"True. But we must see to getting you off this planet alive, so my FireWorld does not perish in a glorious burst of energy.

"I don't see how we can manage that. Any minute they'll notice Dortan has stopped breathing. Then it'll be 'off with her head.' I'd prefer 'off with my head,' now that I think of it, to a slow roast over the fire pit. Can I hope?"

Roebor winced as Shannon bandaged his shoulder. She glanced at him.

"Sorry, I—" *His eyes.* What was it about them?... The blue seemed devoid of flame.

"What's wrong? You're not—"

"No, I will not die. Dortan fought well, but he was never the warrior I am. Or used to be."

"What's wrong? Please tell me. Let me help."

"I see that I have beaten you to the solution to our current dilemma." He waved toward Dortan's body.

"What do we do about him?" Shannon asked.

"The solution lies right in front of you, as it did with Bale. The considerations alone have changed."

Shannon grabbed the fur on his leg. "You mean you're thinking of inhabiting Dortan's body?"

"Yes. This time I have no choice. Your life and the life of this twin solar system depend on it."

"You'd be older."

Roebor shrugged. "With the longevity of dragonpanthers, that matters not."

"You'd have to become Gold Clan."

"I know. Do not try to dissuade me. I can think of no other option. In Dortan's body, I can at least hope to get you off this planet in one piece. If Dortan remains dead, you have no chance at all, of that I can assure you."

"Roebor. . . ."

"Come, let us do it now while my courage holds. Bandage this head wound. The rest, I will manage."

Shannon bandaged Roebor's forehead and one stomach wound that gushed blood.

"Enough. We must hurry."

"What will I do without you?"

He laughed, deep in his chest. "I think you will manage, little one."

She grabbed his magnificent head and hugged it fiercely.

"Ow. I am wounded, puny Earth thing. Go easy on me."

"You can be happy?"

"I can be happy. I will fly! Flying was always the joy of my life. I will have that back. I can endure the rest."

"I'll miss you."

"And I, you." He stood on his rear legs and lifted her into a great bear hug. He held her for a long time. "Now hurry, take me to Dortan's body."

Shannon flowed back to Dortan's body with Roebor and returned to her own without a word. A squeeze of his paw, a kiss on his nose, and she flowed away. She didn't dare delay; she wasn't sure she would leave Roebor if she lingered long enough to truly absorb what it would mean to lose him.

When she looked outward again, a crowd, including Pak and Faldan, had gathered around her and Dortan. The smell of the horse pack accompanied them.

She blinked. "Stand back, everybody, give him room. The experience of coming back into his own body after so long in my brain will disorient him."

The gathered faces inched back, although not far.

"It may take him a few days to recover from what he has experienced, as you might imagine," she added, hoping to give Roebor some breathing room to become Dortan.

Roebor stirred, stood, and shook his russet head, followed by a quiver of his entire body.

Sighs of relief spread around the arena. A few onlookers clapped, a few whistled and cheered.

"What was it like, Dortan?"

"I will have to wait to answer such questions, my friends. My thoughts jumble and whirl in my head right now. I feel as I did after I fought in the Great Challenge all those years ago. It has left me reeling. Forgive me. But I will say now that I shall never be the same." He slanted his eyes at Shannon and winked.

Faldan studied him. "You do seem transformed. Would you recommend that any of us try it?"

Roebor laughed, "No, Faldan. Although I found it fascinating, the way I feel now prompts me to say I wouldn't have risked it if I'd known I would feel so disoriented now. But I will have stories to tell as long as there are ears to listen."

"And what of the Earth thing? Do you believe her account of what happened to Tidak and Bale?"

Roebor's voice grew sad. "I yearn for someone to suffer for Bale's death. Someone should burn for him! Although I wish I might blame her, I cannot. I know her memories now. I understand her well enough. She does not deserve to burn for Bale or Tidak."

Faldan nodded and checked with the other council members behind him. They nodded their assent. "So be it. The Earth thing has answered for Tidak and for Bale, and the Council deems her answers satisfactory. Do you agree, Dortan?"

"I agree."

"Do you agree, Pak?"

"I agree." Shannon searched for him. He stood near Dortan, Jal by his side.

"Do you agree, Pip?"

Heads turned toward a form huddled in the corner of the arena floor with two other females. *Pip.*

"I cannot contest it."

"Then I declare the matter settled. We will permit the Earth thing to return to her world and we will dedicate the day to the mourning of Bale. Come Dortan, let us find you food and let you rest while we make preparations for Bale's rituals." Faldan padded to Roebor and continued on by, expecting Roebor to accompany him.

Roebor gave Shannon a long look. *I have always had much love for you, puny Earth thing. Be well.* He lifted her to her feet with two gentle paws. Taking care with the injury Dortan had ripped into her back, he patted her. Then he whispered, *May the gods go with you,* and he turned and disappeared into the throng that surrounded him.

And with you. I love you. Shannon blinked back tears as she stared after him.

Jal appeared at Shannon's side. "I will accompany you to the portal. I am glad Dortan relented. The lust for revenge has always run strong in the Gold Clan. It has caused much strife on the Island."

"Thanks, Jal." Shannon ducked her head so Jal wouldn't see her tears and added, "Dortan underwent a change during his experience in my mind, I think. I hope so, anyway."

The dragonpanther laughed sadly. "Too much to hope for, I fear, Shannon of Earth. But I shall keep my eye on him for signs of such a miracle."

"Roebor was an exceptional being. I'm glad to have known him. I know the horror of his execution overshadows everything now, but one day, I hope you can be happy. Thanks for befriending me."

"You befriended Roebor on your planet. I befriended you on mine to honor him. Elementary."

"Well, I think he would love you all the more for it. In the meantime, my injured leg can't bear my weight. Can I use your leg for a crutch?"

"I can do better than that." She scooped Shannon into one of her front paws, taking care not to squeeze Shannon's injured leg as she took flight.

They reached the portal area near the boulders where Shannon had first hidden on FireWorld just days ago.

How impossible that seemed.

Jal exhaled a large cone of fire skyward. It revealed the portal, in the same way that casting Shannon's colors would have done.

Who would have thought?

The dragonpanther lifted the paw that held Shannon to boost her to the portal and released her. Shannon tumbled in.

When she disembarked at RiverWorld, Essi and Toss stood ready to greet her—and to treat the vicious wound on her back.

CHAPTER TWENTY-SIX
Reunions

"YOU KNEW I WAS COMING," she said to the Seladorans, still trying to process the loss of Roebor.

of course, shannon. we have news. toss finds perfect dead world for shannon, if shannon needs. also, essi makes progress searching for future of shannon. essi sees shannon cannot return to ocean city until after one more day in alaska. Not more yet, but this much is good, yes?

"Yes, to both of you. Tell me more about the world you've found."

essi talks for toss who still not speaks. nothing but two dead worlds in solar system of dead sun. no solar systems close by, dead world has no atmosphere. temperature frigid.

"So, I arrive, and boom, it's over. Perfect. We'll keep that in our back pocket as a last resort. Show me which portal leads there."

Toss took them to the far end of the portal cave and pointed to a burning window low on the wall.

"Second column in, bottom row. Got it. Keep working on my future, Essi. I'm afraid you must come with me now, though. We can't risk any more shark incidents if you try to come later after you've figured out how I'm going to contain the power—or let it blast."

essi comes. toss comes, too?

"I have plenty of room at the inn right now, so sure."

Essi cocked her head. *where roebor is?*

"Back on FireWorld. I'll tell you the story, but let's get going. Luke and Dr. Moon will be waiting for me."

* * *

Shannon landed on her feet on the pier, exactly where Dortan and his gang had departed from Earth with her in tow. Her bad leg buckled, and she fell with an anguished cry.

This bad-leg-landing business was getting old.

She took stock of her surroundings. It was still dark, but the crutches had disappeared. Shannon didn't know what day it was. She'd lost time, surely, as she had when she went to help Roebor. Luke and Dr. Moon might have left for Ocean City already.

She pushed to her knees and onto her good leg. By the time she limped to her apartment, she'd thrown up once and stopped to cry three times from the pain.

She'd never complain about crutches again.

Her apartment smelled stale and empty as if she'd abandoned it some time ago. Perhaps she'd been gone several days. She opened the back door to let in fresh air. Someone had placed her duffel and her crutches by her bedroom door and stocked her shelves, along with the refrigerator and freezer. *Luke?* Had to be.

She needed to eat. She'd get the food going and then call Luke. Taking a reheated pot roast, steam-bagged vegetables, a package of rolls, and a chocolate cake to the couch one item at a time on one crutch, she blessed Luke for his freezer-stocking wisdom and sat down to call him.

The clock read two a.m. She called anyway.

"Shannon! My god. Where did you go? I've been out of my mind. Are you okay?" A police radio crackled in the background. So, Luke was home in Ocean City, on night shift duty. Recovered from the injury to his arm.

Alive.

Shannon gripped her cell phone in white-knuckled hands and closed her eyes. To hear his deep voice again! She savored it. She wanted him to talk for hours about anything, anything at all, so that she could sit and do nothing but listen to him.

Well, nothing but listen to him and eat.

"I'll tell you all about it but first I need to know what happened after you left the *New Moon* on the helicopter, spewing blood everywhere."

"Oh, that worked out fine. Dr. Moon radioed ahead and arranged for an emergency blood drive. Volunteers from the construction crew and the hospital staff, especially the nurses, and even some townspeople donated blood; so much, they didn't have to airlift me on to Juneau. A night in the hospital, and I was good to go."

"I was so scared for you, Luke. I thought you were going to leave me."

"I'm not going anywhere, cara." His voice caressed her battered spirit. "But speaking of leaving, what happened to you? The infirmary didn't want to release me the next morning, but Dr. Moon couldn't find you, just your crutches out on the pier, so I checked myself out to look for you. Where were you? You're okay? No new injuries?"

"Well, I wouldn't go that far." She adjusted her position to ease the pressure on her ravaged back. She told him about the kidnapping. "How much time has passed since I disappeared?"

"Eleven weeks and three days. I'd almost given up hope." The line went silent.

"I'm back, Luke. Everything will be okay."

"Yes, everything *is* okay now."

"Wait. Did you say *eleven weeks?* That much time leaked from the wormhole? Less than a day has passed for me. That leak's getting worse."

"I'm sorry that I'm not there to help you now. I had to come back to Ocean City to report in, although they've placed me on light duty, but Moon stayed to oversee the project, and as far as I know, he's still there."

"Okay, I'll call him. You're sure you've recovered?"

"I'll be fine now that I know you're safe. They didn't hurt you?"

"Mostly bounced me around some. I did take a cut to my back, but it'll heal. Hey, did you stock in the food here?"

"I did."

"Thanks. I needed it. Nice of you to have it all waiting for me."

"No problem. It was my way of telling myself you would come back, you weren't. . . ."

"They frightened me, that's all. And my bad leg took a few hits. But otherwise, you can sleep easy tonight. I'm sorry you had to go through that."

"As long as you're alive, cara, I'm good."

"How is Narci after all this time? Is she all alone at the house, the poor baby?"

"No, I brought her over here. She's fine. Say hello, Narci."

Shannon heard a soft meow in the background and laughed. "Tell her I'll get home as soon as I can. One other piece of news—Roebor left."

"Left? He's not in your mind anymore? That's great—I mean, where did he go?"

"He fought Tidak's father Dortan to the death in my mind and won, which put me in a touchy spot. The entire Island was standing around, waiting for me to put Dortan back into his own body. So Roebor took over his body."

"He's a dragonpanther on FireWorld again, but in the enemy's body."

"Precisely."

"But he prevented his world from going ka-blooey."

"True. I don't want to, but I'd better end this call so I can get in touch with Moon. I'll let you know when I'm coming down, okay? And thanks again for the groceries. I'd be flat out on the floor without that cake. You sure you're okay?"

"I'm great, cara." Luke clicked off.

She rang Moon. He answered on the fifth ring, sounding eighty percent still asleep.

"Dr. Moon? Sorry to wake you. I wanted you to know I'm back, and I'm okay."

"Shannon! We feared the worst. You disappeared so long ago. Alaska State Troopers held out scant hope they would find you alive. What happened?"

"Kidnapped. By aliens from the same world as the one we hunted here in the Gulf and the one at the site of the coast guard cutter explosion. I owe you an explanation. We'll have tea, and I'll tell you the whole tale. In the meantime, my official line is that kidnappers held me, but I don't know who or why. Okay?"

Moon was quiet for a moment. "Yes, I shall remain mum. I see the delicacy of the situation."

"Are you here on the Project or in Ocean City?"

"By your question, I presume you have returned to the Old Dickson?"

"Yes, I'm in my apartment. I've already called Luke."

"I regret to say I returned to Ocean City three days ago. Several important matters will keep me here for a week or two. Our plane is unavailable tomorrow, but I will send it to bring you home the day after. Will that suffice?"

"That would be great. Much appreciated."

"It is the least I can do, given your help in stopping the alien from killing more whales. I cannot express our indebtedness to you."

"Did the feds give you any trouble over the destruction of the creature?"

"We explained to them in no uncertain terms that we could not avoid its demise because it threatened lives. In the end, they acquiesced. And be sure to remember, per the government, the incident never happened."

"What incident?"

* * *

"So, you foresaw my future, Essi. You told me I'd have to wait a day before going down to Ocean City, and tomorrow's the day I have to wait. Well done. Any luck finding anything else about my future?"

essi not finds anything yet. essi keeps trying.

Shannon slept less than an hour before another power surge awoke her. Her ongoing insomnia increased the odds she'd soon lose her temper and, along with it, lose control of her power, which grew more willful every day. *Face it: She needed to use Toss's fail-safe portal as soon as possible.*

After she had eaten breakfast, she called Tourmaline Kulkarney.

"Darling girl! You're alive. Where have you been?"

"Kidnapped. Aliens. I'll tell you all about it. But first, please tell me our buddies Blacksilver and Torra don't know about my absence."

"I would tell you that, but I don't like to lie—to my clients. I'm quite comfortable prevaricating with opposing counsel, judges, juries, small children, and those to whom I owe money."

"How'd they find out?"

"After their unfruitful discussion with you on the *New Moon,* they hoped to fly right out to California. But their chartered plane didn't fly at night, so they took rooms at the old Dickson hotel, as did I. Thus, we were all still in our pajamas when that charming boy of yours turned the entire old Dickson upside down searching for you in the wee hours of the morning."

Shannon laughed.

"Luke accused Blacksilver and Torra of spiriting you away to Guantanamo for water-boarding. After he finished with us, he tore apart the new Dickson, and thereafter, he moved on search every inch of the town."

"I'm sorry I caused so much trouble."

"Nonsense. I, for one, found him quite thrilling. No wonder you want to keep him."

"So, what do we do about the HSD agents? My official line is that unknown kidnappers took me for unknown reasons and brought me back. What else can I say?"

"Hmm. I believe I just remembered receiving a ransom note and paying off the kidnappers. Thank heaven they released you. How much did we pay out?"

"Let's make it five hundred thousand, and hope nobody checks our bank accounts."

"If anybody asks, I keep that much in my wall safe at home."

"You're good, Tourmaline Kulkarney. I should be home the day after tomorrow. I'll write you a check for that amount to pay you back for 'the ransom money.'"

After finishing her call with Tourmaline, Shannon used her crutches to travel back to the pier to contact Juneau.

Where are you, sweet girl? Have you gone home?

Home.

You and the baby are well?

Well. Happy.

And the rest of the pod?

Also well. You left?

Yes. Captured.

Safe now?

Safe. Thank you for coming to help the whales.

For you, would come.

I love you, Juneau.

Juneau loves Shannon.

Goodbye, beautiful girl.

Goodbye.

Shannon turned to leave the pier when a faint echo followed Juneau's farewell. *Goodbye.*

The baby!

She squeezed closed her eyes. She wouldn't see them again. She stood alone at the end of the pier on her crutches, looking out into the darkness. So many partings. The strong smell of the tar on the posts that supported the pier assaulted her nose and repulsed her, but she didn't move. Now Roebor had entered into a new life that most likely wouldn't bring him to Earth again. Salesti was gone. She would soon lose Luke. The universe seemed cold and empty tonight.

She turned and slowly made her way to bed.

Shannon stayed in her apartment the rest of the next day, reporting her return to the state troopers, speaking to no one else for fear of losing her temper.

Inevitably, her thoughts returned to the power. Did Salesti entrust her with the power because it was confident Shannon would have the nerve to discharge it on a dead planet?

Maybe so.

Death.

Not the first time she'd faced it. It never got any easier. She didn't want to die, whatever Dr. Kelly Killian might think. She and Luke had become close again; she longed to explore life with him. Narci had many good years ahead of her, and Shannon wanted to be the one to enjoy them with her. Essi aged more rapidly than Shannon did; she yearned to enjoy her company as often as possible. Roebor. She wanted to keep track of how he was handling his Dortan identity. Juneau. She would never outgrow her love for the whale or her concern for Juneau's survival in the wild. And a baby beluga she might have watched grow up! And she'd just won a real shot at enjoying Becky's friendship after so long.

She regretted leaving all that behind her.

PART FOUR

IN BETWEEN

CHAPTER TWENTY-SEVEN
Kidnapped Again

MOON'S PLANE PICKED UP SHANNON ON SCHEDULE and deposited her at the Ocean City airport, from which she Ubered home. She'd changed on the plane from her heavy Alaskan wear into her roomy shorts and a tank top.

She never made it to the front door.

Blacksilver and Torra met her at the curb as she paid her uber driver and forced her toward their unmarked car. She struggled as they pushed her along.

"Shannon Kendricks, I am taking you into custody on suspicion of carrying out acts of domestic terrorism," Blacksilver said. His face assumed the look of a smooth mask, but the lilt in his voice betrayed how much he enjoyed this.

Out of nowhere, Shannon's raven flew shrieking, as only a raven can, into Torra's face and clawed his cheek. He let go of Shannon, swiping his arms in the air in a futile attempt to chase the bird away. The bird swooped in for a second time, raking his talons across Torra's shiny, bald head. Shannon twisted and tugged to free herself. No luck: Blacksilver held tight to her other arm.

At the noise, Luke and Gumshoe shot out of the house, as Blacksilver pushed Shannon's head down and into the car, throwing her duffel bag and crutches in on top of her. Torra plunged in right behind her, slamming the door.

The raven fluttered against the window.

Blacksilver gunned the motor and raced from the curb.

"Is that your bird?" Torra asked, taking out a handkerchief and wiping blood off his face and head. "I ought to sue you."

"*You* ought to sue *me*? I think you've got that backwards. We'll see what Tourmaline Kulkarney has to say about it. And you better not have hurt the bird, either." She turned to watch out the back window as Luke reached the curb seconds too late and whipped out his notebook to take down Blacksilver's license plate number. Gumshoe stood in the street barking at their departing car.

She touched the back window with her fingers. *Luke.* She longed to hold him again, to *feel* through her fingers that he was warm and safe and alive.

She turned back to her current tormentors.

Roebor, what do you—

No, Roebor couldn't consult with her now. She was well and truly alone. She missed the big guy.

Stay calm. Stay calm. No adrenaline. Breathe in, two, three, four. Breathe out, two, three, four. Breathe in. Do. Not. Explode. Breathe out. Do. Not. Explode.

"Where are you taking me?"

"To an undisclosed location. A matter of national security."

"This can't be legal. I haven't engaged in any terrorist activities. When can I call my lawyer?"

"We've informed her of your status, not that she can do anything about it," Blacksilver said from the driver's seat.

"What terrorist activities?"

"One: blowing a hole in *USCG Willow* in an unsuccessful attempt to escape custody."

"I wasn't in custody. And I didn't try to escape. I merely sank with the boat."

"Two: engaging in unlawful genetic manipulation to create a bat cat for use against the United States of America."

"What? How did you come up with that? Genetic manipulation?"

"Three: engaging in unlawful genetic mutation of a second creature, which escaped, thereby threatening an endangered species as declared by the United States of America, and destroying the evidence thereof before we could capture—"

"Oh, come on, that's not—"

"And four: leaving the country for purposes of terrorist training from which you have now returned."

"You made that up."

"So, where were you?"

"Kidnappers took me for ransom, which my attorney paid."

"And the so-called kidnappers reconsidered and let you go?"

"Because Kulkarney paid the ransom."

"How much?"

"Five hundred thousand."

"And did the so-called kidnappers happen to operate out of a terrorist training camp in southern Iran?"

"Try not to be ridiculous. And you have no proof to back up that statement. What's really going on?"

"Tell us how you bombed the *Willow*, and we might be able to make the rest of it go away."

"Yes, you could make the rest of it go away because it's all b.s."

Blacksilver drove east out of Ocean City while Torra placed a black bag over Shannon's head.

"Really?"

No one spoke for the next several hours until they jerked to a stop, and someone, probably a guard, asked Blacksilver for identification and gave them permission to continue.

A creeping chill settled over Shannon. Roebor couldn't help her now. Nor Luke, nor even Tourmaline. For so many years, she'd fought for the ability to stand alone, to be completely independent. Now she would sacrifice her damaged leg if any of her friends could be with her to help her through whatever was about to happen. To help her keep her world safe.

She feared they'd throw her into a dark, dank cement cell, with glaring lights and loud, offensive music playing in the background, and they'd drive her mad—

But when Torra whipped off her bag and her eyes adjusted, she was blinking at white-painted cell walls, a door with a small window in it, a neatly made cot, and a divider, behind which a toilet awaited. *Oh.* Calm, clean imprisonment. *So far, so good.*

A fine overlay of body odor did permeate the room, but Shannon didn't mind; she expected to sweat copiously herself. Because of the power.

Blacksilver turned to leave. She said, "I know you've heard this refrain, but I must eat something. Please?"

"We are aware of your needs, and a meal will arrive in a moment. Do you wish to make any further statements at this time?"

"I am incapable of genetic engineering, and I don't know anyone who *is* capable of it. I categorically deny I created or arranged for the creation of either of the two alien creatures that have popped up in recent days. I have engaged in no terrorist activities at any time. I categorically deny I planted or otherwise detonated a bomb anywhere. I have just returned from being kidnapped. At the time of the explosion, I only wanted to get off of the boat for food, of which you had deprived me. How's that for a statement? And I wish to see my lawyer."

"Sorry. She won't get in here, guaranteed."

A knock sounded on the door. It opened from the outside, and a uniformed soldier said, "Sorry to interrupt, but the prisoner's meal has arrived. Also, her lawyer has permission to speak with her while she eats. Alone."

"What? That can't be right. Let me see the order."

Tourmaline Kulkarney sailed in wearing an emerald green dress that reached her ankles, with a matching bolero jacket. Her hat, also emerald green, featured a nest of small, pointed green and black striped feathers. The scent of the day overpowered all within its sphere of influence.

Well chosen, Tourmaline.

Kulkarney dropped a white document into Blacksilver's outstretched hand and pulled Shannon over to the cot.

"Let's sit down, my dear. Are you well? Have they tortured you? Has either of them put their hands where they don't belong? Tell me everything, darling."

Blacksilver finished reading the order, grabbed Torra by the arm, and said, "You won't be here long, Kulkarney. Then she's mine." He slammed the door behind him.

"How did you get in here? Blacksilver seemed so sure they wouldn't let you in."

Tourmaline waved a dismissive hand. "I've been around long enough to know a few important people in important places. In this case, a certain general who was once a handsome private, not unlike your dashing young man. Envision a tall and graceful girl with a feather in her hat, a moonlit night, et cetera, et cetera. We've kept in touch. But let us not dwell."

The uniform who had brought Tourmaline returned, pushing a cart with two shelves laden with food. Tourmaline stopped talking. He pushed the cart to Shannon. "Knock when you finish, ma'am, and I'll come get the cart."

When he had departed, Tourmaline continued. "Here's what I've learned." She lowered her voice and leaned close to Shannon, who had already opened several covered dishes and started consuming the contents. "The government needs an ironclad nondisclosure agreement from you regarding both aliens. They also want to know the cause of the explosion on the ship, and they believe you know something about it because of the other two explosions. I don't believe they care where you disappeared to, but they're willing to hold that over your head until you tell them what you know."

"Can you get me out if I sign the nondisclosure agreement but protest my innocence on the explosions?"

Tourmaline reapplied her lipstick. "As long as they continue to feed you well, let me try. How is the food? Edible?" She swiped her finger through Shannon's mashed potatoes and grimaced. "Instant mashies. I must speak to the general."

"Believe me, when you're as hungry as I am, it matters not at all." Shannon scooped in a large spoonful of the potatoes.

* * *

Two days passed without further word from Tourmaline. Neither Blacksilver nor Torra showed their faces, but her polite young soldier brought in three squares a day, and the feds did provide her with enough to feed three people, which meant it sufficed for Shannon. Barely.

In between meals, she lay on her cot, resting her leg and foot, and wracking her brain for a way to contain her power. She tried fortifying the barrier behind which the power throbbed and pushed, but the power still leaked. She tried erecting extra barriers, fourteen to be exact, but still the power leaked. She tried creating more caverns like the one holding the power, but couldn't devise a way to safely relocate any part of the power to the additional spaces.

Without Roebor, with Essi deep in concentration trying to see into the future, and with Toss voiceless, the halls of her mind echoed, hollow and empty. So, she spent as little time there as she could, except to experiment with any possible ways to distribute the power.

More and more of it leaked out each day.

Sleep still eluded her.

On the third day, Tourmaline returned in palest blue. The one feather on her small pert cap was an enormous ostrich plume.

"I've made considerable progress. They've dropped all references to the aliens and your recent absence, accepting our arguments and proofs. They've conceded they don't care what explosives you might have used to save yourself from the shark or to save that precious baby whale from the alien. But they won't budge on the boat explosion. I have argued until I am chartreuse in the face that you can't confess what you don't know a damn thing about, but they aren't buying it."

She rubbed her throat and paced.

"We need a believable fabrication for a late confession. Let's see. . .You were. . . carrying a small explosive you'd picked up at the new Dickson site. . . You planned to use it to. . . eliminate debris still clogging the area where the UnderWater Complex collapsed, so Juneau could swim there with her baby. . . The explosive happened to be in your run-about when the bat cat crashed into it, and you placed it in your pocket because you abandoned the boat. . . Yes, I see it now. You carried it in your pocket. . . needing food left you agitated, you flicked at it as you demanded something to eat, and you felt it getting hot. . . You begged them to let you go on deck to throw it overboard, but they wouldn't let you, so you dropped it. It tore through the floor, and. . . we can't say why they didn't find traces of it; that's on them."

Tourmaline glanced at Shannon, who stared in naked admiration.

"Yes, you're good, Tourmaline. Give that story a try."

That night, Shannon tossed and turned on her cot. Sweat soaked her shirt and drenched her face and hair. Her skin radiated heat as she suffered through the long hours of darkness.

After her soldier had taken the breakfast dishes away the next morning, she turned inward to visit Essi.

The Great Room, too, had overheated to an alarming degree. Despite the dark covering she'd created, the light had again become so bright she couldn't bear to open her eyes.

She must finish this. Escape, take the portal and move on to the dead world. It was time.

She wanted to contact Luke to tell him goodbye. She cast her colors, juiced by her power, directing them west toward the ocean and searching for Ocean City. . . She cast miles and miles, spreading north and south as she searched to the west. . . *There, Ocean City.* Now, where was Luke?

She found him at home in bed, sound asleep, his schedule reversed because of his night shift.

She whispered his name.

He shot out of bed. "Shannon?"

I've cast my colors to find you. I'm sorry to reach into your mind like this, but I'm out of time. The power will blow any minute now. I haven't the strength to fight it anymore.

He sat down on the edge of the bed, shaking his head to clear his thoughts. "You sure you're out of time?"

Very sure. I'm going to have to break out of this prison and take my portal to RiverWorld. Toss found the perfect place for me to let the power go. So. . . so. . . I love you. I've loved you since the day you found me on the rocks after I first got zapped. I tried not to love you, so you'd stay safe, and now, at least I'll know you will be safe from extraterrestrials. Be happy, Luke.

Before she could withdraw the colors, Luke called out. "Shannon, wait. I'm coming with you. There's nothing here for me without you."

You can't know that.

"The hell I can't. You left me for five years, and again last year. I was a dead man."

Shannon hesitated. She controlled the situation. She could decide for him. The right choice would be for him to live. No doubt about it. If their roles were reversed, he'd want her to live.

But if their roles were reversed, she'd want to make the choice, just as Luke did.

Could she bear to let him come with her, knowing he would die?

Should she deny him the choice? The choice to die for no better reason than because she must die?

No. Luke would not die for her. That was a step too far.

CHAPTER TWENTY-EIGHT
Escape

NO LUKE. I DON'T WANT YOU THERE. I WANT YOU TO LEAVE ME ALONE. She withdrew from his mind and laid back onto her pillow, her eyes and nose burning.

* * *

Shannon lay curled with her knees to her chest on her cot, concentrating on holding back her power and trying to devise a way to escape.

The door burst open. In strode Blacksilver.

"You have the worst timing of anyone I know."

"What's that supposed to mean?"

"I don't feel well; I have a fever. It may be contagious."

"I don't believe you."

"No, of course you don't. Come feel my forehead."

Blacksilver marched over and placed the back of his hand on her forehead.

"You do feel warm, I admit. All right, I'll get right to what I want to say. I'm here to talk about your attorney's last offer."

"Talk to her. You aren't permitted to talk to me."

"You keep forgetting, Ms. Kendricks. The rules of civil law do not apply in terrorist cases."

"Fine. Hold me here forever. Tourmaline told you what really happened, that I was carrying the device from the New Dickson, and I lit it accidentally. Now, if you would leave me alone with my misery—and on your way out, maybe give me something I can upchuck into?"

Blacksilver slammed his fist down on Shannon's table. "Tell me what kind of explosive you detonated on the ship that I didn't see and that left no trace."

"I don't know. I picked it at random from the storeroom at the Dickson. Have you asked them?"

"We have someone inquiring as we speak."

"Good. Then you don't need me. I don't know anything about explosives. Are you going to accept our proposal?"

"I don't know yet."

"Right. Could you leave, then?"

Blacksilver lifted her by the front of her T-shirt.

"Hey—I'm warning you, that isn't wise." The power beat a rhythm in Shannon's temples.

"Do you think your threats mean anything in here?" He shook her. "You've been jerking me around ever since the boat explosion. I'm tired of it." He shook her again.

Hold it in, hold it in. . . be calm. . . .

"Please let me go, Mr. Blacksilver. I haven't intended to jerk you around. You have my word. But some things, I can't explain. Why can't you accept that?"

"Because I know different. And I'm done being Mr. Nice Guy. In here, you're nothing but meat for me to pound."

Really?

As if to prove his point, he shook her a third time, then shoved her head into the wall behind her. It hit with a crack. Lightning spiked in Shannon's vision.

She snapped.

Use it, but control it. Control it.

I want to make a deal, she said to the power. *Don't fight me now, and I will let you out within the next few hours.*

Let us out? Now. Let us out now, now, now.

This is not the place, my home world, but we will travel straight to a different world I don't care about, and you will be free. Don't fight me now, and I won't fight you.

Why? Why today?

I don't want you with me anymore. But I will fight you, and I will win, if you try to free yourselves on my world.

The biggest lie she'd told yet.

A hissing sound arose from behind the barricade.

Had she failed to convince them?

Shannon clenched her fists. If they pressed her, at least she'd go down fighting—

We stay if you let us free today.

Shannon's grip loosened. *Thank Odin.*

With the gentlest pressure she could apply, she touched her fingers to Blacksilver, sending him flying over her table, crashing into the door.

She'd spent some time in custody studying the layout of the facility. By her reckoning, her windowless cell faced the back wall of the building.

Turning, she aimed her power at the outside wall. It blew apart like a wedding cake shot through with a cannonball. She staggered to her feet, grabbed her crutches, and climbed through the debris, pushing aside the larger pieces that blocked her way.

For good measure, she turned and aimed her power back toward the room to push the debris back inside, so the explosion would appear to have come from the outside, blowing inward.

The rubble had buried Blacksilver, but she could hear him scrambling to free himself.

Careful. Just enough to create the deception. She piled a load of light debris above Blacksilver, taking care to leave air holes so he could breathe, and pushed more debris back inside the building. *That should hold him.*

It would take them a few minutes to figure out she'd escaped.

As quickly as she dared, she pushed on her crutches around two corners to the parking lot. No one had come searching for her yet. They must believe the explosion had buried her in the room along with Blacksilver.

The first car she came to, a 2006 Honda SR-V, would do just fine. She smashed the driver's side window, pushed the lock switch, and climbed in. She sent power to the engine; it turned over and started humming. Passing the guard's booth with the broken window rolled down, she waved as she drove by, placing her hand between her face and the guard's view of her. The guard's attention remained riveted on the billowing smoke and dust coming from the far side of the facility.

* * *

The landscape rolling off to either side of the road consisted of sage and dirt.

No place to hide.

She floored the gas pedal and sped down the highway, heading west.

Soon, sirens arose behind her. Her time had run out.

Screaming to a halt, she leaped out of the car, pointed at the road, and pushed her power. The asphalt flew apart with a clap of thunder. Dirt underneath the asphalt spewed into the air, and a hole sixty feet wide and twenty feet deep appeared in its place. Concentrating on an imaginary line extending from the hole, she created a rip in the ground, like a sixty-foot-wide earthquake crevice. It extended both directions as far as she could see.

That should win her a few extra minutes.

Shannon cast her colors in a wide circle into the sky, searching for her portal.

There.

The portal lit the sky about a hundred feet south of her. She returned to the car, drove it off into the brush, and bounced her way over to it.

Five minutes later, a convoy of vans and cars, sirens roaring, arrived at Shannon's barricade. The crevasse stopped them cold. Agents and soldiers poured out of their cars.

After a short consultation, three vans reversed and returned the way they'd come. Perhaps they'd plotted a way to circle around using back roads to approach Shannon from the west side.

What a mess.

She glanced in her rear-view mirror. Her eyes, always large and round, seemed huge now and glowed with white-gold light rather than her usual green.

That couldn't be good.

* * *

Now that she must leave Earth for the last time to demolish herself on a distant world alone, she lingered.

Just another minute.

She shut out the sirens and soldiers. She shut out the dust and the sage. Images flooded her mind. Luke, his warm hands in hers, his face leaning down to brush a kiss against her cheek. Narci, staring at her with those knowing sapphire eyes. Juneau and her baby. The beautiful world that would survive because she was leaving it.

She took a deep breath.

Ready.

The sight of a shiny dot in the distance caught her attention. It rapidly grew into Luke's bright white car, glowing in the morning sun.

He wasn't supposed to be here. He was to be safe. To be alive.

She pulled herself out of the SR-V. She must leave before he reached her.

Luke bounced and scraped his way through the sage and stopped parallel to her car with only a few feet in between them, his car between the agents and Shannon.

She moved around the front of her car toward the portal.

But shots rang out from the clustered vehicles on the road to the east as Luke climbed out his driver's side door. Luke ducked, crawled back through his car, and opened the passenger door. She dove back to her driver's side of the SRV and climbed in.

"Your portal's here?" he asked as he crouched in the space between the vehicles.

"Right above your car. But what are you doing here? How did you know where to come?"

"I called Tourmaline. She's always had a soft spot for me."

"No, absolutely not. You can't come."

"Absolutely yes. I am coming."

Bullets continued to whizz over their heads. Luke ducked back to his car and grabbed binoculars from his front seat. He performed a quick scan.

"How did that crevice get there?"

"The power. Why are they shooting at us?" Shannon asked, her leg once again hurting like the dickens and making her queasy.

"The power did *that?* I don't think they're shooting to hit us. They're trying to keep us pinned until reinforcements come in, either by air or the same way I came."

"Do you see Blacksilver over there anywhere?"

Luke adjusted his lenses and studied the faces in the growing crowd. "Yep. Never say die, that's our Blacksilver."

"Good, as much as I hate the guy, I didn't want to kill him when I knocked down the wall of my cell."

"When you what?"

"He started getting rough with me. He banged my head hard against the wall, and you know how dangerous that was, so I tossed him across the room, knocked out the wall of my cell, and walked away."

Luke stared at her.

"Do you see any pattern to their shooting? Something to give me—and not you—enough of a pause to stand up for a few seconds?"

Luke watched for a minute. As he studied the shooting pattern, the *chop chop* of a helicopter sounded in the distance along with sirens coming in from far off to the west.

"Too late. I have to go now." She touched his arm. "Stay down."

"*We* have to go now." They stood between the cars.

Luke turned to Shannon, a wild look on his face. He wrapped one long, muscular arm around her and pulled her to his chest.

"Let me go, Luke. You can't come. I. . . I want you to live."

"I love you. Will you marry me?"

Despite the desperate mess they were in, she grinned and blushed.

Luke grinned back.

And yet, she didn't answer the question. She tried to pull away.

But she was tired and weak and sick. She was no match for Luke.

"On three," he said. "One. Two. Three." He stepped on the floorboard beneath the car door, bringing Shannon with him, waited a beat for four shots to angle off his front fender, and lifted her high. She pointed her arm in perfect alignment with the portal. It pulled them in.

At the last second, as they passed into the portal, Shannon sent a beam of power down to rip her borrowed car to shreds, destroying Luke's shiny, white car. For a while, perhaps Blacksilver would believe they'd died in the explosion.

"Oh man," said Luke, "I loved that car."

CHAPTER TWENTY-NINE
Solution

AN INSTANT LATER, THEY TUMBLED OUT OF THE PORTAL in a tangle and hit the cave's rock floor. Luke's heavy body landed on top of Shannon, and she cried out.

She looked up at Luke. "I'm never going to speak to you again for pulling this stunt."

They clambered to their feet and took a moment to get their bearings.

Luke checked out the walls of blazing portals. "Surreal. Which is our last exit?"

Shannon refused to point out the portal she'd memorized. "I'd like to say goodbye to the salestis."

Luke lifted his palms, fingers splayed. "As you may have guessed, I'm in no hurry."

Shannon and Luke worked their way toward the Selador River meadow where the salestis lived. Luke held her by her waist, so she needn't put weight on her bad leg. They hadn't yet reached the bend in the River when Magenta buzzed toward them.

"Magenta! I'm so glad to see you. We haven't found a way for me to contain Salesti's power, so I've come back to use a portal to a dead world. I wanted to say goodbye."

The salesti flew close to Shannon's face, studying her white-gold eyes.

yes. power of shannon about to escape. magenta sorry for this. But other salestis fear shannon now. magenta thinks best for shannon to say goodbye from here.

"They won't thank her for what she's doing? That's—" Luke frowned in the direction of the meadow but held his tongue. He and Shannon couldn't see the salestis from where they stood, but they could hear their humming and see their multi-colored auras.

Magenta's tiny kitten face sagged. *salestis sing for shannon, though. listen. these songs for shannon.*

They sat in the tall grass to listen to the songs of the salestis. The songs reminded Shannon of the music that Salesti and Essi used to hum. Their music always lifted her heart. These new songs affected her in the same way.

She would die in a few minutes. Would that last second before jumping into the portal prove a terrifying one, full of regrets and sadness, of hopes unfulfilled? As she listened to the salestis, she smiled and shook her head. *No.* The music felt like Luke to her, as if they sang *him,* and with him in her heart during that last moment, she would be okay. She just needed to find a way to keep him on RiverWorld when she left.

The humming quieted. Luke arose and helped Shannon to her feet.

magenta comes to cave of portals with shannon to say goodbye if shannon allows?

"Excellent."

They had reached the lower steps of the temple when Essi and Toss charged toward them on a brick path from the Seladoran dwellings.

shannon. essi learns something about shannon. important.

Essi gasped for air, still breathless from her run.

"Take a second to catch your breath, Essi."

Essi panted for another beat or two, and said, *essi not see how shannon controls power, but essi sees shannon in future. shannon on earth. shannon sits with narci in lap. shannon talks to lady with big feather on head. shannon has no white in her eyes. so shannon must solve problem. must release power safely.*

"So, you're saying, don't throw myself into the portal to nowhere quite yet?

yes.

"But I must, Essi. Every minute I remain here now that I'm this unstable, I'm endangering RiverWorld, and you and Toss, and Magenta. Or Earth, if I go back."

but. . . .

"Let's sit here on the steps and think it through," Luke said. He thought for a few minutes. "Hey? If Salesti could see the future, so can Magenta, right? Then why can't Magenta tell us what Shannon does to take care of the power?"

All eyes turned to the salesti.

"Did you see me blow up on a dead world, Magenta? Is that why you haven't spoken up?" Shannon asked.

no, no, shannon. magenta not sees that, but magenta not sees anything else shannon does to send away power either. magenta not understands this at all. magenta should see but not sees.

The others continued to look at Magenta.

"Okay then," Shannon said. "Roebor thought Salesti chose me not only because I had some residual power already, but also because she knew something about me the other salestis didn't. Magenta, have you thought of anything Salesti might have known?"

salestis know almost nothing about shannon. magenta learns fun things all the time about shannon. gifts of shannon. friends of shannon. travels of shannon. good heart of shannon.

Shannon rubbed her forehead. They'd gone over and over this ground. She'd love to believe Salesti had known a way for Shannon to dispose of the power and live to tell the tale, but if such a way existed, they'd failed to find it.

"All our actions have brought me here at this time and this place at the critical moment. Let's say that Salesti knew *that* would happen. Say Salesti knew I would offload the power from here. How could I do that safely?"

The group sat without conversation for a while.

"I'm not seeing it," Shannon said.

"Wait a second," Luke said. "A minute ago, Magenta talked about your travels. You know what Salesti knew about your travels? That you lose time in the wormhole. There's a leak. Could that have anything to do with it?"

"Luke! The wormhole! We've been thinking I have only two choices: I must either die on a lonely star to expel the energy or learn to control it. Maybe there's a third option. Magenta, is there any way I can stop at that point in between segments of the universe where the leak is? What if I poured my energy out that hole? Maybe Magenta couldn't see the solution unfold because it happens outside of time and space—in the wormhole."

The tiny creature flew back and forth, buzzing.

magenta knows magenta can stop between portals, can make shannon stop. magenta not knows what happens to energy if shannon pours it out leak.

Luke said, "Roebor would know."

"Right. Back to FireWorld."

The group rose from the steps and hurried to the portal cave.

CHAPTER THIRTY
Consultation

SHANNON LANDED ON FIREWORLD much as she had the first time, except this time, the pain of landing sliced through her body. The suns had set, and a multitude of stars stretched across the sky. She rolled onto her back and stared at them as the pain in her leg subsided.

Not a familiar star among them. No North Star. No constellations. No Jupiter or Mars. No Milky Way.

In the dark, with the wind off the sea of fire carrying the smell of sulphur across her still form, Shannon reached out to Roebor.

"Roebor, are you awake? How are you?"

Shannon! You have returned to FireWorld? Have you gone mad?

"So, you're awake. How are you doing?"

I have fared well since you left. My comrades blame my time in your mind for my oddities and memory lapses. It would not fare well for you if they found you. Why did you come?

"I don't plan to stay long enough for anyone to find me. I want your opinion on a solution for the power problem. I can't control the energy now; I'm in danger of exploding any minute."

You mean to explode here? Roebor asked, his voice unbelieving.

"No. Never. Essi has seen enough of the future to predict that I live and return to Earth, but she can't see how I offload the power. We've hit upon an idea—trying to expel it out the leak in the wormhole the salestis made for me."

Brilliant! Who thought of it?

"A group effort. Magenta—do you remember her?—believes she can stop in between portals, and I can stop with her, but we don't know what will happen if I do expel that amount of energy out the leak. Would I inadvertently destroy a solar system? Would I destroy RiverWorld or Earth?"

Hmm. My answer would be theoretical. We know wormholes exist now, but we do not know much about them. Few use them other than my dragonpanthers and a few salestis. Or that used to be the case until you came along.

"But what's your best guess?"

Not all wormholes behave the same. That said, we know the primary common feature of wormholes is that they traverse ripples or folds in the universe, moving an object from one distant location in the universe to another, a journey which might otherwise take a billion light years of travel. In addition, the wormholes arriving and departing from RiverWorld seem to be quite unlike other wormholes, with unique properties.

"You can't help me?"

I did not say that. My astrophysicists hold that as to the cave of portals and their wormholes, nothing exists in the gap between portals at all except the fifth dimension, upon which energy has no effect. So, if they are correct, you can dispel the energy through the leak and harm no other living worlds or creatures.

"And if they're wrong?"

If the theories are incorrect, or energy spills within the wormhole, the power could damage the portals, destroying the connection between Earth and RiverWorld. That scenario would mean your death. I am sorry, Shannon.

Shannon nodded. *We have a chance with that method, anyway, and no chance otherwise, so unless you would recommend against it, I think I'll roll the dice.*

Take the chance, Shannon.

"Uh-oh. I see dragonpanthers. And I appear to be glowing in the dark, so I'd better get going. Thank you. I hope I can come again sometime. I miss you already."

Goodbye, Shannon. Send me word, if you have a chance, to let me know you have survived. I shall pray to all the gods. And Shannon?

Yes?

I believe in you.

CHAPTER THIRTY-ONE
Power Struggle

SHANNON CATAPULTED OUT OF THE PORTAL and into Luke's arms.

"Nice catch."

"Thought I would try to spare the leg for a change."

"And you did. Okay, kids, listen up: Roebor thinks the odds favor success—no harm to any living worlds. Magenta? We need you for this operation to work, but it's risky. If anything goes wrong, an exploding wormhole could trap us all. Now would be the time to tell us if you have any second thoughts. Take a minute to think about it."

Magenta buzzed and flew in tight circles.

"Toss and Essi, if Magenta agrees to try this, I need you to clear everyone from the portal cave and the temple, including the steps, and stay back at least as far as the huts in the valley, in case the wormhole explodes and damages the portal cave. And also, I need you to come here and give me a huge hug."

Essi hurried into Shannon's open arms and hugged her tight. Thoughts of Essi filled Shannon's mind: Essi as a cherubic young lavender child arriving on Earth to change Shannon's life forever; Essi, shielded behind Shannon when the aliens came for her; Essi, transformed into a beautiful young woman in five of Shannon's years; Essi, emerald eyes sparkling, delivering the prediction that Shannon would survive this day.

At last, Essi stepped back, and Shannon welcomed Toss into her arms. "Thanks for watching over her, Toss." She whispered in his ear. "Toss, can you do me a favor? Luke can't come into that portal with Magenta and me. You must hold him back at the last moment."

Toss, who hadn't spoken a word since he'd returned from captivity in an alien mind, nodded and whispered, *sh-shannon be safe.*

Toss spoke! Shannon's lips parted and tears formed, but she blinked them back. She stepped away from Toss and grinned at him.

"You have one last chance to step out, too, Luke. Provided I don't destroy the portal, if things don't go according to plan, Essi can take you home afterward."

"If you die, I die, whether I'm with you or not. Since I have a choice, I want to be with you."

Her heart crushed inward as if the croco-saurus were squeezing it in his seven-fingered grip.

Magenta had ceased buzzing. *magenta ready.*

"Thank you for this. You're the best."

magenta thinks now-dead salesti knows magenta becomes friend of shannon and magenta helps like other friends help.

"I'm glad to have you as a friend."

"You're glowing as if your insides are on fire," Luke said to Shannon.

"Time to do it."

Shannon stepped to the portal to Ocean City, and Magenta flew over to rest her four tiny paws on Shannon's shoulder.

"Luke!" Toss said, stepping toward him.

Startled to hear Toss speak at all, Luke turned back toward him.

Shannon held up her arm.

Luke realized his mistake and lunged for Shannon's waist.

The portal pulled her in.

* * *

The familiar sense of falling out into Ocean City had always followed right on the heels of a jump into the portal at RiverWorld. This time, her body jerked hard, as if restrained by a seat belt in a fifty-mile-an-hour crash.

The thwarted gravitational pull sucked the air right out of her. She gasped and tried to suck in air, her windpipe rasping. She sucked in again. And again. The third time, her chest loosened, and the air flowed deep into her lungs. *Thank you, Odin.*

She jumped as Luke spoke. "You okay?"

She nodded. "I'm okay. Are you? And how did you get here?"

"Your braid was flying out behind you when you jumped. I grabbed it."

"You're okay?" she asked him.

"Perfect."

"I'm never speaking to you again. You aren't supposed to be here."

Still, Shannon must put her anger aside and concentrate now.

Lacquered black greeted her on every side. She listened—nothing but absolute quiet all around her. Heavy, oppressive quiet.

She examined her fingers: they glowed. In fact, her entire body glowed with white-gold light so strong it shone through her clothes. Even in this inky dark, she could make out Luke's form in the light emanating from her.

"A beacon in the night," Luke said, staring at her glow and backing up an inch or two.

"More like a nuclear bomb. Magenta? You okay?"

magenta fine. but magenta not holds shannon and luke here long. The voice came from Shannon's shoulder. The sudden stop hadn't moved it an inch.

leak here, it said.

"I can't see anything; how will I know where to aim the power?"

magenta guides arm. give it.

Shannon raised her hand to her shoulder, and the diminutive salesti stepped onto it, activating her tiny hummingbird wings. Guided by Magenta's fuzzy paws, Shannon's hand slid forward until it extended as far as it could stretch.

another step, Magenta said.

Shannon peered down past her feet. Nothing but an inky void. Another step could take her over an unseen edge to empty eternity. She took the step.

good. Magenta flew back to Shannon's shoulder.

"Better get it done, Shannon. You're looking like the girl with the x-ray eyes."

In her mind, Shannon inched the barricade open, taking care to keep the escaping light under control. Luke gasped. A beam of white-gold light, a foot in diameter, flowed like molten lava from her fingertips straight out into the void.

The power pushed at her; it pushed hard. It strained to burst through the barricade all at once in every direction like an exploding sun. Shannon pushed back.

Let us out, out, out. . . all at once, free us, free us, free us.

She wrestled the power to where she wanted it, flowing, blazing, in a single beam out into another dimension, escaping time and space forever.

On and on, the power poured out until Shannon's arm wavered. Luke stepped forward, his chest to her back, reached around her, and steadied her arm with both of his. "We'll do it together."

make beam hurry, magenta not holds shannon and luke still much longer.

Shannon opened the barrier wider, beating back the power's desire to escape its constraints, battling its wish to burst from her mind all at once, everywhere, in glorious abandon, killing them all.

It whispered her name. It knew her. *Good, good. . . open, open, open. . . free us and Shannon can sleep. . . sleep. Shannon can sleep.*

Its whisper made her drowsy. She longed to rest. She hadn't slept much for days now. . . so tired. . . .

Yes, Shannon, rest now, sleep now. . . .

"Luke, talk to me, talk about anything. The power wants to put me to sleep so it can erupt. Please, help me stay awake."

She slapped her own cheek and jerked her head to shake the cobwebs free. She opened the gateway several inches more, but still, she didn't surrender to the whispering pleas to let it all go.

Luke's voice, low, gentle, steady as Gibraltar, pulled her attention from the sly clutches of the power back to the beam that flowed from her, and to Luke's two big, square hands on hers, to the glow of her skin, waning now.

Shannon was running out of strength. "I'm not sure I can keep going much longer."

"We can, and we will, for as long as it takes," Luke said.

His words buoyed Shannon. She set her jaw and pushed on.

"Magenta, how much wider can the beam of power be?"

bigger, until shannon hears rip. rip not good.

"Rip not good. No, I imagine not." Sweat poured down her forehead now, into her eyes, her mouth. Her shirt clung to her, and her sweatpants dripped.

She returned her attention to the barricade. The door itself was warping now. Cigarette-sized holes had appeared all over its surface, from which miniature beams of white-gold escaped.

"I'll open the beam wider. Can you listen for the slightest sound of a rip and let me know?"

She slid the barrier wider; the power urged her on.

Open all the way, all the way, all the way.

She moved the door again, another two inches.

Yes, Shannon, yes. More. More!

"Hold it—I hear a crackling hiss. I think it's at full throt-tle," Luke said.

Shannon shut out the whispering of the power and the blinding light radiating from her palm until the steady beat of Luke's heart at her back drowned all other sounds, all other senses.

Hold and listen. Hold, listen. . . .

* * *

"Magenta's at the end of her strength, Shannon. We have to quit."

Shannon glanced at her skin; the glow had disappeared. A tiny amount of power hovered behind the barrier, but it didn't press to escape. The whispering had ceased. The remaining power had mended the holes in the barrier.

"Shall I keep you?" Shannon murmured with cracked lips to the power left behind. "Will you work with me?"

Yes, came the reply.

"The power's gone. Let go, Magenta."

The words had barely escaped her lips when they tumbled onto her picnic table.

* * *

"Well done, Magenta. Salesti would have been proud."

The tiny creature buzzed a tired, contented song.

well done to shannon and luke. magenta only holds shan-non still. luke holds shannon and shannon does hard part.

"Let's just rest here a minute. I feel like Raggedy Anne, only with half her stuffing missing," Shannon said.

And that was the truth. But she had expected to be exhausted. Anything else? Could she tell the power had dissipated? She listened to her body. Yes: the fever that had plagued her for days had lifted; the tingling up and down her legs had quieted. The tension in her shoulders and back that she'd hardly registered had vanished, leaving her feeling luxuriously loose and relaxed. And her mind felt at peace as if a great war had been fought and won.

She took a deep breath. The breeze flowed in from the ocean, carrying its familiar scent, a scent she never thought she'd smell again. And there was the back door of her house in her neighborhood in her town, all so mundane and familiar, yet all so refreshing and wonderful, because she was alive and she'd returned. And Luke was here and—where was her Narci? She'd expected the cat to beat them to the picnic table since Narci could sense when they were coming through the portal.

She called the cat's name and waited. Nothing. Narci wasn't here.

"I wonder where she is," Shannon said.

"Depends on how long we've been gone in Earth time."

magenta goes home now.

"Wait, Magenta. What can I do to thank you for helping us? Without you, we could never have used the wormhole leak to get rid of the power. I would have exploded in a grand finale on a dead planet. Do you need anything? Want anything? If it's within my power, I'll get it for you. Or do it for you. Or be it for you. You name it.

Magenta's tinkling laugh danced into the clouds. *salestis need nothing. salestis ask nothing. not salestis' way. and shannon saves riverworld. is special gift to magenta because other salestis not kind to shannon. salestis, who fear nothing, fear power of shannon, and yet shannon not destroys salestis. this is gift for magenta.*

"That's not much of a gift. I would never hurt the salestis, let alone destroy them."

because of who shannon is. shannon is gift enough. now, point up, let magenta fly home.

Shannon, too tired even to cast her colors, lifted her arm and pointed skyward to the point the portal should be. Salesti flowed down from Shannon's mind, through her body to her arm and back up to her fingertips. In the next instant, she was gone.

Shannon reported their conversation to Luke, who'd heard Shannon's half.

"You're the gift. Very poetic. Strange little creatures, aren't they?"

"Strange and mysterious and wonderful. I think I have enough energy to make it to the kitchen. I'm hungry. How about you?"

"I could eat," he said. "A whole cow."

Luke found Shannon's extra pair of crutches and helped her disentangle herself from the picnic table. To Shannon's surprise, the backdoor was locked. But she kept a spare key under the fourth decorative stone from the left along her back fence, and in a matter of minutes, they had entered a kitchen that smelled very much abandoned.

"We need to find out how much time passed. Let me find my laptop. It was June 27th when we left, right?"

Luke had gone straight to the cupboards to start a meal going. He called out to the living room where Shannon had headed to retrieve her laptop. "That's right."

"*Odin's eye.* Luke, you won't believe this."

He walked out from the kitchen, holding a can of tuna in one hand and an open beer in the other. "What?"

"It's May 16th. We lost almost a whole year in less than a day."

CHAPTER THIRTY-TWO
Fabrications

"LET ME RECAP," Luke said. "I've been away from work eleven months, and I can't explain my absence. So I'm toast. The world thinks we died in the car explosion, and our funerals were splendid affairs." He took another gulp of his beer. "My dog is a year old and won't remember my face."

Shannon nodded, finishing the last graham cracker in the box she'd eaten for dessert, and tapping the laptop screen, which displayed a beautiful photograph of Luke's large extended family gathered around a gravesite.

Luke continued, crushing his empty beer can and tossing it into the trash, "And I can't explain to friends, family, or feds how it could possibly be that I *didn't* die in said car explosion or how I could possibly have escaped all the law enforcement there that day."

Shannon flipped the computer window to another tab, showing the fiery remains of Shannon's stolen car and Luke's burned and broken vehicle. Dozens of army regulars, state troopers, county deputies, and plain-clothed men in black stood around the wreckage.

"Now, you, on the other hand, don't face such a rosy picture. You must answer for not only your disappearance but also for your escape from a federal detention facility by spectacular—and again mysterious—means. And after you try to explain that away, you still have to answer for the ship explosion they hauled you in for in the first place."

"Worst of all, we have no idea where Narci and Gumshoe are," Shannon said.

"Yes, and that."

"I vote we call Tourmaline Kulkarney right now."

"Do it."

Shannon dialed. Kulkarney answered.

"Brace yourself, Tourmaline."

"I have braced. You are?"

"It's me, Shannon. Back from the dead."

Tourmaline's voice turned frigid. "You either have a revolting sense of humor, or I have a hotline to heaven, which I doubt, although I can imagine receiving a few calls from the other realm. What do you want?"

"Luke's here too, and we'd like for you to come over as soon as you're free."

"Prove you are who you say you are. Tell me something no one but Shannon would know."

"Easy peasy. You came along with me to visit Roebor in my mind."

Shannon held the phone away to protect her ear from a shrill scream.

"No details over the phone. I have an appointment in about fifteen minutes, but I'll be right over afterward—to your house, right? Leave your gate unlatched, and I'll come in the back. I must hear everything. Oh, and I shall bring your darling kitten when I come. I shall miss her, you know."

"You kept Narci for me? Thank you so much!"

"It was my pleasure. She's a little darling. But I must say, I occasionally had the strangest feeling that she knew exactly what I was thinking."

Shannon laughed with a little hiccup at the end.

Shannon clicked off. "Who'd have thought? Tourmaline and Narci. I'd also like to call Moon. I trust him."

"Okay, but warn him that until we figure out how to deal with the authorities, he can't let word get out."

She dialed. "Dr. Moon? I have pleasant news for you, I think."

"If I didn't know it was impossible, I would say I recognize this voice."

"And the impossible becomes the merely improbable because this is Shannon Kendricks."

"But how? Over twenty law enforcement officers saw you die."

"Very long story. Which someone who has seen aliens and knows that telepathy is a thing might believe. We have to deal with the HSD people and others, so you can't tell anyone we're back yet. But we'll talk more, okay?"

"I look forward to it. I believe I will go fix a pot of tea. Good day, Shannon. You have given an old man excellent news, indeed."

She clicked off and turned to Luke. "What about your parents?"

"I want to go break the news to them in person. Now, if that's okay."

"Go right away. I don't want them to go an extra minute thinking you're dead. Take my car. If it runs."

"Safer to catch an uber ride. I'll go down the block to call it. I'd like to stay here tonight. We don't want anyone to see us yet."

"Good idea. It's weird how they left everything here just as it was when I left. I'm surprised they haven't sold the house and given all my things to Goodwill."

"With your gambling proceeds and Roebor's gems, your estate is huge. My guess is that it's sitting in probate."

"What a mess."

* * *

"So, the truth is out as a defense. We must concoct a different, more ridiculous story that fits the facts and that they will believe." Tourmaline paced the floor of Shannon's living room. Dressed in flowing silver, a turban on her head with a thin, three-foot-long feather trailing, she hadn't said much more since arriving an hour ago.

She had freed Narci from her cat carrier, and Shannon's blue-eyed baby had remained nestled into Shannon's side ever since.

Today had been a tough one for Shannon's injured thigh. It throbbed and ached, and sharp pains shot down toward her knee. She shifted once again to try to find a comfortable position for it. She'd better get serious about her treatments.

Tourmaline had listened with fascination to Shannon's tale, stopping her to curse at Blacksilver's heavy-handed tactics. "Wait until I'm finished with him. He'll wish he'd stayed buried in the rubble."

Now, however, she'd moved on to the question of how to dig Shannon and Luke out of the unfortunate hole in which they found themselves.

Luke had come back from his parents with sixty pounds of energetic Gumshoe in tow. It turned out the vet (yes, *that* vet) had taken in Gumshoe, then released the dog to Luke's parents at their request. They'd wanted something to remember him by. "He recognized me right away," Luke said, a wide grin on his face.

Gumshoe sat at Luke's feet, chewing on the toe of his boot.

"First, we must tell them how you got away. I don't suppose either of you can fly?"

They shook their heads.

"Turn invisible?

"Shrink?

"Induce mass hypnotism?

"We've played our abduction card already; it might be too soon to try that one again." Tourmaline tapped her long, silver nails on the wall as she paused. "But we'll keep it in reserve."

She walked a few more paces. "A variation on that theme might do, however. Some government organization, very hush-hush, top-secret, black op, and all that, took you for questioning about the aliens.

"We admit you were familiar with the dragonpanthers, which is why the super-secret organization nabbed you, because. . . because. . . ."

"Because I found Bale as a baby and raised him in my unfinished basement until he grew too large, and that's when I meant to turn him loose, but he panicked and died?"

"Not bad, not bad. It needs tweaking, but I can work with it."

"But wouldn't this organization have stolen Bale's body?" Luke asked.

"Spoilsport." Tourmaline shook her silver-gloved fist at him.

"They couldn't reveal themselves, so they had to let the body go, which is why they needed us to tell them everything about Bale," Shannon said.

"Thin, but acceptable."

"So, in they swept under the cover of the explosion, they set off and spirited you away in a car? Jet? Hot-air balloon?"

"In a helicopter that flew us out inside the earthquake crevasse Shannon made," Luke said.

"Except Shannon didn't make the crevasse, the secret government agency made it, so their helicopter could rescue you at the same time as it prevented the feds from reaching you."

"Do we know if they have video footage of the incident?" Luke asked.

"If they do, and if it doesn't show what we say it should show, why, the secret agency doctored it," Tourmaline said. "Obviously. All right. I'm satisfied the secret agency whisked you away. Now, why did they keep you so long, and why have they released you unharmed now?"

"Punishment for not revealing the alien?"

"Possibly, possibly."

"They had a baby, too, and they wanted to see if I could establish contact with it? They kept us there all this time, but the baby died, and so they let us go?"

"What if it's not a U.S. agency but Russian?" Luke asked.

"And now we're afraid for our lives, so we're asking Blacksilver for protection?"

"Are you kidding? He wouldn't give us the time of day."

"Precisely," Shannon said.

"Concentrate, darlings. We now have your means of escaping the amassed law enforcement at your disappearance site, and the explanation for your lengthy absence. What about the minor issue of the explosion in your cell? And, if they're still harping on it, the ship explosion?"

"The agency was trying to snatch me before Blacksilver could, hence the vessel explosion, but I surprised them by taking off for Alaska, so they had to wait. And as soon as I got back, Blacksilver snatched me first, so they had to break me out."

"Why didn't they grab you when you got out?"

"The. . . operative charged in to finish off Blacksilver, per his orders, but when rescuers arrived, he had to pretend he was part of the rescue forces until he could slip away?"

Tourmaline continued to pace, nodding to herself, mumbling something now and then, until she stopped, at last, towering over Shannon and Luke, who sat together on the couch, hands clasped.

"I'll be back first thing in the morning with your scripts. Memorize them, then burn them or eat them. Do not leave them around for snooping eyes. I know someone who knows someone in an off-the-books government organization. I'll have a fact or two to legitimize your claims. Get a good night's sleep. We go live in two days."

CHAPTER THIRTY-THREE
Resolution

"HELLO, I'D LIKE TO SPEAK TO MR. DAVID BLACKSILVER, PLEASE. This is Tourmaline Kulkarney. . . Oh, I believe he will find the time to talk to me. Tell him Shannon Kendricks has returned and sits right beside me at this very moment." Tourmaline patted Shannon's jiggling good leg. The attorney wore shimmering gold today, from hat to ankle. Her feather and shoes were black, as were the buttons on her dress.

"See if he doesn't—Oh wonderful. Yes, I'll wait." Tourmaline winked at Shannon. With her hand over the phone, she whispered, "I'm recording. You won't miss a thing."

Tourmaline broke the news to Blacksilver that a Russian agency had taken Shannon and Luke overseas against their will the day Shannon left the detention facility. The foreign agency had recently released them in eastern Europe. They'd found their way to the States and wished to discuss matters with Blacksilver at his earliest convenience.

Blacksilver cleared his calendar. He found it convenient late that very afternoon.

* * *

"Bale was such a cute. . . bat kitten," Shannon said, rubbing the fresh bandages Doctor Singh had applied after her treatment earlier this afternoon.

Shannon had warmed to the spinning of her ridiculous tale. *Odin knew,* her story was the only colorful touch in a shabby, depressing room.

She sat at a scratched gray metal table in a space configured for interrogations. A large darkened window spanned one wall for unseen observers, and a camera hung from high in the wall in the corner. Nothing else interrupted the dismal emptiness of the room. The walls were painted a sickly institutional yellow-gray, although, for reasons unknown, a lush gray carpet covered the floor. The room's negative vibes hit her so forcefully she swore she could smell the sweat of wave after wave of the accused lingering here.

She'd worn a sleeveless navy-blue dress and her navy sandals for the occasion. Tourmaline sat to her right. They had taken Luke somewhere else for questioning.

"He had enormous eyes back then, dark blue until he was about six months old. I would stare for hours at those beautiful eyes. And his paws were *so* big compared to the rest of him; I laughed so much about those paws. He used to trip over them."

Shannon had been talking for the better part of two hours now and was recounting her fictitious early days with Bale yet again. She sniffed as if holding back a tear.

"And his ears! Oh my gosh, so big for his little golden face. You saw how his fur shimmered in the light, right? Well, it glimmered even more when he turned about four, maybe because that would be the age of maturity. I'm not sure. I'd see him curl into a ball in the sunlight, and I'd watch his fur shimmer when I ran my fingers through it. His wings, though—very tiny compared to what they eventually became. Did you see the wingspan on my baby? Now, I saw my abductors' bat cat for a short time each day until its death, but. . . ."

* * *

". . . . I didn't love it when Bale learned how to spew fire, though. You'd cottoned on to the fact he could do that, right? Silver blue flame. Scared the daylights out of me the first time he roasted a piece of beef. He made quick work of my curtains one time when—"

"All right, enough reminiscing," Blacksilver said. "The facility where they kept you. What can you tell me about it?"

"As I said last time you asked, nothing much. They gave me a room much like the one you put me in, except nicer—an actual bed with a mattress, soft blankets, and sheets. Everything in pale yellow, of all things. Would that be a psychological warfare thing? Pale yellow to make me happy enough to identify with the enemy?"

Such poppycock.

"Never heard of that, I'll ask around."

"Anyway, they took me only one place—the chamber where they held the young bat kitten. I never learned where they found her. I suppose someone discovered her the same way I discovered Bale—she may have walked right up to them. They wanted me to make contact with her. To establish the kind of relationship I had with Juneau and with Bale. But, Mr. Blacksilver, that was one sick bat kitten. I felt so bad for her. I worked with her, as I had with Bale, and we made excellent progress, but about a month ago, she died.

"Are you sure it died?"

"Oh yes, I saw her. We went down for my morning session, and she had expired overnight. I cried bucketsful."

"Then what happened?"

"Well, I feared for my life, I can tell you, because they didn't have any need for me anymore. But they took me back to my cell, and the next day they took us out in a truck, drove for a day, and let us go. I hadn't seen Luke in all that time. He told me he'd been training with their special forces."

Tourmaline had decided that a story that separated them made it less likely that either one would slip up on a detail of their captivity.

"Why would they let you go?"

"I have no idea. I'm just grateful they did. Maybe they let us go because we couldn't really prove anything or point you to their facilities. Anyway, back to your question about the building. Other than going down to the baby's chamber, they never let me out. When they didn't take me down to work with the baby, people would come in to talk to me about Bale every day, and every day, I would talk about him as I'm doing now. They wanted every detail. Then a different guy would come. And he would want the same details. I would tell them the same thing all over again."

"You can't tell me anything else?"

"No, I saw nothing but the bat kitten chamber and my cell. I can say I lived in a sparsely furnished concrete building. I had no window, no exercise yard, no group showers, which was a lucky thing, I guess. I had a bag over my head going in and out, same as when you moved me. Oh—another thing different from your facility—I had a nice bathroom. Kohler. Seriously. In yellow. A shower and tub and tiles around the sink. Very cheery."

"How do you know they were Russian?"

"I saw the Russian alphabet on various things, like the bottom of the pottery in which my food came. And some people who visited me had accents so thick I never understood them. If they weren't Russian, they were from one of the similar places, Belarus, Kazakhstan, or whatever. I assumed Russia because it would have the resources and sophistication to pull off the kidnapping, right? They sure fooled the agents and troopers, didn't they? As I understand it, our people never saw the helicopter at all. Were you there when the agents nabbed us?"

Blacksilver coughed. "No, I didn't make it there in time."

So. It embarrassed him to admit he had been fooled. And he *had* been fooled, although not by Russians, and not in a way he could have detected. He was still being fooled.

"I thought I would die when all the law enforcement officers started firing, Mr. Blacksilver, no joke. And then, *poof*, in an instant, the Russians helicoptered us out through the crevasse they'd made. How did they create that thing, anyway?"

"I don't believe our scientists know. Did you see anything?"

"No. I heard a noise like a train and stopped to figure out what I was hearing. That's when I saw the crevice in the rearview mirror. It looked like an earthquake had hit. It stretched out for hundreds of feet, right? And how wide was it?"

"Over a mile long and sixty-four feet wide in most places."

Shannon whistled. "Anyway, as glad as I was that they rescued me from the gunfire, it turned out to be a case of 'out of the fire, into the frying pan.'"

"So, you remember nothing else about the facility?"

"Institutional carpet covered the floor. Brown. But otherwise?" Shannon shook her head.

"Let's go back to the explosion at the detention facility. You didn't do that?"

"No. You must know that. Your people searched me to within an inch of my you-know-what when I came in there and didn't find anything. I guess the same people who kidnapped us caused the explosion. They must not have had many operatives outside, though, because I walked right out of there and found a car to get in and drive away without being stopped once—by them or your people."

Blacksilver glanced down at his notes when Shannon made her last comment.

"But I have a vague recollection of a guy coming in over the rubble as I was leaving. Do you remember him? I don't think he even saw me. It was all smoky, and my head hurt; I was in shock, but I remember him. Maybe he was the bomber. I think he wanted you out of the picture."

Blacksilver started tapping his foot under the table as he pondered his fabricated close call with death.

* * *

"I thought my blasting cap accident caused the explosion on the boat because I couldn't think of any other explanations that made sense. And I still think so. But, yes, it could have been the Russians, I guess."

* * *

"No, I never would have hurt Bale, and he never would have hurt me. He couldn't fly; that's why he crashed, poor baby. He tried so hard. . . Could you give me a tissue, please?"

Shannon dabbed at her face.

* * *

"I'd gone out in my kayak on the calm waters between Ocean City and Green Dog Island early on New Year's Day, so I had the shoreline all to myself, and Bale swam right to the kayak and stared at me with those baby blues. He looked so tiny then. I hunted all around for his pride or whatever you would call it, and I'm sure nothing else like him was out swimming that day.

"I scratched him behind the ears, and he followed me back to the marina. As easy as that, I became the proud mama of a bat cat."

* * *

"Yes, we *all* wanted to examine the body of the alien in the Gulf of Alaska. Perhaps the foreign agents decided if they couldn't have it, you couldn't either, and sent in a submarine.

Too bad our government didn't believe Dr. Moon, who's a very bright man, you know. You could have sent a submarine up there, and it might have chased off the Russian sub, and we'd have had a chance to examine the alien, don't you think?"

* * *

After five grueling hours of interrogation, Blacksilver took a break for a late dinner. He promised that when they'd finished eating they should be able to wrap things up in short order.

The five of them, Shannon, Luke, Tourmaline, Blacksilver, and Torra, sat at a round conference table. When their food arrived, they discussed the chances of the Ocean City Orcas, the local soccer team, this season, but everyone soon drifted off into their own thoughts. Bent over their plates, staring at their dinner entrees, all five wore the marks of the interrogations, visible in extra lines around the mouths, smudges under the eyes, pallor in their faces. Shannon couldn't see her own face, but given the others, hers must be a sad affair.

* * *

Having eaten in a hurry to de-emphasize that she'd eaten three times as much as any of the men, and five times as much as Tourmaline, Shannon reached for the dessert boxes in the middle of the table. At the same time, Blacksilver, who sat across from her, reached for a new napkin from the pile next to the desserts.

Their fingers touched.

...It all fits. I mean, who could make up shit like that? Raising a baby dragon? Who would believe that? Except I saw the thing myself. Escaping that car explosion? I'd have said no way, except here she is. Russians? Why not? Our people didn't open that crack in the earth, and it was too damn convenient for a natural earthquake.

Shannon jerked her hand back as if she'd received an electric shock. Somehow, she'd tapped into his thoughts. Not only did she know the words he was thinking—rather than the images and emotions she'd always received before—but she could still hear him after breaking physical contact. Every single word.

Jesus. I'm not a leper. She doesn't have to jerk her hand back like that. I mean, what's the big deal? I bumped her hand. Okay, so I roughed her up a bit at the detention center, but I hadn't even started in on the serious stuff. I guess I did crack her head pretty good on the wall. She could still be touchy. But Jesus. . . What should my next move in this case be? The boss wants me to let her go. Should I? Tempting. I landed the assignment I wanted in D.C. Time to get out of this backwater. But I don't like letting her off. It's the principle of the thing. If she would freaking apologize for jerking us around, I might—

Shannon stared at him, her mouth falling open. She shut it. *Need to break the connection now!*

"Anybody else want dessert besides me? Luke? You guys?" She took Luke's hand under the table and concentrated on its wonderful square strength. She'd honed the practice of staying out of Luke's mind over the years and blocked any thoughts of his as automatically as she wiped her nose when it dripped.

He smiled at her. "No dessert for me. You can have mine."

She listened: silence from the mind of Blacksilver.

Thank Odin.

As she and Jose Torra dug into their chocolate brownies with fudge and whipped cream, she said, "Mr. Blacksilver, before we go back on the record, I wanted to say I'm sorry."

You want an apology, Blacksilver, you pissant, you shall have one.

"You two agents scare ordinary citizens, you know. You forget that. And when people get scared, they do dumb things, like hold information back, thinking they'll get in more trouble if they tell the truth."

"It's always worse to withhold information. I hope you've learned your lesson," Blacksilver said.

"Oh, yes, definitely. I understand it made your jobs harder, and I'm sorry. If you gave me a do-over, I would admit to you back on the *Willow* that Bale belonged to me. But I felt so bad he'd died, poor guy, and I'd gone into shock, I'm sure. Being food-deprived didn't help."

And that's on you, you grasshopper.

"Plus, I thought it didn't matter one way or the other, since I don't know where my poor Bale came from. I hope someday you can be less angry at me. Because I regret not coming clean earlier." Tears formed.

She stole a glance at Luke. Although he stared back at her stone-faced, he developed a slight tic in his right eye, as if he thought she might be laying it on a tad thick.

Blacksilver appeared unmoved by the water in her eyes, but Torra buckled.

"Hey, it's all right, Shannon. We get it. The big guns come into town, and the locals always get nervous. But you've told us the truth now, so we forgive you." Shannon's eyes strayed to the long double scar visible on Torra's bald head, courtesy of the raven. *Excellent work, Bird.* She returned her eyes to Torra's face before he could notice that she was staring at his puckered pate.

Blacksilver cringed and threw mental daggers at his partner, but he didn't correct Torra, and Torra never looked at him, oblivious to the fury in his partner's eyes.

She blew her nose on a napkin.

Luke gave her a handkerchief, his face still expressionless. She didn't have to read *his* mind to hear him thinking, *really?*

She turned back to Blacksilver. One direct lock on his eyes and his thoughts played for her again, clear as day. *Loki's luck.* She must figure out a way to control this.

...Torra, you wuss. When will you learn to keep your mouth shut. . . Still. I think she means it. . . Okay. I'll grill her for another hour when we go back, so she remembers who's boss here and maybe I'll assess a steep fine because of the coast guard cutter explosion even though it sounds to me like her Russian friends pulled that off, and then, all right, case closed. D.C., here I come.

Shannon stared down into her dessert. *Another hour? Blacksilver, you cockroach.*

However, against all odds, she and Luke would get out of this mess with their hides—and their lives—intact.

Still, she now faced a fresh hurdle: her new and improved mind-reading skills.

* * *

When Blacksilver turned them loose at last, Tourmaline, Luke, and Shannon wasted no time escaping Blacksilver's office. Tourmaline stopped them in the lobby of the Federal Building and, standing on the sleek black marble, gave Shannon a huge hug. A single rainbow-colored feather jutted straight forward from Tourmaline's hat and curled down at its tip. Shannon avoided poking her eye out on the offending plume by ducking left at the last moment.

Shannon said, "We owe you so much, Tourmaline. I can't tell you how much I appreciate you. You'll stay in touch, won't you? We can have lunch or dinner, right? At least until I head off to work at the New Dickson when it's ready."

"Yes, my darling, so long as you bring this scrumptious man of yours along with you now and then, and so long as we stay out of your mind and keep away from aliens of all varieties. Can you make that happen?"

"Promise. Well. . . maybe I can't promise anything about aliens, but I'll do my best."

Tourmaline let out a long sigh. "I thought as much. And child, if the New Dickson loses its allure, you will always have a third career on the stage awaiting you. I loved your performance in there—fabulous, astonishing, tour de force. Bravo. Wherever did you learn to lie with such guileless perfection?"

"With all the alien business, I've had many, many opportunities to practice." She glanced at Luke. He stirred and shifted his feet as he listened to this discussion of Shannon's wonderful ability to lie.

"But I'm out of the alien business for the foreseeable future and won't have any need for stretching the truth," she hastened to add.

"Stretching? Sweet child, you took your scissors to the truth and cut it into itty bitty shreds. Which you then sprinkled all over unsuspecting Messieurs Blacksilver and Torra like confetti on a parade."

Tourmaline spotted the uneasy expression on Luke's face at her praise of Shannon's ability to prevaricate. "But, as you say, no need now. No need whatsoever. No, everything's quite finished now. All wrapped up. Complete. Done. Finito."

The attorney gave Luke a long hug as well, a long, tight hug, and broke away at last. Climbing into her tangerine-orange Bentley Continental GT, she waved airily, and screeched out of her parking space and into the street.

* * *

"Did you mean any of that?" Luke asked as they drove to Shannon's. "That apologizing all over yourself at dinner?"

"Not a word. That beetle nearly knocked me unconscious. I didn't owe him an apology. But I. . ." Shannon swallowed. ". . . I bumped his hand when he reached for a napkin just as I went for the dessert menu. Imagine my surprise when I could hear his thoughts. It continued after we stopped touching. Losing my power might have curtailed my ability to do that—I expected it to, but I heard his thoughts better than ever."

Luke kept his eyes trained on the road, did not glance over at her. But did his fingers tighten on the steering wheel?

"Anyway, he was thinking that, on the one hand, a fresh assignment awaited him as soon as he put the wraps on our case; plus, his boss wanted him to let us go. On the other hand, his small-minded, petty, juvenile desire to make us pay for stonewalling him tempted him to stay and make us suffer."

She waited to see if her barbs about Blacksilver would get a chuckle out of Luke.

Nothing.

"But he started thinking that if I would give him an apology, he could move on. So, I gave him a whopper, and he let us go."

"You touched his hand, and you could read his mind."

"Like he was saying it out loud." *Right. Enough of that topic.* "Can we stop for food?"

"That's the first time it's happened since we came back from the wormhole?"

"The only time. I didn't expect it. Food?"

"Sure. You haven't read my mind since we came back?"

"No, never. What's Tourmaline's plan for when you meet with your boss tomorrow?"

"Pretty much the same story. Convincing Captain Chen should go down as smooth as bourbon after what we've pulled on Blacksilver."

"Smooth as bourbon?"

"Quiet now."

Shannon smiled, and pointed at a highway chain restaurant fast approaching on their right.

* * *

"I'm back on the force. Starting Monday. Have to go through a medical and shooting test at the range and all that, but I have four more days of free time before I report," Luke said as he came in the door from his appointment with his boss. He'd left hours ago. Shannon had spent the afternoon worrying that matters had not gone as well as they had with Blacksilver and Torra.

But now Shannon squealed and jumped into a full-body hug, her crutches falling to the floor.

"I suppose I can move back to my place now," he said. "Since we're no longer on the lam."

Shannon dropped her arms and hopped back.

What did he want her to say? Did he want to move because he wanted to escape her telepathy? *One way to find out.*

"You could. Or you could stay here. See how it works out to come and go in the open?"

Luke studied her with those wonderful brown eyes, his thick lashes lowered in thought.

"I think it's time to fish or cut bait."

"What?"

"Will you marry me? Not 'Will you let me live with you?' Not 'Do you love me?' because I know you do."

"Busted. Yes, I do."

There. She'd said it.

"And again—will you marry me? No matter how scary your life becomes, you won't ever run out on me again? You'll still love me if you read my thoughts someday, and I'm grumpy or thinking the things that flash across people's minds, but they'd never say out loud? You'll learn to filter out the nonsense in my brain and not let it bother you?"

Shannon stared at him. No words came. No thoughts came. She had frozen like an angelfish in Antarctica.

Narci, who'd been dozing in the front window on the wide mahogany ledge, jumped to the floor, meowed once, and ran for the back patio. *Magenta,* she said to Shannon.

Shannon's wits returned to her enough for her to say, "Narci thinks Magenta's coming."

Shannon hadn't picked up her usual forewarning of Magenta's arrival. But she attributed that to Luke's distracting words.

"Magenta can wait."

Luke wrapped his arms around her and held her in place. Shannon's face flushed pink.

"Let's catch Magenta when it falls. I need a minute to think. You raise several excellent points. My telepathy could cause terrible problems. I don't know if I can do that to you."

"Wrong answer. This is about *you*. Do you know if *you* can live with these problems? I already know I can." He sighed. "Go on, go catch the little nuisance."

Shannon grabbed her crutches and followed Narci onto the patio. She cast her colors—

But no colors appeared. No portal appeared. Shannon tried again. And again.

She panicked.

Why couldn't she cast her colors? She couldn't function without them: they defined her; they made her worth something.

Worth something.

Could she still contact Juneau?

Juneau? Can you hear me?

Far away, a reply: *hear you.*

Thank Odin. If she still had Juneau, she could bear anything.

Good enough, sweetheart. Stay safe.

Shannon knew the portal's approximate location, so she raised her arm—and felt nothing. She checked with Narci, who sat on the picnic table, staring at her. "Has Magenta come down?"

Narci meowed. *Yes.*

So. Her communications with the cat, sparse though they were, remained intact.

Shannon laid her head on the picnic table and flowed into her Great Room—

Except she couldn't.

Meaning she couldn't see Magenta. Meaning she couldn't see Essi unless Shannon went to RiverWorld.

"Magenta! I can't cast my colors. I can't come into the Great Room. But I still have a bit of power; I know I do. What's wrong with me?" Shannon held her breath waiting for an answer she hoped she could hear.

magenta not knows. magenta senses not much power in shannon. maybe not enough for color casting, flowing into mind.

"But I can still read minds."

magenta wonders if shannon always can read minds but does not know this until essi and salesti visit. or maybe power opens doors that always exist.

"So, I'll never cast the colors again?"

magenta not knows. something for shannon to find out. if no more casting colors, maybe power opens more doors for shannon that already exist. help shannon learn new skills.

"Can I still use the portal?"

not unless magenta or essi takes shannon.

Shannon sat at the picnic table, stunned. All thought fled from her mind. Blood rushed to her stomach, like a prickling of ants. Her head pounded. Then the thoughts flooded back in. All of it, gone. The colors, her Great Room, traveling to other minds, and bringing others to her mind.

She felt the wild impulse to *fix* it, to rush out and find a way to bring it all back again. But with her next breath, she could feel deep in her being that no fix existed, there would be no bringing it all back.

She'd be worthless if a new set of aliens came to Earth.

Helpless.

She'd grown accustomed to winning the day, to stepping up at great cost to herself. To doing the impossible. Could she adjust to being. . . ordinary?

Well. Except for the mind-reading.

And the voracious appetite.

And the hair and eyes. She pulled her braid around to inspect it—still silver blonde.

And Juneau and the baby.

Yes. She could adjust.

"Well, Narci, looks like you're my eyes and ears on the portal from now on. I'm counting on you."

Narci stared back at her, unblinking, her sapphire blues giving away nothing.

"Whatever you came for, Magenta, I'm probably not equipped to help you anymore. I'm sorry. I still owe you so much."

shannon not worries. magenta needs no help from shannon. comes to give shannon message from roebor. roebor tells shannon roebor does well. roebor flies and hunts and swims in sea and roebor happy. also, roebor finds more pretty stones for shannon. stones coming now.

A sack the size of a soccer ball fell from the portal and would have caught Narci beneath its weight if the cat hadn't scrambled out of the way.

"You okay, Narci?"

Narci licked her paw with great concentration as if she hadn't nearly been beaned by a bag of jewels.

"More diamonds," Shannon murmured, hefting the bag.

no, roebor says stones different. roebor chooses for shannon.

Luke came out from the kitchen with two cups of coffee and sat next to her.

"Where did the bag come from?"

"What color are my eyes?" Shannon asked him.

"An unusual shade of dark green as always; why?"

"You're sure?"

"I've been tested: I do not suffer from color blindness."

"It must be that I didn't lose the unusual eye and the hair color when I lost the power because it was Essi who caused them to turn," she murmured.

"What are you talking about?"

"I can't visit my Great Room anymore. I can't cast my colors. I can't see the portal. Am I still giving off my special scent?"

"Yes, same as always."

Essi and the lavender lightning had given her the scent, not the power. "That's the one I might not mind losing." Sure, her mysterious, exotic scent was her best quality. Sure, she would become pedestrian, boring, uninteresting without it. But she'd always feared it, too. Because of Luke. "I always wondered if the scent bewitched you, if you fell in love with it, and not me."

Luke barked out a laugh. "You're joking. You thought I loved you because of your perfume? I love your perfume, sure, but I never loved you because of it. I love you for a million reasons, all mixed together. You're brave, you're crazy, you push through the worst adversity when it counts, you're smart, you laugh funny, you love Juneau and Narci. You're well-organized, you have this cute habit of running your fingers down your braid when you're nervous, you have—I don't know how to say it—an air of innocence about you that's somehow basic to your nature, whatever you've experienced, and you're open to new adventures, lord knows, and your hand in my hand fits in mine just right. I like watching you eat, it's—"

"Okay, I believe you." She smiled, turning pink. "But besides my normal human flaws, and I know I have plenty, I can still read minds, including, on a bad day, yours."

"Minor flaw."

"Magenta said I might discover other paranormal skills."

"Unimportant."

"I can't lead us to rare whale species anymore."

"Don't care."

Dare she believe him? He could love her if she were no longer powerful, no longer able to save whole worlds? He could love her despite the. . . drawbacks?

If she accepted him, she'd have to trust him. She'd have to let him in. After everything she'd suffered. . . could she do it?

In the years since Essi's first visit, she'd freed Juneau against all odds, she'd defeated ancient aliens and earthly opponents, she'd helped Roebor take the virus that could have killed all of humanity off the planet, defeated Tidak and Bale, rescued Roebor from a painful death, faced off against a shark to save Essi, and rid the universe of Salesti's immense power without obliterating any planets. Or herself.

Yes, she'd learned to face her fears.

Shannon could do this. She could let Luke in.

She opened the sack she'd been bouncing in her hands, and a pile of emeralds spilled out onto the table.

"My god. They're beautiful," Luke said. "Did you rob a jewelry store I didn't hear about?"

Shannon ran her fingers through them and picked up a large and lovely emerald. "They're from Roebor." She looked up at him and smiled. "Would a macho police officer allow a girl to fund her own honeymoon?"

Luke eyed the jewel. "Heck of a honeymoon. But you deserve it. Did you have a destination in mind?"

"I know of a place where you can swim with blue whales off Sri Lanka."

"All right, then."

"All right then." She leaned toward Luke and closed her eyes.

The End.

WITH MY GRATITUDE

Thanks for coming along on this journey of Shannon's with her. It would be great if you could leave a review at your favorite site. Want updates about what comes next? Go to AuthorCathyParker.com to subscribe to my newsletter.

[I'll give you a hint: a free prequel!]

ABOUT THE AUTHOR

Now that Cathy Parker has finished this trilogy, she hopes to embark on a new adventure to foreign shores. This adventure, however, should not interfere with her writing endeavors, as her hoped-for destination's climate includes a rainy season—just perfect for settling in at the keyboard and imagining a new tale into life.

Please visit her at her website, AuthorCathyParker.com, where she hopes to chronicle her successes and spectacular failures at finding her way in a new and different culture.

www.ingramcontent.com/pod-product-compliance
Lightning Source LLC
Chambersburg PA
CBHW051528100726
47898CB00005B/1610